DESOLATION ISLAND

Adolfo García Ortega was born in 1958 and lives in Madrid and Barcelona. He is a translator, literary critic, journalist and former editorial director of the prestigious Spanish publishing house Seix Barral. His critically acclaimed novels have won many prizes. *Desolation Island* is his first book to be translated into English.

ADOLFO GARCÍA ORTEGA

Desolation Island

TRANSLATED FROM THE SPANISH BY

Peter Bush

VINTAGE BOOKS
London

Published by Vintage 2012

2 4 6 8 10 9 7 5 3 1

First published with the title *Autómata* in 2006 by Bruguera, Barcelona

First published in Great Britain in 2011 by Harvill Secker

Vintage
Random House, 20 Vauxhall Bridge Road,
London SW1V 2SA

www.vintage-books.co.uk

Addresses for companies within The Random House Group Limited can be found at: www.randomhouse.co.uk/offices.htm

The Random House Group Limited Reg. No. 954009

A CIP catalogue record for this book is available from the British Library

ISBN 9780099516934

The publication of this work has been made possible through a subsidy received from the Directorate General for Book, Archives and Libraries of the Spanish Ministry of Culture

The Random House Group Limited supports The Forest Stewardship Council (FSC®), the leading international forest certification organisation. Our books carrying the FSC label are printed on FSC® certified paper. FSC is the only forest certification scheme endorsed by the leading environmental organisations, including Greenpeace. Our paper procurement policy can be found at www.randomhouse.co.uk/environment

FSC
www.fsc.org
MIX
Paper from responsible sources
FSC® C016897

Printed in Great Britain by Clays Ltd, St Ives plc

A Esther, ani ohev otach, ahev,
m.v.k.p.t.

Only the invisible moves us.

Théodore Jouffroy

It was a life stripped of the present moment.

Antonio Muñoz Molina

I

I HAPPENED TO BE IN MADEIRA ON NEW YEAR'S DAY morning in the new millennium and it was there I met Oliver Griffin, a Spaniard in all but name, who accosted me on the sea-view terrace at the Carlton Hotel and used all his charms as a seductive storyteller to engage me in a series of relaxed though private exchanges. He invented and drew islands, because it was the activity he'd found most interesting in life to that point, or so he said when he started to talk garrulously about himself as if we were two old acquaintances, which we were not. I now realise no third party would ever have thought we were, I certainly didn't feel I was, but Griffin's warmth immediately captivated me as if he were unveiling the hidden designs behind his strategy for seduction. That activity of drawing islands, he stressed, modulating his words quickly in an almost monotonous lilt, could easily have turned into a full-time profession and given him the reputation of a fool. In the event, he had earned his living as a history lecturer, he added, only to abandon his academic career when an unexpected inheritance from San Francisco resolved his economic problems, just like Flaubert's Bouvard, he added.

He had drawn the island that was his obsession, for that's how he described it from the start, hundreds of times in recent years. It was a necessary exercise to ensure he didn't forget the place, he said, as though he'd invented an island that was his alone, however real it might be in some part of the world. He drew it to give it specificity while he awaited his opportunity to travel there, when it would assume a physical and geographical reality. Sketches of the forty-seven fjords, nine canals, fifty-six capes, eight gulfs and twenty-three beaches thus emerged repeatedly from Oliver Griffin's fountain pen on whatever piece of paper was at hand, wherever he was, in hotels, bars, trains, airports, friends' houses, hospital waiting rooms: it was simply an exercise to help him remember, a highly elaborate mnemonic device to chase off other thoughts. Many people solve crosswords, whereas I draw islands, I mean, simply that one island. I became so expert, he added, I could even draw it with my eyes closed: its rugged, elongated coasts, with a range of peaks and troughs like a graph charting Stock Exchange share prices or a dyspeptic seismograph, set obliquely, leaning westwards, like a Tower of Pisa in reverse. Griffin located purely from memory the names of the most important sites on the island – a total fantasy, he said, for, however much he remembered seeing it in one of the books he had consulted in the National Library in Madrid, he hadn't retained their precise positions: Cape Desire, Cape Pillars, Port Mercy, Beaufort Bay, Cape Cut, Port Churruca, Mataura Cove, Barrister Bay . . . names nourishing a desire that impelled him towards a strange, profound encounter with himself from the day he was born, he said, one he had yet to decipher, like somebody who comes across a letter addressed to himself but written in a foreign language.

He had spontaneously sketched islands from early childhood. He was familiar with those irregular shapes his fingers drew extraordinarily slowly, as if he'd always known the direction they should follow: islands, not ridiculous circles *manqués* he surrounded fluidly with dashes and slender strips of horizons, suggesting the idea of a sea. Unknown to Griffin and outside the realm of his experience because, like me, he came from an inland city, as I admitted to him, and that sea was as imaginary, threatening and enthralling as a secret. With the passage of time, he developed an interest in antique books of ingenuous, tinted islands, which he searched out, paid the high prices demanded, and admired, studied and collected as if fate were inexorably leading him to them.

Those Books of Islands fascinated him, he said, because they were totally unreal in their descriptions and colours, and still were today, I fully agree, added Griffin, who, like myself, believed those descriptions to be as fictitious as any novel. Books of Islands, he said, like maps, were texts I read in my adolescence with greater enthusiasm and empathy than literature, because I felt they raised a curtain in my imagination like scenes in a film, revealing realms of fantasy, which they undoubtedly were, while my finger ran over sites, promontories, coastlines, and a residue stuck with me, a sensation lodged in my head immersing me in happy, escapist suspension of disbelief. I suspect those Books of Islands related to actual islands, though that soon became irrelevant, they could be fake, invented islands for all I cared, Oliver Griffin said casually. Besides, islands, or so I've read, he continued, sometimes stay or at least become invisible. It is their destiny, whether or not this is mythical, to be lost in remote corners of the world, either because they are wrongly located or fell into oblivion when the scant maritime traffic they saw evaporated. Now they only exist in the feverish minds of lunatic sailors, islands appearing on no maps, islands nobody survived to recount their longitudes and latitudes, inaccessible islands, shrouded in ethereal mists or preserved by strange tempests at the epicentre of which they live on and flourish on the margins of time. Even islands outside the possibilities of history, like the one described in Cervantes's *Persiles and Sigismunda*, the island inhabited by King Kong, or even Robinson Crusoe's: islands that are invisible, in a word.

Invisibility, he continued, that was so important in relation to my own life and name, also shaped my island: first it was fiction, then reality, and then fiction again. Like my name, he stressed. And Oliver got up from his chair on the sunny terrace of the Carlton Hotel where we were admiring the blue sea, and, like a man plucked from a previous century, though he couldn't be more than fifty-five or sixty, introduced himself ceremoniously à la Melville, as he pointed out, parodying the 'Call me Ishmael' in *Moby Dick* with a 'Call me Griffin', followed by an affable smile and handshake as he awkwardly bowed his head. He added that he was as invisible as the islands he drew or at least tended that way, not because he was antisocial – he clearly *was* an affable fellow – but because he felt an affinity with the way everything in his life turned into literature, a family trait that was apparently hereditary. Or rather, he said, short-circuiting my confusion, I am metaphorically invisible, since my name is the same as Griffin, the Invisible Man, if you recall, the protagonist of H. G. Wells's novel of that name. Via an inevitable association of ideas, as I told my interlocutor, I remembered that Georges Perec, my favourite writer, had wanted to use the name in a film called *Vous souvenez-vous de Griffin?* I see, Oliver commented, after admitting he was familiar with Perec, though not with that particular fact. My full name, by the way, is Oliver Ernesto Griffin Aguiar, my father, Sean, was an Irish engineer from San Francisco and my mother, Matilde Aguiar, was a famous radio broadcaster from Madrid and both are still alive, if divorced: each live in the city of their birth and wish me Happy Christmas, in the morning and at night, respectively.

The island that had obsessed Griffin for years, the one he called his own, was Desolation Island. The whole story he recounted in Madeira on those warm January days that ushered in the new century stemmed, in turn, from the only remaining trace of the life of another real or fictitious man, who was definitely invisible, since only his name, John Talbot, remained, or perhaps, as Griffin remarked, only his death remained, that took place many years ago, because it was all we know about him, or at least all that Herman Melville decided to mention in Chapter VII of *Moby Dick*. The lips of Ishmael his narrator spelt out the inscription on one of the marble, black-edged gravestones embedded in the wall, on both sides of the pulpit in the New Bedford chapel, the Seamen's Bethel, that still exists today in Bethel Street, Nantucket:

SACRED
To the memory
OF JOHN TALBOT
Who at the age of eighteen was lost overboard,
Near the Isle of Desolation, off Patagonia
November 1st 1836.
THIS TABLET
Is erected to his Memory
BY HIS SISTER.

'In this same New Bedford there stands a Whaleman's chapel, and few are the moody fishermen, shortly bound for the Indian Ocean or Pacific, who fail to make a Sunday visit to the spot', Griffin quoted Melville in a trance, confessing, as if he were indeed in a trance, that he'd entered that chapel some time ago after reading that page in his favourite and much reread novel, because the words, Desolation Island, gave meaning to all his previous life and would do so to all his subsequent life, as he was about to tell me. I searched for Desolation Island, Griffin said, on maps, in Books of Islands, in whole libraries, but which of the three Desolation Islands in the world was Talbot's? I started to invent one: although Melville says it is in Patagonia, it could just as well be the island of Tristan da Cunha, also known as Desolation, facing the coast of Patagonia. Mine, the one I later located at the western end of the Straits of Magellan, perhaps appeared suddenly, by mistake, when I hadn't intended. But that island – who'd have thought it? – said Griffin was already linked to my life in the strangest of ways, and the fact it caught my attention when I was reading *Moby Dick* was simply a natural epiphany in the unfurling of my existence that was bound to happen sooner or later.

Chance or fate determined that that island I'd read about, an invisible isle to me, the invisible man, was my grandfather's and was held to be so by my family for years. It was the Desolation Island where an extraordinary, fantastic, inert monster had appeared five hundred years ago, at least according to the press headlines of the time, which came into my grandfather's possession and that I still have, said Griffin, duly dubbing the find a monster. In fact, the body or object that emerged from oblivion was a metal object, an artificially wrought human figure, found on Cape Cut, on Desolation Island, in 1919, and that Graciela Pavic, its discoverer and the curator of the Salesian Museum in Punta Arenas, restored and cleaned for years until it assumed the presentable state in which it appears in the photo my grandfather Arnaldo had taken with my grandmother Irene, when they visited the museum on their honeymoon in the Straits area. That journey took my grandparents as far as Valparaíso, which was also the destination of the ship which took me to those parts years after, said Griffin, flourishing his hand after a long pause that anyone else might have deemed a contemptuous silence.

He then handed me the photo of his maternal grandparents, all spruced up and smiling, standing in front of the camera embracing, like a friend, both sides of a metal automaton whose unnerving smile and face gave it the features of a disfigured warrior. I scrutinised those seemingly strange people. This photo has accompanied me through life, Oliver said, breaking his silence, as if waiting for the moment to reveal its inner secrets and tell its story. And seemed, Griffin continued, to have been there for ever, inciting one to travel, as Baudelaire writes, and its moment had come when I read that epitaph in Melville's novel. This photo had been my family's gateway to something extraordinary, and had been shut away at some point, had been severed, locked in an inexplicable, orphan state, hibernating between bundles of photos of cousins, brothers, sisters, relatives, weddings, travels and monuments, and now it entered my life by chance, I forget how. Perhaps it fell on the floor when I opened a wardrobe drawer, but the fact is it *did* fall into my hands, and I grasped it as if I'd been expecting it all along, because I found it soothing, a photo subtly evoking mystery and desire that led me constantly to imagine a mythical place that had been non-existent and fictitious until recently, I could almost say, until I decided to retrace my grandparents' footsteps. It was a place that attracted me but I'd yet to receive the appropriate summons, a final excuse to give meaning to the words written on the back of the photo, which in my youth sent me into a wildly exotic, symphonic mood, as in the lines of the poet of the sea, Brauquier: 'For those of us who have seen nothing, the map of the world is full of names of cities that float on our lips like exotic scents.' Griffin then showed me the other side of the photo and I read what his grandfather or maybe his grandmother had written: 'Punta Arenas, 1923. Salesian Regional Museum. Figure from Desolation Island, lost for five hundred years. It is frightening.' When that photo came into my possession, said Griffin, I already loved islands and drew them when I played at inventing places. Until the photo also became invisible. Invisibility became a feature overshadowing my childhood and whole life: to be called the Invisible Man is a heavy burden and legacy and I'd no idea what I'd let myself in for.

Over time my grandfather found out more about Graciela Pavic, Griffin continued, keen not to leave any stone unturned in his story and indifferent to the din of daily life in Funchal where we plunged as we talked. Although they never returned to Punta Arenas, he said, they did occasionally write to her, and must have developed something of a friendship in the time they spent in the Straits while their boat, the *Santander*, turned round. She told them about how she walked down to the port every day and headed to a vantage point in the city in order to survey the whole of Catherine's Bay, where her husband and two sons had died in a fishing boat. It happened on a summer's day in 1918. Arturo Bagnoli set sail with his two sons, aged seven and nine, to lever mussels off accessible rocks on the north coast, as they often did, very close to land and quite safe, but on that miserable day currents in the rough sea dragged the boat out to the centre of the bay and a storm broke, immediately capsizing their fragile vessel. Remains of the boat were swept southwards, onto a cape at one end of Useless Bay, but the bodies never appeared. Grief at losing all she had on that tempestuous morning sank Graciela into a deep depression and for years she undertook a long, random pilgrimage to islands, coves, bays, harbours, caves, searching that rugged coast for the bodies of her husband and children. The only thing she found in the end was the automaton that she refurbished with such passion, Griffin said, as if it were a beloved soul she'd saved from sentence of death, decomposition and worms. Gentle, melancholic Graciela Pavic, he went on, poured out her despair in long letters to my grandparents when she realised that she would never find them, however vigorously she explored and renewed her faith each morning when she looked at photos of her husband and children: they had died, and she with them, because every remaining day of her life would be a day lived in retrospect, in the most desperate rush imaginable to recreate every single moment they had shared.

Oliver constantly thought about Graciela Pavic, or reinvented her, because it was obvious he'd never met her, and simply transformed her into his symbol of desolation, since, as he said, desolation was etymologically an absence of consolation, from the Latin *solacium*, or absence of pleasure, if we followed ancient Occitan *solatz* sung by the earliest troubadours. The void is desolation, he pensively added, a desert where aggressive devastation, like an aggressive disease, attacks everything, starves life and withers the tiniest buds of hope, and that's what Graciela must have felt in her soul as she went from cove to cove, island to island, cranny to cranny, searching for her dead children, with only the reflected solitude of that landscape in her mind where suddenly, a miserly glint vanquished the waves, a dull spark from a tin corpse that was built to strike fear into cormorants, seagulls, ingenuous Indians and myopic sailors from its cliff-top eyrie.

2

I USED TO MEET GRIFFIN IN A CAFÉ ON THE AVENIDA Zarco, named after the founder of the city, opposite the palatial home of the regional government. If there was no rain to deter us, we walked up the steep slope to the Fortaleza do Pico, but the breathless Griffin never stopped talking and telling stories that weren't always his own. Madeira fascinated him, and he knew things about the island that nobody, or almost nobody, knew. When we passed one of the low stone houses abutting the Church of Santa Clara, Griffin told me it was where the great mariner, not to say pirate, Carteret was held and threatened by his men, on the expedition of another pirate, another mariner, by the name of Wallis, when he'd come to Madeira to repair his boat, the *Swallow*. Inexplicably, perhaps because he'd run out of gold, Carteret decided to stop the repairs and set sail with the boat as it was. Nine men mutinied and took him at swordpoint to that stone house, from where they kept watch on the bay, but Carteret persuaded them to put down their weapons, surrounded as they were by loyal crew, and pledging, so they say, to show mercy towards the rebels. That proved to be a lie and they hung the nine men from the yardarm after they'd dislocated every bone in their bodies. The story of Carteret and Wallis made a deep impression on Arthur Conan

Doyle, according to Griffin, when he was in Madeira in the winter of 1881, although he'd certainly heard about it before coming to the island. However, Conan Doyle was really astonished by the uncanny sight of a lunar rainbow in the bay, something I also saw one night, said Griffin, when I observed the city from one end of the seafront, its houses lit up on the mountainside where Funchal is built.

Griffin and I stopped at the top of the castle, the famous Pico, and looked down at the city from its battlements, at the beach as far as Barreirinha, the marina, with its yachts and sloops, and the big boats moored by the long, crowded Pontinha quay. On one of those excursions that generally led to a fishermen's café or the Rua da India or one of the tourist restaurants on the Cais Novo, Griffin started to tell me about his voyage, unleashing a torrent of stories and characters that spilled into each other, and time always seemed to pass incredibly quickly when I was with that extraordinary inventor of places and life-stories for all and sundry.

One morning when we'd drunk two iced coffees at Os Ingleses, a bar near the cathedral, and couldn't decide which of the usual watering-holes to visit next, Griffin said, I was here in Funchal some five years ago and stayed at the Calcamar Hotel on the Rua dos Murças, while I waited for Afonso Branco, the captain of the merchant ship *Minerva Janela*. I had contracted to sail with Branco, through correspondence with his shipping company, boarding in Lisbon, but I arrived late and the *Minerva Janela* left without me. I was told to fly to the boat's next port of call, given that I'd paid in advance for my passage, and to wait there. I did just that, said Griffin, but arrived four days before the boat reached Madeira, time enough for me to fall in love with the island and this city, Funchal, a beautiful, resonant name, that, as I read in a book by Casimiro Ortega the botanist, is the name of a variety of fennel, *Foeniculum vulgare*, that grew on the banks of the island in 1707, when it was discovered by another botanist, Hans Sloan. I roamed the granite breakwaters that skirt almost the whole of one side of the city that overlooks the sea, while the other side is practically vertical, with streets that slope like ramps. I have spent many hours on that promenade, sitting at the end of the quay with the red and white beacon, watching all manner of vessel set sail, merchant ships, container ships, Russian cruisers, Japanese whalers, the island's rubbish collectors. As a result, Griffin went on, I can agree with Paul Morand that ports aren't at all poetic, or at least that such poetry is the invention of armchair poets: a port in itself is filthy-dirty, and its only beauty is brought by the voyager wanting to experience departures and arrivals, dreams, when all's said and done, because a port's only reality is its boats, and I now believe the true port is the one conceived from the open sea and not from land. He fell silent for a moment. I remember, he then said, another boat I almost embarked on, also sailing to Valparaíso, to the same destination as the *Minerva Janela*. It was the *Soliman*, a black, rusty sand transporter, but I was put off because they anticipated it would be a much longer trip than the *Minerva Janela*. Besides, the Philippine captain inspired no confidence whatsoever, and though this might seem incredible, he looked like a one-eyed, toothless character from a novel by Salgari. When the *Minerva Janela* finally arrived, I was in the port, as usual. Its huge hold was carrying tree trunks from Africa, timber from Nigeria, Senegal, Sierra Leone, and, wherever you looked, columns of containers like massive tower blocks, secured by thick ropes and chains. Oliver Griffin suddenly broke off and said goodbye, confident we would meet again the following day. I was so shocked by the abrupt way he'd interrupted his flow that I hardly had time to respond and lingered there awhile, semi-paralysed, with most of the day looming before me, a day that now looked irremediably empty without that fellow's enthralling conversation.

I met him in the same spot, Os Ingleses, the following day when he launched forth without even the briefest exchange of pleasantries. No doubt, said Griffin, before starting a now familiar routine, I learned most about Funchal from John Byron, the poet's grandfather. As I read in his book, Byron spotted Madeira on 14 July 1764 and immediately he set foot on its soil he was won over by the springtime warmth of its climate and the crisp winds that blew across the island at certain times of day. In his list of the island's virtues, continued Griffin, he most praised its marmalade and cider jams and the scent of sugar-sweet violets that hit him the second he left behind the stench of the port. I have often remarked how the most experienced sailors act like sleepwalkers on dry land, entranced as they are by the wildness of nature, and Byron was no exception as he marvelled at Madeira's leafy trees, especially its laurels, as red as the island's celebrated wine. Curious by nature, his favourite science being botany, all the rage in the eighteenth century, he left his ship in the hands of the second officer and with the sole company of a nun who was free to speak to foreigners, so Byron claimed, he devoted several days to studying the smooth leaved *Laurus magnoliaefolia maderiensis*, named by Lamark, his friend the expert botanist in Kew, or the fleshy fibred *Caladium*, a plant with a two-colour leaf, deep red on its back and bottle green on its edges, that invites you to take a bite and taste its dry sting, as Byron himself noted.

For my part, when Oliver launched into a rapturous commentary on things wild and fabulous, I sometimes tried to bring him back to what I believed was the core of his narrative, his journey to the Straits of Magellan. But nothing could stop his flow; on the contrary, as winter follows autumn, and autumn spring, a new shoot of a story was born with each fragment of his tale. That's how I discovered that the *Minerva Janela* – as Griffin decided to tell me when we were crossing the Casino Gardens on our way to the Sheraton – was a 480-tonner, a 120-metre-long merchant ship that became his home, or rather his world, for a number of months. After leaving that boat and returning to the life he had led before his long voyage, he was beset by a strange melancholy and recurrent fond memories of his companions on his voyage to find Desolation Island. A boat is a live being, Griffin suddenly commented in the bar at the Sheraton, and that's why it can have a dark purple, gloomy air, as in a photo that's been deliberately darkened, or can be a cataclysmic sight from land, yet breathe an exhilarating vitality from the sea, like the sweat exuded by an athlete.

I could never, Oliver confessed, forget that morning five years ago when I saw the *Minerva Janela* moored to the bollards on the Pontina wharf. It was the picture of an untameable beast languidly hiding its real self like a person whose acquaintance one has just made. Twenty and a half metres across, six deep, a top speed of eighteen knots, recounted Griffin, nodding towards the port where similar ships were anchored. It could go even faster when swept along by a favourable wind. That morning the *Minerva Janela* seemed to be asleep, as if waiting for a word, order or command. It was breathing, if one can say that about a ship in port, which I think one can. It's what ships in port do: they breathe as we do when we are dreaming. Its hull was dotted with rust, which didn't seem to be the result of neglect as much as wear and tear, particularly around the capstan; it wasn't a beautiful vessel, rather it seemed unpleasant or at odds with my state of mind, and unexpectedly vulnerable. However, these impressions vanished as soon as I saw the modern plastic-covered Navsat carapace for satellite connection, an eye-catching elegant grey and aerodynamically lined. Piles of containers dominated the boat, each a murky orange, and generally rusty, battered and worn. A dog barked at me from the deck, said Griffin, welcoming or perhaps threatening me, it had yet to decide.

We changed direction when we left the Sheraton the second Griffin entered one of his silences and started climbing the steep Rua Aranhas to the Palacio de Sao Pedro. Shortly after we'd reached the top of the street, Griffin remarked that it now houses a strange kind of aquarium, though it was Carmen Polo de Franco's residence when she visited Madeira in 1955, and many of the elderly in the area still remember how she was astonished, not to say stunned, to discover there was a famous Madeiran homonym of her husband, the Generalísimo. Griffin was sure she was angered by that unexpected revelation. At least, he continued, one deduces that from a letter written by Doña María de Borbón, the king's mother, who from her gilded exile in Estoril considered that famous collector of necklaces to be a fraudulent and uncommonly stupid witch. Everywhere one looks, said Griffin, one sees the name of Francisco Franco: on boats, schools, squares and hospitals; there's even a museum named after him and his brother Henrique, or maybe it's his son. I'm not sure and frankly I don't care, but I imagine Polo de Franco with a big scowling smile and I find that amusing. Then abruptly, though not impolitely, Griffin shook my hand and headed downhill. I didn't follow him because I realised that, for one reason or another, as far as he was concerned, the day's session was at an end.

3

WHEN I MET GRIFFIN A FEW DAYS LATER IN THE OS Combatentes restaurant on the Rua Ivens, he launched into his childhood experiences, as if we'd not been apart for a minute. In 1955, the year when Carmen Polo de Franco was astonished or stunned in Madeira, said Griffin, I was astonished or stunned in my classroom at the age of seven or eight. I shall never forget that day, he said, lowering his voice before pausing. I was late for class, my school's long corridors and empty galleries were extremely distressing, and made me feel both guilty and vulnerable, and years after, when analysing that state of mind, I've always attributed my lateness, that was frequent at the time and no doubt the result of my mother's inability to wake me up and give me breakfast, to a powerful sense of being set apart from my peers, my companions and the rest of the human race in general. Moreover, my name emphasised that difference, if not a sense of rejection. I don't mean the fact I was related to Wells's Griffin, that invisibility that turned me into literature, because I imagine nobody around me, let alone myself, had read or knew anything about the English writer. No, I'm alluding to the fact that I had a foreign name, and those silent corridors heightened a contemptible sense of alienation that might have felt nightmarish had it not been true that I was completely awake during every second that brought me closer to the classroom door. I remember knocking and someone I couldn't see opening up. As the door receded, something untoward entered my field of vision: I wasn't facing the usual lines of attentive classmates sitting at their desks, but reorganised rows with all manner of stuffed animals set out on the desktops. There were lizards and snakes of all sizes, two huge crocodiles held aloft by two iron bars, small chickenish birds, brightly coloured pheasant-like birds, plump poultry, long-shanked fowl, a kind of two-headed sheep, Galapagos Island turtles and others as tiny as a fingernail, bottled frogs, dozens of boxes of butterflies, others with fireflies or poisonous Tierra del Fuego scorpions, and my empty desk stood there with the item the teacher had assigned me, the Patagonian penguin or Chilean partridge, the words 'discovered on the northern shore of the Straits of Magellan', exquisitely written in black Indian ink on a small label stuck to its wooden base. I recalled that skinny, forlorn bird and its stiff feathers the moment I saw the photo of my grandparents with the automaton from Desolation Island, and subsequently have often thought about the sequence of coincidences that brought me to that remote part of the world and how one was undoubtedly that stuffed Patagonian penguin, an unequivocal sign that destiny spreads its nets wide and catches its prey in the end, for good or for evil, said Griffin. These specimens were on loan from the city's Museum of Natural Sciences, he continued, on the occasion of a festive event so they could do the rounds of classrooms at that time, and had been collected by the famous Scientific Commission to the Pacific, led by that exceptional man Almagro y Jiménez de la Espada. After the Great Exhibition in the Botanic Gardens greenhouses in May 1866, it was decided to take the splendid South American fauna on tour in Spain, and they were displayed in Sevilla, Valencia, Barcelona, Valladolid and Madrid, whence, continued Griffin, they erupted into my school life almost a hundred years later. I must acknowledge that on that morning in 1955 the idea of foreignness again surged within me, in the shape of a keen desire to travel, to see the world, to be someone else, and, he went on, it had been nurtured by the novels I was already reading, being such a precocious reader. Over the years I incubated the idea further, and my reading nourished it to unsuspected levels, to the point that they became part of the web of coincidences that were to dominate my life. Thus, in 1978 I once again found stuffed items from the Scientific Commission to the Pacific where I'd least expect to find them, in a place I had gone for literary reasons, because of my long fascination for Gustave Flaubert, my favourite author, said Griffin. I discovered a pair of stuffed birds from Patagonia, very similar to the penguin I'd found on my desk in 1955, in the Museum of Natural History in Rouen, where, pure fetishicist that I am, I happened to be searching for the Amazonian parrot Flaubert had rented for a time as a model for Loulou, in *Un cœur simple*. The parrot was with other Latin American stuffed birds, on the top of shelves in a narrow attic in the museum, and, level with my eyes, I distinguished in that great assortment of birds, those Patagonian specimens with labels attached to a leg by a piece of string that said 'Spanish Commission to the Pacific, 1862–1866'. It may seem incredible, but it is absolutely true, Griffin declared categorically, before referring to Flaubert's journey to the Orient with Maxime du Camp, a friend from his youth.

I couldn't identify any obvious connection between Flaubert's trip and the central thread in Griffin's story, if there was one, given his tendency to go off at a tangent, but the appearance of the words Cape Horn mid-flow restored formal coherence to Griffin's narrative, as he noted that Flaubert and Du Camp left Marseille on a boat bound for Alexandria, the Nile, which they boarded on the morning of Sunday, 4 November 1849. The captain's name was Rey, Griffin said he'd read somewhere, a strange, aloof individual, and his second-in-command was Lieutenant Roux, with whom Flaubert soon struck up an excellent relationship, much better than the one he enjoyed with Du Camp, who was fatuous and vain, as is well known, Griffin commented. Young Roux entertained passengers by spinning tales of dangerous voyages and adventures that took place around Cape Horn. However, Gustave was most struck by a tragic incident involving an albatross, perhaps a relative of the many albatrosses in that attic in Rouen's Museum of Natural History, next to the Amazonian parrots he'd rented and my Patagonian penguins. Roux apparently related how on one of the voyages around Tierra del Fuego in a brig on which Roux himself was serving as an able seaman, a man fell overboard, a surgeon from Limoges he'd just been playing cards with, and before they could throw him a lifebuoy or do anything to help, a huge albatross swooped down on his head, attacked him with its wings and beak until it had submerged and drowned him, and perhaps did so – such was the argument Roux used to lighten the tragic tenor of his tale, said Griffin – to wreak revenge for the death of the albatross rhapsodised fifty years before by Coleridge in his *Rime of the Ancient Mariner*. Perhaps that explains why, Griffin concluded, it was the only sea voyage Flaubert ever made, because he was afraid that one day the phantom of that or another benighted albatross might swoop upon him. He mentioned it briefly in *L'Éducation sentimentale*, by way of exorcising it, when Frédéric Moreau his alter ego has him merely 'journey' and 'return', in a three-line paragraph resuming his reflections on gloomy steamers, cold dawns, vertiginous landscapes and short-lived loves. And that's all, added Griffin, lamenting such literary miserliness, given the hugely eventful nature of any return sea voyage: as Kafka wrote in 1913 to his beloved Felice, there is never a dull moment at sea, and I, who have travelled the seas, can confirm how very true that is.

After we'd lunched and walked along a good stretch of sand, Griffin resumed his flow, but once again he didn't focus on his own story. Griffin said that earlier, when mentioning the albatross, he'd suddenly remembered a poem by Baudelaire, whom he read assiduously in the vain hope of learning all his poems by heart, that's devoted to the huge seabird 'that inhabits the storm and mocks the archer'. Griffin went on to say that Funchal had also enjoyed the pleasure of Baudelaire on its streets, and he suggested I should accompany him to the house of one Filipe Pereirinha, an antiquarian whose great obsession had been the gradual conversion of his business into a local museum, something he'd completed a mere five years ago, when Griffin set out on his voyage in the *Minerva Janela*; by visiting the Pereirinha Museum, that is, the antiquarian's house, I saw with my own eyes how it had been devastated by an accumulation of dozens of glass cases with countless, probably thousands, of objects that I reckoned were old rather than antique, big and small, ridiculous or predictable, letters, photos, paintings and model boats, huge bony whale jaws hanging on walls here and there, flags, coins, medals, books, prints, clocks, weapons and dozens of other categories. To his great surprise, Griffin continued, and to mine now, he found a note written by Charles Baudelaire, dated Madeira November 1841, addressed to the head of the Fishermen's Guild that was influential at the time in the politics of the port, in which he begs them passionately to let him sail for Europe, a letter Filipe Pereirinha or his son Antonio had bought at an auction, his son who emigrated and became wealthy in that same Europe Baudelaire was desperate to return to.

It had all begun a few months before, in 1840, on 19 April to be precise, Griffin recounted in that local museum, when Baudelaire's stepfather, General Jacques Aupick, told Alphonse, the poet's elder brother, that it was time 'to rescue our Charles from the slippery pavements of Paris', a euphemism that covered the pernicious company he kept, namely whores and drug-addicted poets. On the initiative of the Family Council that regulated Charles's life, it was decided to send him on a long sea voyage, a journey that would be both pleasure and punishment, and could be to the Caribbean islands of Martinique, the coastal cities of the Indian Ocean, or even Indochina. They resolved he should go as far as Calcutta and that the trip must last eighteen months including the voyage and stays in the area. It was expensive, 5,500 francs, almost double any other journey to Asia, but Aupick and the other members of the Council considered it a good investment, even though it meant requesting a three-year bank loan. The indomitable Charles set sail from Bordeaux, in the *Paquebot-des-Mers-du-Sud*, that raised anchor on 9 June, a three-master, 450 tons, and a merchant rather than a passenger ship, 'lined, riveted and pegged with copper', as advertising leaflets specified at the time, added Griffin.

Charles had been allowed on board because the skipper, Pierre Saliz, was a friend of Pierre Zédé, who in his turn was a friend of the frosty General Aupick. Charles took along the complete works of Balzac as his only source of entertainment, and had already begun to devour them when on 8 August they rounded the Cape of Good Hope. That day, and over the next twenty-four hours, a vicious storm that seemed to centre its wrath on their vessel alone, its turbulent waves twice the height of the ship, battered the boat to the point that it almost capsized. According to eyewitnesses, Baudelaire helped the crew carry out emergency measures, and even acted in the face of danger like a sailor skilled in manning the masts. The serious damage done to these, the rigging and sails forced Saliz to dock for longer than planned in Mauritius and Réunion, and Baudelaire eventually disembarked in the port of Saint-Denis de Bourbon.

Saliz departed for Ceylon some days later but failed to persuade young Charles to accompany him. The poet's vehement refusal was more than the old skipper's patience could take, yet he'd noticed in Charles, continued Griffin, the symptoms of an acute attack of melancholy that Saliz feared might lead to suicide, and consequently he negotiated with Jude de Beauséjour, the skipper of the *Alcide*, a return passage for his young protégé. But the *Alcide* was also in need of repair and it was two to three weeks before it could set sail. Baudelaire spent that time in the company of landowner Gustave Adolphe Autard de Bragard, to whom he was introduced by one of the *Paquebot-des-Mers-du-Sud*'s officers on one of their excursions around the island. Autard de Bragard, a law graduate, was a cultured man and he invited Charles to stay with him until he could embark on his return voyage, but what really led Baudelaire to accept his kind invitation was the beauty of Emmeline de Carcenac, Mme De Autard, the landowner's wife and an ardent fan of Gautier's poetry, as was Baudelaire himself, and he wrote a sonnet to her in which he describes her as 'the Creole lady whose charms go unnoticed', predicting that if she went to Paris, every poet would be her slave. Young, romantic, svelte, Emmeline was infatuated with the poem and the poet, said Griffin, but although she lived for weeks in the grips of an exciting seduction, perhaps the greatest passion of her life amid the tedious routines on her husband's plantation and the boredom of grey colonial life, she would never see him again after the *Alcide* sailed away on the tide of 4 November, would never walk the streets of Paris or meet its poets, those potential slaves to her charms, because Emmeline died on the high seas sixteen years later, on 22 June 1857, said Griffin, almost forty and less beautiful I expect, in a boat that was finally taking her to the metropolis, a few days before Poulet-Malassis the publisher put on sale *Les Fleurs du mal*, which include the poem inspired by the woman who would never read them.

When the *Alcide* reached Madeira, its captain decided out of the blue to change his destination and head for New York, something that upset Baudelaire's already stressful plans. Driven crazy by a desperate need to return to France, he paced the streets of Funchal and didn't leave the city, searching for a boat where he could buy his passage or endebt himself further. It was at that point when he was so distressed and neurotic that he must have written the letter asking the Fishermen's Guild to help him by authorising him to embark on the *Mima*, a three-master from Genoa that was en route from Bahia, the same letter Griffin and I saw in the flat display case in the Pereirinha Museum. The strange thing about this story, said Griffin, is that, after he'd crawled from tavern to tavern pleading histrionically, trying to understand the locals and begging them for information about boats bound for Europe that had moored in port, and after he'd almost boarded the *Mima* as a stowaway, which he didn't, simply because the boat's destination was Genoa and not France, Baudelaire finally went back to the *Alcide* a few days after it had anchored when its skipper had received a counter order to sail to his original destination. On 16 February 1842 the poet disembarked in the port of Garonne, near

Bordeaux, loathing the idea of making further voyages, which he never did. He hadn't finished reading Balzac's complete works, said Griffin: people even claim he lost a volume or two on the journey.

4

THE CREW OF THE *MINERVA JANELA*, FROM CAPTAIN Afonso Branco down, hardly went ashore while it was anchored in Funchal when Griffin joined their number as the only passenger on that voyage. They comprised eighteen men of different nationalities and were sailing under a Portuguese flag. Branco, said Griffin, was middle-aged, short, robust, with handsome features, very short, greying hair and a taciturn manner. He was a natural giver of orders that he never reiterated, with whom I maintained a cordial, respectful, if distant relationship. His frequent silences meant he trod a fine line between seeming at a loss and being rude. His First Officer was Luiz Pereira, a close friend of Branco's from his adolescent days and he was swarthy and much warmer and open in his dealings with me. Second Officer Fernando Grande was a total extrovert, a cheerful joker who never lost his cool in dangerous times. The other two officers were a Galician boatswain, Rodo Amaro, who was older than Branco, a hale fellow well met overseer, and Olivier Sagna, a French purser from Bordeaux, Baudelaire's point of departure and return. Olivier Sagna could be petty-minded, but was always honest and scrupulous in his work. The remaining crew were electricians Paulinho Costa and Tonet Segarra, engineers Pedro Ramos and José Amuntado, head of the engine-room Macedonian Pavel Pavka, whose second-in-command was the much tattooed Charly Greene, plus six sailors, including the unforgettable black Mbuyi Kowanana, from the Ivory Coast, and finally the cook, Michel Bergeron, dubbed Tidbit by his colleagues despite being as thin as a rake, another sailor who haled from Bordeaux like the purser.

I befriended them all on the voyage, added Griffin, even though spending several months in a confined space on a boat with eighteen men is not the best recipe for relaxed cohabitation, and each individual's character gradually and inexorably unrolled like a coil of barbed wire. Additionally, characters changed for many logical reasons, the climate, the isolation imposed by the sea or the inevitable sight of the same faces hour after hour: in the end, against the odds, an atmosphere of freedom predominated. The only invariables were authority and discipline, the basis for a well-run crew, Griffin concluded in a night-time bar on the Rua do Seminário that allowed us one last glass before they closed shop: without a hierarchy that everyone on board respected absolutely, life could at times have been quite intolerable.

The night before we left port, after I'd introduced myself to Branco on the bridge, Griffin went on, and clarified why I hadn't been able to board in Lisbon, as Branco himself had planned, due to a delay beyond my control, First Officer Luiz Pereira accompanied me to the cabin he was to share with me, and gave me the top, very narrow berth, where a built-in shelf next to the pillow displayed calendars of naked women, mixed up with novels by Philip K. Dick, and six or seven novels by Jules Verne, said Griffin, including, I remember, *The Children of Captain Grant*, where the action appears to start on Desolation Island, in the Straits of Magellan, *Twenty Thousand Leagues Under the Sea*, *A Winter Amid the Ice* and the *Survivors of the Jonathan*, books that had always fascinated me as a boy to the point of obsession, like the journey I was about to undertake in that cabin, where fifty years later I again had access to books that had shown me what real-life action was all about. Pereira had just left the cabin to work with the harbour pilots on the various manoeuvres for the boat's departure, and I relived the feelings I'd felt when, on the cusp of adolescence, I read those books that transported me to a different, imagined, longed-for world, like someone hoarding their most treasured moments, and it was then that I thought I had an inkling of how my whole life had been a preparation for that moment, in a huge ellipse before I could confront the great voyage of my dreams I'd read about in Verne, that I had always thought impossible, said Griffin, and that was now about to start, as I rocked in the belly of the boat.

The languages I'd learned, added a self-engrossed Griffin, the history books I'd studied in my long professional career, the short journeys I'd made in small boats, the geographical associations I'd joined to enjoy the pleasure of hoarding the cards they issued, the maps I'd bought in all the cities I'd ever visited, the islands I'd invented and drawn ad nauseam, above all, my island, that Desolation Island, unconsciously guiding the tiny steps I took were, Griffin said, only links in a chain that had finally connected in that cabin and become simultaneously beginning and end. In the confined space that would be my home in the months to come, reeking with the smell of engine-room oil and grimy damp, I could never have felt more real than when immersed in the fantastic reality of the fictions that were my memories. I switched on the small electric fan Pereira had given me before he left and an acrid smell permeated our narrow cubbyhole, coincidentally triggering the aroma from my dreams. Like Raymond Rousel, Griffin commented, I had an infinite admiration for that unique genius, Jules Verne.

However, I wasn't as lucky as Rousel who met the maestro in Amiens where he'd lived since 1871 and obviously I was never able to shake his hand, though I embrace Rousel's final eulogy, said Griffin, as if it were a ritual prayer in a religion I worship: 'Blessed be this unrivalled master for the sublime hours I have enjoyed throughout my life reading and rereading him.' Blessed be Pereira who'd brought those books on to the *Minerva Janela*, as Baudelaire had brought Balzac along 'to read them time and again and learn about the wide, wide world', Griffin said, Pereira used to say in awe. We left the bar on the Rua do Seminario where the barman had generously allowed us to sink a last glass alone behind closed doors, while he swept and energetically stacked chairs on tables. Griffin bid me farewell in the doorway not without first wishing me the best of all possible nights.

Griffin and I resumed our conversation, his monologue in fact, a few days later when we breakfasted in the Carlton Hotel and as the day had dawned with a heavy downpour of large drops of rain, he thought it his duty to tell me about the weather on the day of his departure five years earlier. The barometer was very low, said Griffin. It rained more heavily than now because there was a squall, but the wind was a north-westerly and Branco waved to Pereira, who in turn communicated with the tugboat skipper over the radio. Fernando Grande implemented subsequent orders, but the pilot had drawn alongside and wanted to come on board to talk to Branco. The squall wouldn't abate until midday and he advised an evening departure that the captain fixed for 2000 hours. Nobody went ashore and nobody left his position in case they were needed for the manoeuvres to leave port. I looked out from my porthole at the beaches on the Avenida do Mar and the yachts in the marina on the other side of the bay battered by a strong wind that blew sheets of rain across the choppy sea, and fantasised about being one of the tourists who were really marooned in shops and on terraces where photos of Michael Jackson and Madonna coexisted with images of Virgins and vintage views of island villages, like Câmara de Lobos, Machico or Caniçal. The boat was swaying a lot but I felt no signs of seasickness. It was 10 October, my birthday, something I'd curiously forgotten until then. On the other hand, I did remember what Chateaubriand wrote when he saw migratory flocks of birds in October, said Griffin, and felt October was a month afflicted by a nameless anguish forcing the weather to change and wanted to have wings or be one of the clouds scudding through the sky in order to fulfil his irresistible desire to flee, flee at all cost, to be in some way invisible on land, as happened to Melville's Ishmael, and was now happening to me in my quest for Desolation Island. I know that for a fact.

The *Minerva Janela* set sail at the time agreed. Motorboats sped across the bay on a surging wave that startled the hundreds of birds, mostly seagulls, bobbing on the sea to soar in the bright pink orangey light that on 10 October created the strange feeling one was under an artificial vault, as on a lighted stage, something I've rarely seen more than once in my lifetime. The boat hooted two or three times in the harbour. The scant tourists on the marina looked up. It had stopped raining, continued Griffin, and within hours I was soon under the spell of the monotonous rhythm of the waves, the subtle changes in the currents, visible on the silvery surface, and suddenly, by the time I decided to look out, the clouds hid the moon and it was pitch black out to sea, the only lights being on board. I went on deck and peered over the stern rail, said Griffin, I began to discern the constant noise on the *Minerva Janela*, the track-a-track-track that was to be my background music for the next few months and became part of my thoughts. I saw night descend on the high seas, a real balm to the spirit, as inevitable and genuine as deep mourning. After we'd finally left beautiful Madeira behind us and bid farewell to the last glimmers from the Punta da Cruz lighthouse, I looked out on an expanse of shadows, the disturbing darkness of a turbulent sea, and felt more invisible than ever in the middle of a void where everything was as invisible as I was, even the wake stretching behind the boat, that one intuited rather than actually saw, as it broadened out inanely behind the boat and transmuted into a kind of lagoon within the sea.

5

ARNALDO AGUIAR, GRIFFIN'S GRANDFATHER, WAS A magician and conjurer who made bodies disappear or cut them in two after sawing the box where he'd encased them. He performed under the artistic name of Samini and nothing now remains of what my grandfather did or possessed, Griffin told me when I saw him a few days after he'd recounted his departure from Funchal on the *Minerva Janela* and after vanishing, like a genuine invisible man, from island life, without leaving his bedroom, no doubt. Griffin resumed quite naturally, as if no time had elapsed since our last encounter: When my grandfather Arnaldo set out in 1923 on that honeymoon voyage to Valparaíso with my grandmother, he wasn't yet 'the Great Samini', or even 'the Famous Samini', simply 'Samini' and only in the sparse theatres where he performed. I've always thought that he conceived the idea for his best act, curiously, one in which he made his partner invisible and proved that invisibility in a series of tests, when Graciela Pavic showed him the automaton in Punta Arenas. Over time he elaborated an act that involved his helper entering a device with a remotely humanoid form, at first similar to an Egyptian sarcophagus, later like a space robot with a head and torso, via a door which he would open so the public could verify nobody was there, or that it *was* in fact the same person in a state of 'molecular modification', as grandfather described it, explained Griffin, a modification granting him the privilege of seeing without being seen, of performing without anyone knowing the kind of action he was about to perform, or mind read, spy or watch, and thus, to the audience's amazement, at an order from my grandfather, the invisible person hurtled against a table and moved it centimetres along, displaced cups of coffee or the belongings of spectators, extracting a wallet from someone's inside pocket, or slipped off a lady's necklace who would whimper in delight or fear. All this happened if it was a nightclub or dance hall, because if it was a theatre he invited members of the audience up onstage, where they at any rate would witness the climax of the act, the moment when he caused the invisible man to dress, item by item, gradually, and, in their hypnotic state, they first see trousers without feet walking by themselves, or a shirt waving its sleeves without arms inside, and then see him become fully dressed, but a being who was completely hollow, empty, headless, evaporated, the real fictitious invisible Griffin from Wells's novel, it's a fact, the invisible Griffin who had to walk around bandaged from head to foot in order to assume volume, about whose literary existence my grandfather was probably totally ignorant: at most he might have seen Whale's famous film starring Claude Rains, and of course in the era when my grandfather invented this act, he could never have imagined that his daughter, my mother, continued Griffin, would marry a Griffin, a visible, flesh-and-blood Irishman. I don't know how my grandfather's trick worked, but it turned him into showbiz's Great Samini. Sometimes, the machine that made people invisible was shaped like an automaton with human guise and the transformation mysteriously took place in its interior. The figure's facial features, from the many photos I have seen, came more and more to resemble the automaton from the Straits of Magellan, so great was my grandfather's obsession with that lost dummy. As far as I know, nothing remains of any of that, said Griffin who'd suddenly gone all gloomy as he stared at the rainy Funchal evening.

Much to my surprise, Griffin launched into a monologue of lamentations in a voice that became increasingly subdued and I felt like a stranger at his side. I only managed to grasp a single thread that was too private and too profound, which he no doubt rehearsed repeatedly, one about the passage of time and how, over time, and Griffin raised his voice as he reiterated the word 'time', an entire universe of intense feeling and people gradually disappears. What happened to the friends my grandparents and parents had, a self-engrossed Griffin wondered, and their worries and heartache, what they thought was and wasn't important, the articles they bought, the items they lost or broke, every challenge to move forward, every minute of endeavour, their triumphs and failures, what happened to their moments of happiness, days of good cheer, all their pleasures and emotions? Everything fades, said Griffin, nothing remains: there are only people who inherit possessions, businesses, companies and houses. Though that's not my case, he said, nothing remained and nothing will remain, not even children, and if we children do remain, we then cast off the past, destroy it, erase it, render it invisible before our own eyes, or simply forget it. Life is quick to dissolve into oblivion, into nothingness. When Griffin said his piece I thought he was crying while his eyes receded as he watched the grey clouds coming from the south-east, whence a path had opened up for the *Minerva Janela* when he'd departed five years ago.

My grandparents reached Punta Arenas in the southern summer of 1923, said Griffin, recovering like someone chasing off ill omens, and I don't know how long they stayed, or whether or not my grandfather ever performed as a magician in the local theatre, though he must have tried out some conjuring because he wasn't famous and was contracted to give a single performance on the Mercedes Estate, near the city of Porvenir, on the Tierra del Fuego, on the initiative of Graciela Pavic who had spent her childhood there. They had their photo taken with the automaton in the Salesian Museum in Punta Arena before or after that performance, I'm not sure precisely when.

However, my grandfather did write a letter on the Mercedes Estate, according to my grandmother Irene, noting that the main residence was at the end of a long flatland leading to a beach that overlooked the Straits in a place called the Way of the Whitebait. On the day he performed using handkerchiefs, card tricks and the odd experiment into telepathy, a hydroplane landed, a Breguet XVI, and it made a deep impression on him because a Spaniard was piloting, although it belonged to Aeroposta Argentina, the airmail line linking Europe and South America. As a man who was crazy about aviation, my father tried to find out more about the flight and the plane. However, the pilot had made an emergency landing, wasn't in a talking mood, and simply repaired the Breguet and took off again. In order to alleviate my father's sense of frustration, the owner of the Estate, Don Esteban Ravel, Graciela Pavic's friend, as crazy about planes as my father, added Griffin, agreed to take them all, Graciela included, back to Punta Arenas in his own aeroplane, a Latécoère 26, the only one in the whole area, piloted by Don Esteban himself. Flying over the Straits of Magellan was a unique experience for my grandparents, nigh on an hour's journey, in the gentle glow of a long January twilight, in midsummer, as they flew south, towards Dawson Island, and then climbed along the coast of the Brunswick Peninsula, and its narrowest stretch, the mosaic of the roofs in Punta Arenas suddenly appeared in crepuscular shades of blue, yellow, red and green, like a large patchwork quilt.

6

THE NAVIGATION BRIDGE OF THE *MINERVA JANELA*, continued Griffin, changing the subject and returning to the account of his voyage on the merchant ship, occupied the entire fourth level of the aftercastle and had twelve large windows tapering down in size either side of the central and biggest window. Hieratic Captain Branco was always on the bridge with First Officer Pereira and Jordao Navares at the helm, an austere, taciturn soul from Cape Verde, with a scar-covered face that led Second Officer Fernando Grande and Paulinho Costa and the other sailors to nickname him Acab. Sometimes Rata, Tonet Segarra's ugly dog, slipped in, sniffed around, and then sprawled on a folded blanket put there by Branco. The dog and I got on very well: whenever he saw me, he barked and flashed his teeth, a gesture I always reciprocated. A kind of visor or eave protected the cabin windows, above which were radio and radar aerials, satellite receivers and lightning conductors; even so the windows were almost always streaming with water swept up by the wind. The green anti-glare glass meant the navigation bridge was usually dark even by day, so the radar screen could always be read at a glance. Jordao Navares, alias Acab, normally had little to do, although he kept one eye on the lever of the engine order telegraph in order to pass on Branco's orders and the other on the radar. The boat was steered by automatic pilot, said Griffin, and unless there was an indication something was amiss a few miles on, whales or perhaps a fishing fleet, nobody steered manually unless the boat was about to dock.

I used to wander unrestricted on board, said Griffin, but there were places I rarely went. For example, I wouldn't go to the cargo deck where the black sailor Kowanana worked, although I could always see him from my vantage point sunbathing in his swimming trunks and listening to U2, the Cranberries or George Michael on his Walkman. Very occasionally I descended to the boiler room, the deepest, most loathsome spot on the boat, where Pavka the Macedonian ruled the roost, also wearing headphones, as he studied and shouted out tenses and phrases in Portuguese. On the other hand, I spent long spells leaning on the side rail on the second deck, my favourite spot, added Griffin, surrounded by wet ladders, cables, hoses, battery lights, pullies, winches, ropes, looking at the immanent greyness of the heaving Atlantic we were advancing through. When I was there, I perhaps felt I was somehow breathing at one with the boat and imagined I now belonged there.

Once I was familiar with the ecology of life on board, its rules and routines, my thoughts began to expand on their own and I amused myself by imagining my grandfather's life, the incidents on his voyage or remembered the hundreds of books I'd read and the true or false stories (I didn't mind which) inspired by the automaton of Punta Arenas, and recreated the stories and adventures of all those ships and sailors who had passed through the Straits of Magellan in the last five hundred years, as if it were the funnel to the world, on that same route I was travelling then, much less poetic, I must say, than one might think, with an appalling climate and constantly being pulled this way and that. Or I drew islands, *the* island, Desolation Island, that never abandoned me: I'd draw it in my mind, as I looked down at the waves surging monotonously. At other times, mid-morning, after I'd jotted down a few notes or read a magazine, because Captain Branco had yet to decide what tasks to allot me so I didn't feel too idle in the long months the voyage would last, I'd go up to the bridge to chat with Branco and listen to him giving his strangely brisk orders, 'Full steam ahead' or 'Forward a quarter'. If he was busy, I watched Fernando Grande calculate distances on the big maps in the map room, in a spectral red light that gave us both a pallid, almost translucent look, curiously enough, almost to the point of invisibility. 'In three days, four max if the storm they're forecasting is bigger,' Second Officer Grande would say, according to Griffin, 'we shall see Santo Antao, 16 degrees north and 24 west, the first of the Cape Verde islands. You take a peek,' and Grande twisted the compass that was open to the right degree two or three times over the map before one end fell precisely on the point marking Mindelo on St Vincent Island, our first port of call. 'Right, we'll be there in three days in the evening, if Branco doesn't tell us to speed up.' Then he dragged me out of the map room, said Griffin, and to the crew's lounge where Tidbit, the ship's cook, had laid out tins of tuna and a few beers, and showed me photos of his children and wife. 'She's only one,' said Grande, adding that no self-respecting sailor has only one wife. 'Of course, you must be married to one who's the official widow,' he joked, said Griffin, 'but you need others to console her.' After laughing at his own wit, he called Tidbit and told him to save the tuna for the sailors and fetch the contraband caviar, because they were officers. Then Pereira would join the party, almost always with a Philip K. Dick novel under his arm, and I'd spend many mornings or evenings with the two first officers, talking of everything under the sun, keeping boredom at bay or sharing our tedium.

When we reached this point in his yarn, Griffin preferred to change landscapes before he continued his peroration, as our conversation meandered for hours wherever we happened to be in Funchal, and time passed and neither of us noticed. It was late, as he pointed out, and thinking I saw an anguished frown flit momentarily across his secretive brow, I began to anticipate one of his brusque farewells, but not so, on the contrary he suggested we continue elsewhere. I was delighted and we split the taxi fare to Câmara de Lobos, a few kilometres outside Funchal. We can dine there and I'll tell you about an interesting coincidence, one of the many fate weaves, said Griffin mysteriously. I will tell you about Brunswick and the way this name is linked to the existence of the automaton of Punta Arenas.

Then I remembered he had mentioned that name earlier, when recounting his grandfather's return journey by air from the Mercedes Estate. Brunswick. The Brunswick Peninsula. Griffin uttered these words several times in the taxi, averting his gaze, perhaps trying to stage-manage a sense of drama. And then you have the Duke of Brunswick, Griffin went on, as if he too were alone, before falling silent on the rest of the drive and only speaking when we were finally sitting on the terrace of a summer-season restaurant, surrounded by German tourists, opposite a small, filthy promenade divided off by ripped car tyres. Griffin glanced at the menu and then continued: I think I may have already mentioned the Brunswick Peninsula, on the Magellan, where one finds Punta Arenas. When I mention that name, the third Duke of Brunswick inevitably comes to mind, an individual marginal to my story, though an item he commissioned to be built certainly is not.

He lived in a castle in Dolna Krupa, which is now in present-day Slovakia, at the turn of the sixteenth century. He was passionately interested in mechanical devices and every kind of machine, clock or construction with automatons. He was also, and no less intensely, a wheeler and dealer who liked to engage in politics, and never from the sidelines. Automatons were all the rage at the time in the courts of Rudolph II of Habsburg in Prague, and his uncle Philip II in Spain. Moreover, both were patrons of Juanelo Turriano, the great engineer of such toys from the days of Charles V, whose fabulous inventions were admired throughout the West. Cabinets of Wonders were equally fashionable, containing mechanical models, small and large, that imitated any movement in nature or art, birds that opened their wings and beaks, tritons that dived in and out of fountains like dolphins, musicians who played their instruments or even blew them, warriors who clashed swords and blacksmiths who struck anvils. That intermeshing of gears, cogs, counterweights and limpid metallic sounds obsessed the duke who was such a crazed collector of clocks he even integrated them into his panoply of weapons and ducal ensigns and offered small fortunes for machines that operated with absolute precision.

He was also characterised by extreme envy, added Griffin, and with either sublime or non-existent discretion he persuaded the great maestros to build him a replica or duplicate of each unique item they manufactured for those more powerful than himself, however expensive and inimitable the contraption might be. Subsequently, the high value of these items in his castle collection was always relative, depending as it did, to an extent, on the fact they were mere copies. When their authenticity was questioned, the duke asked why were his the copies and not the ones belonging to the other owners that were officially declared the originals, because in fact there were always two of every automaton or clock the renowned engineer built, and neither possessed less value in terms of manufacture, design or artfulness, let alone the precious materials used. As a result, the duke argued, said Griffin, some items – his – were a reflection of those originally commissioned, and as is the case with mirrors, it's very difficult, not to say impossible, to distinguish the real from the fake, given that reflection and reflected are identical.

You could see in Dolna Krupa, for example, Griffin recalled, creations like that well-known Christmas scene, the so-called *Weinachtskrippe*, commissioned from Hans Schlottheim in 1585 by Christian I, the Elector of Saxony, or *The Tower of Babel* that Schlottheim made for Rudolph II, or *The Vessel with Fanfares*, also for the same emperor, which, they say, he gave to the Sultan of Istanbul; the duplicate devices the duke owned included Langenbucher's *Chariot of Victory* and the celebrated *Cabinet of Pomerania*, by Hainhofer, that purported to be the complex, miniature summation of all the sciences, mathematics, optics, physics, astronomy and geometry, not discounting the myriad small crannies with secret chambers and traps located within the artefact.

Driven by his sickly desire to possess an exact copy of whatever original was commissioned in this fashion, the duke even requested, under sworn oath, a copy of everything built by Melvicius of Prague, the great, ageless, possibly Jewish genius, renowned from the times of Emperor Maximilian, who was over a hundred when he died – that is, if he ever died, Griffin speculated – the teacher of the Turrianos, Acquaronis and Schlottheims, of engineers whose fame spanned almost two centuries and whom Philip II secretly asked to forge a whole army of male automata to fortify the Straits of Magellan, something he obviously never succeeded in doing, not even with the help of Sarmiento de Gamboa, the creator of the first two settlements on the Straits, the man the king ordered to transport the one hundred and eleven automata he'd planned to set around the islands under the naïve pretence they would seem threatening, and not even with the help of Melvicius, who, conversely, out of pride or feeling a personal challenge, strove to manufacture the best, most complete, perhaps most awesome, android automaton of his era. When the duke's spies informed him of this project, said Griffin, he ordered, bought, bribed and even tortured old Melvicius to ensure he kept his pledge to give him a copy of whatever emerged from his house, and thus manufacture, also in secret, a second automaton. The existence of this second automaton stayed hidden for years after the deaths of the respective protagonists.

Sarmiento, on the other hand, was in the know, and when he travelled to the Straits, he took with him not the hundred and eleven in Philip II's scheme of things, but the only one, one might say, manufactured by Melvicius, or at least one of a pair, but this is meat for another day's tale, said Griffin, who was beginning to show signs of fatigue, perhaps because of the wine we'd drunk at nightfall in that restaurant in Cámara de Lobos. One of the reasons for my voyage was to find out which of the two automata existed today in Punta Arenas, and if you want to know whether I succeeded, for the moment I will only say that I did and I didn't, in equal measure. I still wonder if we should think of them as two originals or two duplicates, and whether in the end it makes any difference. Whatever their reality was, Griffin continued, it is a particularly strange coincidence that the geographical location of that automaton carries the same name, though I'm not sure it was to honour that duke who commissioned copies behind everyone's back in such a relentless and oppressive way. Anyway, this only came to light centuries later and belongs in the public domain of a mere handful of historians, said Griffin, and I fear they're as secretive as Melvicius ever was, so it is as unknown to ordinary people as the story of that automaton.

7

I WONDERED WHAT SURPRISES MY VOYAGE AND, IN particular, my final destination held in store, Griffin added when we returned to Funchal late into the night. Many of the crew were well acquainted with those haunts because they'd been to the Straits before, the odd one, like the slightly greying boatswain, Rodo Amaro, had even worked on the San Gregorio Terminal oil refinery, way up the coast from Punta Arenas, and Charly Greene, the fair-haired engineer, spent a winter on the barren island of Lenox, south of Navarino, where there was only ice and snow, because he fell in love with a Scottish biologist and penguin lover who had established her research camp there. Pereira, for his part, was the only one who had really sailed round Cape Horn.

'I was on a containership belonging to Mobil Oil,' Pereira told Griffin, 'and I can say that the west winds blew as fiercely as they did five centuries earlier, a year before or ten years later on, as if you're pummelling against a wall that makes the most powerful engines splutter and wheeze and sometimes you feel almost vertical as the waves push the keel of your boat up high. From my cabin,' Pereira went on, 'battered by icy winds and the endless downpour, I saw the barren island and awe-inspiring cape, the real end of the world, and my only thoughts were of

Jules Verne, Richard Dana and the nineteenth-century whalers, and I told myself I was alone in experiencing that unique moment in the world, that life is only tolerable if one can say elatedly "I'm really living this",' said Griffin, concluding the first officer's little speech.

Then he said nothing until we reached the hotel, where we said goodbye and left to chance a possible encounter the following day. Predictably, we met in the morning in the usual café on the Avenida Zarco, and Griffin immediately started to talk about Punta Arenas. It's a strange city, he said, as he summoned the waiter and ordered our drinks, splendid hotels and buildings that look as sinister as the KGB's Lubyanka, no doubt housing the local authorities, and a wide range of streets and houses that exude extraordinary colour and vitality. There are beautiful, elongated red dusks, the likes of which I'd never seen before, and areas as commonplace as you'd find in Madrid or Quebec that people consider featureless, with McDonald's and Fuji or Kodak photo-shops. I can also describe details of a couple of hotels and restaurants that are as magnificent and expensive as any in Paris. These weren't the places recommended to me by the likes of José Amuntado, Paulinho Costa – whom I befriended very soon after I started mingling on board – or even the highly conscientious Rodo Amaro, perhaps the most honest and Catholic member of the *Minerva Janela*'s crew: they mentioned places in the Zona Franca or Barrio Hortícola, which I of course visited, dives full of sordid, melancholy charm, like a tango or whatever. The Ribeiro establishment, between Briceño and España, was one such bar with green lamps over customers' heads, panes of dark glass in the doors and amber lighting that gave a veneer of intimate warmth to the grimy wood, a would-be American bar where the owner, a tall German blonde with a wooden leg whose looks did her real age credit, pointed to the posters decorating the bar, circus posters or something similar, where a troupe of acrobats, including herself, the lame blond giant asserted, perched high on the trapeze, and I remembered what Cortázar writes in his book on John Keats when he says he met a female acrobat who'd been burnt by the moon in Punta Arenas. Reasonably enough, I asked the big blonde on the high wire, now on the other side of the bar, if not of life itself, like all of us who were there on the other side of the world, in that southernmost city, on the actual frontier established by Sarmiento de Gamboa, the brilliant sailor and magician, added Griffin pursuing the long sweep of his stories, but she didn't know of any Cortázar, nor, as far as she knew, had the moon burnt anything apart from her heart, that is, if the moon had two big dark eyes like the Chilean who deceived her. On the other hand, she had heard of the Great Samini's invisible act, though I didn't dare tell her he was my grandfather, when I asked her if the name meant anything to her.

Punta Arenas is a strange city, Griffin repeated, a city that is invisible and remote for almost everyone, and exists only for people who really want to go there, because it isn't on the way to anywhere, except to *my* island, to Desolation Island, and is as invisible as the journey there planned by Antoine de Saint-Exupéry that he never made, on his famously truncated 1938 expedition from Newark, New York, to Punta Arenas, 14,000 kilometres by plane across the whole of America, as a fellow recounted to me in the old German acrobat's dive, a man who was drinking pisco, that thick, yellow liquor, taking long, slow sips, and wiping the sweat from his brow every now and then. Saint-Exupéry's flight should have been a heroic feat for France and the writer, a world-famous ace aviator, who left Montreal on 14 February 1938. Two days later, when he was flying over

Guatemala City, the Simoun he was piloting crashed and was completely wrecked. Saint-Exupéry miraculously survived, although it took him ages to recover from his broken legs, arms and ribs, as well as the infections he contracted.

The expedition ended there, thousands of people felt hugely disappointed, and it became a myth, a kind of invisible happening was the term employed by the man sipping yellow pisco, said Griffin, emphasising the 'invisible', because the whole city of Punta Arenas had come out to welcome the French pilot with all due pomp and ceremony, and a friend was waiting for him here, whose name he'd probably forgotten, a Chilean from Antofagasta who'd worked with Saint-Exupéry for Aeroposta Argentina in the early thirties. 'That Chilean,' continued the man sipping yellow pisco, 'was my father and the day Saint-Exupéry, the invisible hero, didn't appear in the sky, my father lost everything and it changed his life and easy-going manner because he'd bet everything he had on his old mail-plane co-pilot landing at 1600 hours, not a minute earlier or later, exactly five days after he'd set off from Canada. It would have been a heroic feat, if he had brought it off, that's for sure.'

The yellow pisco guy, who never divulged his name, then showed me the spot where the landing had been planned, a strip improvised at the Miraflores aerodrome, which was equally invisible, or so I told him, said Griffin, and now had been transformed into an ice rink, close to a small, stony beach, a rather useless rocky waste, where, according to that same man, parts from bodies thrown live into the waters of the Straits during the Pinochet dictatorship washed up, and that too was invisible for everyone concerned, he said, added Griffin. The exact location was the Asmar dry dock where you can now see a very different set of corpses, once famous boats, like the *Hipparchus*, *Falstaff* or the Scottish ship *County of Peebles*, which have been stripped and now act as a breakwater.

'At the lowest part of that breakwater you'll find the so-called "Pilots' Beach" because they threw the wretches from military planes or helicopters down onto those beaches, and after a time, at least in two instances I am aware of,' continued the yellow pisco guy, 'in 1974 and 1976, remains started to wash up on that spot with the tides and currents, remains that were simply skulls and bones, as hollow as the automaton in the Salesian Museum' – and Griffin emphasised the fact the man had referred unexpectedly and casually to the automaton in his photo – 'and were washed away and disappeared for good in the city's naval base.'

Occasionally we sailed past merchant ships and oil tankers on the high seas that belonged to companies as important as ours, said Griffin after a pause when his attention seemed to be distracted by the news in a local newspaper someone had left on the chair next to him. The *Minerva Janela* belonged to Texaco, though it was registered in Lisbon, something I never realised until I'd been on board for a while, and when we passed another similar boat, the English *City of Liverpool*, Branco had a friendly conversation with its captain over the radio. Olivier Sagna told me they were all friends, and that the boat was brother to the *Minerva Janela*, and both belonged to the all-powerful Texaco & Co. But at the time, before and after our brief stay on Cape Verde, Griffin went on, we saw a huge amount of traffic on the sea and ships hooted that belonged to companies like Evergreen, Exxon, Amoco, Mobil or Chevron. I have very vivid memories of the day we sailed past the *City of Liverpool*, a lousy day as far as I was concerned. I was helping Sagna and Amaro to remove rust from the lifeboat moorings with strong stripping agents, the smell from which, on top of the constant stink of putrid tar and foul fumes, was making me feel sick, said Griffin. When Sagna noticed I'd turned a deathly pale, he forced me to wear a safety mask and told me that the fumes that sometimes came up the passageways from the bottom of the boat were from the diesel engines. More than once, Sagna added, they'd been forced to extinguish fires in the area around the boilers caused by the engines' poor combustion. 'You must have seen the burn scars on Pavel's arms, or the riveter gloves Charly always wears.'

Even so, despite the mask, I was ill, terribly seasick, and finished up in my cabin, almost unable to open my eyes or avoid feeling endless turns churning round my head whenever I moved. I had a dreadful two days during the storm that Fernando Grande had previously warned me about in the map room. In the murk I remembered how my seasickness was in fact more serious, Griffin said, it was a final symptom of panic, of neurosis prompted by the uncontrollable angst I felt at the inescapable idea I was at sea, in the middle of the sea, at the *epicentre* of the sea, abandoned and alone in the heart of that heaving, ravenous void, and that reality was appalling. Everything fell and flew from one side to another, everything was flung through the air, Pereira's books, his family photos, zinc and plastic containers, everything, absolutely everything. It was total chaos for two days when I was prostrate in bed in a terrible agony, sicking up my guts while I inevitably fasted. I had no clear notion of the time that had passed when I did recover finally: the storm had died down, and I could hear the crew shouting cheerfully in passageways and on deck, happy to see dawn break over Cape Verde.

8

IF OLIVER GRIFFIN WASN'T A TRAGIC, OR RATHER dramatic, character in his search for the island he kept drawing, if only mentally, or hadn't been possessed by that acute sense of invisibility his strange surname absurdly sentenced him to, or by his compulsive need to relate, or at least relate to me, a perfect stranger, the whole of his voyage in the most minute detail, with amazing erudition and powers of recall that increasingly put me in awe of him, since I'd never before met a man like Griffin, if it weren't for all that, I mean, Griffin would evidently have been, if only for initiates, a kind of authentically Flaubertian Bouvard (as he'd defined himself on another occasion), thus relegating me to the role of Pécuchet in that famous novel where two rich, lonely men explore human knowledge and its attendant stupidity. I personally resisted the idea because both characters are comic takes on ingenuousness: Griffin and myself were hardly that. Nonetheless, it was practically impossible to hold a conversation with Oliver because the moment he opened his mouth his words were transformed into a monologue delivered by someone reading a text as if it were inscribed in his brain rather than if he were improvising, and I realised I wanted to find out more about him, about his life, personality, loved ones, past and present, and assumed that would all emerge naturally from Griffin himself, but gradually I was forced to accept that his life was also invisible.

On the many days we spent together, seeing each other almost daily, he revealed next to nothing about his private life and I concluded the invisibility that haunted him had invaded his personal memory to such an extent he avoided narrating anything so subjective because it simply wasn't evident in his recall of his past. It wasn't that it didn't exist: it was merely transparent as far as he was concerned. Conversely, Griffin was becoming someone I needed in a way I found hard to pinpoint. I needed to listen to him continuing his story and learn the ins and outs of his quest for that automaton, chimera, island, identity or madness, whatever you want to call it, a seafaring Quixote for whom I was Sancho Panza, a silent witness to his fathering of stories within stories that in turn lived within other stories. Such was my need that the days I didn't meet Griffin or didn't make the appointment we tacitly agreed the previous day, I wandered through Funchal with a nauseating feeling of irritation and emptiness. Such days were barren wastes.

Days after he'd told me about his dismal experience of being seasick in a storm, I met him again opposite the port. Time on board ship is a hard test and pushes you to the limit of wanting to strangle your cabin mate, said Griffin as we walked side by side under the ever-present palm trees on the Avenida do Mar, without any preamble, despite the interlude, so for a few seconds I almost thought Griffin was adopting the pose of a man dictating an unusual set of memoirs. Yes, time on board boats is hard, he repeated, because often time is all you have, time, lots of time, vast amounts of time, acres of time to digest and parcel out, to think and waste, to work and get bored, to unleash your imagination until you see phantoms or memories that appear as if they were hallucinations. It's scarcely surprising, continued Griffin, that in voyages of yesteryear horrors were sighted that were figments of the imaginations of passengers and crew: slimy monsters, unknown creatures that in fact dwelled in their nightmares, beings that Freud would have fished from the depths of their minds because they were nourished by the subconscious and the darkest of myths, myths as dark as the pitch-black sea whence those monsters surged, the darkness surrounding ships, and myths triggering the most incredible panic. That is why for the sake of one's reason one must measure out one's time on a boat and know how to fill it before it devours one, Oliver continued.

And he recalled how, for example, Tonet Segarra played a tenor sax in his free time and did so with brio because he'd played with an orchestra on tour in Germany, and that José Amuntado tattooed Pedro Ramos, his colleague in the engine room, uncomplicated tattoos, landscapes with palm trees or naked women, and that Jordao Navares read hunting magazines and sometimes, with Bergeron the cook alias Tidbit, read Batman or Mafia comics, or that Kowanana, when not listening to his favourite music on his Walkman, donned his Adidas tracksuit and punched a sandbag. There was a time when, historically, every ship carried an hourglass, Griffin went on, with a span of thirty minutes. They were called sand-glasses. The majority of such hourglasses were made in Venice, in furnaces on the island of Murano, and were very fragile and had to be stored in places that were protected against unstable weather. Nonetheless, a well-stocked boat carried spare hourglasses because they often broke, and it was the duty, or one of the duties, of the cabin boys, to measure out the life of the boat in four-hour shifts, watching the bottles of sand and turning them round so they could begin anew.

I remember how before arriving in Lisbon, where the *Minerva*

Janela had waited for me in vain, I visited naval museums in the different cities I passed through. It became a mania I couldn't throw off, and in my free time, when invited to give some lecture or other in cities that were seaports, I never missed the opportunity to meander in airy museum rooms and feed my imagination on objects from the oceans. I saw all kinds and sizes of model boats, from ones you could hold in the palm of a hand to those with life-size figures in galleons and sailing ships from two or three hundred years ago. I have in mind one in particular, in Rotterdam, in the Leuvehavenstraat, that I found fascinating. It took three hours to reach the Maritiem Museum Prins Hendrik de Rotterdam from the train station. I visited it one morning six years ago and saw the famous *De Buffel*, one of the first battleships. In the museum's glass cabinets and rooms I found many curious items worthy of my attention, but concentrated almost exclusively, for a long time, said Griffin, on the fabulous recreation, almost an eighteenth-century *tableau vivant*, of the bilge, the rock bottom of a boat, and its impact on the health of passengers and crew. It was a papier-mâché effort that included a married couple in contemporary dress holding handkerchiefs to their noses, the husband supporting his pallid wife, and several sailors in actions relevant to their function in such a space, scrubbing the timbers with a long brush, emptying buckets of filth or sealing cracks in the wood with tar.

The realism of the scene made a deep impact upon me, and when I read the description on the nearby wall about the source of the reconstruction, I saw, said Griffin, that it had formed part of a series of 'live scenes' created in 1910 to demonstrate, with real actors, various moments of daily life on a boat, with exact replicas of the furniture and rooms on the *Boothmeier*, a Swedish schooner from Gothenberg that was exhibited whole in the Universal Exhibition in Barcelona in 1929. The copy was notable in the detailed way it showed how pestilence and sickness spread from that disgusting spot to ports, cities and countries. Boats have always been unhealthy dens of putrefaction and stench, refuges for colonies of rats, said Griffin, and still are, hence the scrupulous routines for cleaning the *Minerva Janela*, and our purser Olivier Sagna's paranoid obsession, always insisting that everyone, officers included, worked hard when it was time to polish decks and passages, clean engines and gears. And it all rose up from the miasma in the bilge, as I could see in the cross-section reproduced in that Rotterdam museum. From bilges, fetid places, Griffin emphasised, real sewers, final resting homes for all rotten rubbish and food, the excrement that didn't drop straight into the sea but came from poop deck latrines euphemistically dubbed 'the garden', and the water filtering through its leaking joints, that was the source, said Griffin, of infections that turned into epidemics when they reached port. That is why people said they feared evil brought by sea, why Nosferatu comes off a ship and why plague comes by boat. And I remembered, continued Griffin, what Eugenio de Salazar wrote about the water or substance he saw coming out of the bilge pumps: 'Neither tongue nor palate would want to taste it, nor nostrils smell it, nor eyes see it, because it spills out into a hellish hell, and stinks like the devil.' The *Minerva Janela* didn't have a bilge properly speaking, at least not like boats in the sixteenth and seventeenth centuries, but the engine area, behind the last double thickness walls in the hold where Pavka worked, stank in a way I've not experienced since, and I still carry that smell in my head, from my occasional visit down there. 'I'd describe it as a disgusting, all-pervasive smell or sensation that's very peculiar, akin to rotting algae and fish,' said Pavka, and the Macedonian added that on big merchant ships it was difficult to coexist with such an unheard-of cocktail of smells if you don't know or accept its nature, I thought that was a wonderful way to describe it, Griffin concluded.

9

NOTHING IN LIFE IS THE SAME AND YET EVERYTHING is linked, and conjurers' tricks are no different, as in the illusions my grandfather Arnaldo created, where everything was interconnected, what the world calls coincidence, chance or destiny. A handkerchief extracted from a lady's handbag becomes a dove in a magician's top hat, a gentleman's wallet a rabbit in a brightly coloured box and a burning rope a stiff, freezing stick. If I am here today, said Griffin, if I embarked on the *Minerva Janela* voyage I now recount to you, it is because I have a very distinct 'loathing of domesticity', as Baudelaire wrote and experienced in his own flesh, and it's a sentiment I heartily endorse. I refer to the fact that, like my favourite French literary fetish, though quite differently, because he never used to leave Paris, and we've seen how his truncated passage to India ended in a hasty, stressful return via Madeira, I never set up home, never feel at home, am always in transit. Passing through houses, Griffin said with relish, when I supposedly lived in fixed abodes that I have now completely forgotten, passing through people and experiences. If I experience something, I file it away mentally in order to remember later, a long time after and enjoy, but it's a one-off moment that I never repeat.

I'm now into my fifty-seventh year and still feel that I have always been moving on, leaving many if not every door closed behind me. I don't hold on to friends, in fact, today I haven't a single one I can appeal to or call, no relative or loved one, Griffin added clinically. Suddenly, one fine day, I stop ringing my friends, acquaintances or lovers, I congeal at the least reminiscence, as if I were in a ferry taking me to another island while they stay on shore. Obviously they still exist, or existed after I walked out of their lives, I mean they haven't died, and I'm sure they must be happy or sad wherever they are, but I've never seen them again. They are lodged in a memory or simply belong to the past, that invisible place in time. I've always fled (no, the right word isn't 'fled', but left behind, insisted Griffin), as if the only way to go was forward, which is how I see it. As a child I spent ten years in a good, reputable school, and from the day I left I've never ventured back. I have no childhood friends, at most, I recognise them when I bump into them, generally in strange places, but it isn't mutual, or so it seems, which only reinforces my feeling of invisibility. I went to university, taught over many years, worked in various countries and cities for many more, and always, at the end of each phase, I've turned the page on those things in my life, and never looked back or left any trace. My offices have always been places that are alien to me, without personal photos or links to my private life. After I've left them, I could perfectly well not return and it wouldn't matter one iota, nothing of mine would be there and, over time, I would miss nothing whatsoever from the place. I have married twice and never heard again from my exes, and they've heard nothing of me, I suppose. I live in the present continuous tense, in terms of my relationships with people and things, said Griffin. When for an almost imperious reason I have gone back, I have felt only a mixture of nostalgia and alienation that wasn't necessarily painful but it wasn't pleasurable either. Consequently, I've created a kind of invisible life for everybody, myself included, where each episode can be invented, because it wouldn't be any less palpable than the truth that is itself unattainable, or rather has been erased.

I was thinking such thoughts in my cabin, when Cape Verde was spotted in the distance, Griffin remarked after a prolonged pause when he appeared to be absorbed by an inopportune memory. I will now tell you about my cabin, he suddenly ventured. Although there was no overgenerous use of space on the *Minerva Janela*, I couldn't complain, said Griffin, and we all had enough room to put our things, however violently storms and surging waves hurtled our belongings to the ground in motley heaps. As far as I knew, nobody ever stole from anyone: that was a sacred rule and perhaps the one carrying the harshest penalty if it was infringed, because a sailor who stole, however trivial the theft, never worked on another boat; every shipping company would duly hear about his record as a thief. The cabin I shared with Luiz Pereira was an officers', and I had two racks for my clothes, a desk, and, though it was very small, some three metres by seven, a washbasin and shower, when the usual was one bathroom per two cabins.

I've already mentioned that I slept on the top bunk, next to a porthole looking on to an aluminium ladder, in a covered area of the cabin deck, at the top of a hatchway through which black Kowanana sometimes would emerge, smiling and nodding in my direction. But at that particular moment, when I looked through the porthole, I didn't see the white teeth of the man from the Ivory Coast, but glimpsed an imposing, distant basalt mass, even blacker against the mid-ocean light, of what was surely Santo Antao, the first of the Barlovento Islands, which meant we were now only a few miles from the archipelago discovered in 1460 by the Genoese Antonio da Noli and his Deputy, the Portuguese Diogo Gomes, that was said to be 'belonging to Cape Verde' because it was some ninety leagues from the real Cape Verde, a crag situated on dry land now known as Senegal. Lines from Rimbaud's 'Drunken Boat' immediately rang in my head: 'I have seen starry archipelagos and islands and their delirious skies opening to the sailor', and as a result of those peculiar associations of ideas, when we sailed closer to the island, then passed it by, I remembered, for example, how Dr Henry Moseley, a passenger on the *Challenger* on its 1872 voyage, had written that, when seen from the sea, the coast of Santo Antao and later San Vicente, our destination, comprised barren, desolate peaks and beaches that reminded him of Aden's desert wastes, said Griffin. Aden! Why Aden? wondered Griffin excitedly, why did he compare it, relate it to the place where Rimbaud fetched up in those same years, obsessed with discovering the gardens of Zanzibar, an island he unfortunately never reached, but longed for as passionately as I longed for my Desolation Island? How strange that I remembered Rimbaud's poem as I was recalling Moseley who was indirectly associated with Rimbaud, and that Rimbaud and I were connected by 'starry archipelagos' for which we'd abandoned all else! Everything is linked, though nothing is exactly the same, Griffin reiterated.

And I also remembered, he continued animatedly, or rather saw with my own eyes, the sandy mist cloaking the waters between the islands for mile after mile that has been described by many narrators who have sailed there, a mist that sometimes originated from the cloud of smoke from the volcano on Fogo Island, in the archipelago's Sotavento Islands, or from winds containing fine Saharan sand. They were clouds of sand over the sea. I saw that, because the strength of the sun had changed and the wind had turned torrid and dense, spawning a silty foam on the waves that splattered over the whole surface of our ship. Then, from the stern rail, given my singular affection for Books of Islands, I remembered what Alonso de Santa Cruz says in his *General Compendium of the World's Islands*, that these islands, where all vessels took on supplies of water, cotton, salt and mutton (on condition that they left the sheep hides behind), the place, without entering into details or distances, where Pomponius Mela in antiquity located the house of the three Gorgons, the infamous Stheno, Euryale and Medusa, the daughters of Phorcys and Ceto, a trio who were the favourite monsters of ancient poets. Even Santa Cruz recognises, continued Griffin, that the word Gorgon in Greek 'sounds swift and terrible', swift and terrible like Perseus who went to those islands, as I did now, and brought back the head of Medusa, she of the adder tresses, who turned to stone everyone she looked at. What objects, beings or persons, good or bad, valuable or tacky, bold or cowardly, were those rocks before they were petrified by the Gorgons' gaze, that, on the *Minerva Janela*, next to Sagna and Amaro, the sailors who'd come to have a smoke next to me, drawn by the sight of that black coast I now saw as barren and scorched to a cinder?

Once, in Hamburg, I saw Friedrick Wüstenfeld's edition of one of the four existing copies of Al-Qazwini's thirteenth-century *Cosmography*, said Griffin, and the Happy Islands are there. They may be the Cape Verde islands but it is more likely they are the islands of Madeira, the Azores or Canaries, islands which in any case appear in Ptolemy, and were considered by Al-Qazwini, like Ptolemy before him, as the end of the world, the final edge, an enigmatic, surely attractive yet lethal place, where the happiness their name alluded to was derived from the leisurely lives of their inhabitants and visitors, if they had any, and the absence of any need to make an effort to survive, since nature provided all and nothing but bliss was in demand, a world full of pleasures and riches, where death, after joy or desire, was guaranteed. Death, said Griffin, no doubt accelerated by Medusa's capricious gaze.

The *Minerva Janela* reached Mindelo, the capital of San Vicente, arriving from the north-east nine days after leaving Funchal. According to Griffin, it was Wednesday 19 October. The boatswain Rodo Amaro did his duty, said Griffin, and supervised all the tasks involved in docking with the port pilot, an individual who came on board dressed impeccably. He was Manuel de Novas, in a peaked cap and yellowy-khaki safari jacket, a blend of sailor and soldier, although he owed his fame on the islands to the fact he was one of the composers of the songs of Cesária Évora, that most universal of Cape Verdians. The bay was littered with the remains of boats that had run aground years ago, their rusting hulks transformed into playgrounds for adolescents sporting the football shirts of Oporto and Boa Vista.

The port of Mindelo is very large and dirty and used by all manner of vessels in need of fuel, an oasis they visit like thirsty animals. We moored by a breakwater covered in detritus, potholes full of oily water and unappetising layabouts watching a handful of workers sweat over their labours. Captain Branco assembled us all to announce cheerfully that we had a free day and that he didn't want to see us again till the next morning, said Griffin. He was excessively paternalistic and recommended two things, one was the use of condoms 'even if only to ask the time of day', as he put it, and the other was that we should sleep in a good cheap hotel, the Residencial Sodade, on Franz Fanon Street, because the rooms had a bathroom, television, hot water and, above all, a minibar. Then, he addressed me, said Griffin, adding that the views over the Porto Grande bay were magnificent and there was a cinema nearby. Branco stayed behind on watch duty, with Second Officer Fernando Grande, and Greene, the second engineer. The rest of us left the ship. I abandoned the others in an elegant, colonial brothel Jordao Navares knew on the Rua Angola, a strikingly clean, anachronistic, if down-at-heel place. They all headed to the Bar Je t'aime to drink grog and beer into the early hours, 'because it's a place where European women hang out', said Sagna, always according to Griffin.

After I'd left them I meandered around the more respectable streets, occasionally venturing down alarming avenues with scabbier housing than the rest, their every façade chipped and flaking. I strode along the Avenida Amílcar Cabral, to my right the beautiful bay with small boats on the beach and to my left stalls selling mangoes and tapioca. It was almost dusk by the time I reached the Fish Market, a large building inhabited by cats and nobody else at that hour. Very beautiful women were reclining on the overgrown grass at the end of the beach. I spent the rest of the day on the terrace of the Casa dos Liquores listening to 'Miss Perfumado' over and over again on a jukebox people kicked as they slotted a coin in. Night fell and I decided to go back to the boat. It was so very wretched and depressing, said Griffin, and when I tired of listening to Cesária Évora repeat 'terra de felicidade' and thinking about the Gorgons, inhabitants of these Happy Isles, I decided to share a taxi with Pedro Ramos, whom I'd come across filling his rucksack with pirated CDs in a music shop.

The *Minerva Janela* departed the middle of the next morning for the Sotaventos Islands and Santiago Island, and by the evening was in sight of the black beaches of Tarrafal dotted with German sunshades. It still had to sail along the whole coast of the island, said Griffin, to reach Praia, the archipelago's capital. It took an hour and a half to unload two containers in a manoeuvre straight out of a silent film. I watched the movements of the crane with Amaro and two sailors. The boatswain took photos of the cargo for insurance purposes, in case of fire or accident. That night Branco decreed that nobody should sleep on land because he wanted to set sail at dawn. I stood on deck and enjoyed watching the reddish glow settle on Praia, a wonderful time for spiritual calm and burning temperatures, said Griffin, when I felt what Baudelaire wanted to feel, *hors du monde*. Jiménez de la Espada, the leader of that expedition whose finds, to my astonishment, were exhibited in my school that morning in 1955, had experienced that very same moment, when he reached the island on 22 August 1862 to get coal supplies from the only source on offer, an English company. To tell the truth, everything at the time was the property of the English, the coal, the wells for drinking water, the scant shops, the land, the boats, everything, said Griffin.

While they unloaded the large orange containers, I saw the city's brown arid wastes extending before me, a few trees you could almost count on the fingers of both hands, and the high torais, blackish plants that grew to a man's height. Like Jiménez de la Espada, I also noticed how beautiful the natives were. 'I never imagined a black woman could be as beautiful to look at as some of these islanders,' wrote Jiménez, said Griffin, and I remembered the whores in the Nicolau, and the waitresses at the Casa dos Liquores, whose green eyes and black skin had fascinated me, and the women stretched out by the main street in Mindelo, next to the Fish Market. And if I looked further on, towards the back of Praia I saw only basalt, black basalt everywhere, bare basalt rocks. In the lower reaches of that brown blackness, next to the Ribeira Grande beach, Jiménez de la

Espada found a grave, said Griffin. It was anonymous, though well cared for, with a small square section marked off by a wooden fence and a wrought-iron gate that led one to a well-trimmed, bright green lawn contrasting with the basalt and growing around the gravestone where the initials E. B. had been carved, and doodles drawn that intrigued the Spaniard. Jiménez de la Espada often wondered who might be resting there, said Griffin, and must have wondered for years because he left without finding out, but fifteen or twenty years later a cousin of his, Jonás Alberto Jonás, whose name was repeated simply on his mother's whim, Griffin remarked, paid him a visit to persuade him to sell a property that belonged to his family to an Englishman who wanted to settle down in the north of Spain where Jiménez de la Espada's family owned a heath overlooking the Cantabrian Sea. The Spanish scientist and explorer didn't obstruct the sale, but out of mere curiosity he decided to meet the new buyer, related Griffin. They were introduced in due course and, after a pleasant conversation on the subject of birds, the Englishman and ornithologist confessed he was buying the land so he could bury the remains of his mother who had died on the high seas shortly after giving birth to him. The Englishman recounted how his parents were on their way to Cape Town when Elisabeth Behevor, his mother, went into labour in the middle of a storm near Cape Verde and died the following day, much to the despair of her husband, Aloysius Behevor, who could do nothing to prevent it. They decided to bury her near Ribeira Grande, and her husband, said Griffin, set aside a sum of money for the grave's upkeep, and put a local parish priest in charge, a Spaniard, who put all his tenacity into the task. The priest had just died and the young man wanted to bring his mother's grave to Spain, the country of the man who had looked after her so attentively for so many years.

Excited by such an extraordinary coincidence, Jiménez de la Espada recalled that he could vouch for the priest's attentions, since the grave was the very one he'd seen on his voyage, and then realised the doodles on the stone were a way of expressing the fact a woman was buried there who'd died in childbirth, according to the customs of the Wolofs, the nation from which the natives on that island were descended, as the young Englishman would reveal.

We didn't even stay a day on Santiago Island, said Griffin, taking a deep breath. Before dawn on the next day the *Minerva Janela* sailed from the port of Praia, opposite the María Pía lighthouse, on the other side of the small island of Santa María, when the lighthouse was still flashing intermittently. Branco had given precise indications to Luiz Pereira and Jordao Navares to head for Pará and the Amazon estuary in Brazil, towards the Equator. But something horrific happened. A mere three hours after the sun's blinding light filled the sky, an accident took place that was to make its mark on that voyage. We entered the uncertain, arbitrary, relentless, violent sea Conrad writes about, and my friend and the ship's electrician Paulinho Costa died. There aren't usually accidents on this kind of ship, Pereira told me later, explained Griffin. I don't know what happened, an incident, a tragedy, a misfortune out of the blue, or perhaps it was down to lack of balance, disharmony, the shifting sands of life, I don't know, death pure and simple was what it was, but remind me to tell you about it some other time, said Griffin. And yet again he was gone.

10

AS FAR AS THE EYE COULD SEE, ONE SAW ONLY OCEAN, said Griffin in Os Combatentes on the Rua Ivens, where we'd planned to have lunch, as usual. Ocean on all sides, not the blue, peaceful ocean we now see in Funchal, but a rough sea, the colour one only finds in the sea, that doesn't exist in the rainbow, maybe green, greenish red even, maybe yellowish grey, swathed by banks of fog that appear suddenly, at any time of day and under the brightest sun. The light then coalesces into a huge, blindingly white metallic wall a few metres ahead. Yes, when we sailed from Cape Verde, we were surrounded by a sea that bodes ill, turbulent waves sustaining every degree of intense movement, that seemed to speak a language of grief and absence, indeed, 'grief and absence', the words I heard Fernando Grande utter when he presided over the ceremony to bury Paulinho's body at sea, in the midst of the solitary ocean. What is the strange motive that drives human beings to embark on long voyages, said Griffin, is the eternal question every man boarding a ship asks himself across the centuries. And there is no easy answer. It is the question Defoe puts on Robinson Crusoe's lips ('Who are you? And why would you want to travel by sea?' said Griffin raising a finger), and the one Melville implants in Ishmael's mind when he sees the *Pequod*. And when

I asked myself the same question, all I could imagine was an irrational impulse similar to the one that drives suicides or generates phantoms of self-destruction. That dark, obtuse idea, born in my head, grew most painfully at the sight of Paulinho's body, wrapped in sheets secured by ropes and about to be cast into those indifferent waters alien to all that is human, and the end of *Moby Dick* came to mind 'and the great shroud of the sea rolled on as it had rolled on five thousand years ago'.

Griffin then told me about the accident, as he'd promised he would. The accident, he said, happened in the engine room, the stinking territory of Pavka, the fine, upstanding Macedonian. Everything was so different only an hour earlier. Paulinho and I stood on the poop deck and watched the tenuous shadows from Santiago Island disappear into the distance. The barometer had risen slightly and the sky was a blend of clouds and blue patches. The heat had started to feel oppressive and Paulinho had told me about the hurricanes further south, en route to Pará, our destination. He said a favourable westerly wind should drive off the squalls that often blew up at that time of the year. I'd accompanied him when he went to tighten the davits to the lifeboat winches, so if there were heavy seas, the waves smashing against the sides of the boat wouldn't loosen them and the spray wouldn't rust the launch levers. While Paulinho was doing that, said Griffin, under direct orders from Captain Branco, I tried to tie down any loose objects I saw on the deck so they didn't collide when the boat tipped this way and that, a useful task I supposed, but hardly heavy duty, simply a time-filler.

I really liked the first-rate electrician and affable joker Paulinho Costa. He was an inlander like me, and in my cabin or in the narrow passageways between the columns of containers we'd often talked about the absurd spell the sea exercises on men from the interior. And about submarine films, his favourite and mine, that were usually so technical and claustrophobic, and above all so alike, as Costa would say. Despite being so youthful, still under thirty, he had two children he talked about with great love and enthusiasm and Ana, a sad-faced and sad-limbed wife, whose photo he showed me on several occasions. Costa had a generous manner that invited you to trust and like him.

That morning, when we were both in the poop, he was finishing his routine checks, said Griffin, when a distorted voice summoned him over the intercom to the engine room where there was an electrical fault in the fuel-oil supply. He left me to watch the sea by myself, with no sign of land on the horizon, simply that ominous metallic haze. I remember it was 10 a.m. and a few minutes later I heard a thunderous explosion at the bottom of the boat. I was still paralysed in that same spot when I saw Pavka clamber out of the hatchway and run to the ladders to the bridge. He was covered in black grime and giving off smoke as he ran past Fernando Grande, Pedro Ramos and Kowanana, who were all rushing down to the engine room.

The boat suddenly stopped and a deafening siren started to wail, like a histrionic voice from an echoing megaphone. The whole crew was on alert and ready to extinguish any fire that might have started. I stayed silent in my position in the poop. I didn't know what I should do. Then I saw José Amuntado walk past me looking on edge. I grabbed his arm and asked him to tell me what had happened. He told me in a wretched voice that a spark had caused a generator in the pressure chamber to blow up and one of the steam valves had burst when a burner overheated. 'Brother,' he said, 'young Costa's head was inside. It exploded. The fucking valve hit him right in the temple. Bang! Like a bullet! That's what happened, brother. A bastard spark, a bastard valve and bastard bad luck.' I remember, for some reason, perhaps to put out of my mind what Amuntado had just recounted so as not to imagine Paulinho Costa below decks, that I thought about something idiotic instead, that the man sounded like a woman I'd once met at a supermarket cashpoint, and I almost smiled when Amuntado headed off again, said Griffin. The following day Branco ordered Fernando Grande to do the honours at the funeral ceremony. Costa would be buried on the high seas, as he'd have wanted, or at least that's how the crew responded, when Rodo Amaro the boatswain reluctantly took a quick vote.

It's strange how accidents happen, said Griffin. They strike suddenly, then it takes ages to find out what really happened, what small, if fundamental, change has taken place in the universe. They are interventions by fate that come unrequested, and present themselves as faits accomplis, as in childhood. An accident curtailed my grandfather's career as a magician. He stumbled, his box of swords fell on top of him and he sustained various cuts, nothing serious, but the audience laughed, laughed at the clumsy old conjurer whose tricks were so obvious. He gave it all up a few days later. An accident destroyed Graciela Pavic's life. Her husband and children drowned. They were never found and she was always looking for them; there wasn't a day in her life when she didn't search the beaches and coves in the Straits. An accident brought the automaton of Desolation Island into the light of day. Accidents modify, reveal, change, transform and turn the lives of people and things upside down. Accidents are the real God.

Somebody on the *Minerva Janela* said the accident that cut short Paulinho Costa's life would bring bad luck and it was true, I can't really say why, said Griffin, though it was clear from then on that our voyage was suffused with shock, sorrow and a strange malaise. None of us could prevent a sombre mood reigning over our free time in the dining area or lounge, and anywhere on board suddenly became a good place to talk about marine misfortunes and accidents, the crew's favourite topic after Costa's death, a way to frighten off evil spirits, some reckoned. Captain Branco had known another Portuguese electrician, on another boat owned by the same company, whose legs had been amputated at the knee after a similar accident to the one that killed Paulinho. 'When pressure valves burst,' said Branco, 'they embed themselves cruelly in whatever they hit and are red-hot, so penetrate easily. That fellow was lucky, because he survived. Costa wasn't.' Fernando Grande related how he'd seen a container in the upper reaches of the ship come open and empty out part of its cargo, fake Suzuki motorbikes made in Shanghai, on the heads of three sailors, literally burying them alive. Their bodies were also thrown overboard the following day with full honours.

Pereira was the only one who didn't believe in fate and claimed he'd never seen an accident on his voyages in different boats. He even criticised his colleagues for exaggerating. 'Boats are very safe places,' said Pereira, 'and what happened to the unfortunate Paulinho Costa was a one-in-a-thousand chance. Like throwing his body into the sea. I'd have preferred to take him to the first port, or return him to Cape Verde. His widow had the right to a funeral and to put flowers on his grave whenever she felt like it.'

Branco said he was right, and the company was insured for such extreme circumstances, but it was usual for sailors on board to vote on whether the unfortunate person should or not be put to rest in the place he died, however terrible his death. 'That's always been the way, from the time of the great whaling ships, a kind of tacit law. It's a question of fate: if death comes to you on the high seas, on the high seas you must stay,' said Captain Branco. Pereira nodded, then cursed the sea, 'It devours us even when we are alive!' and banged his hand on the maps table, said Griffin.

But the business of bad luck was at the very least worrying: three days after the Portuguese lad died, Kowanana lost a finger, his little finger, sliced off by the loose end of a steel rope he'd not seen whipping past his nose, and that same night the sea turned rough, a squall tossed the boat up and down and a sudden rush of water swept purser Oliver Sagna overboard. As the cry of 'Man overboard!' went up, the engines were shut down and the lifeboat launched, with Pereira and two sailors aboard, while the rest of us leaned over the port and starboard rails, peering in the dark at the waves lashing the helm. It took four hours to rescue the purser on a night that was a real bitch, said Griffin. Sagna was still alive, but shaking violently and prey to painful cramps hitting his whole body.

After that, calm was restored to the *Minerva Janela* for several days and an iridescent, multicoloured sunset reconciled me with my passionate need to be there and nowhere else in the world, the nightmare of invisible folk like myself. Perhaps Paulinho's death, Kowanana's finger and Sagna's suffering were the price of sacrifice, rather than coincidences, that had to be paid to an angry god of the sea who'd been disturbed in his sleep, as second engineer Charly Greene, our resident Welsh expert on goblins, bars and legends, opined. But Paulinho Costa lived on in our thoughts and nothing about the voyage was the same thereafter. We were one less, and it could happen to any one of us.

II

I DEVOTED EVERY THINKING MOMENT TO MY ISLAND over the next few days in order to fight the sadness and silence oppressing the ship. I sat on the deck under the bridge, oblivious to all around me or perhaps prompted by it, and drew the island, once, twice, thrice, a hundred times, first in my head, picturing its shores, trying to imagine what it would feel like to set foot there, and finally on paper. I made lots of drawings. Here's one, said Griffin, holding out a sheet of paper. He handed me a fine drawing of Desolation Island that afternoon when we met up. I'd been expecting him to tell me about that island for some time but had decided against asking him to, because I'd have felt ridiculous saying 'Tell me more,' as if I wanted him to disclose his dreams and desires, and that could only happen when he wanted, when he'd decided it was timely to insert it into the peculiar inner order of his account. Besides, it might be true or a lie, like the whole of his story so far, or wholly extracted from a pile of books: at the end of the day, who cared?

I took a quick glance at the drawing, before he launched off. There were two other Desolation Islands in the world, apart from the one in the Straits of Magellan, said Griffin resignedly, as if relating something he'd said lots of times before. One of the two is in fact several, the Kerguelen Islands or the Islands of Desolation archipelago. The other is Tristan da Cunha, equidistant between Patagonia and the Cape of Good Hope. I have studied them. I even tried to draw them and retain them in my head, but I couldn't, they didn't really interest me, at best, I've seen them in all kinds of Books of Islands ancient and modern, and they definitely don't appeal. If you want the Kerguelens, read Poe and his *Narrative of Arthur Gordon Pym*. He tells you all you need to know about those islands, their discovery by Baron Kerguelen in 1772 and baptism by Cook years later as the Islands of Desolation. Or read Verne and you'll see how he recreates the colouristic atmosphere and geography of those islands in the Indian Ocean in *The Sphinx of the Ice Fields*. Then Griffin's face brightened and he pointed to the paper I was holding with his Desolation Island drawing. This is the one that matters to me, he said. Look, and he nodded at the piece of paper, the coast looks like a comb or a fish's backbone, with so many fjords, inlets and shallows that cut into the land: just see how long and deep they are.

After my voyage on the *Minerva Janela* was finally over when I arrived and set foot on Port Mercy, on the north side of the island, my much anticipated feeling of elation gave way to tremendous disappointment: it was a monumental déjà vu, as if I'd often been there before. I didn't experience any new pleasure, simply a repeat of what I'd felt so frequently over recent years, as when I invented an island for myself in private on the ship's deck. I then asked Griffin to make an effort to tell me what he felt, when he at last landed in that place he'd conceived of as an idea, because there could be no doubt that Griffin's Desolation Island was basically that, an *idea*.

As I made my way over the island, Griffin resumed, on a not particularly cold day under a leaden sky with the full range of greys one might expect, I began to identify the landmarks I had drawn on my sketches, Seal-Hunters Cove, Apostle's Rock, Mataura Cove, Milward Peak. I struggled through desolate vegetation that switched suddenly from extraordinary leafiness to barren plains that led to scary woods, believe me, skirted by layers of blue ice licked or lashed by the waves from the Straits. I remembered those oh so true words Commodore John Byron had uttered about that spot: 'This coast is encircled on both sides by high mountains almost entirely covered in snow.' There was no brightness, at any moment it threatened to go dark: it was a gloomy, twilight atmosphere. On the other hand, at no stage did I feel dry or parched; the island's character was dismal and damp. The air was flecked with rain or it was raining horizontally, ineffably. If I opened the palm of my hand and waved it in front of my face, it was rapidly covered in drops of rain that with the low, overcast sky deepened the disconcerting sadness mentioned by all travellers who have sailed that way.

This is what I saw.

The immense mountain ranges create a no less immense spiritual solitude: there is nothing and nobody, only labyrinths of fjords, narrow channels penetrating even the small beech-tree woods, their green jars with the green cypresses in an adjacent wood, and they contrast with the eerie arbours of magnolias halfway down a mossy hillside striated with sky-blue ice, like the ice of the glaciers spread across the whole strait. Occasionally one hears the isolated shrieks of parrots, though one can't imagine where they can be, perhaps on the shore opposite, but that's so remote it doesn't seem possible, perhaps it's the breaking ice that's screeching, moans borne through the air like bird cries, ghostly sounds, the same that must have incited Sarmiento de Gamboa to hatch the ridiculous notion of strewing the coast with automata, whose presence, together with those inexplicable natural shrieks, would strike atavistic fear into the hearts of English and Dutch sailors, the enemies of the Empire, said Griffin.

He also heard an incessant noise that waxed and waned depending on whether the wind blew from the north or south, the movements of thousands of penguins on icy beaches or the dirty, ugly rocks on the coast of Beaufort Bay or Cape Caves. I stretched out to rest on a bed of black undergrowth and was soon soaked and trembling: an intense cold driving into the marrow of my bones. I couldn't put these impressions into my drawings, but I can point to where they happened. And Griffin excitedly put his finger on places that meant nothing to me.

Have you ever seen arborescent ferns? he then asked, but he didn't let me reply he never did. I was surrounded by those prehistoric plants, probably the most resistant on the planet. Did you know that they have survived glaciations and earthquakes, changes of era and ecological disasters? Lying on those bushes, looking up at the sky, I saw a majestic pair of albatrosses, crabs in beaks, fly by. I had reached my island; I had at least reached Desolation, the end of everything, the final end! I tried to raise my spirits so as not to undercut the value of being there, at the centre of my idea or my island, what did it matter? but I couldn't obliterate the banality of that moment, and felt only contempt for myself.

Yes, this is what I saw: memory can't erase that. He pointed again to the sheet of paper in my hand and added: This is the savage and imposing Cape Column or Columns, on the exit to the strait, the end of Desolation, the end of my dream. Its owes its name to the fact it is high and vertical like a column, and it really is, said Griffin, absorbed by one of his recurrent abstract musings. The great voyager Bougainville describes it as a mass of stone crowned by two bigger rocks like castle turrets that lean north-westwards. I stood there for a long time, battered by the icy winds, thinking about Graciela Pavic and the way her grief had condemned her to a living death sentence, and how that was where she found the automaton because she went there, almost out of desperation, to search for the bodies of her children and husband because someone, a Yamana or Alaculoof Indian woman, told her she might find their remains in those distant fjords where they might have been swept by tides and melting ice, and also because that was surely the only place she hadn't looked. I remembered how she almost died on that occasion, because her boat, like her lost family's, also capsized there, and when she reached the coast, on the land between Cape Column and nearby Cape Desire, chance led her to see the strange glint from the rusty automaton on Cape Cut.

Yes, I saw all those places, I saw them for real, and I saw them as John Narborough must have seen them centuries before when he sailed there and named the island Desolation after its barren rocks, valleys of ice as ancient as the world, its wind-whipped sides and horrific steep and solitary wooded gullies, from which Narborough claimed, according to Griffin, it was impossible to extract wood to make torches. And I was in St Felix Bay, on the lighthouse of which (the lighthouse at the end of the world! Can you imagine, Jules Verne again) I celebrated reaching the end of my dream, remembered Melville once more, when he speaks of lost islands and says that real locations aren't marked on any map. That's what I felt about that island, that it was on no map and only existed in my drawings as it existed in reality. In 1860, old Herman Melville, now into his forties, had begun to write poems, and sailed on a merchant ship captained by his brother Tom. He relates how the boat rounded Cape Horn and that the next day, when he was standing on deck, near the four Evangelists, at the western entrance to the

Straits, as engrossed in a poem about Greece as I was absorbed in my drawings on the *Minerva Janela* after the death of Paulinho Costa, someone told him to look back because he would see the majestic sight of the lofty, double promontory of Cape Columns at the end of Desolation Island. And Melville looked back. Did he see, as I would many years later, the place where Melvicius's automaton awaited his fate? We shall never know.

12

I EVENTUALLY GAVE THEM ALL A DRAWING OF THE island, Griffin continued, because I sketched dozens on the days I got so bored and despondent. The first and I think the only person who asked me what it was and why I did it was Pereira, when he was rod-fishing from one of the starboard decks, the day dolphins were jumping and tempting all kinds of fish to the surface under a blistering sun. Captain Branco had demoted him somewhat arbitrarily because of disagreements over the speed and management of the ship, but Pereira preferred not to talk about that because, after all, Branco was his friend. Quite frankly, said Griffin, Costa's death changed the captain's mood, that is, if he ever had such a thing, and now he always seemed to be angry, and had added a disconcertingly aggressive tone to his already harsh character. But several things happened before that.

The first was a big row between the captain and his second officer, Fernando Grande, as a result of a misreading of the planned route, which had taken the *Minerva Janela* miles to the south of its intended itinerary. When the captain realised what had happened, he shouted to Pereira and Grande to come on the bridge. Pereira came in and sat down on a chair. Branco squared up to Fernando Grande in front of his first officer and insulted him furiously, oblivious to the fact Navares could hear. The pilot was very upset by the violence of the confrontation and his cheeks reacted to the boat's constant vibrating, but he kept his eyes glued to the sea opening before him. I was also there, but I felt protected by my sense of invisibility that was most helpful in that situation, because nobody noticed me, not even Pereira who told me about the scene later on. Once he'd grasped the enormity of the miscalculation, Branco decided to recover the ground lost as soon as possible by backtracking to the point where the error had kicked in. Fernando Grande, on the other hand, believed it would be more practical to head due north until the ship reached the latitude they'd deviated from. Griffin pointed out the second officer was ignoring Branco's timely observation that that would involve a great risk of collisions with other vessels in those waters and the dispatch of an unnecessary SOS, if only as a cautionary warning, and that would cause excessive alarm, then endless communications to inform all and sundry of the ship's longitude and latitude and their apologies. 'In other words, it's a hell of a mess and all your fault,' exclaimed Branco, still agitated by the situation he now had to sort out. Conversely, if they turned round and went back to the spot where they'd begun their deviation, they would have to do none of that, because no other boat was on that route, according to his sailing chart, and people would merely assume the journey was taking longer, since Fernando Grande's error had simply added a few more days to their whole voyage.

Branco accused Grande of being incompetent 'in every circumstance and moment', and the second officer defended himself by saying that, for heaven's sake!, it was the first time he'd done anything like that and everybody is human and if he wanted he could slash his wrists, but what was done was done. Branco: It's the kind of mistake a novice or alcoholic makes, and you're on your way to becoming a complete failure. Grande: I don't drink, but if you were suggesting the contrary, with due respect, that should be decided on land and in private. Branco: Don't be so headstrong and let's decide this in terms of time and money. Grande: You would save both by heading north. Branco: I don't want more problems, we shall turn round. Grande: Sailing for the sake of it is hardly what appeals to me or, with all due respect, to the rest of the crew. Branco: Nobody sails for the sake of it, we're all here doing our duty, as per our contract, and obviously earning money, and the sooner the better; this is a merchant ship, not a liner. Grande: You don't need to remind me of the difference, I am only too aware of it. I will only add that my error is a direct result of the stress caused by the death of our Portuguese colleague. Branco: Issue the immediate order to change direction over the next few days, today is Tuesday, and by Friday or Saturday we'll reach where we should be now.

That was how Branco ended the argument, said Griffin. The captain sought Luiz Pereira's agreement, but the latter stayed in his seat, legs up and with his heels on the winch control panel, preferring to be neutral, even ironic, saying he was sure nobody on board thought they were on a cruise and that both options, going back a few miles or heading north, were valid, and consequently, the captain's decision should be enforced, because all else would be mutiny. Fernando Grande saw he'd lost the spat and slammed the bridge door behind him in a pathetic, impotent gesture. When they were alone, Branco berated Pereira for not giving him more enthusiastic support, but thanked him for reminding Grande of his place in the pecking order. The *Minerva Janela* immediately prepared to about turn.

For a few days we had an extraordinary sense of return: we were retracing our steps, and it was like reliving the past. I again thought of Paulinho's death, but also of his inevitable resurrection over time, of Cape Verde and the whores in Mindelo, and Madeira, a breathless retracing of steps to that moment when I entered my school classroom and saw the stuffed animals from Jiménez de la Espada's exhibition on display.

The next thing to go wrong, said Griffin, was a dangerous fire in the galleys, introducing a parenthesis in his story so he could take a breather on the terrace at the Carlton Hotel where we'd met that afternoon. Bergeron, alias Tidbit, the cook, was busy jotting his dreams down in minute detail in a few moments of lucid recollection, something he did daily but erratically like a man obsessed, and was unable to extinguish an unexpected column of fire that flared up from the large frying pan and spread to the cables of the loudspeaker system above the extractor fan. It must have been about 7 p.m. and most of us were waiting for dinner. Several boxes of biscuits and bottles of olive oil burnt and the extractor couldn't entirely absorb the black, billowing smoke that soon filled the whole area of the cabins, kitchen and dining room. There weren't enough extinguishers on hand and several sailors brought more from other decks to help Tidbit, who was frightened by the way it had spread so quickly. Once the fire was put out, he found the loss of what he called his book of dreams severely traumatic. I tried to console him days later by telling him that, as everyone knew and as Freud had already pronounced on the subject, recording one's dreams was basically an onanist practice that brought on paranoia, as demonstrated by the many celebrated suicides who had often been adepts, so in the long term the fire might prove a providential liberation. Bergeron, alias Tidbit, who'd begun a new notebook that very day, looked at me incredulously because he didn't know who Freud was or what I was talking about. I shall never forget Tidbit's face. As his tears welled up he thanked me for my kind words. I still don't know if they were prompted by the fact his eyes were still irritated by the smoke or the loss of the dreams he'd filed away in the notebook that had disappeared. On impulse, I gave him one of my drawings of the island, which he glanced at in a perplexed, questioning manner. I left him in that state to go off with Pereira, who was heading to the second deck when the cry went up that everyone had been waiting for, 'Dolphins to starboard!' He was carrying a fishing rod.

Pereira asked me which island it was and when I was about to tell him, said Griffin, he cast out his hook and line and spoke of the bad luck Paulinho's death had brought. 'Rather than bad luck, I'd call it a loss of harmony, something like losing control, as drastic as going in the wrong direction the other day or the fire in the galleys might have been. If either of those incidents had prospered, Branco would have had a nervous breakdown, I know him only too well and his firm temper is a mask, a disguise. He would have made the crew pay for it and we'd all be praying to God for a ship to appear on the horizon to take us in tow and get us out of this tub as soon as possible.'

Pereira had got hold of a folding chair and was wearing a T-shirt imprinted with the faces of Mick Jagger and the Rolling Stones. 'I am on holiday, today is my day off,' he said ironically, avoiding any allusion to his disagreements with the captain, although later, in our cabin, said Griffin, he discussed it again at great length over a game of draughts. When he reeled in his line, he repeated his question about the island. I said it was Desolation Island in the Straits of Magellan, sure he must have seen the southern face of Desolation, as Melville had, but a hundred years later when he'd rounded Cape Horn towards the Pacific in a Mobil containership. However, it wasn't so, because his route took a lower latitude, quite a distance from the coast.

'Did I miss out on something wonderful on that island?' asked Pereira. I don't know, I answered, I've never been there, and I only draw it as I've seen it in Books of Islands and atlases of the area. The island fascinates me because of something I saw in a photo of my grandfather. It's where I'm headed now. 'From Punta Arenas, I suppose,' said Pereira, casting out his line again. Yes, from Punta Arenas, I retorted, said Griffin. 'I don't know that island, but I do know others just as sheer, that are really so forsaken and desolate they bring on grief,' said Pereira, 'although I think Rodo Amaro has visited the place. He knows the whole of the Straits and has even lived there.'

That wasn't news to Griffin. The boatswain had told him as much one morning when he accompanied him to check the damp levels in the partitions in the second starboard hold, but when he'd spoken about the island, Amaro confessed he hadn't stepped foot there because he never went to the other side of the Straits. 'My obsession is Ferraris, not islands. I couldn't care a shit about them,' Rodo had said brutally, with a smile.

'What's the size of your Desolation Island?' asked Pereira. I don't know, Griffin answered, I shouldn't think it's more than a hundred and forty square kilometres, why? 'Just in case you can buy it,' smiled Pereira. I laughed at such a stupid idea but it was obvious the first officer wasn't joking. 'So why do you make those drawings? Blast, there's no fish today, the sea's in no mood for giving me presents!' Pereira looked at him for the first time since they'd been talking on that deck that reeked of kerosene or petrol, like the whole ship, and put his absurd rod to one side. Griffin told him that as far as he was concerned they were a kind of language, like his own language that allowed him to express himself or his desires. We all have invisible lives that begin to surface once the right conduit is found, he said, mine is reaching that island, as if it were an act of physical possession, a sexual act or affirmation. I draw the island so as not to forget the object of my desire, so as to dream about it: to draw is to caress. 'So I see: a variation on love. Some people love dogs and others love islands. You belong to the second camp.' I told him that, although he'd been joking, he was quite right, love was what was at stake, and Pereira and I both laughed and leaned on the starboard rail until the sun started to burn.

13

THE LAST TIME I MET GRIFFIN HE'D TALKED ABOUT love, but only about his love for the island, as expressed in his obsessive drawings. What love isn't obsessive? he commented when he said goodbye. The next time, I was strolling through Funchal on the off chance, although our encounters had little that was chance about them: we sought each other out: he wanted to continue his story and I wanted the pleasure of listening to him. When I saw him again, as I was saying, I remember he mentioned Graciela Pavic, though not immediately. He launched into a tirade about love. He mentioned the love or loves he'd enjoyed, though he didn't like talking about his two wives, Roberta the sensual redhead, then Elsa the calculating brunette. They suddenly disappeared, and that was that, end of story. However much love there might have been between us, I am happy to think their departure, without acrimony or contempt, ensures that all our pleasant memories, the erotic ones included, won't go down the sewer of sentiments that have died the death. There's always a smile to look for, a caress to put a name to, a hazy, nondescript memory to pinpoint that's so hazy it must be a tactic to ensure survival.

However, the only passionate love Griffin thought he'd enjoyed in real life was with a Frenchwoman, Fabienne Michelet, who was in her mid-thirties when he met her in a hotel in Riva during holidays when they both appeared on their own, powered by an unequivocal urge that led to their meeting, just like Kafka in that same city: it was love at first sight. That happened far too long ago, said Griffin, although not a day goes by when I don't think of her or the moments I lived by her side. Her face, body, voice, laughter, words, gestures, my irrational, frantic desire to be close to her and my inability to imagine other circumstances could exist when we weren't together, the excitement of the chase, the anguish when we couldn't find one other, all that took place in an intense period of under twenty days, the length of the holidays we extended as long as possible. After that, a couple of rushed, passionate dates in airport hotels, letters promising a rendezvous that was eternally postponed, a week in Paris, then three days in Bordeaux where she had relatives, a weekend in Nantes, where she lived with her lawyer husband – a carefully contrived tryst with all the piquancy of a furtive, literary act, a perilous, provincial love-game – and finally in Madrid, haphazardly, on the slightest pretext, an excuse that never arose, the journeys were never undertaken, six months, one year passed by and the last letter that I kept and always carried with me until I tore it to shreds on the *Minerva Janela*, one announcing her imminent arrival. 'I'll call you the moment I leave. I can't stand being without you any longer,' Fabienne wrote, said Griffin.

I really thought she loved me because I loved her. But she never called, never wrote again, and nor did I. Why? It would have been a reproachful letter and that wasn't my style. I waited and then forgot rancorously. Only a few months later, I had terrible doubts, perhaps Fabienne hadn't kept her promise because something beyond her will, outside her control, had prevented her. I even thought she might have died. Then I acted like a lunatic for days on end imagining, in the vaguest of hopes, the most incredible, frustrating incidents: an accident in the taxi taking her to the airport or station, an assault in the street, rape, burglary in her own home, followed by paralysis giving way to aphasia, prolonged amnesia, a coma, one of those comatose states when individuals sink into unconsciousness, are still alive but sleep like vegetables and wake up after fifteen or twenty years, a formal, civilised pact with her husband who'd discovered our adulterous relationship, or, perhaps worse, she'd been murdered by him in a onset of passion, coldly, or by a contract killer . . . the range of possibilities was infinite, absurd and a constant torture. Finally, faced by the evidence of the abyss, I preferred to believe (though not entirely, I always leave a flickering light at the end of the tunnel of life's desires) that Fabienne had died, convinced it was natural causes, a heart attack, sudden illness, a swift, fulminating cancer, and nobody could tell me because nobody knew I existed. Yet again invisibility controlled an area of my life, yet again I became transparent as my individual, petty story unravelled.

I visited Nantes several years after being in love with Fabienne, said Griffin. The reason for my visit to the city is irrelevant, I expect it was an academic engagement, lectures, a conference, something of no matter. Might it have been my fetishist love for Verne? Perhaps. Whatever it was, I couldn't resist the temptation of finding out where Fabienne had ended up. I only knew her surname (I sent my letters to a post-office box) and didn't know if Michelet was her maiden or married name. I tried to interrogate the waiters in the famous La Cigale Brasserie on the place Graslin, asking if the surname Michelet related to a particular lawyer, but they couldn't help; they knew no lawyer by the name of Michelet. I found no joy in the telephone directory or municipal census. My instinct told me to go to the cemetery. I now interrogated the woman in charge. I managed to see several mausoleums that were built to Michelets of different genealogies, but no date coincided with Fabienne's, so I gave up my search, as I was going to leave the city the following day.

I returned to La Cigale and from where I was sitting noticed I was near the Grand Hôtel de France. Ensconced in that hotel, I later found something that both surprised me and reminded me of the figure of Graciela Pavic and the automaton from Desolation Island. I came across the story of Jacques Vaché, champion of black humour, friend of Tristan Tzara and André Breton, famed as a founder of surrealism with the least surrealist creations, a mere handful of poems and letters. He was born in Nantes and died young, as was right and proper, from an overdose of opium in the Grand Hôtel de France, place Graslin, as recorded in an old police report signed by Inspector Laroze on 7 January 1919, which was framed on a wall where I stopped and read it. Vaché was twenty-three on the day he died. He was tall, slim and handsome and his good looks and ephemeral elegance were ambiguous in the extreme. He belonged to one of the city's leading families, from which he must have eventually inherited a large fortune. The war that had just ended left many youths with a bad taste in the mouth because of the excesses and deep emptiness it had spawned, exacerbated by their hatred of injustice and patriotic fervour, as in Céline's famous novel. Vaché enlisted as an army interpreter for the North American troops stationed in France at the end of the First World War and never saw active service. He died with twenty-two-year-old Paul Bonnet, a rank-and-file soldier like himself, who had booked room 34 on the second floor. They were embracing in their underwear, uniforms heaped on an armchair, and sexual scandal added to the furore over their deaths from overdoses of opium. The censors imposed a silence: they were soldiers in the French army. Corporal A. K. Woynow from the North American Supplies Division was with them and supplied the pipe for burning up the opium. Woynow survived because he smoked much less than his friends and woke in time to raise the alarm by shouting down the corridors of the hotel. A couple of hours earlier it had been all joy and provocation, their hearty laughter echoing in the gloomy reception where they'd just ordered ten cups of hot chocolate, a tragicomic excess, because they'd each bet they could resist a similar amount of opium. They were half naked, which didn't mean they'd decided to commit suicide for romantic reasons, as Woynow, still in a state of shock, was quick to point out to the police. They purely and simply hated their uniforms, said the US citizen, Griffin remarked. Poincaré, the President of the Republic, sent a letter of condolence to the family the week after. He declared that Private Vaché had died for the Fatherland. What has all this got to do with Graciela Pavic, you will be wondering? Well, the date. My thoughts flitted to Graciela, said Griffin, because on that day, Monday 6 January 1919, when the young French soldier died, possibly at the very same time Woynow was shouting down the hotel corridor, Graciela Pavic found the automaton on Desolation Island. I remembered that coincidence of events, time and date as I read the report on the wall in the lobby of the Grand Hôtel in Nantes, and it made my spine shiver as it always does when I think about Graciela.

Oliver said nothing for a few minutes. I didn't ask him about Fabienne. I realised the story of that love had finished there, on his trip to Nantes; alive or dead, he simply believed she'd vanished from his life like his two former wives, a set of memories to recall at will. I wanted to find out more about Graciela Pavic, but Griffin talked about Upland Geese as we walked. He told me that one night, when dawn was about to break, he heard a noise coming from the sea. He looked out of his cabin porthole on the *Minerva Janela*. Directly in front, said Griffin, I could see the silhouette of a large moribund Upland Goose that was perfectly visible in the glow from the bluish light. It had thrown itself against the deck kamikaze style. When I was a child, he went on, my aunt took me to the park near our house one afternoon. I spent a long time looking at how the birds in the highest treetops kept heading dizzily towards the ground only to fly up when they were a foot or so from the ground. I don't what kind of birds they were: their acrobatic flight was exciting and I looked on in a hypnotised, almost horror-struck state. That image came to mind when I saw the large grey-brown bird on the wet deck. It was strange to see in such tropical climes, the crew later told me, but flocks of migrating birds were now flying over the ship all the time 'making song-like sounds', as Kowanana remarked. Upland Geese are often mistaken for Patagonian geese, but they are also found in Tristan da Cunha and have even been seen on St Helena, much further north. According to myth they are monogamous birds that always fly in flocks. And if one Upland Goose dies, its partner flies as high as it can, then hurtles down, never opening its wings to glide, in a plunge to the death. It is suicide. I think Upland Geese and Graciela Pavic have something in common, I'm not sure why, perhaps because I associate suffering caused by loss with the infinite desolation that gives its name to that island I keep searching for. Pedro Ramos bludgeoned the goose to death with an iron bar. 'Its flesh is inedible,' said Tidbit the cook. It was thrown into the sea like poor Paulinho Costa, though quite unceremoniously. A minute earlier, as I looked at the dying goose, I thought of Graciela Pavic, said Griffin. And that was the occasion Oliver told me part of her story.

She was blond and beautiful, all bright-eyes and glowing cheeks. The curls of her hair shaped into a halo where someone like me could lose his reason, said a deeply pensive Oliver. Or like my grandfather. Her face was angular and firm-chinned with round cheeks and fleshy lips that broadened out her smile. Her eyebrows were thick and expressive. I deduce all that from photos I inherited after my grandparents' deaths along with the letters and everything else linked to Desolation Island. Graciela is by herself in the one I now have in mind and it's a full-length portrait. She's smiling slightly and doesn't seem totally in control of her movements, as if she is willing her soul to flee while her body remains, and she does whatever the photographer asks: the pose is quite natural: she's staring into the lens, stooping consciously, knowing she will be looked at, imperceptibly lifting her chin and perfectly modulated face. It's a black-and-white photo from before December 1923, the year they met her, in her house perhaps, or the museum, or the place indicated in the gold label stuck to the verso:

STUDIO
PHOTO-PORTRAITS-WALTER
CALLE NOGUEIRA, 7
PUNTA ARENAS

Graciela Pavic is in her element in the photo. It was a present she sent my grandparents two years after they visited Punta Arenas. It carries an affectionate, entirely informal dedication on the back: 'For Irene and Arnaldo, heartfelt friends, master and mistress of my dreams, magicians. Your Graciela. A cold August day in 1925, thinking of you always.' Did Graciela like the magic, dinner jacket and top-hat conjuring tricks? Hence the years of contact and letters between her and my grandparents, though they never met again? That relationship was in itself magical, my grandfather Arnaldo would say, said Griffin. I've always carried that photo with me, I'm not sure why. There are other photos that were taken on the same day as the photo with the automaton, in the museum. Despite her age Graciela's face retains its elusive beauty and her hair its flowing spirituality. My grandfather met her when she'd just hit forty and he once told me she was the most strikingly beautiful woman he encountered on the whole trip to Valparaíso, with the exception of Irene my grandmother, naturally, with whom, in retrospect, she bore a close resemblance. I imagine her as tall, though not overly so, wistfully melancholy, though not overly so, an expression that can fake a show of happiness at will or seem exaggeratedly blissful. That was how she hid the effort she was forced to make to curb and conceal her irremediable grief.

When she discovered that my grandfather was a magician, she cherished a bond of sincere, enthusiastic sympathy and salvaged from deep down a taste of childhood, something she'd quite lost, from when she was a girl and travelling circuses sporadically came to Punta Arenas in one of the Chilean mail-boats linking Santiago and Buenos Aires. They performed in the city's theatres, cafés and squares. Perhaps what my grand-father told her about the world of magicians and the theatre helped Graciela recover a distant *frisson* of childhood excitement that kept her awake all night. Graciela was descended from Dalmatians from Dubrovnik in Croatia that was then part of the Austro-Hungarian Empire. Miro Pavic, her father, was a petty criminal who migrated to Tierra del Fuego in 1890 with his wife, Veronika Jergovic, and their elder child, Ivo, who was one year old. It was claimed gold had been found in those solitary southern fastnesses. Miro Pavic had been jailed in

Zagreb for pickpocketing and knew that, sooner or later, his future would be the gallows if he didn't embark on an adventure somewhere else in the world. It didn't matter how far he had to go, he told himself in his kitchen in Dubrovnik (where boats from Trieste made their first port of call before going to Palermo, Genoa or Marseille and thence to the republics of Argentina or Chile), as he peered at a newspaper caricature representing a gold digger who'd struck it rich above a caption that read:

He made a new start at the end of the world!
You can too!
Come to the new California!

Distance is in men's hearts but especially in their heads, Graciela said her father liked to remark, explained Griffin. A few weeks later Miro set off with his family in one of those Italian vessels, perhaps the famous transatlantic liner *Alessandro Camondo* that transported thousands of his compatriots to Patagonia and Tierra del Fuego. Dalmatian migrants to Chile and other southernmost regions suffered the most dreadful conditions. They weren't even worthy of third class and travelled crammed in holds where a flimsy metal structure had been installed on three levels, said Griffin, with dozens of narrow cage-like iron beds with no conveniences, washbasins, linen or blankets. It was all lamentations, sea sickness, sighs, rows, fights, knives, bad blood and they suffered innumerable hardships on gloomy decks policed by sailors bristling with arms, an asphyxiating home for the emigrants for almost two months: many died on journey. When the Pavics finally reached South America, little Ivo had a temperature and swollen glands. They settled in Fort Bulnes and later in Punta Arenas and had three other children before Graciela came into the world in 1895. When she was four, Veronika, her mother, died of dysentery and inconsolable sadness because she would never again see her beloved Adriatic Sea. By then they were living on the Mercedes Estate.

14

MIRO PAVIC STARTED WORKING FOR THE RICH landowner Don Laureano Ravel on the Mercedes Estate in Useless Bay. It was the very same place, Griffin said, where my grandfather, on his honeymoon in 1923, performed a private magic show before flying to Punta Arenas in the Latécoère 26 that belonged to Esteban Ravel, son of Don Laureano and new owner of the estate at that time. A newly born babe, Esteban was barely slavering when Miro Pavic was rescued in 1891 on that huge farm after he experienced one of the most dramatic incidents in his life. As I said, Griffin added, it was gold that drove the emigrants to Tierra del Fuego and gold that immediately motivated Miro Pavic when he reached the Straits of Magellan. He left his wife and tiny son Ivo in Fort Bulnes and joined forces with a fellow called Pacheco he'd met on the *Alessandro Camondo*. Pacheco was a petty criminal like Pavic, but more of a gold seeker, and the two men went off to Puerto Natale in the northern Chilean cordillera. There they found chaos: thousands of prospectors in camps sprawled over the town and foothills and dug all over. Many were Jewish and Lebanese American prospectors from the exhausted veins in California and Nevada. There were good and bad, though the distinction was quite irrelevant given that they were all unscrupulous, said Griffin; everyone carried carbines and cartridge belts and used knives to resolve their problems. Miro believed the place was a den of murderers who killed each other at the slightest excuse. The rumour went up that gold had been found on the Beagle Channel, near Lenox Island in the south of the region, so many headed there.

Miro Pavic and Pacheco joined those who, as the settlers and adventurers got wilder and wilder, began to organise gangs to exterminate the natives on behalf of southern landowners in Tierra del Fuego, whose flocks of sheep were being attacked and rustled by Ona, Alaculoof and Yamana Indians, all now known by the common name of Fuegians in the press of the time, said Griffin. It was well-paid, regular work, whereas prospecting for gold was a lottery, or worse, Russian roulette. One of the most important of these ranchers was Don Laureano Ravel, a former lawyer in Santiago and an ex-general.

At the time he had contracted the services of a Scotsman, Alcydes MacLenan, to get rid of the Indians. He was from Edinburgh, where he'd preached the Gospel until he'd almost been strung up after being accused of rape in a Highlands village. He was forced to make his escape on the first boat he found in port and didn't ask where it was going. MacLenan's cruelty soon made him infamous, because he'd slit open the guts of dead Indians to profane them, and gave his men an extra bonus if they tabled the ears of all the Indians they hunted down, Graciela explained in a letter to my grandfather. But his reputation soon rested on an episode in which Miro Pavic was the protagonist, after he'd enlisted in MacLenan's gang with his inseparable buddy Pacheco. That was how Pavic almost lost his life.

They rode out with MacLenan and his gang in search of a tribe of Fuegians they wanted to teach a lesson. They took along large provisions of alcohol to get the Indians drunk and strips of beef they'd injected with strychnine. The presents would in principle enable them to approach the Indians peacefully. The policy of the ranchers, in Don Laureano's book, was to make them hungry and feed them poisoned meat, which they gratefully devoured. The expedition set out from Porvenir, where they loaded up their provisions, and a couple of days later rode into the Sierra Balmaceda. In a skirmish with Ona Indians on the northern bank of the O'Higgins River several men were wounded, although Pavic told his daughter Graciela that they killed all the Indians. Most of the gang wanted to turn back, because they didn't really know where they were riding: the Indians had been exterminated and they hadn't found any settlement, so why go on? The Scotsman said they should dump the meat there and then because it was an onerous burden. Some of the men protested over the meat, Pacheco included. 'Animals might eat it, and other animals those animals and their meat could end up in the stomachs of our miners,' he said. MacLenan retorted, reiterating his order, 'And Indians might eat it too. Throw it down here and it can fulfil its purpose.'

Then the Scotsman voiced his intention to ride on a few more days to prospect for gold. He'd been told it was a good area. But few shared his opinion. It was a very dangerous time in winter and they thought it was absurd to insist on looking for gold when in spring, with the thaw, they'd only have to stoop down to fish it out from the banks of the streams. MacLenan said that was precisely what he meant: they should grab the gold when there was no competition. They couldn't agree and the gang divided in two, wrote Graciela. MacLenan, Pacheco, Pavic and two others preferred to stay in the area and look for the precious metal. They knew that the much-feared Julius Popper, who'd come from China when he heard the word 'Gold!', so Griffin said, was digging a rich vein in Lago Vergara, in the southern parts of the mountains. Perhaps Popper hadn't exhausted it or perhaps there were other veins thereabouts. The rest of the men returned with the wounded to the Mercedes Estate.

Maclenan and Pavic's group exhausted all their supplies after a week looking for gold on MacPherson's Crag. 'We shouldn't have been so quick to poison that meat,' the oldest lamented, an Argentine by the name of Orlando Valle. The fifth man in the group was a fifteen-year-old Chilean. They knew him only by his nickname of Blondy. He never said anything, so they assumed he was dumb. On day eight the weather changed and snow covered the whole crag and temperatures dropped to below zero, something for which they weren't equipped. 'I could stand all this if I'd found some decent gold nuggets,' exclaimed a querulous Pacheco, who was in a bad state. Pavic agreed those hardships would have been worthwhile if at least there was some reward. The fact was they hadn't found a single trace of gold.

MacLenan was furious with himself because he knew he'd been responsible for a miscalculation. Then, when they were searching for a safe haven against an icy storm that blew up unexpectedly, the five men fell into a deep hole, the walls of which were a hundred per cent ice. They were stuck there for a week. In that time, the Chilean lad, who'd knocked his head when falling from on high, never recovered consciousness and died. They'd consumed all their supplies before falling down the hole, and although they could slake their thirst by patiently melting the ice, hunger pursued them and was a permanent threat. At the bottom of that hole they didn't know when it was dawn or dusk; they couldn't defecate, though old Valle never stopped and turned it into an unhealthy latrine; their clothes were always wet and the walls of ice were always cracking loudly.

'This prison isn't safe,' said Pavic, who read in the eyes of his colleagues that they weren't overjoyed about landing there as a result of the lunatic hunt for gold. They all experienced frostbite. Pacheco cut off three black fingers from his right hand and felt no pain.

'If we don't eat, we soon won't be able to move and won't have the strength to climb out. We'll all die,' said Pavic cold-bloodedly, assuming the leadership after MacLenan sank into sheer despondency and only prayed and mouthed threatening quotations from the Bible, as if he was out of his mind.

Then Miro Pavic looked at the dead Chilean lad and added, 'Snakes and worms will eat him. Wouldn't it be better if he fed us, so we don't meet the same fate? Wouldn't that be nobler, as far as he's concerned?'

They overcame their repugnance and for three more days, the time it took them to climb the icy walls to the rim of that pit, they fed on the flesh of Blondy the Chilean, which Miro Pavic cut off in strips. When they finally emerged, they encountered Don Laureano and his posse who'd set off from the Mercedes Estate in search of the lost band of men, alarmed they'd been so long in those harsh wastes without showing any signs of life. The four men were completely faint and unrecognisable under their beards and shoulder-length hair. They said nothing about what had happened, which they'd sworn to keep secret for the rest of their lives, but someone blabbed, because before long MacLenan's reputation for cannibalism spread far and wide. Subsequently, Miro Pavic told his daughter that story that did nothing for his pride and weighed heavily on his mind. MacLenan recovered and went back to being the cruel Indian hunter who pulverised foetuses. Then Don Laureano appointed Pavic as his overseer and entrusted him with the administration of his estate. Miro Pavic thus became his right-hand man.

15

GRACIELA MET ARTURO BAGNOLI, HER FUTURE husband, in Santiago, where she was one of the very few women who had gone to study in the capital. That was due to the generosity of Don Laureano Ravel, who made the money available to Miro Pavic so his daughter could go to college. At about the same time, they started pronouncing the *c* at the end of her surname as a *k*, abandoning the original Croatian sound of *sch*, Griffin felt bound to explain. In Santiago, young Graciela fell passionately in love with Arturo, whom she describes in her letters as being of average build with bright honey or dark amber eyes, an unruly moustache, clean-cut features and a charming, intelligent gaze. They soon married in secret, although Don Laureano Ravel was privy to the deed, but nobody in the Pavic family found out until much later and on the Bagnoli side, the closest relative present was his cousin Gaetano, who acted as best man. Arturo later wrote a letter informing the rest of his family in Italy of the good news. They both continued their university studies, Medicine and History respectively, but Graciela soon had to give up hers when she became pregnant with little Pablo, the first of their two children.

Arturo Bagnoli, like Miro Pavic, sailed to America as an emigrant in an Italian boat, the *Emma Salvatores*. He came from

Caserta, like his cousin Gaetano Orticolo and friend Stefano Farnese, two young men who also joined the adventure on the high seas. The *Emma Salvatores* was a down-at-heel boat that combined sail and steam power. It plied the route between Naples and Río Gallegos in Argentina, the final goal of Italian emigrants, and a route people claimed had inspired Edmund de Amicis. Stefano Farnese got off in Río Gallegos, and in due course became mayor of the city as well as a fanatical supporter of Mussolini. After Graciela lost her family, he often asked her to let him help her, and said she could rely on him to help her remake her life in a less painful location, but she refused to contemplate the generous offer from her husband's old friend. The real reason was that she could never relinquish the hope of finding a trace of her beloved family after the accident and if she had no choice in the end but to give up all hope, she'd at least derive consolation from the fact that life near the Straits of Magellan thrust upon her the obligatory role of the guardian of a large cemetery in which each cove, fjord and beach might be her children's graves.

She even came to believe, and confessed as much to my grandparents, that God had sent her the warrior automaton, a *golem* or *ronin*, to help her protect and look after that huge tract of cemetery. While he was telling me this in Funchal, Oliver Griffin was reminded of the keeper of the cemetery in Nantes, a small, doughty woman, who looked like a peasant and whom he'd asked about the whereabouts of Fabienne Michelet's grave. She told me the place was too large for her to remember the details of every person buried there, said Griffin. I asked her, Was it perhaps as big as the Straits of Magellan? The woman couldn't think what to reply or didn't know what I was talking about.

Arturo and Gaetanos' final destination was much further

south, 'on the boundaries of our dreams', as Arturo Bagnoli called those arid, depopulated, moribund, austere yet intoxicating lands, abandoned by the hand of God like my Desolation Island, or why not his very own island, for I expect he nourished a savage primeval instinct pushing him further and further to the edge, to the island-shaped frontier, stopping in Punta Arenas, at the centre of a circle whose field of action was a natural world as difficult to explain as the fact he found himself marooned there. I often think I identify with that man, Griffin confessed, someone as invisible to me as I was to him, and in my life I've sought what he found in a much shorter span, and I don't know if my journey there was self-propelled or driven by the fact I was Graciela Pavic's resurrected husband, intending to appear unawares, over seventy years later, to deliver myself up as a sour-tasting present that had got lost in time, an absurd present, now everything was resolved and Graciela Pavic was certainly dead. Just as somewhere in the world, a present awaits me, a present that lost its way in the perverse, capricious circuits of one punctilious postman after another, a present sent twenty years ago by Fabienne Michelet the day she wrote, 'I'll call you as soon as I leave. I can't stand living without you any more.' Arturo Bagnoli and I embarked on a journey to the world's end and that's the link between us.

When he finished Medicine, he and Graciela, now twenty-five with two children (the second, Gaetano, was also born in Santiago), decided to settle in Punta Arenas. There they had their home, friends and future. A nameplate would soon be on the door proclaiming 'Dr Arturo Bagnoli', the pride of Caserta at the world's end. They couldn't foresee their happiness would last only three years. One summer's day in 1918 the locals told Graciela they'd found shattered fragments of the sloop *Good Luck* that Arturo had fitted out that morning to go mussel fishing in Catherine's Bay. He'd taken his sons Pablo and Gaetano with him. Everything indicated they had drowned when a storm suddenly broke and then vanished as quickly as it had come. Graciela opened her mouth to say something but couldn't find the words. She could only think about children, children galore, other children, but never her own. And that led Griffin to recall a story that made a deep impression on him when he heard it, a story also set in Nantes, Oliver added before continuing.

One day in November 1766, Bougainville's expedition was preparing to sail in the frigate *La Boudeuse* from the river port of Nantes, where the Loire broadens into the Atlantic. It was a large four-master with twenty-six cannons, which they'd loaded with trinkets to trick the Indians and trade with them. A good part of this junk comprised big and small coloured glass baubles. Pierrot, a nephew of Captain Bougainville, had accompanied his parents to the port to bid farewell to the expedition. He was five years old and mistook the bright bits of glass overflowing from a small barrel that had unfortunately been left open on the quayside for coloured sweets and toffees. Little Pierrot wasn't listening to anyone, and just played up and down the quayside. When his parents took their eyes off him as they waved their handkerchiefs in the wind at *La Boudeuse* that was sailing out of the inlet towards the Saint-Nazaire estuary, he put a handful of baubles in his mouth. His death agony lasted three days and nights; the boy died from the bleeding they caused. Bougainville knew nothing of this tragedy until his return, and when told, the great French sailor, far from expressing sorrow, shrugged his shoulders in resignation and said: 'A righteous punishment from God for the numerous times we gave those trinkets to Alaculoof children in the Straits of Magellan.' Graciela had met Alaculoof children, perhaps the last before they died out for ever, and perhaps she was thinking of those children when the locals told her the boat carrying her husband and children had sunk. Griffin said Graciela Pavic stayed silent for days after that: she felt thoroughly depressed; they could hold no wake, funeral or ceremony, so there could be no respite or mourning. And when the bodies failed to appear, everything slowly fell into oblivion, that gateway to loneliness.

Hope surged in Graciela and led her to search tirelessly. She began to contract indigenous canooers who went out in skiffs made from animal hides to the area where the accident took place and then she went further abroad to the most distant coasts, like Dawson Island, where MacLenan and her father had slaughtered Indians years before, and then even more remote coastlines, like the Clarence, St Inés and Desolation Islands, until she'd wandered the whole territory of the Straits in journeys that took months and years, in benevolent weather or in the midst of cruel tempests. Nothing held her back, not even the skeletons of whales and remains of disembowelled wolves and minks which was all that she found. People began to make fun of her or pity her in her madness. She was rallied by rumours, by clues, real or false, she picked up and investigated personally to the bitter end, but only exhausted herself in the attempt.

It was like the time she was almost shipwrecked near Cape Columns, on 6 January 1919, the day Jacques Vaché was dying, when her eyes saw what from a distance looked like a human form. She thought it might be a mummy or something similar, a natural embalming brought by good fortune, or even a body preserved intact by the ice and low temperatures. It soon revealed itself to be a strange kind of metal figure, rusty scrap iron emerging from the shadows of history. It was obviously derelict. It didn't seem very tall, though she then saw that half its body had sunk below ground. It was camouflaged by the lichen and moss covering the rocks on that hill, most of its surface rusted and only the briefest glints from the silver and yellow steel remaining betrayed its existence.

Graciela badly bruised her hands crawling up. From close quarters it looked like a real warrior in armour who'd died at the end of a battle, and for a moment Graciela imagined she might find a skull and skeleton inside. The possibility startled her, because if that were true the man must have died several centuries ago. However, the face was disfigured and expressionless, the flat mask scaring and brutal and long, long ago a clumsy Dr Frankenstein must have inserted the parts for eyebrows and eyes and the mouth and jaw. It had been given a rough coat of paint and the paint had disappeared. A visor over the forehead and helmet structure over a potential head convinced Graciela, Griffin went on, it was definitely not a human being, but a simulacrum. An imitation of human life. An artefact.

Her remaining doubts were dispelled when she leaned over the figure and saw its arms were articulated by a delicate internal mechanism with cogs and chains that was now completely unusable. Graciela noticed its chest was riddled with holes, perhaps bullet holes, but fired by what weapon and when? She concluded it was an automaton, and expressed her astonishment aloud, as she began to realise it might be a notable find for the Salesian Museum in Punta Arenas where she'd worked as a restorer ever since she'd arrived in the city. She decided to clean and restore it and find out its origins and history. She stared at it lingeringly, abandoning all trivial thoughts, letting herself be carried away by the spell of that most unreal moment.

You won't believe it, said Griffin, but Graciela was experiencing a strange feeling, an irresistible attraction. She took pity on, or even better, however ridiculous it seemed, fell in love with the metallic body that refused to surrender its secrets, though she immediately regretted even contemplating that possibility. She shook her head, just in case she was dreaming. 'What could be more prisoner of itself than an automaton? What freedom can there be for a being created never to possess such a thing?' Graciela mused philosophically, restraining her more eccentric impulses. Wasn't she also a kind of soulful automaton, after that miserable summer's day in 1918? Nevertheless she intuited, shamefacedly and a touch reluctantly, that that unimaginable automaton might be the rope end to pull her out of the pit of grief where she was mired and give new meaning to her life. What's more, it was true, added Griffin, she made it the centre of her universe, as one deduces from the letters she then wrote.

My grandfather always said he and my grandmother faced a strange, beautifully reconstructed metal figure that was quite repulsive, although he found it fascinating, especially considering, as he was intent on finding fame as the Great Samini, it suggested a marvellous act of magic he would later invent. Graciela took excessive care of the automaton, never saying a word about the unnatural feelings it aroused in her on Desolation Island that she thought were horrific and perverse. Nonetheless, something lurked in the shadows, since she behaved towards the automaton like any deranged woman, whom people forgive her slight misdemeanours, might with a plastic doll. Quite unconsciously Graciela talked to the automaton, cleaned it, referred to it as if she were convinced it was flesh and blood. 'As if it were a son or lover,' Esteban Ravel once remarked, her powerful friend, the owner of the Mercedes Estate who was secretly in love with her, as became obvious from Graciela's letters, Griffin told me. The automaton came to take the place of her dead family, because, in a short span of years she had lost husband and children, father and brothers. In 1923 she was alone in the world, and prevaricating about whether to go to Dubrovnik and meet relatives she'd never seen, a journey she kept postponing for the rest of her life.

16

IT WAS NECESSARY TO GO WAY BACK IN TIME, TO moments that have fallen into oblivion but no doubt existed, to dig out the history behind the automaton that infatuated Graciela, Griffin explained, since it had to have a history despite its metal body and complete lack of will. Does anyone know, for example, Oliver asked imperturbably, that the idea of a fake army of automata was hatched by Maximiliano Transilvano, secretary to Charles I, when he heard Pigafetta talk about Patagonian giants – which is what his captain, the great Magellan, called them – when he returned and told his monarch the story of the voyage on which so many perished, including Magellan? I was struck dumb for a while. What could I say? Oliver Griffin's inquisitive eyes stared me out: he was so proud of the knowing tone of his question. Griffin was only testing on himself the rhetoric or rehearsed curiosity he used to hook yours truly, by demonstrating that history is a trickle of time on a drip feed and no gushing flow. It was his way of questioning the way men's memories were handed down over the years, and marvelling at its frailty. After his previous question, he asked others that were less profound and more ridiculous that revealed the immense shadows of history where a time-traveller like himself could meander, that felt palpably invisible, since every testimony or memory is invisible, particularly testimonies and memories of what never existed and that make up a catalogue of deceptive possibilities, Griffin the historian concluded. With no rhyme or apparent reason, as if testifying to his usual semi-absentmindedness, he embarked on a series of questions that were inopportune and unrelated to the coherence of his thesis but nonetheless 'illustrative', as he eventually described them. They only made me feel impatient and ill at ease . . . Does anyone in fact know, he asked, that a woman, possibly by the name of Amelina Barreto, wife of the architect of the Souza Barracks on the top of Funchal's highest peak that houses the garrison that protected Madeira from pirates, decided to poison her husband, probably Manuel de Flandes, though that's of little matter, and that the idea led her to attempt the operation repeatedly until he finally died from the strychnine she put in a mushroom and lamprey stew, however emphatically the island's most famous doctor stated on the death certificate that it was death caused by dropsy? Griffin fell silent and shrugged his shoulders.

Or else, he muttered: does anyone in fact know that the fiancé of that young woman walking past now, here in this Funchal hotel, at this moment in the afternoon, had a grandfather who just died peacefully, possibly yesterday, in bed at home in Lisbon, yet this man, the miserable coincidences of life!, killed with his own hands, though nobody remembers now, Communist peasants on the frontier between Portugal and Spain in the distant era of the Salazar dictatorship? Silence again.

Or else try this one: does anyone know that Miro Pavic, Graciela's father, ate human flesh in that cave on MacPherson's Crag where he was trapped for a week between the walls of ice? No comment. When he asked if anyone knew that Antonio

Pigafetta, registered under the name of Antonio Lombardo, a mere supernumerary, on the expedition that became the first voyage around the world in 1519, was in love, secretly or not, with the great Fernando de Magellan, I was reduced to dumb silence, a silence that deepened and would soon be broken again. Well, what does it matter if anyone knows or not, what matters is that I know, said Griffin, crossing the threshold of darkness where he always headed when talking to me, as if in a trance.

Maximiliano Transilvano, from Transylvania, Emperor Charles I's renowned private secretary, listened attentively to Antonio Pigafetta on Christmas Day in 1522 during the exchange between the frivolous and haughty Italian and the king who'd just arrived from Worms. And while the young man talked, one could imagine the events on that voyage he later described in a letter although he'd never been on board ship or known any other society beyond greasy Parisian parquet or Valladolid's loathsome mudflats, where they now found themselves. A polyglot in legal issues and a political visionary, Maximiliano Transilvano then imagined the Patagonian giants, 'those cannibalistic, fearsome Indian giants', as he called them in his letter, lacerating Spaniards with their arrows and poisonous darts, and glimpsed the dangers that the situation described by Pigafetta might pose for the Catholic future of the Empire. The real long-term threats were the English and the Lutherans, however much the Emperor preferred to fear France and only wanted to think about defeating this neighbour. The idea came to Transilvano straight away, but he said nothing; it was a single moment when he forgot Pigafetta's lively narrative. Why not create a fake army, was what he was thinking, said Griffin dramatically, a new, unheard-of war machine comprising thousands of small devices of war to terrify non-baptised giants and greedy Englishmen alike? And he had a fleeting, dazzling vision of blinding flashes from the polished silver cuirasses of an army arrayed on the high, jagged peaks of the mountain ranges on the coasts of the cruel Straits that the Italian chronicler described so vividly, provoking unmitigated panic or at least deterring the enemy from making frantic attempts to occupy lands conquered for God and the Pope by Charles the Holy Emperor.

Nonetheless, that image vanished at once from his head that now filled with other, more routine worries, although the sage Transilvano was never to forget, said Griffin, the inspired shaft of thought he'd had that Christmas Day. And it is preserved in letters where he mentions to another court correspondent his idea of fortifying the newly discovered Straits with thousands of sturdy metal figures attached to posts and looking almost human, scowling terribly, some moved by a device that made them seem what they weren't, sufficient to frighten onlookers duped by the mirage. Several years passed before Philip II implemented the secretary's idea: Transilvano never saw either of the two automata that were, in the end, fashioned into reality by Melvicius's hands.

Indeed this whole story of the automaton is a love story, Griffin said resolutely and unexpectedly, before he rehearsed his ethereal love of Madeira, Graciela's sweet love of Arturo Bagnoli, his grandparents' life-long love of each other, his intense love of Fabienne, his absurd love of Desolation Island, Graciela's lunatic love of the automaton, his forbidden love of Li Pao . . . And decided to speak of other loves. What Transilvano couldn't imagine, said Griffin, was that Pigafetta, the bearded man recounting in his macaronic Italian spattered with French, Spanish and Latin the most fabulous journey ever made in that epoch, loved Magellan who'd been his leader and captain, and that afternoon, seated at the other end of the long table stained by wax that had spilt over from the candelabra, was trying to conceal the pain caused by Magellan's death, that was now rather subdued since it had occurred in Mactán eight months before, though he still felt in turmoil. Not very much is known about this love and inevitably, like all banned sentiments, it is today open to all manner of prurient interpretations; at the time it could only inhabit the head of a Pigafetta afraid of betraying himself, who avoided any tell-tale words or gestures and shut himself behind the bolted door of prudence. I've fantasised for years, continued Griffin, about this homoerotic relationship, and have always felt warmly disposed towards Pigafetta, in a way I know is at once appealing and distasteful. And on the high seas, aboard the *Minerva Janela*, my fantasy grew apace as the idle days on deck brought me closer to South America.

When I was on the high seas I thought of him not as a faded, historical character but as a lover who'd lost his love, and at the same time I thought about Li Pao, man or woman, my Li Pao, the Chinese transvestite I loved who disappeared from my life overnight and whom I'll tell you about later: my thoughts compelled me to bring those two individuals together in strange burials from a real or fictitious past that my mind constructed. And I thought about Pigafetta, and then about my forgotten, ephemeral love for Li Pao, when I saw another flock of hungry birds fly over our boat from the leeward side one morning. It was a raucous alert: we were close to the coast of Brazil, even if it was still three hundred and fifty miles away. Luiz Pereira, the first officer, had forewarned me in our cabin. 'The shit-eating birds will soon be upon us. They dive into the sea like swords,' he said. It was then I thought of Pigafetta, because he spoke of dung-eating birds that flew after others, until 'the latter got rid of their detritus which the birds in pursuit immediately consumed'. They were literally shit-eaters, as Pereira called them. It was curious biological activity that caught the eye of Pigafetta who must have stood aboard like me, looking at the same ocean, but five centuries earlier. At that moment, when Brazil was not yet in view although one sensed the presence of the South American coast of that huge oceanic lake, the spectacle of exhausting acrobatic flight was in full swing over the *Minerva Janela*, over the high towers of containers, the great picopardos, and bluish carabillas, featherless naviles or pájaros romos, the exotic names of some of the coastal species that Pereira taught me. Some were birds that never settle on the sea and are swept this way and that at the mercy of the wind. These were my favourites, but I never discovered their real names. Nobody on board liked them.

After we'd sailed within a few miles from the volcanic Isla da Trindade in Brazilian waters, and a coastguard patrol boat came from the island and skulked close by until Captain Branco gave them our registration number and the dates of our itinerary, the sea changed. I saw Fernando Grande and Amuntado make more frequent checks that our cargo was secure. They waved to me from the rigging, while I remained on the second bridge and clung to a lifebuoy rope. I noticed the birds had suddenly disappeared and the waves on the high sea were now crashing against the helm; the boat was never-endingly pitching and heeling, rising and plunging fifteen and twenty metres at a time. I felt a terrible seasickness in my stomach, something I thought I'd got over. During my last bout of nausea, I had been forced to spend the whole time on my bunk, and hardly ate a thing. It was a tailor-made slimming diet. I did the same now and could see the grey waves sweep the deck with spray and heard the dull moaning of wind, as constant as the disturbing noise from the boat itself. I tried to concentrate on thoughts that would transport me far away, said Griffin, because seasickness is a misfortune that can lower anyone's spirits: there is no way out, it is a rat trap in which one would prefer to lose consciousness and wake up in another life: we cease to be human beings and are transformed into a yellow sewer that longs only for death. So I returned to Pigafetta and love on Magellan's expedition. My hypothesis is that that turbulent, passionate love, so tacit yet so virile, trapped in that abominable passage, was the real cause of the famous tragedy of San Julián, which in turn I believe was rooted in the jealous rivalry between him and the Royal Inspector Juan de Cartagena, the rebel who stood up to the Captain-General in the middle of the voyage, and who I consequently became fond of, because he was a star-crossed hero marked by misfortune and disappointment in love, a helpless hero forced to fight against Magellan's mighty power. From my bunk I concentrated on recreating a previous episode that took place on the coasts of Guinea and confirmed my bold suppositions.

Elated and unwearied by the day's story-telling, Griffin began to tell all as we climbed Funchal's steep streets, towards the Caminho das Voltas, in the vicinity of the Botanic Gardens. The expedition had departed from Sevilla, led by the *Trinidad*, on 10 August, St Lorenzo's Day, but the five ships didn't set sail until 20 September from Sanlúcar de Barrameda. It was the year of grace of 1519. Fernando de Magellan's reputation as a misogynist was already on the tongues of gossips slandering him as an invert, as they had so often said before, in that port, in Seville or Lisbon, or earlier, in distant Calicut in India. Now, as they were about to set off, the rumours in the taverns of Cadiz singled out Cristóbal Rabelo the young page, still almost a child, who always accompanied him, who died by Magellan's side in Mactán clinging to his hand, whereas the great explorer had always acted coldly and elusively towards Beatriz Barbosa, with whom he'd contracted an appearance-saving marriage of convenience. Cristóbal Rabelo embarked on the *Trinidad* as his servant, against the wishes of Beatriz who was appalled by the constant sight of Cristóbal embracing her husband or sitting on his knee, wearing few or no clothes at all. On the other hand, he left her on land, on the pretext that it would be a long, hazardous journey, as it was reasonable to predict, holding unimaginable dangers, and he refused to countenance those who advised him to let women travel on board. Never ever, said Griffin, but nobody ever discovered why. He didn't want women near him, but he couldn't stop sailors who liked to dress up as women, that was very common on long voyages at the time, or the presence of those secretly called sodomites or sodomitic, adepts of practices the Inquisition punished with the death penalty, though they were tolerated on board. All in all, Magellan's puritanism was only a studied way of hiding his own real inclinations, argued Griffin, and he adopted a harsh attitude that a small band of favourites knew was a façade. Consequently, it shouldn't surprise us if Pigafetta's love was requited in some way by the captain. On the other hand, Pigafetta never returned the love of Juan de Cartagena, captain of the *San Antonio*.

On that Christmas Day in Valladolid when Pigafetta recounted the entire adventure of the long voyage to Emperor Charles, that same day when Maximiliano Transilvano conceived the idea of the creation of an army of automata, Juan Elcano, master of the *Concepción* and survivor from the voyage, gave a very different account to his monarch, and separately. It was much less colourful than the Italian's version: among the episodes he related, as Transilvano noted and even mentioned later in one of his letters, said Griffin, was a sequence devoted to their brief stay on the coast of Guinea, in the middle of October 1519, the first year of their expedition. On that occasion, after they'd been there several days stocking up on wood, meat and water, Magellan suddenly ordered the arrest of Captain Juan de Cartagena, whom he had had a fierce argument with days before. It was deep into the night when they quarrelled; they spoke loudly, in private, although many sailors knew their violent exchange was provoked by jealousy over the young Italian. I wish many of us had covered our ears, Elcano told Charles I, said Griffin, or had been fortunate enough to be deaf from birth. 'As well as Juan de Cartagena, I was also instructed to arrest,' Juan Elcano related his police role in these events, 'a man who was wearing strange clothes when he was seized. I expect they were a female's, and I found that disturbing and repulsive.' Elcano could barely remember the name of this sodomite, as he repeatedly told the emperor, Transilvano noted later, but he guessed he was probably Simón de Asio, a friend of Captain Gaspar de Quesada, whom he knew by sight. He did know he was an ordinary sailor, Elcano asserted, always according to Griffin.

There on the sand, with only a prayer of endorsement from the chaplain of the captain's boat, Magellan gave the order for the transvestite to be beheaded in the presence of all his men. Simón collapsed. Quesada cried and begged for mercy, as did Cartagena, but Magellan took two daggers from his sleeve and demanded Quesada and Cartagena decapitate him there and then. The astounded Juan de Cartagena refused, and Quesada preferred to stab himself rather than kill his young friend, to whom he was united by love. When both men refused, Magellan arranged for the sentence against the transvestite sailor to be carried out on the beach. The role of executioner fell to Elcano. A black pool of blood soon spread around the lifeless torso of wretched Simón de Asio and the captain-general ordered everyone to file past without averting their gaze. According to Elcano, they then made a bonfire over the pool and burnt the two parts of the body separately. A thick, greyish smoke rose in the sky for several hours. An attempt was made to dismiss Cartagena from his position as commander, but Esteban Gómez, Magellan's pilot, who was popular in his time and a sworn enemy of the captain-general, subtly suggested that such a decision would lead the various crews to rebel, a mutiny that in fact later erupted, led by Cartagena, in St Julian's Bay, where they spent the winter. Why did Magellan and Cartagena quarrel that night, and why did that acrimonious argument unleash such butchery? Griffin wondered. Perhaps it was their love of Pigafetta, or the fact they both desired the adolescent Cristóbal. And why, despite all that, did Magellan pardon Quesada and Cartagena when he could have taken advantage of the favourable circumstances to order a legal, righteous execution without having to fabricate elaborate excuses? These ruminations saved me from my seasickness as I lay prostrate in my cabin, my rope in a well, Griffin concluded, bringing his story to a climax in front of the entrance to the Botanical Gardens.

17

WHEN JAMES WHALE SHOT *THE INVISIBLE MAN*, HIS favourite film and mine, in 1933, said Griffin days later in our favourite café on the Avenida Zarco, it was ten years after my grandparents had their photograph taken with Graciela Pavic and the revamped automaton, and several years before Saint-Exupéry began his short-lived long-haul flight to Punta Arenas. One day, after seeing the film yet again, I started to research the life of Whale, which I've always felt was remotely similar to Magellan's. James Whale was forty-four at the time, almost the same age as the Portuguese mariner, and he loved David Lewis the way Magellan loved Pigafetta. Lewis was an actor who'd been his production assistant and then a screenplay adaptor in Hollywood. Lewis would sometimes show up at shoots and stand completely still behind Whale next to the spotlight supports, making no noise at all, until the director, sensing an unsuspected presence behind him, swung round. As he did so, Lewis synchronised his reflexes, turned round quickly in tandem with Whale, and stood behind him again, creating the illusion that in fact nobody was there or perhaps, if somebody was, he must be invisible. They began joking it was 'Wilhem's game' in homage to Verne's character, Wilhem Storitz, who, like Jack Griffin in the H. G. Wells novel Whale was adapting, drank a beverage concocted from a secret formula in order to become invisible at will.

But that prescience that there was an absent presence was no joke. We invisible folk know that only too well, Griffin went on, we're expert at startling people. We know when it happens and know when we are off radar. I have often felt off radar like that, unseen, not even sensed, and yet I *was* there, for heaven's sake, in flesh and blood, wanting something to happen, for someone to shake my hand or give me a hug or merely say, 'Hello, it's you, how are you, what do you want, what would you like?' And I've also seen the tremendous shock on people's faces when they suddenly and unexpectedly discovered I was standing behind them, quite unintentionally, as a result of the silent, feline way I move. How often have I heard, 'Where were you, I didn't see you coming, I didn't know you were here,' and so on! I'd stand a few centimetres away from the back of their necks and hold my breath. People would be slow to realise anyone was there. 'Anyone would think you were invisible!' my mother or father used to say, and I finally created a personal art out of those strange appearances and over time, as with Jack Griffin in the film, it represented the inexorable fulfilment of fate: my name guided me there, and it was my duty to refine the technique of really invisible folk. I managed to pass unnoticed in dozens of social gatherings, with friends and teachers, in conventions and in class; during exams students looked everywhere trying to spot me because they didn't know where I'd appear, though *they knew* I was there. That is the invisibility that has always haunted me.

Occasionally, Whale didn't like those jokes played by David and his bad timing could ruin a whole day's filming. However, given his introvert nature, it was only to be expected from a haughty, refined Englishman, as long and lean as a reed, who shot every single sequence in a shirt and tie, quiet as the dead, concentrating on his actors' diction. The ungovernable Whale never got excited or revealed his emotions in public and simply told David to stop behaving like a little kid. When they met, almost the moment Whale arrived in California in 1929 in the depths of the Depression, James had just hit forty and David was twelve years his junior, but obviously he was no little kid. Magellan's Cristóbal Rabelo *was* a little boy, but neither Whale nor Lewis had remotely heard of him, Griffin made that crystal clear.

The production company had asked a special favour of young David to take out an English director who'd just come to Los Angeles and was famous because his play, *Journey's End*, was *the* great box-office success of the decade in London's theatre land. David did so on several nights taking him to dine at the Delmonico, Thelma's Tavern and Ruffo's, where the stars used to drop by. At the end of a month Whale grabbed him by the shoulder, kissed him on the mouth and swore he was the only person he'd ever catch a plane for if he were sick and dying at the other end of the country, a thing he certainly would never do for his mother. Within twelve months they were living together on a hill in Los Angeles, near Sunset Boulevard, very close to where Whale committed suicide not so many years afterwards.

James's father was a miner like the ones Jules Verne portrays in *The Black Indies*, his mother, a puritan as strict as Magellan, who dressed him like a hermaphrodite on Sundays and took him to church in Dudley, near Birmingham, in the heart of the Midlands mining area, where James was born on 22 July 1889. Whale fought in the First World War as a non-commissioned officer in the Battle of the Somme and was taken prisoner by the Germans in Steenbeek. As a prisoner of war he discovered his aptitude for drawing that he soon developed as a therapy against angst in those filthy camps. Over time his drawings became his individual way of tackling in advance situations he might find himself in. The state of invisibility, for example, remarked Griffin. Hundreds of pencil sketches of scenes in *The Invisible Man* existed before he started shooting, many of which were never filmed or only filmed in his head, at most in dreams, sketches in which Wells's character's presence is palpable because of swellings in clothes, curtains or a cushion, or lines traced in the air that denote a voice emerging from nothing. How strange he should draw invisible men and I should draw islands. Not even in the plural: he drew the invisible Jack Griffin and I drew Desolation Island.

But to return to his time in the Great War, continued Oliver, while James was a prisoner in the Karlsruhe camp he made thousands of drawings he subsequently sold for a good price in London after the armistice. This allowed him to enter the world of the theatre and meet two men who would become men he loved: Bob Sherriff and Colin Clive. Whale's entire life takes place among men, or, to be more precise, among *those* men. First, however, in 1923 he tried to marry Doris Zinkeisen, a Scottish artist who lived in Liverpool, to maintain appearances, like Magellan and Beatriz Barbosa, but it didn't work out. Curiously enough, Griffin went on, my Li Pao was also a painter of dragons by day, though by night he changed his name and occupation and became Mae Jing, though that's another story. To go back to Bob Sherriff, he earned his living as a playwright and scriptwriter and had managed to establish good relations with theatre impresarios in the West End. He'd written the wartime drama *Journey's End*, which immediately struck a chord with Whale and the whole of British society between the wars.

Bob was pleasant and extremely active and most people considered him to be Whale's permanent partner, though nobody fantasised about a relationship of a sexual nature, however much those scheming showbiz artists were keen to grasp at any straw of suspicion. The actor they both selected for the lead role was, in his turn, a young man who'd spent time in the trenches and endured the mental stress of war, Colin Clive, an insecure, passionate fellow, whom Whale was to give several leading roles, including one that immortalised him as Dr Henry Frankenstein. As soon as Whale saw the svelte, beautiful Colin, he fell in love; however, it wasn't requited, at least not as immediately as James wished, because Colin also liked women and was reticent about acknowledging his passion for men.

As far as Clive was concerned, his relationship with Whale was both a source of strength that helped his self-confidence and a torture for someone with such a weak character, to the point that whenever the director tried to leave him, Colin collapsed and took to the bottle. I wonder, Griffin added, if that might not have been Magellan's attitude to Pigafetta, if he'd survived in Mactán and he and not Elcano had gone around the world, and if he and not Pigafetta had been the one to tell Charles I of the prodigious feats performed on that adventure. But our subject is Whale, almost five hundred years later. In 1933, the year *The Invisible Man* was filmed, the relationship between him and Clive was not at its best or had already been poisoned for ever, and Clive was prey to a depression he tried to cure by resorting to whisky. According to the press, it was not unusual to see him completely drunk in late-night bars.

Depression was a state he would frequently slide into when he was with Whale, himself a manic depressive, and I can't but help think, said Griffin, that James's melancholy originated in the murky, oppressive skies over Dudley, the black faces of the miners and the sad childhood of prayers and privations James carried as a lifetime burden he could never fling off. Clive seemingly wanted to return to London; he couldn't stand the glitter of Hollywood, where he felt totally drained and Whale, rather than hang on to him, encouraged him to go. Just like that, a cold blast of wind without guilt or remorse. Anyway, he'd already chosen another actor for the role of my homonym, added Griffin.

It was none other than the then unknown Claude Rains, an English actor whose career was a blank to everyone and whose face didn't yet appear in film-star photo albums across the United States. One day Whale called Clive and told him not to worry, the role wouldn't allow him to shine: he'd have an uncomfortable bandage around his head all the time. 'I should engage a beginner, said Whale, Griffin told me. Colin got the message but didn't return to England: he married and became an alcoholic. When he died a few years later in the summer of 1937, Whale decided not to go to the funeral ceremony or related memorials. He didn't like the dead, ceremonies for the dead, or the words the living intone to the dead, words the dead never hear, invisible words, I mean.

Bob Sherriff never left Whale's side and adapted Wells's novel for the screen, he also approved of the choice of Rains, whom he met at a party in the house of the producer, Carl Laemmle. 'You'll be amazed by his ability to find a voice for everything,' he told Whale. And in fact Rains's voice *does* predominate in *The Invisible Man*, because his face makes its first appearance only in the film's final, static close-up. James didn't know him and had never heard of him, but he soon found biographical details to delight him, like his date of birth – Claude Rains was born in 1889, the same year as Whale – something that was important to Whale, a secret fan of Cabbalistic games and mathematical games with numbers. Moreover, Rains was a Londoner, a provenance that always made James feel neurotic, given his own humble mining background which he tried to conceal, to the point of inventing a Scottish genealogy for himself, an antiquated rural nobility totally bankrupted by a licentious rake of a forebear from Inverness. For James it was about class, and especially the upper class, however cockney Rains's accent might be. And naturally Bob was right: in the four months they filmed, Whales was fascinated by Rains's modulated voice, which could be extremely tender and extremely sinister, particularly when in his role as raging mad Jack Griffin, he got angrier and angrier and reached a smouldering pitch of spite that scared the entire film crew.

Bob Sherriff once brought a suitcase stuffed with books to Whale's house. 'Here you are, this might help you understand what invisibility involves,' he announced, dropping the case on a sofa. He poured himself a drink and told Whale to read the novel by H. G. Wells and all his fiction, and other books on the same topic, to get himself in the right mood. They were all in Bob's old suitcase, even those Wells presumably read in order to write his *Invisible Man*. 'That's all I could lay my hands on,' Sherriff added. He also handed him an old photo of Wells taken when he was fifty, posing straight-backed, complete with moustache and bushy eyebrows, opening a hefty tome in his library. I imagine Whale in Hollywood bars and cafés at night, probably alone at a circular table at Ruffo's, sipping his inevitable cocktail of gin and berry liqueur and reading cheap editions of *The Secret of Wilhelm Storitz*, by Verne, Wells's master, or *The Invisible Murderer*, Philip Wylie's horror novel, using Wells's photo as a bookmark, while he sketched and racked his brain for tricks and devices to create on camera the extraordinary special effects sparked by that secret formula.

A few years ago, Griffin said in passing, I read in the catalogue of a famous auction house that they were going to sell a tablecloth of Whale's drawings where the words THE INVISIBLE MAN appeared next to his signature. It must certainly have been a tablecloth from Ruffo's and from the time when he went there and read those books amid the hustle and bustle of the star system. How could he film the invisible? What techniques could he use? Film twice and superimpose the images? Film against a black background that would absorb the light? The problem was finding the right light, as in Verne's story of Storitz, finding a substance to break the light into new, different, unheard-of elements. The persistent paranoia began to oppress Whale who let his daily routines slide and never rang his friends. David reproached him for being so offhand. Might it be true that invisibility drives you mad? What was behind those absences and that longing for the abyss the reserved Whale felt more and more drawn to? Mere depression and disgust because he could see his father's face that was always black with coal dust?

As he began to prepare the film, Whale's preoccupation with lunacy, his real obsession, deepened. After he'd said that, Griffin threw another raft of questions at me: Have you seen his films? Have you seen the madness on the faces of those buried in the trenches, the madness on the faces of those who end up being monsters, the blind madness of fear? Is an invisible man a monster? This is the key! Was the automaton Graciela Pavic found a monster? Who is monstrous and who isn't? Griffin kept asking, absorbed in one of his pensive moods, at the back of the café where we were sat. But he recovered after a few seconds. They say, said Griffin, now in a lighter mood, that when Wells saw the film, he congratulated Whale for his cinematic version, but reproached him for making a pathetic lunatic out of someone who was in principle only searching for rational scientific explanations, as in the novel.

Whale had driven himself desperate trying to persuade Universal Studios to let him shoot a different version – the one he was developing in those dozens and dozens of drawings he then gave to David – and felt the writer's comment to be insulting and, remembering his obsessive wariness in relation to lunacy, sent him a note with this single sentence: 'Only madmen want to be invisible and I *am* a madman. Yours, J.W.' But Wells reposted spitefully rather than politely with another single sentence over his initials: 'When whales surface they think they are submerged. H.G.W.' Wells thus played with the meaning of Whale's surname and alluded to the director's sexuality that was almost an open secret in Hollywood. Isn't a whale a monster? James must have wondered when he read the note while perhaps waiting for a taxi to drive him far from any public place. What is a fact, recounted Griffin, is that weeks after the première, Whale tore Wells's photo into four and returned all his novels to Bob with a curt 'Thank you'.

Whale's entire universe was galvanised by this film, *The Invisible Man*, that supposedly represented his life's crowning achievement and the heights of bliss. A long decline would set in, leading to his suicide, but that year he enjoyed favourable astrological signs. On this occasion it was again Bob Sherriff who wrote his screenplay. He had finally broken with Clive, out of necessity, but he felt guilty and he'd reached a peak in his love for David, something that neither bothered to hide at parties. 'Your friend is handsome. Like a Spaniard,' they'd tell James. Conversely, his artistic realm gave form to a sensation he was familiar with as a result of his sexual inclination, the sensation of invisibility. And finally, in the bare, desert valleys of Los Angeles, he could locate the story of malign Jack Griffin, redolent of Britain in a ghostly, snow-covered English countryside, even if it was only cardboard, a disturbing scenario for that victim of his own ambition and chemistry (the myth of the magic formula that regrettably has been lost – Oh woe!). I've seen *The Invisible Man* dozens of times, confessed Griffin. A strange vibration keeps drawing me back to it. Perhaps it is simply the coincidence over surnames and the inexplicable allure of the invisible. Perhaps my love for Li Pao, the Chinese transvestite and painter of dragons, unleashed elements kept on a tight rein within me that were connected with elements on a tight rein in the depths of the film. I close my eyes and can see Rains taking off the bandage to reveal his empty head. I shut my eyes and see the snow marked by footprints moving forward by themselves. I close my eyes and see the circle of bobbies linking their arms and holding nets up to prevent wretched Jack Griffin from escaping, so Whale can't escape, perhaps indeed so I can't escape. I close my eyes and see the barn burning and the police eagerly watching the great bonfire. Yes, that's right, Whale liked that story of an invisible man, because he felt he'd been invisible during his whole lifetime when it came to showing his true face, his true body, and that bonfire where everything finally burns is the same bonfire, though quite coincidentally, said Griffin, that Magellan ordered to be lit on the beach in Guinea in order to execute the sailor disguised as a woman whom Elcano had to turn to cinder. In short, it was the same atoning conflagration.

18

WHEN I LISTENED TO GRIFFIN'S TALE, I FELT LIKE someone who spurns a familiar path in a forest, loses his way and begins to walk along unexplored tracks (if there are any) risking getting lost even further, which he then does, though he doesn't feel alarmed, quite the contrary, he enjoys the feeling because it brings fresh places and experiences and he can meander unthinkingly across a leafy, overgrown heath, recognising nothing at all: that was Griffin advancing through life and his narrative. He went on, and on, and on . . . Just as James Whale in Ruffo's read everything that fell into his hands on the theme of invisibility, so Griffin mused on the deck of the *Minerva Janela* about Pigafetta, the sailor he identified with on occasion – who was also really far from being a sailor, since they'd both been smuggled into the crew – who was born five hundred years before in Vicenza del Veneto. Griffin was thinking about Pigafetta as he, like Magellan's ships centuries ago, now furrowed waters sailed by Captain Branco's modern container-ship that emitted a constant rhythm from its poop, a peaceful sound Oliver found soothing. Same bisexual condition, same status as a cosseted passenger, and same role as an invisible, fantasising peeping Tom, he said, referring to the Italian. He told me of his bookish search for Pigafetta's personality, now he'd acknowledged a hypothetical homosexual trait within himself, now he *knew* that Pigafetta was homosexual, which led him to imagine himself as a man of arms and letters from the Quattrocento, endowed with that androgynous beauty one finds in the canvases of Masaccio or Botticelli. Griffin imagined him disembarking in an equally imaginary Barcelona in 1519, a young, ambitious, frenetic and energetic member of the retinue of the Nuncio of Adriano VI, Monsignor Francesco Chieregati, amateur musician and a cardinal.

And at that moment, said Griffin, I remembered it was in Barcelona in the rainy spring of 1957 that I saw *The Invisible Man* for the first time. Suddenly, when I was staring at a void in the ocean, after Second Officer Fernando Grande had told me in the map room that Rio de Janeiro was about to appear in view, on the deck of the *Minerva Janela* I remembered that day as if it were yesterday. I was nine years old. Nine years old! Griffin exclaimed in a state of shock. So strange, more fatal coincidences: nine like Pablo Bagnoli, Graciela Pavic's eldest son, when he disappeared in their boat in Catherine Bay.

My father had moved there for a while, because of some contract or other. A tall, fair-haired, garrulous Irishman, he worked as an engineer on the most diverse and mysterious projects. I only know, or recall once finding out, that it involved building works in the port. I remember little from those years in Barcelona, and it all relates to the port and foreign tourists with sunglasses and waspish waists and frequent rides in motorboats with my parents. I can see my father now, smiling broadly as he holds me tight and points at specific places, boats of every size and colour, and, no doubt, important details I have forgotten.

We lived in an attic on calle Balmes where the huge sandy-coloured terrace was home to three palm trees and small blue tiles. We left home on an April morning in 1957 and walked down into the city, towards the port, heading first along the Ramblas, where we ate pastries near the Virreina, and then along nearby side streets that were dirty and down-at-heel. There were pieces of broken bottle in the entrance to an ice factory and I had the bad luck to step on one when I was putting weight on my instep, and the end of a fragment of broken glass sliced through my trousers. Half a bottle of anis, Marie Brizard or a similar brand, gouged my left leg, at the level of my calf. I bled profusely and my mother must have thought I'd cut a tendon or vein. She was horrified and looked aghast at the flow of blood.

They rushed me to the first local clinic that occurred to the taxi driver my parents asked for help, but it was a sordid Help Centre with hardly any staff. I was scared but sensed my parents were even more so. They hastily closed the gash with three black staples but didn't use stitches so it went on suppurating late into the evening. As a reward for my good behaviour on that dreadful day, my father took me to the Kursaal Cinema on the Rambla de Cataluña. The film they were showing was none other than *The Invisible Man*. How could I forget that! My first memory: it was short, barely lasted more than an hour. My second memory: I was impressed to hear my surname mentioned, but any feeling of identification immediately fused with a powerful sense of alienation. A diabolical cocktail of me and not-me. I heard the name as if it wasn't connected to me. Griffin . . . Griffin . . . And finally, a third memory: compassion or rather an inevitable tragic empathy with that man whose footsteps in the snow were abruptly halted by a bullet that suddenly hung in the air, before lodging in the exact spot where his lungs were supposedly located. I've previously mentioned this overwhelming feeling of alienation from myself that has dominated my entire life, Griffin said, and you can be sure it was triggered by that film.

Do psychiatrists have a definition for this state? Perhaps it's what they call depersonalisation or paramnesia, I have never bothered to find out, Griffin continued, that state in which a sense of being separate from one's own identity is accompanied by an acute self-scrutiny, as if I could observe myself from the outside. That alienation from myself and my own name reached absurd levels: for example, in my memories, Homer's *Odyssey*, Ulysses' portentous voyage that in one way or another I tried to imitate in my voyage to the Straits on the *Minerva Janela* – I even joined the Society of Friends of Joyce simply because of the title of his novel. In that same school where one magical morning I discovered items from the Scientific Commission to the Pacific, we had to read the *Odyssey* and *Iliad* (or was it Virgil's *Aeneid*?) that formed part of the academic curriculum for children and were forced to complete a detailed piece of writing, with sections on what happened, the characters, plot, passions unleashed and human archetypes, plus as many observations as possible inspired by the epic poem. They called it a 'commentary'. But nobody wrote one. Nobody could be bothered. Everybody simply copied; everyone copied a commentary that already existed, which was no doubt a model of its kind or at least useful and valid for the teacher (who was our teacher at the time? Griffin asked rhetorically), that was handed on like a little treasure to which small variants were added from class to class, and from pupil to pupil. But suddenly, when I tried to recall the name of the boy who was the first author of that 'commentary' and tried to bring into the light of day our pseudo-Homer, author of the little pseudo-*Odyssey*, handwritten, stapled folios (with an onion-paper top page, like an imitation book), I remembered something that incredibly I'd forgotten: I'd written that spiel! I was the author of that first version, that first précis everyone subsequently reproduced as if it were their own work. But when had I read it, when had I written it? I couldn't remember. Nonetheless, I did write it, said the self-engrossed Griffin, I had no doubts at all as the memory flooded back: I could see the size of my scrupulously legible writing, could see my mother tapping the top of the pages so they were level, could see the sections I'd underlined in red and blue.

When I saw the light and had full view of that huge creation from my past, the thirty or forty folios my mother stapled between cardboard covers and stuck on a label she'd designed herself, I was back in Barcelona, but it was no longer spring 1957, it was years after the incident with the broken glass and the day I saw Whale's film. It was during a strange period in my life, when I lived as an adult in that city for a number of years, also on my own with no very specific work, like my father earlier. To be frank, I had no work and simply wandered around the city and spent my savings.

Griffin admitted he'd worked for a few months as a night watchman ('My first job as night watchman in museums, which was rather like being in a cemetery') in the Madrid City Provincial Museum. He'd provisionally given up teaching History at the university out of pure tedium and added that he remembered all that when he found himself on a bench in the Rambla in front of the Kursaal and discovered it now showed only porno films, though from the outside it looked exactly the same as on the morning of his ninth birthday.

It was a time, said Griffin, when paralysis entered my life and froze it. I lived in Barcelona, in an apartment where I felt more alienated than ever. I'd abandoned everything and lived almost like a tramp. There were periods when I didn't shave or change my clothes. I didn't talk to anyone, I read books and went to the cinema. Some nights I'd go to a clipjoint with Chinese girls near my place, the Club Pekín. During the day I tried to find traces of my childhood in the city, from the year I spent there, hardly a year in fact, but only made my way to the port with its bars and boats, and the Via Layetana, where my parents had a friend, John, a very thin American from San Francisco like my father, though he was Polish in origin and generally referred to as Palik. He was a journalist on the *Los Angeles Herald*, the newspaper where my father made me read the article on Whale's suicide around that same time. 'To think we saw a film of his only the other day!' my father said.

We spent Sundays in Palik's house. I don't know why but it was always full of actors and actresses who'd start singing when it was time to go and play very melancholy music. On the other hand, as an adult, as I was saying – Griffin went on – I spent my idle hours feeling alienated from my flat, but from the inside, like one of those parasites that live in other animals' shells, lying on a red sofa, in a perennial shocked state of *jamais vu*. I could be like that for years. I lived in a strange mood of nirvana. It took me six months to realise that, but I knew I could stay in that void where I let everything go for another two years, if not six. Or why not nine? Time was irrelevant: it didn't feel as if I was living there.

The furniture was old and uncomfortable and there was hardly any food in the house. I rarely remembered to change the sheets, the television was very old, small and orangey-coloured, with a broken remote control held together by Sellotape. There was a tiny selection of books that were of no interest to me – that's right, *books* that didn't interest me, an anti-library, one I could happily have dispensed with but was too lazy to throw out, and I rarely swept the floor or dusted the furniture, and I never raised the shutters in all those years or put anything in the many wardrobes and drawers with little doors scattered throughout the house, built to order on the instructions of the previous tenant, a German who had suddenly cleared off without leaving a trace, after he'd lived there for twenty years on the trot. I was invisible, and my house was invisible to me, because I couldn't have cared less. Then one night I met Li Pao in the Club Pekín.

19

SHE PUSHED SOMETHING TOWARDS ME AND STOOD up, said Griffin. She'd just sung several Nat King Cole numbers, as she had on my other recent visits to the club. I'd noticed her, behind the bar, pouring out drinks not looking her customers in the eye, tedious, night-time clients who inspired neither respect nor hatred and were searching for their souls, or simply sex. She was much younger than me and that gave me a few advantages. I think I fell in love with her blend of indecisive, ambiguous youthfulness – like a landscape photo that invites you to imagine you're there, whatever it's like in reality, Griffin went on – when you sense a hidden energy that might explode any minute, and I felt I wouldn't mind being engulfed, swept away, annihilated. This came with desire, a tremendous desire to possess her. Or him, given she was obviously a transvestite, a dual sexuality that added to the sudden attraction. What had she pushed my way over the bar, between drinks? A miniature papier-mâché dragon painted gold, green and red. 'The Shao Ming dragon allows you to live to a hundred.' I'd rather not, I said. 'That's a lie. You do want to live for a hundred years. On the other hand, I certainly don't,' she retorted.

I looked around before picking it up, like a weary know-all

teacher or inveterate sceptic, as if afraid of something or needing to think it through. I saw there were very few customers, like other nights, when I'd nothing on in Barcelona and opted to go to the Club Pekín in a loner's peculiar attempt to fight insomnia with one drink after another and inane conversation. But the truth was I always went back to the Pekín hoping I'd meet Li Pao again. The first time I went down those steps and immersed myself in that ambience of see-through curtains, air fresheners spreading a saccharine smell of sandalwood and jasmine, and red lights heightening the sense of darkness (though one could see perfectly well in the chiaroscuro generated by the spotlights over the bar), there was only one customer apart from myself, when they suddenly announced Mae Jing on the small stage at the front. I then realised it was Li Pao's artistic, night-time name and later discovered his real name was Fuong. She was a lot like the young boyish Chinese youth I often passed in the street, whose strange beauty I found disturbingly attractive. We'd both exchanged glances and the occasional smile when we looked back walking past each other, trying to find out where the other was headed. Simply playing games, so it seemed. And suddenly there she was, metamorphosed into a porcelain singer, dressed and made up Oriental-style, wearing a long dark-blue shiny silk sheath of a dress that revealed how very svelte she was, and possessing a voice that was an extraordinary mixture of late Jimmy Scott and early Madonna.

The mere sight of her enraptured me. I felt I was victim and protector, master and slave. She sang unfashionable songs in English – Frank Sinatra, Andy Williams, Johnny Hartman – and Chinese ballads with a shyness that gradually turned to warmth and vigour. That first time she sang only for me, never took her eyes off me, to ensure I saw she was the young man I walked past in the street. When she stopped singing, she disappeared through one side of the stage, and never re-emerged. I waited in vain and left in a daze because the whisky was going to my head. After that, I dropped in several evenings, simply wanting to see her, Mae Jing, the real name, I later discovered, of a legendary Sixties transvestite actor from Formosa, to whom Li Pao wanted to pay his own private tribute, and every night, whenever she did so, she'd stare at me, thus indicating to employees and customers alike that she was singing for me, that there was a special feeling between us. Nevertheless, we didn't speak, because when she finished her act as Mae Jing, she'd always reappear in the small area of the club as Li Pao on the arms of other men, dressed like the other girls at the Pekín, even transmuted back into Fuong, that youthful, androgynous beauty, at once the man and woman I imagined young Pigafetta must have been, except her nails were brightly varnished and lips a deep red. When he finished singing, Li Pao meandered through the club as if she hadn't seen me, as if I'd become invisible for her again. Looking serious, if not surly, she'd routinely work on the other side of the bar helping the other girls in the clipjoint, as if she were seeking to attract me by showing contempt or indifference. Until the day she pushed the small dragon towards me. That day changed everything.

In a voice pleading to be had immediately, she told me she painted dragons, that it was her work in a nearby workshop belonging to the Club Pekín's owner, and that they were on sale in emporia throughout the world. As she spoke, she moved closer and closer. She stared hard at my legs and heaving chest and started to caress my face, arms, hands, though she never looked up once. I didn't move or do anything to stop her. She slowly brought her face close to mine and told me her name.

Not her real name, but the one she'd given herself. 'My name is Li Pao,' she said. She was very fragile and beautiful. Her skin and make-up were pale, not mother-of-pearl, but a very cultivated feminine softness. I felt unerringly drawn towards her. Or him, because I always knew he was the youth in the street, and he knew I knew when he said why don't we go the same way tonight, rather than walking past each other? And he pointed to the exit. I nodded, putting my mouth to his lips. Li Pao kissed me and I desired her more than ever.

Griffin told me he waited outside for nigh on twenty minutes. Li Pao appeared in a change of clothes, jeans, with her hair gathered under a cap on the slant. She was the boy in the street again. Li Pao insisted I go to her house. She quietly gripped my arm, Griffin continued, making me shiver all over. I suddenly became completely passive. A taxi drove by, which we hailed. She was full of a boyish, fitful repartee in the car, even her tone of voice went from sad and light to mature and serious. Then, quite stupidly, I started to wonder how much she'd weigh in my arms. Forty to fifty kilos, at most, I calculated. 'Tell me,' she, or he, said, alluding to my awkward, neutral attitude, as if I hadn't yielded entirely. 'Tell me what you want now, what you wanted yesterday, what you wanted a year ago, what you might desire tomorrow.' She put her head on my side and her hand in my lap. On the way to her place in the Borne, I rapidly recounted my life as an inventor of islands and cultivator of history in the occasional university while fielding the driver's furtive glances in the rear-view mirror. I sensed that journey didn't allow for further revelations, said Griffin. Li Pao also gave me a short version of hers. She was twenty-four, had briefly studied art, wanted to return to Taiwan, the country of her grandparents, where she was heading via Germany and France. She'd been in Barcelona for a year, a city that reconciled the irreconcilable within him, and had been singing for a month in the Club Pekín, a transvestite act, Mae Jing-style, his heroine. He'd come from Hamburg, where his parents lived and where he was born; he'd been raped several times and been committed to a reformatory for theft; he worked as a painter of dragons in an illegal sweatshop to pay for an illegal passport. She earned much more in the Club Pekín and had no regular customers; he only bedded those he wanted to. He didn't usually charge, did it for pleasure and in an act of freedom, but I didn't believe her, said Griffin, convinced she was lying to calm my nerves.

She took out a cigarette and lit it. It was foreign; I thought I saw a Dunhill label. I looked at her smile as if I were reading a familiar text. I recognised that fake smile and honeyed expression, ready to gulp down the next moment of life; it was a cinematic gesture, a smile I'd seen before, but I continued to find it attractive however much I felt it had been rehearsed. 'It's miserable being ashamed of who we are, isn't it?' asked Li Pao, looking through the car window. 'You aren't ashamed, are you?' she asked me to my face without giving me time to reply. 'I'm not ashamed but I still don't know what I am,' I answered. 'Lots of customers at the Pekín are homosexual. They're the sort who come to a place like that, to be with people like me. It's quite normal,' said Li Pao. 'I know it's normal,' replied Griffin. All of a sudden, we were walking into his house, that was as removed from reality as mine, the difference being that I didn't feel *his* was invisible. We went to bed.

That was the first night. I remember her glittering gilt bracelets on the night table, replicas of more ancient ones, etched with shapes of Chinese dragons, her obsession, and mottoes in Chinese as well. I remember my confused feelings of desire and love when Li Pao's face was close to mine and we were kissing and licking and that irresistible impulse (it was sex, of course, the smell of her sex that was stirring me and setting me on fire, and the delicate, pervasive perfume from her terse skin, and a voice telling me 'do it') that carried me into the heart of that initiation as if into the depths of a lake or sea, except that instead of drowning, said Griffin, I realised an unexpected source of air was liberating me, even though I plunged deeper with each kiss and movement, hers or mine; in Li Pao's bed bodies and that kind of intense silence spoke the same language of love. I knew it was an onslaught of love because my desire to see her the following night kept me on edge all day. And the next night, the second night, she repeated the passion of the first: whispering gently in my ear that she liked me, and I told him, or her, that I liked her. We had lots of encounters after that, drawn out, extending far into the morning, making love in vulgar or sublime manner, we didn't mind how: we were innocent and had no hang-ups. Her elastic body didn't conflict with a rather strange kind of violent serenity, the kind displayed by the youths who'd surrounded Pasolini (and who killed Pasolini, Griffin added). And her androgynous beauty, that, as I said, suggested the sensual and delicate image I'd formed of Antonio Pigafetta, but it was also brutal and mysterious, reminding me of the handsome Serb Adan Krupa, a taciturn young man, who always looked far gone and insincere, who helped Bergeron the cook, alias Tidbit, on the *Minerva Janela*, someone I never spoke to. His was a frightening story, said Griffin, before he started recounting it.

Young Krupa, who was probably not as young as he looked, had come aboard as second cook in Lisbon on a Slovenian passport and he too was heading to Punta Arenas as his final destination, 'for family reasons', he told Pereira when signing on. But on the voyage Captain Branco and Second Officer Grande discovered by chance that he was a Serb travelling under a false identity. It was around the time Kowanana lost his little finger, after Paulinho Costa died. For some reason or other, Branco and Grande were looking for Tidbit and without knocking, went into the cabin the two cooks shared. They found neither, but as Branco was leaving the cabin his arm hit against shelving and some books fell on the floor. Envelopes and photos dropped out of an old illustrated guide to Lisbon written in Serbo-Croat, which the captain almost trod on. He stooped down to pick them up and couldn't help taking a look and was surprised by what he saw: photos of armed soldiers smiling, joking and brandishing bottles, perhaps even enjoying a drunken party. The place looked like an ordinary flat, with the usual armchairs and sofa, the usual landscape views on the walls, wallpaper, standard lamps with shades; there was a balcony in the background though in fact it was a huge gaping hole, the doors were missing, blown out and sandbagged; you could see a city, in the hazy distance, houses and streets in a valley, and mountains beyond that. Branco looked closer: lumps of plaster littered the floor; it was a mess. He looked even closer and saw that the soldiers were poorly dressed, some wore T-shirts and caps, others army jackets over jeans and trainers. They were all carrying rifles with telescopic sights over their shoulders, pressed close to their chests like a loved one or in a bottle-free hand. Branco read the Cyrillic script on the back of the photos:

GRHAVIĈA ≠ VRAĈA, SARAJEVA, 1993

A young man in uniform was stood next to one of the soldiers who was boastfully waving his rifle above his shoulder. He wore his collar unbuttoned and a cold smile, a grimace almost congealed on his lips, and he wasn't staring straight at the camera, but to one side of the lens. Branco immediately identified Adan Krupa. That same night Fernando summoned young Adan to the dining room in front of the whole crew at supper and set him a little trap with the help of Pavel Pavka, the Macedonian. Krupa realised he'd been unmasked when Pavka asked him quite naturally about renowned streets in Ljubljana, including one where his brother lived. Krupa got them all mixed up and couldn't even recognise the country's coins or president's name. He fell into every trap Pavka set him.

When Grande finally asked him who the hell he was as he laid the photos he and Branco had found on the table, since it was obvious he wasn't Slovenian, the handsome young Krupa folded and admitted he was one of those four snipers posted in a house in the Vraca district of Sarajevo. Yes, he'd killed people, and yes, he'd been present at torture sessions, or thought he had, he wasn't sure. He hadn't raped anyone ever, he vehemently denied such a thing. But perhaps he had, because he drank a lot at the time and never remembered anything afterwards. In fact, he knew he'd killed people because his comrades had told him, but it was all a blur and he could distinguish nothing with any clarity. 'It was war. Who doesn't go crazy in a war? Nobody's hunting me on that count. I've no warrants or police after me,' he concluded frostily, clearly resisting the powerful temptation to beg for mercy. Suddenly we all moved away and left him isolated and alone in the dining room. From then on the whole crew avoided him, and Bergeron banished him from the galleys. Branco said he wasn't under arrest, 'because there was no warrant out', ironically echoing Adan's own words, but warned him he would be left on land as soon as they reached the next port. Krupa accepted the situation resignedly, but shook with rage. I observed all that in my distant role as a guest, and now I can only remember the handsome charms and icy beauty of that young assassin with the vacant stare, said Griffin.

In the months I was with Li Pao, he quickly resumed, I went back to the Club Pekín on many a night and didn't always leave with him or her, although I spent most nights in his place, far from that strange flat of mine that its previous tenant had strewn with empty drawers, where in a state of paralysis, permanently in a tunnel or simply lying on the sofa, I stared at the ceiling and imagined my remote Desolation Island where I never thought I'd go. Crossing to the other side, never to return. That was the key to my sexuality. I have never felt I was a real homosexual, and in fact my only relationship of that kind was with Li Pao for the short period of time we were together. When I fell in love with him, I'd already separated from Roberta, my first wife, but my love for Elsa, whom I married later, was still way off, and my passion for Fabienne was even further in the future. Although I now doubt the word 'love' can represent what attracted me to Li Pao and think I was more than likely aroused by the sordidness of taboo sex, the perverse shadows of the Club Pekín and that curiously hermaphrodite body housing man and woman in one. But I soon noticed my passion for Li Pao was yielding to an imperceptible but inevitable boredom. How does love come? How does love go?

My anticipated exit, Griffin said, happened one night when I held my breath in front of the entrance to the Club Pekín and kept my hand on the door handle, under wintry rain, the same day, though thirty years later, when my father left, when he abandoned my mother and me and disappeared to Los Angeles. I held my breath, said Griffin, and didn't go in. In fact, it was impossible to go in. Destiny took on the visible shape of a drunken individual (like Krupa in Sarajevo raping but forgetting he'd raped) who opened the door violently and walked out, knocking me backwards on to a dustbin. That took me further from the Club Pekín, and when I stood up, I took three or four steps backwards, then more and more and was now in the entrance to my house, went upstairs to my flat and again entered a parenthesis, during which I drew islands time and again, invented the shapes of islands, coves, capes, gulfs, volcanoes, beaches, crags and coasts. And a week went by when I opened the door to no one and left the phone off the hook. Then all at once, without realising it, a month slipped by and then another. And once again, two months later, I was back gripping the Club Pekín's doorknob, debating whether or not to go in, perhaps hoping another drunken customer would emerge and throw me into the gutter, and thus distance me once more from the lost object of my desire and love.

I uttered her name as soon as I was inside and talking to a waitress I knew who'd recognised me, another beautiful Chinese woman who always had a smile on her funereal lips. 'Li Pao has gone,' said that waitress with the mournful mouth. And I felt relieved, said Griffin, felt I wouldn't now have to explain anything, or tell her of my lack of love, or now perhaps, even better, I was spared having to hear the words 'lack of love' on her lips and the decision she'd finally taken. I remembered her athletic vigour and the things she'd come out with, all of a sudden, 'You are so beautiful', 'How was that?', 'Did it feel good?', 'Are you enjoying yourself?', 'Do you want to smoke?' Or her obsession: 'Do I give you what you want?', 'Is this what you like?' 'Yes,' Griffin replied, 'that's right and you're what I love.' Then she was no longer there, or it was the beautiful Chinese woman with the lethal lips saying that.

Voids to fill and voids to confront. The bitterness or sadness when love dies. Learning to live with it is the only way. When she disappeared, I forgot most of my past with her almost immediately. Gradually I recovered or returned to moments at her side, details as when suddenly someone remembers the face of another person encountered on a train journey, one never to be seen again, yet it's a face that appears unexpectedly in memories, that comes in without knocking and goes deep inside, and you wonder whether that person you know nothing about, except that they exist, is alive or dead. 'Sometimes,' Griffin said Li Pao would say, 'sometimes I want to die. That's all. To disappear.' She often said that. Perhaps she fulfilled her dream. Perhaps she, or he, is now dead.

Griffin's love for Li Pao didn't last very long. Five or six months. She didn't love him as much as he loved her, he confessed. Then she went back to Taiwan, after revisiting other European countries. Another theft, Griffin told me: she stole from the illegal sweatshop owner, who also owned the Club Pekín, stole the passport it had been such an effort to pay for with those countless coloured dragons. Griffin said she could have stolen it from the club's owner at any time and that if she didn't do it before it was because she liked pretending she was the mythical – in her lights – Mae Jing, singing for an invisible man like myself.

20

THE SWIMMING POOL WAS THE PROBLEM, BECAUSE Whale never liked swimming pools, Griffin told me on another occasion. He had one built at the age of sixty-four simply for the pleasure of seeing young naked bodies dive in. And it was *the* problem because it was a luxury that would lead to his demise. The day the builders finished, Lewis stood and looked at it when it was still empty and predicted it would do James no good whatsoever, or he at least felt it boded ill. It was the day he finally left him for ever. Faced by the enormous depths of that empty vessel, they both commented it shouldn't stay like that, lest some drunken guest fall in at night. But Whales's vanity had begun to balloon ages before, when he turned fifty, and was intolerable in the extreme. He didn't like growing old: like all hedonist lovers of beauty, he watched his body change and thought it the highest, most scandalous toll life had ever exacted. He hated mirrors and blushed in front of them now he was forced to embrace worldly hypocrisies and still love that body of his. He sometimes laughed at himself, but generally David Lewis found him grimly lethargic and depressed while he acted as if he were living a grotesque repeat of his adolescence. He argued with his cook, his gardener and his chauffeur, then became capricious or spiteful, kicked over furniture to show he was angry, smashed objects which had only recently moved him to tears, tore his favourite photos to shreds and even banned any discussion of his films at home unless he initiated it, particularly at parties. However, everything suddenly accelerated in one of those parties he started giving after his fiftieth birthday when David, his steady partner from June 1929, heard him relate an incident in his own life as if it had happened to him. It was a reasonably entertaining story, Griffin related in turn, the protagonists being French archaeologists and Wallace Beery and Maureen O'Sullivan, who were lost in the depths of the El Paso desert. Apparently Berry wanted to play a practical joke on them and pretended to be the President of the United States travelling incognito on an amorous fling with his lover. The French people didn't really swallow the ruse although Berry's face seemed really familiar (but from what and where?), and Maureen perfectly assumed the role she'd been assigned, covered her face, avoided being photographed and simply kept repeating: 'My God, sweetie, they've recognised us! They've recognised us!' Wallace rang David and told him to come and confirm his fake identity and spin the joke out. The only drawback was that David was in Hollywood, over four hundred kilometres away. When he arrived, almost twenty-four hours later, Wallace and Maureen had left, though the group of French archaeologists was still there. David Lewis approached one of them and lowered his voice to a confidential pitch, but they could all hear him: 'You haven't by any chance seen the President of the United States around here? It's vitally important we find him. He's disappeared.' At that moment he took a publicity photo of Berry out of his pocket and the French looked at each other totally nonplussed before confessing he had been with them the previous day.

But, hell, that was an adventure he, David Lewis, had experienced. Whale was stealing it from him and telling his guests so *he* was the centre of attention! And that wasn't the end of it, Griffin said, these borrowings became a habit for James whose life, in any case, was totally colourless or enclosed in a tedious, self-absorbed artistic bubble, and so he began to inject into his biography actions and incidents lived by his lover and companion David. Consequently, Lewis had to listen repeatedly to Whale rehearsing his own favourite anecdotes: the episode with the police as a result of a broken headlight, or a fascination for idyllic sunsets, red, ecstasy-provoking Californian suns, or the cringe-making performance by a particular actress caught in a politician's embrace, or David's strictly personal experience on the liner *Athenas* en route to London, in 1939, when he had an extrasensory impulse when hypnotised by a Spanish magician (the Great Samini?) who effortlessly lifted him up with two fingers, a man weighing in at over 120 kilos. That looting of his experience by the old Faun who thus began to feed parasitically on his young lover's life, was the fruit, Lewis immediately grasped, of Whale's need to give himself a life and avoid feeling empty and at a loss, but that didn't make it any less irritating for David who couldn't think of a way of putting a stop to the habit. Then one day he had a bright idea. In 1940, the failure of *Green Hell*, which would be the last film Whale would sign off, was threatening to plunge the prickly director even deeper into despair. David turned up at the house he shared with Whale at 788 South Amalfi Drive with a weighty package, a big surprise for the old man. He'd just been to Michael's Art Supply, the best art shop in Los Angeles, and bought everything a painter could need: dozens of canvasses, brushes big and small, tubes of oil-based paint, boxes of watercolours, wax sticks, coloured pencils, sharpened charcoal, thinners, sketchbooks, hundreds of sheets of paper, an easel, two palettes and two packets of cotton wool. He handed it all to James as a present to help him develop a new start in his life.

And he did just that, with rejuvenated enthusiasm, recovering the vitality that had enabled him to survive the Great War, thanks to David's gift to his artistic self. He turned half a greenhouse into a luminous studio and started to fill his life with paintings and reproductions of paintings, landscapes and portraits, at any time of day and on all his journeys along the coast, to Santa Barbara or Santa Monica, as far as San Francisco. In 1941, he slammed the door on the cinema, fed up with the whole scene, and never returned to see if there was any fallout. Day after day he transformed his depression into a hedonist lifestyle, surrounded by young men, pleasures and free spending, that he confronted, as is natural, without a care in the world and with the best intentions of a platonic peeping Tom. But something still tortured him: the definitive loss of his youth and beauty and lack of access to young bodies, whether Li Paos or Pigafettas, a forbidden fruit that required a physical effort that was now beyond him. He felt annihilated. He wasn't worried about not being rich, but he was no longer young or handsome and couldn't stand his ageing, greying features.

He spent ten years in that foggy decline of troughs and titillations. He finally distanced himself from David in the spring of 1951. The break was tumultuous and accompanied predictably by a violent, hysterical row that erupted when David refused to go and live with James in Paris, far from Hollywood, in a different life with a new identity, wholly devoted to painting. David refused and wouldn't even contemplate going to Europe for a holiday and that led to a sour parting of the ways. James went by himself. Upon his arrival in Paris, the real goal of the trip, he rented a flat on the rue Sufflot, opposite the Panthéon, immediately met a cultured young idler in a Poussin Exhibition at the Grand Palais and soon became his permanent shadow. He was Pierre Foegel and twenty-four, the age Li Pao confessed to being in that first taxi that drove us to his house and a new love, said Griffin.

James and Pierre toured Italy and its museums. They visited every single one at their leisure, because they fancied the lot – Florence, Milan, Rome, Venice, Bologna – and Whale fell in love as much with the great Italian painters as with young Foegel. He spent his days copying the originals in the galleries where their works were exhibited. When he returned to Los Angeles a year later, he had to extend his studio within the greenhouse. In fact, the greenhouse disappeared to give way to a replica of a heterogeneous museum contrived by an amateur and countless paintings adorned the mansion's corridors and sitting rooms. There were more or less successful copies, or at least ones you could savour, of Masaccio, Andrea del Sarto, Raphael, exercises in chiaoroscuro by Masolino di Panicale or Ghiberti, perspectives by Uccello, drawings that strove to capture Leonardo's melancholy. In Bologna he wanted to buy a Primaticcio, but was told it was a fake, in Venice he mixed Madonnas by Padovanino with landscapes by Veronese and in Florence bought up all the Ghirlandaio reproductions he could find.

Painting, travel, the sun and Pierre's love made him forget the cinema and his films completely. He would only speak very occasionally of *The Invisible Man* when prompted by a house or face he'd seen in Lombardy or Tuscany. Back in California, in 1953, James forced David to leave the house for good, but Lewis delayed his departure because Pierre, who was coming to fill his place, stayed on in Paris putting the finishing touches to his move and saying goodbye to his mother, the widow of a gendarme vegetating in a hospital in Nantes (the city of Fabienne, the city of Vaché!). Whale's life now centred on the silent, deferential Pierre. It was then he commissioned a swimming pool, although he hated them. To fill the void in his house – especially when Pierre returned to France for long periods – he resurrected his parties for young ephebes. From December 1956, at the age of sixty-seven, everything changed, and dark omens of approaching demise were flagged: he started to have health problems, his brain was failing him, he was afraid he might be hospitalised, might lose control of his body and life, and could already see himself as old and paralytic in a geriatric residence: James couldn't tolerate such total dereliction.

Griffin remembered what Li Pao would say, and often wondered whether he perhaps had done just that: 'Sometimes I want to die. Disappear.' Another drastic variant on the theme of invisibility, he commented sardonically. Subsequently in 1957, on 29 May (how could I ever forget, said Griffin, the moment my father told me to read the news in the *Los Angeles Herald!*), he got up, washed, had breakfast and went down to his desk: 'to the people I love . . . ' (on the envelope of the note he left behind) '. . . I have had a wonderful life but it's all over now.' And he added, 'The future offers only decrepitude and pain.' People often ask: who knows what goes on in the head of a suicide? Perhaps tedium at copying one painting after another, or the memory of a love went through Whale's. Which one? Clive, in the end? David? Pierre? He was alone in his mansion, went to the swimming pool and threw himself in head first into the shallowest water. The impact on hitting the green-tiled imitation seaweed mosaic at the bottom left him unconscious. He drowned. The housekeeper who came in the afternoon found him afloat hours later. His ashes are in the Forest Lawn Cemetery in the Glendale district my father visited the following year.

My father, Sean, said Griffin, left home for a Mexican woman he'd fallen blindly in love with a year after I sustained that horrific gash in my leg. A love like old James's and young Pierre's. Who can tell, all love starts the same way. Her name was Analía Soler and she was an actress who went by the name of Perla Chávez; I think she died unknown and penniless. You can't really say that Sean scarpered. He simply left us, Griffin explained, that's true, but it was really a deal my mother and father agreed, because there was no divorce at the time and my mother, who scented Sean's love for Analía straightaway, wasn't going to go along with the public humiliation such deception implied.

When my father went, Matilde, my mother whose beautiful voice made her the stuff of legends, started to work as a radio presenter thanks to my grandfather Arnaldo Aguiar. For many people it sufficed that she was the daughter of the Great Samini the conjurer for all doors to open wide. She became famous because she was *the* voice on radio advertisements in the Sixties. She never remarried and we never went short, even Sean, soon reappeared in the shape of a monthly cheque towards my studies and clothes, and later, when I finished at university, he came to Madrid to see me. I sometimes imagine my father arriving in Los Angeles on that Sunday in May in 1958 when he got off the plane on the other side of the world. He enters Perla Chávez's house dragging a huge suitcase behind him, almost a trunk that contains his whole life and a couple of photo albums of me, and sits on a sofa by a picture window opposite the house they called 'Boris Karloff's' where the actor perhaps lived whom the district knew as Mr Death because of his face, and that James Whale must sometimes have visited, when passing through Glendale (his last resting place), in order to see his old friend.

My father lingers and looks out of the window, unsure what that house represents, before thinking more practically and ringing a handful of people, childhood or family acquaintances, all Irish: Irishmen and -women who are now also Californians and oblivious to the strange family life that Sean, the youngest of Graham Griffin's children, left behind in recondite Spain, fine citizens and drinkers in San Francisco, not too far away. And Sean thinks of looking for work again and rings them up. His cousin Clark, for example, who is almost a brother to him, the one he hobnobbed with as a young man and who finds him work as an engineer in the Pacific & Co. Shipping Company a few weeks after he arrived. I imagine my father on that sofa in Perla's house, still in his overcoat, as I also imagine Arturo Bagnoli after he left the *Emma Salvatores*, his face flushed by all he can see that's so new and exciting, yet deadened by melancholy, aware he was living on that frontier that's both the end and beginning of something else. A sharp sense of being an outsider as well as a hero, and why not? Another variation on the theme of invisibility. Did my father also know he was invisible, that, shall we say, he bore the same Griffin stigma as I do? I'm sure he never conceived such an absurd idea, even when we saw Whale's film together – I remember how my bandaged leg brushed against my father's trousers that day – and he didn't even notice the identical surnames.

When I was almost ten and Sean went off with Perla, whose films I never saw, continued Griffin, I felt panic-stricken and began to hoard the most miserly objects and souvenirs of him I could find around the house. There weren't many, to tell the truth, and almost all were impersonal. There were childhood and adolescent photos, and I then thought how I was invisible to half my family, to half my uncles, cousins, grandparents, people who were strangers, despite the blood links, on the other side of the ocean and about whom I knew nothing at all, as little in fact as they knew about me. However that image of someone 'making a new start', as if he were waking up after a drinking session or a nightmare, sitting on Perla Chávez's bed or sofa, his mind at a loss, said Griffin, is what reconciles me to my father and prevents me from hating him. I cannot and should not speak rancorously of my father: on the contrary, he arouses a degree of unusual warmth. Starting from scratch again, recommencing from whatever point we've reached in a previous life, whatever comes up, love, a job, a family, a dream, beginning a different life as someone else – in fact or in the end – is part of the malleable human fragility we all carry within us, said Griffin. When he was an old man and retired from the Pacific & Co. Shipping Company, I visited him in his caravan in Pasadena, where he lived with his current wife, another Spanish woman. Sean gripped my hand and said: 'I'm sorry. I think I've always been starting things I've then left unfinished.' Perhaps he thought he'd been on the mad side and wasn't a good role model for a son like me, but by that time in our lives, it wasn't about setting an example; since my life was also cast and in a way I knew that the old man I was scrutinising from head to toe in Pasadena, his every wrinkle, strip of skin, hair, blemish, was to come to me eventually, because all in all I'd done what he'd done, time and again I'd started projects and adventures I'd left unfinished.

21

WE REACHED THE PORT OF NITERÓI IN RIO DE Janeiro on 29 October, at a gusty 7 a.m., said Griffin when I next met him on the streets of Funchal. The *Minerva Janela*'s entry into port was delayed several hours because a Russian boat was blocking Dock 34, the dock the harbour pilot had assigned to ours. He was an affable man who, once aboard, greeted us almost gleefully and shook our hands as if he were repaying an unknown favour. The whole docking manoeuvre was in the hands of Fernando Grande and Rodo Amaro, the boatswain. After issuing all due instructions, Captain Branco had retreated into his cabin and, like a distant, impossible child of Ahab, only emerged to give out the duty roster and suggest a hotel in the city, the Belvedere, although as always we could stay wherever we wanted, 'provided we didn't import any larva'.

As it had been raining non-stop for several days, the port of Rio was awash with huge puddles and yellow mud, said Griffin. The power shovels emitted black smoke through their long, vertical exhausts and were protected by rainproof material; their drivers, like all the port workers, wore home-made plastic ponchos over their naked torsos. Those of us with no specific tasks on the boat that day watched the docking manoeuvre from the gunwale. We could hear Amaro and the odd sailor shouting,

'Pull! Stern ropes three and four!', 'Open to poop and ease forward!', 'Stop flush!' It was a fascinating language I didn't understand, at once brusque and concise.

After the manoeuvre was completed, I saw Greene and Kowanana, the first to leave, come down the gangway, kitbags over their shoulders, and I thought how the crew leaving ship in port is a kind of short-lived excision or amputation, like a surgical removal of a body part, an arm or a leg. Boats are strange variants of a live being. Pigafetta had related that when he was in the Land of Verizon, said Griffin, the natives said rowing boats were daughters of the caravels and that when they drew alongside, they did so to drink from their udders. They were suckling! A lovely idea, isn't it? They thought boats were living beings. And they *are*, reaffirmed Griffin, I think that too, and when I look at any port, like Funchal's now, it sparks an uncanny emotion: I see new forms of life on the quaysides, however absurd it may seem. That's why the departure of each sailor, if only for a few days, is like a traumatic amputation from a live organism. That was what the future held in store for young Adan Krupa: a genuine extirpation that would sever him for ever from the *Minerva Janela* and our hearts. Skulking in his cabin, the swarthy Serb waited for his moment to abandon ship. We all knew he deserved it and did nothing to help him. How self-righteous we were!

When it was my turn, I felt quite peculiar stepping on dry land after so many days on board endlessly pitching from side to side. It's as if you're walking on a slope, said Griffin, your legs wobble until you become used to being on dry land. I tottered off the *Minerva Janela* with a typical sailor's drunken gait. Branco had given us three days' leave. I accompanied Luiz Pereira and Rodo Amaro to the Belvedere in a taxi. It was towards Ipanema on a steep side street, Rua del Jardín de Alá, at the end of Avenida de Copacabana. We drove through Avenida de Sá Vargas Freitas o Ataúlfo de Paiva where naked beggars ruled the roost and jostled with ordinary citizens and wary tourists. A single topic obsessed the newspapers and our conversation with a black taxi driver, an oldish, fair-haired guy, wearing a shoulder-strap T-shirt and toffee-coloured sunglasses, who bluntly introduced himself as Paipinho: 'mad cows' and the Creutzfeld-Jakob syndrome. The subject was headline news and Amuntado, who was also in our taxi, decided to get out before us in a street near the Belvedere, because he was going to his sister's house and was very worried by the sickness attacking English cows and by the millions of animals being sacrificed: he felt it was the beginning of the end. 'Food is rebelling against us,' said Amuntado. 'Let's be honest: it's a reasonable revenge for the building of so many slaughterhouses for cows, sheep, kangaroos or men, it makes no odds.' Paipinho endorsed his views, adding that was why he and his seven children had gone vegetarian. 'Or better still, poor,' he said with an ironic smile. 'You bet the poor don't die from eating mad cows, no siree, nor mad kangaroos. Or even healthy beef, to be on the safe side. I can assure you: my children won't die from any such thing. Of course they won't. At least that's what people are saying round here at the moment.' I ignored him from that point on and looked out at Rio's commercial district we were driving though. It took an hour to reach our hotel.

The Belvedere was an old hotel from the Forties, clean enough and with not many rooms. Sailors from Europe and journalists stayed there. The building was on three floors with balconies that looked on to the street. It was almost all painted white and bright green and that gave it an even more tropical air. It seemed full of light, and smelled of disinfectant and turpentine. Every room was air-conditioned, its high point of luxury. After trying out the bed and glancing at the minibar and bath, I suddenly felt anxious: what was Branco going to do with Krupa? Paipinho was still in the Belvedere and I asked him to drive back to Dock 34, where the *Minerva Janela* was moored. I wanted to find out whether Branco would hand him over to the police or simply sack him, as he'd promised, said Griffin. When he saw me, the captain objected to my unexpected return; he saw no need for me to accompany him, Grande and the Serb to the company offices, since the captain intended leaving him in the hands of Texaco. 'These are internal matters,' said Branco. But I told him I felt I'd signed up to the boat and all that implied and had been deeply affected by the case of that youth. I didn't want to hate him for the rest of my life. 'But in my view he is hateful,' said Grande. Branco agreed. 'Will he cause trouble?' Griffin asked. Grande said: 'I don't think he's up to that.' The captain finally agreed I could be present, though he added: 'I don't know what you're hoping to see.'

It was then I caught sight of Krupa with his luggage and belongings on the second covered deck: he was waiting for the captain and looked sheepish and silent. I tried to engage with his eternally vacant, frightening beady-eyed stare, but realised his face was so swollen he could hardly open his eyes. Branco looked me in the eye, not his usual pleasant or severe self, but questioningly. He seemed to be saying: 'I don't know whether or not you understand, but I couldn't care less what you think anyway. Life's like this.' Fernando Grande stepped forward and seized Krupa's arm and began to lead him down the gangway. He was afraid he might fall down after the beating he'd been given, because the Serb looked drugged up. When he walked past me Grande said: 'It's only right, on behalf of all those who are no longer with us because of this wretched bastard. My hand hurts, but he'll get over it. We forced him to swallow a tube of pills so he wouldn't complain too much during the formalities. You coming?' I followed them off the ship.

Texaco & Co.'s offices were in the administrative area by the port entrance, quite a way from Dock 34. We drove there in one of the tankers. Branco simply sacked him from his crew in the offices because 'of fraudulent identity papers'; that was considered a serious charge. 'Is that all?' asked an individual who introduced himself as the head of the office without looking up from the report. 'That's all,' replied Branco. Then he added: 'You will see from my report I suggest paying him half of his wage this far, and that the other half be retained as a fine. And remove him from the company's payroll, in case he crops up in another Texaco boat somewhere in the world.' 'Let's sort this guy then! He's scrubbed!' said the head of office, trying to be sociable after reading the report. Krupa sat at the back of the room, cowering and indifferent to his fate, after all, it was only another parenthesis opening and closing in his life. I didn't give him another glance, although as I was leaving, he looked up like a good boy and we nodded peremptorily at each other. Captain Branco had something else on his agenda. 'We had a fatality after leaving Cape Verde. It's in the other report. His name was Paulinho Costa,' Branco informed the head of office. 'I need another sailor, an electrician if possible, and that's more urgent than ever, now the Serb is no longer with us.' The head of office said he'd send someone in the morning for his approval. 'How long will you be in port?' 'Three days,' answered Branco. Branco and Grande left the office and walked back to the *Minerva Janela*. I looked for Paipinho, but he'd gone. I took another taxi back to the Belvedere.

The day after we docked, Griffin went on, Pereira and I went to the old district of Lapa to see a friend of his, also from Porto

Alegre, who owed him money, but we couldn't track him down. 'He's got away with it again, as he does every year,' grumbled Pereira, said Griffin. Lapa, particularly one narrow street that cuts across it, the Rua do Riachuelo, is full of prostitutes, and has been for years, and is a popular area with sailors and travellers of all nationalities. We met up with a rather tipsy Kowanana and Greene in a kind of lounge with mother-of-pearl furniture that doubled as a internet café and snake shop, because the walls were stacked floor to ceiling with glass-fronted boxes where one or two reptiles snoozed, each one with a label and dollar price. The sailors sat at a table with four women opposite a bottle of bourbon, and grimaced ironically at us before averting their gazes, a touch of boyish embarrassment on their faces. Or at least that was what I thought. Their expressions simply betrayed a lack of savoir-faire, something I'd felt after leaving my job at the Provincial Museum in Madrid and was infatuated with Li Pao. When I was with him or her, said Griffin, I inexplicably blushed when I saw someone else giving us the once over with a shocked look on their face. On such occasions, I couldn't avoid staring at the floor and letting a sense of moral unease surface, no doubt the dying embers of prejudice. That day in Rio de Janeiro's Lapa district I noticed that one of the four women, who were all dark and not particularly beautiful, the one who said she was Cazilda Canabrava from Minas Gerais and was caressing Charly Greene's head with her eyes shut, was very like Li Pao, or perhaps it was merely her oriental, androgynous features that seemed familiar.

My first thought was it would be too much of a coincidence if that encounter were of his or her doing. But I soon resigned myself to the fact that I'd not see Li Pao again; after a few years went by, I forgot her entirely. I scrutinised the prostitute simpering next to Charly and dismissed any connection with my old love. I'd no doubt that Cazilda was a woman, said Griffin, I mean a woman with an unambiguously female sexuality that set her apart for ever from the Li Paos of this world. Perhaps because I'd been stirred by the vision of that young woman, who'd all of a sudden bestrode our Welsh second engineer in that lounge-cum-reptile shop, or perhaps because she'd rekindled hot-blooded memories, I settled back in our taxi to the Belvedere and told Pereira about the sexual ambiguity of men and women in voyages of old.

We talked about sex on ships, about whores Pereira had known and loved, and the harsh conditions imposed by long voyages without docking, on which some women always travelled disguised as men, if not vice versa: men who, after weeks and months of enforced abstinence, dressed as women or acted like women, like poor Simón de Asio whom Magellan had had beheaded in Guinea. It made me think of Baré, the young man or woman and affectionate servant and lover of Philibert de Commerson, the renowned botanist and explorer, who accompanied Bougainville on his expedition, the one, Griffin reminded me, when little Pierrot died in port after swallowing those coloured glass baubles.

In 1764, after Commerson vehemently rejected the possibility of becoming Voltaire's secretary for the rather eccentric reason that the philosopher was fascinated by his agricultural knowledge but appreciated none of his other scientific qualities, he was unexpectedly widowed after a cruel birth and took into his service a young woman by the name of Jeanne Baret or Baré, the daughter of a Ferney pig-farmer. Two years later, he travelled on *L'Étoile* on Bougainville's expedition as the king's naturalist, and if we remember him today it is because he discovered the bougainvillea he named after his captain. But what I want to relate, Griffin went on, are the hatreds and rivalries and consequent revenge taking, because there was another doctor on the expedition, Vivès the surgeon, who was of a very different character to Commerson. While the latter was passionate, irascible and sometimes violent, as Bougainville noted in his diary, Vivès was a thoughtful introvert, with an inevitable tendency to harbour rancour. That rancour, fruit of the envy and jealousy experienced by men of science competing for fame and glory, led Vivès to betray the young servant Commerson took on all his botanic expeditions, a boy answering to the name of Jean Baré, who wasn't particularly handsome or ugly, very old or very young. He accused him of being a woman. Which was what she was, as she confessed, giving her real name as Jeanne, and her age as twenty-seven. She had embarked out of love, without the consent of her Philibert, her master. She even tricked him with her male clothes, and he didn't even recognise the woman with whom he'd shared two years of his life. Commerson admitted the young woman had been his lover before they set sail. Fear that the presence of Jeanne Baré might incite the crew to mutiny forced the expedition's leaders, in a council meeting on board *La Boudeuse*, to decide to abandon the couple on the island of Mauritius in the Mascarenhas, next to the island of Réunion.

This is the island Baudelaire visited years later on his way to Ceylon, though he soon scurried back to the quaysides of his Seine and their hashish smokers, bored with languid colonial life and loathing the sea and seasickness. Five years after they were found out, said Griffin, Commerson the botanist died in the arms of his beloved Jeanne, and she returned to Paris and had to wait for 1789 to die as a wealthy monarchist, sliced in two by the edge of the guillotine.

I have sometimes thought history can be written backwards and have fantasised that perhaps Pigafetta, like young Baré or

Baret, was a woman disguised as a man, and not an effeminate man, as I presume he and the hapless Simón de Asio were, or perhaps he was simply beautifully androgynous like young Li Pao, and perhaps, Griffin rhapsodised, Cristóbal Rabelo who'd died with Magellan and been inseparable from him, was his bastard son, a child he'd had years before with Pigafetta the woman, lurking under her male garments, and even loving in a manly way a feminine Magellan. But history says differently, said Griffin, the absurd may be possible but remains absurd.

At the end of our leave, we returned to the *Minerva Janela*, where changes had been introduced. Krupa's dishonourable dismissal was followed by the departure of a deeply depressed Pedro Ramos the engineer. His irascible temper had led him into fights in port that were governed by no rules of fair play and he ended up in hospital in Pirajá with a fractured skull. He had to recover from a bad fracture to the inside and outside of his head. I shall always remember good old Pedro Ramos's rucksack full of pirated CDs and his skilful breaking of birds' necks at a stroke. Branco thought it was timely to accept his resignation to prevent his mental state becoming infectious and leading us into fights and aggressive behaviour. ('I've seen crews at each other's throats as a result of the destructive, negative bile issuing from one man,' pontificated Branco during a meal far from Rio de Janeiro, said Griffin), or before Ramos threw himself overboard on one of those grim days we faced on the high seas before reaching the entrance to the Straits.

These two and the deceased Costa were replaced by one extra hand, since Tidbit, the cook, said he needed no help in the galley. Texaco sent a sailor Branco knew from other voyages: Nemo Caporale, from Sao Paolo, a strong, tall, smiley man with a bald pate that was always hidden under a woolly cap, a theosophist to boot, as he insisted on introducing himself. Theosophy put the human soul at the centre of the universe that was a reflection of the universal soul, around which God, the spirit, death and the extrasensory, all supernatural elements, revolve. When I asked him to elaborate his philosophical position, Caporale told me he believed in the occult, and was a disciple of the doctrines of Helena Petrovna Blavatsky, the great Hindu Brahman who founded the Theosophical Society in New York. 'In short, like the Jews, we theosophists are contrary and immune to the papacy in the Vatican and all that Catholic baloney of Christs, crosses and trinities,' Caporale riposted smiling broadly like a man who is happy.

After leaving the port of Rio de Janeiro as an electrician, he spent the first days in the holds, one side or the other of the engine room, studying the boat's circuits and connections. He liked to spend his free time gabbling on with me. I thus discovered that he was very fond of the horses and stuck photos of his favourite racehorses on the empty spaces on the walls of the cabin he shared with Amuntado, horses he'd watched race and win, and had even groomed: he'd handwritten their names on their photos in the manner of fake dedications: Fundador, Chanclos Fruit, Rebelde and Sakvat Truli. 'I want to buy one or two purebreds and win the Sao Paolo Grand National one day,' he liked to daydream.

Caporale's comment, strangely, made me think back to my father's life. I hardly knew anything about Seán Griffin's family when I was a child and adolescent, at most I presumed my grandfather Graham had died when Sean was a child, but I did once remember, when Caporale was telling me about his love for horses, that my father's cousin, Uncle Clark, the one who'd secured him a job with the Pacific & Co. Shipping Company of San Francisco, and with whom he felt brotherly links ever since he'd been an altar boy at Old St Mary's Church (my father, in his cups, would recite: '*Corpus Domini nostri Jesu Christi custodiat animam tuam in vitam aeternam*. Amen. *Rorate Coeli desuper. Et nubes pluant justum*', a Latin ditty I also learnt by heart), my Uncle Clark, I was saying, over time, thanks to his successful business, or perhaps luck at the card table, presented my father with a racehorse that was called, uncannily I felt, Invisible. From that day when Clark was so generous, Sean didn't miss a single race and spent his Saturdays at the racecourse, with or without Perla Chávez, watching Invisible race.

Griffin seemed to be overcome by emotion and interrupted his story for a few moments. I had just befriended sailor Nemo Caporale, a happy theosophist who claimed to descend from the house of Savoy, said Griffin ironically, reordering some of the shards of his narrative, taking a deep breath and launching back into his tale. We were like two peculiar islands in the centre of that island of the *Minerva Janela* that was also in the centre of islands I ceaselessly drew or invented, unconsciously, mechanically, on paper, that Caporale really liked. Once at the end of a day, when we were alone in the reading room, he told me he used to wonder what the world would be like after you're dead. It was a kind of game, an exercise in imagination that he enjoyed playing when he closed his eyes before going to sleep.

It was a more popular sport than I credited, because Graciela Pavic and my grandfather Arnaldo played the same game, said Griffin. In one of his letters to her in the Thirties Arnaldo wrote: 'Have you ever fantasised about what the everyday world will be like after you're dead? Try to imagine it, think of your friends, the people you can see and who see you, think of the lives of the things that have belonged to you so far,' Graciela told my grandfather, by return of post, that she'd started to imagine that from the hateful, unfair day her whole family had perished. When Caporale told me about that game he played recreating the world that might exist after we've all turned into dust, I thought of Li Pao and whether he was dead or alive, who could know? and took from my pocket the paste dragon he'd given me when I met him. I'd always kept it and right then, mid-ocean, with that stranger I was beginning to feel akin to, like a twin, I decided it was high time I got rid of fetishes tied to unfinished stories. But Caporale wouldn't accept Griffin's present, despite his persistence. And to my astonishment, right there in Funchal, Griffin did what he'd done five years earlier on the boat: he took Li Pao's small coloured dragon out of his pocket – the aforementioned red, green and gold object – and handed it to me. It's yours, he said, it's a present, so please don't reject it. I took it, kept it and inspected it closely as soon as Griffin left.

22

LET'S GET BACK TO GRACIELA PAVIC. GRACIELA TOOK her automaton from Cape Cut, where she'd found it, to the Salesian Museum in Punta Arenas on that same gusty 6 January, and it was a struggle, as she told Griffin's grandfather years later. After gazing at it for ages and experiencing that ineffably amorous impulse, she had to extricate the figure from the hard, almost frozen earth. It seemed unmovable, as if rooted there, which was almost the case, as Graciela soon saw, because the lichen and plants around its lower half had penetrated inside, gripping it like bindweed. First she used her hands she'd already bruised in the climb up, but was forced to abandon that method when she almost lost a nail and was bleeding. It was too deeply embedded and she started to search for razor-edged, sharp-pointed stones to help her dig, wondering how far down the rusty iron man was buried, only half of whose body was visible. She found nothing of any use and had to go back to the small inlet where she'd tied up her boat. She had various useless tools but did have an axe capable of opening a trench, so she dragged back up the wind-beaten hill, axe in hand, to where she'd left the android.

She excavated a hole around the buried artefact, but when she bent down to pull it out she saw a large cylindrical shape lower down, not two legs, ending in what looked like two feet or at least a good imitation. She had to widen the perimeter of the hole she was digging a good deal further before she could finally extract it from the pit where it had been lodged four centuries earlier. She used the axe to sever the roots of the plants that were stuck to it. When she tried to lift it, she realised the automaton weighed more than she'd imagined. Now she could see the whole artefact next to her feet, she thought it was encased in a ridiculous, stiff skirt like an iron tube, said Griffin. The whole device was more an imitation medieval knight in Arthurian armour, of the crude kind sold to fairground side-shows and displayed like a genuine Aunt Sally.

It was almost a metre and a half tall. And as Graciela was by herself, *she* had to drag it down to the boat, or even carry it in her arms, intensifying the strange feeling that her undertaking was beginning to resemble a rescue, although she was alone and terrified by the wild thoughts flying round her head. She thought quite absurdly that she'd just given birth to that creature. Pure madness. That dead or dormant body, whether human or inhuman, would now revive again, it must, Graciela told herself. Nonetheless it took her four years to repair it. Many more, in fact.

When she reached Punta Arenas, she left the automaton in her boat hidden under canvas, unconsciously expecting something to happen. But what? Nothing ever happened in her life apart from the desperate quest for her dead family or their remains. And wasn't that waiting itself a permanently interrupted happening? wondered Griffin, once again apparently talking to himself. Two days later, when she'd prepared a space in the museum laboratory and notified the authorities of her find – and they merely sent a small note to the local press, who didn't print it in any of their editions – she went back for it the same morning, accompanied by Kuller, the German museum attendant and volunteer weekend fireman, who pushed an elongated barrow with two large spoked wheels on each side.

Before Graciela left the harbour, she glanced across the bay, as she always did and would do for the rest of her life, in case she suddenly woke from her nightmare to find her husband and children rushing along a quayside and into her arms. Reality won out and there was no new awakening. Nothing had changed.

A huge middle-aged man with a fine head of white hair, an honest, lay Salesian, Kuller lifted the automaton on to the barrow and covered it with a blanket. His movements were imbued with gentle piety. Graciela helped tie it down and walked on one side of the barrow to steady it when it tipped turning a corner. They moved quickly and discreetly down the sloping Punta Arenas streets to the museum and nobody once looked askance at the load they were pushing. Nevertheless, said Griffin, she had to make a big effort to kill the temptation to think they were body snatching, because in a way that's what it looked like.

By the time Arnaldo and Irene, my grandparents, disembarked from the *Santander* on 10 December 1923 almost five years later, the automaton had been refurbished, though not entirely, and was on display in the room the museum set aside for the History and Fortifications of the Straits. 'Android found on Desolation Island, *circa* 1500', read the succinct metal plaque on the pedestal where they'd stood it, tucked in a corner by a visitors' thoroughfare, next to the door to the Botany Room. She'd invested more than four years in the slow repair process, the final goal of which, as far as her obsessive determination went, would be to make the automaton as mobile as its creator had wanted. To get that far, Graciela spent months building and dismantling each part with an iron discipline, day after day, studying its entrails, striving to understand its workings, carefully cleaning each small cog, polishing and re-polishing each pulley, each pivot, each tooth, each wire, each chain, each rivet, each hook, each wheel, big and small, and rebuilding the broken elements time and rust had rendered unusable. However, she left the bullet holes in the armour intact: the bullets that she found inside the body and discovered were lead and mid-nineteenth century. She didn't think it would be right to reseal the holes; they were scars that told the story of a struggle, although she couldn't at all suspect what it was.

She soon faced the bitter truth: despite her lively imagination and constant researching in books about engines and clocks and visits to scrap merchants in the port and blacksmiths and engineers, one part was missing, the crucial part that could set the rest in motion as well as the range of actions the figure could perform that she'd studied in relation to the intricate device designed by Melvicius. The automaton's mobility had a limited number of potential movements that were set hierarchically, meaning it could consecutively lift its arms, raise and lower its jaw, extend its forearms and then its wrists while its head twisted to the right, lean its torso forward while its head twisted to the left, make a one hundred and eighty degree turn from its waist, fling its head backwards and apparently seize something in the articulated fingers of its right hand. In a word, it moved like a warrior conceived to instil fear from afar.

All those movements were possible and could be performed consecutively in a single sequence, which naturally and quite intentionally, from a long distance, produced the appearance of real human movement, or could be enacted separately, in distinct phases, thanks to small levers on springs that Graciela gradually discovered strategically placed throughout the body.

However, for all this to happen, the missing piece was essential: Graciela found an empty space at the very centre of the automaton. It was the key part, known as the matrix or fulcrum, and Graciela began to think of it as the automaton's heart. Which was a very precise description, added Griffin.

Naturally, it wasn't a real heart, but its absence left the threatening figure lifeless and static, so the parallel with the human heart couldn't have been more apt, as far as Graciela was concerned. Everything indicated that the key piece, in a complicated combination of inter-dependent actions, triggered off all the other pieces and levers, either all at once or gradually, in function of the potential movements one wanted to activate. That missing piece, said Griffin, was more the province of Melvicius the alchemist than Melvicius the engineer. Or the sum of his two sides. 'An item at once philosophical and real, the bringer of light' Griffin declared, which was how Graciela understood and described it in a letter to grandfather Arnaldo, who, ever a magician, defined it as 'the bringer of light'. Why was it missing? Who'd taken it? Graciela never found the answers to these questions and didn't think them important; she couldn't have cared less. A long time afterwards, in the summer of 1930, that unique item became a reality. It had been necessary to imagine, draw, manufacture and assemble it from nothing and have recourse once again to books, scrap merchants, blacksmiths and engineers in the city, to designs and yet more designs and lots of failures, errors and breaks, until the job was finally given to the workshop of a Hungarian inventor of patents in Santiago by the name of Bakony. Five months later, it had been built and was ready for Christmas.

Graciela was obsessed about resurrecting that metal body, so it worked as it might have worked in days of yore. She had fallen in love, and, blinded by love, she wanted it to be someone who moved. She wanted to kiss the android, shut its eyes and bring their lips together. That's why she rebuilt its face, following the rough-and-ready parts and features old Melvicius, its creator, had left behind. Thanks to Graciela, life was restored to a frowning visage, flat eyes and the hint of a nose, and a mouth subtly marked by a slit that wasn't overly dramatic, where she shaped gently puckering lips from embossed tin plating. She decided to fashion them to remind her of her husband Arturo's lips that she missed – but how could she! she wrote to my grandfather, said Griffin – they were lost with her kiddies somewhere on the floor of the bay. In the event, that cold, mysterious pout, devised by a lunatic impulse, never left that non-existent mouth. Nonetheless, Graciela tried to use coloured paints to soften the coldness of the iron face's total inhumanity and instil a touch of authenticity, even though it seemed excessive, and it worked. But the paint couldn't hide their mutual loneliness. The automaton's solitude was integral to its make-up, given that it was born to that end, created to exist in the desolation of Desolation Island, said Griffin. The solitude of Graciela, who'd not been born to such a state, was another matter. She fought acquiescent solitude and wishfully imagined she was waiting in a time capsule for Arturo and her children to reappear at any moment, that it was all a harrowing nightmare or incident that had been wrongly interpreted by the locals and their cruel, pitying voices, and that their death wasn't death but a long voyage her husband had been unable to tell her about before he sailed to the other side of the world, to distant Dubrovnik, whence Miro her father and Veronika her mother had come, or perhaps Arturo had taken his children on a different voyage, an equally long haul, to the city of Caserta, full of relatives and songs she'd never seen or heard and could now never imagine, because Arturo left before they could share those dreams of different streets and worlds. Graciela began quite unconsciously to act like a new, modern-day Penelope, weaving and un-weaving at her loom. Struggling with the automaton's internal mechanism she couldn't understand, she built by day what she destroyed at night, and advanced and retreated in its refurbishment, secretly trying to avoid encounters with oblivion, where outside its gates a small retinue of pretenders had begun to gather. Quite literally so, said Griffin, because it involved the flight of steps up to the museum door, where, as the years passed, two or three young and not-so-young members of Punta Arenas society lingered in the hope of a date or romance with Graciela, whose beauty didn't fade with the passing of time.

Esteban Ravel was among them, although he enjoyed more status and potential, because of his brotherly friendship with Graciela. He was always close by, looking after her, firstly in person, extending his stays in Punta Arenas, restlessly seeking to amuse her so she didn't despair, and, when he had to visit his properties in Tierra del Fuego, employing intermediaries, like the museum's director, who tried to cater for Graciela's most basic domestic needs. Esteban enjoyed another advantage over the other young men, said Griffin: she let him look after her and ignored the rest that she didn't even notice. Esteban Ravel had loved her from his childhood; they'd shared lessons when Miro Pavic worked for Don Laureano; they'd played and grown up together on the Mercedes Estate out in Porvenir, which Esteban, the only heir, now owned. Like a caring elder brother he ensured Graciela didn't go without, and scolded her if she didn't eat or sleep enough, though he had to keep to himself the passion he felt for her and he prayed the woman he so loved would eventually recognise the reality of the deaths paralysing her life, would get over them and create a minimal space for a possible love, perhaps even a second marriage. But it never happened. Conversely, said Griffin, I'm sure Esteban Ravel secretly saw too much of the expenditure Graciela and the museum incurred repairing the automaton. In the years after her family tragedy he frequently visited her: there were times he visited the museum every day and talked to her for hours about the automaton she'd discovered, the object of an obsessive, extreme fascination that occasionally alarmed him. He consoled and cared for her even more in those years when he was afraid she might lose her reason; although that love never came to anything, he loved her to the day she died.

But any hope his love would be requited was shattered a few years after Griffin's grandfather travelled that way and performed his Great Samini act on the Mercedes Estate in 1923. It was shattered after the restored automaton made its first movements, probably the first in its whole existence. This happened at Christmas in 1930 when the engineer and inventor Bakony sent the key part from Santiago to Punta Arenas by mail-boat. In all those years after Arnaldo Aguiar and his wife Irene's honeymoon, Esteban had become reconciled to caring for Graciela as a sick woman, because the more the automaton was refashioned, the more Graciela became disturbed, as if she were no longer in control of herself, and she spent every morning waiting for a part to move miraculously, until she realised its heart was missing, and then she came out of her shell and burst into tears. Nothing can move, can live without its heart, she told herself or wrote in letters she sent my grandfather in her lucid moments, said Griffin, Nobody ever knew, but Ravel embraced the heroic abnegation that comes with love. He switched his residence from Porvenir to Punta Arenas, let slide his livestock and mining business on the estate almost to the point of bankruptcy, went to live in a hotel between calles Bulnes and Maipú, and every night, without fail, dined in his hotel with Graciela, in silence: until Christmas Day morning 1930 when Bakony's package reached the museum. It was an elongated, helical part, over half a metre long that forked in two directions. In the form of a crown, like this:

¥

Or this:

Ж

a cross-section, and cut with differently shaped and sized concave and convex teeth. That same morning when she inserted the new part that gave sense and order to the automaton's every articulation, Graciela locked the laboratory – or rather workshop – door. The part was a perfect fit, but it was some time before she managed to adjust the rest of the cogs and set the main and secondary levers.

When she finished, to Graciela's astonishment and glee, the automaton started moving its arms and head, turning round on itself, raising and lowering its jaw, and articulating its finger-joints. And did so just once. Graciela came out of her rapture and activated the lever back once more, and the automaton repeated all its movements with a measured precision. It did so again. Again and again and again. Esteban, who'd followed her to the museum, watched everything through the keyhole. Graciela laughed, cried, was elated, talked to the automaton and caressed it. Then she stopped and thought for one, endless minute before continuing to insert her fingers mechanically and absentmindedly in the orifices the bullets had left in the android's body. She suddenly cleared everything off the table and sprawled the automaton on top like a lover. Esteban Ravel now watched Graciela leap on to the table, part her legs and sit astride the metal body, kissing its tin lips, moving and convulsing until she climaxed. It was then that he realised she would never love him.

23

I'VE OFTEN REFLECTED ON ESTEBAN RAVEL'S frustrated love. Frustrated by what he believed to be insanity, a feeling that refused to go away. The rich landowner knew Graciela had moments of unreality because she refused to accept the facts, but her love for the automaton was an extreme symptom of a more advanced, if not clinical, state of insanity. He occasionally thought, 'She loves it because it can't die,' and then thought, 'But can you call that a *human being*? Can you call that *love*?' and reproached himself for conceiving such ridiculous ideas. Ravel was moved by a sentiment of sacrifice and never loved another woman, nor did he ever attempt to get Graciela cured or call on a specialist or psychiatrist of the many starting to become fashionable in the burgeoning city. His love was withered by indecision and replaced by a self-denying, discreet devotion to Graciela from afar.

When he saw her mount the automaton with her legs apart in a sexual act that was no less real for being impossible, Esteban Ravel felt something similar to the compassion prompted by the intermittent madness she entered and departed like a fog. But we shouldn't forget that her madness resided in the historical origins of the android. Initially, Philip II's idea of fortifying the Straits with one hundred and eleven identical figures was madness in itself. And although the idea wasn't his but his uncle's, at this point I must mention the figure of the melancholy young monster, Rudolph II of Habsburg, the Spanish monarch's nephew and a great collector of automata.

Rudolph, said Griffin, was perverted, paranoid and lusted after terrible acts, to the extreme of having a female automaton built that he fornicated with in the presence of his courtiers, or so people said. He wasn't vulgar or brutish: he was very refined though infected with a permanent saturnine sickness. The jury is out on whether all his perverse and perverted, dark and twisted longings and love of the occult and spiritualism came from his great-aunt Joanna the Mad, or whether he'd learned all that from his uncle Philip II, with whom he lived in 1563 when he was only eleven and extremely vulnerable. In Satan's great dance in Bulgakov's *The Master and Margarita*, the novelist speaks of him as one of the stellar guests of Voland, the Devil, and refers to Rudolph, as only 'a magician and alchemist', said Griffin, suddenly averting his gaze, remembering the ambiguous fascination the word 'magician' exercised over him, associated as it was with his life by Arnaldo his grandfather, the renowned conjurer, the Great Samini, for the greater glory of such spectacles.

By the beginning of the autumn of 1577, shortly after his coronation, Prague, the capital of his realm, was crawling with a whole retinue of tricksters, counterfeiters, goldsmiths, wizards, magicians, fortune-tellers, readers of entrails, gold-makers, gold-hunters, spagyrists, telepaths, Satanists, astrologists, miniaturists, quack botanists, inventors and manufacturers of mechanical contraptions. Rudolph surrounded himself with all such charlatans and was in his element. His passion for politics was non-existent, obviously, unlike his uncle Philip, who was also a spiritualist who'd taught him the art of governance, but he felt a real passion for power, and power meant only one thing as far he was concerned: possession, the possession of people, the possession of objects, the possession of strange and peculiar objects. When they didn't exist, he ordered their manufacture, spurred by the demands of his deranged, egotistical mind. Subsequently, his desire to collect became a desire to possess everything. It wasn't enough to possess a colossal number of unusual or intrinsically valuable objects or ones endowed with strange magical properties, he aspired to possess everything, absolutely everything, and spared no expense to that end, on the contrary, he put aside huge sums of money, put himself into huge debt and emptied the coffers of his empire.

Naturally enough, continued Griffin, I went to Vienna and Prague a few years ago to see what remained of his collections. I was relieved to see stuffed ostriches were among Rudolph's favourite objects. The ones I found weren't very different from those I'd observe at the end of my voyage on the *Minerva Janela* in the Salesian Museum in Punta Arenas, Graciela Pavic's, as if they were ostriches or similar animals discovered in Patagonia, near the Straits, and presented to Rudolph by his uncle Philip. Rudolph was especially fond of birds. He himself had an aquiline nose and beady eyes, and was airy and light, as if built to make a quick escape. Many noted how Emperor Rudolph II always seemed on the point of flying into space. There were lots of 'birds from the Indies' among the scant objects from his collection in Hradschin Castle in Prague that I visited when it was relatively neglected, to judge by the drab appearance of each room: perhaps some were Amazonian parrots like those that belonged to Flaubert, which I saw in Rouen, said Griffin. He commissioned numerous, bird-shaped automata, even the figure that, according to legend, he ordered

Melvicius to manufacture, with a head shaped like a giant crane's.

Driven by his collector's desire to possess and his perverse quest for the absolute, Rudolph dispatched agents throughout the world to secure him the oddest items and bring him the most daring alchemists. They were half spies, half traders and served under any flag to secure the precious booty they would then deliver to the emperor wizard. I saw all or at least most of the treasures from Rudolph's Chamber of Wonders in Vienna's Kunsthistoriches Museum. It was a cold November morning. Vienna in winter always reminds me of *The Third Man* and I always think I'm going to bump into the pathetic Rollo Martin pursuing Harry Lime in gloomy cafés or getting off the big wheel in the Prater. The streets were covered in snow and snow puts history on hold, said Griffin, as the physical, temporal contours of a city disappear. I'm terrified by the idea I might lose my grip on history. I thought, 'What century am I in?' but soon came to when the idea flashed through my mind that I might be affected by a madness similar to Graciela's or Rudolph's.

I took a taxi from the station; electronic music blared out from its strident radio. 'A hundred per cent contemporary,' I thought, said Griffin, as he headed for the museum. I still remember a handful of really unimaginable objects in the rooms dedicated to the conspicuous monarch: his own horoscope engraved on rock crystal with a tawny lion at its canary-yellow centre, Rudolph's favourite colour, a book on the movement of the stars open at an allegory of Venus (his lifelong obsession; agate goblets (said at the time to be a remedy against gout, an ailment suffered by many monarchs of the day); carnelian goblets (to restore good temper to the melancholy and irascible); whitish lime that reacted to certain poisons with a change of colour (useful, said Griffin, when testing whether one's food had been poisoned); and delicate goldsmithing by the great Jamnitzer, in his youth a pupil of the enigmatic Melvicius. From his Bestiary, I saw *The Gonsalvus Family*, the famous painting he commissioned from his court painter, Dirk de Quade van Ravenstyn, which depicts the sensational freak family of the day, a family of Spanish stock in which every member of the family, except the mother, suffered from *Hypertrichosis universalis congenita*, the disease that causes hair to cover every inch of skin, animal-style. I also remarked the considerable paraphernalia of alchemy in the collection. Rudolph II was fascinated by white candles, retorts, crucibles and vats. In one very special place I saw the profusely illustrated edition of *Das Narrenschiff (The Ship of Fools)* by Sebastian Brant, one of Rudolph's favourite books, a present given him by the eccentric painter Giuseppe Arcimboldi, known as Arcimboldo, when he arrived in Prague as an adult, on his way from the extinct court of Maximilian II, where he'd been the royal portraitist and earned himself notorious renown by painting human faces made of fruit and vegetables, or items like frying pans, glasses, barrels and bottles. Rudolph began to take an interest in Arcimboldo when the latter lauded to the skies the rhyming couplets of Brant's long poem satirising human baseness.

Madness fascinated Rudolph like all things strange, deformed and monstruous. It was the emblem of his century, the stigma of contemporary monarchs and nobles. Giuseppe Arcimboldo introduced himself as a 'painter of the fantastic', but his real passion was mechanical figures and puppets, to the point that he designed sophisticated devices for figures engaged in naval battles in theatrical performances. This drew him like a magnet to Rudolph, whom he accompanied like an inseparable court jester organising all kind of entertainment for him, from the improvised construction of ephemeral sculptures, poor copies of classic busts made from lettuces, cucumbers, pears, grapes and peppers that found their way to the palace kitchens after the divertimento was ended. It was Arcimboldo who put the emperor in contact with Melvicius the alchemist and engineer, whom he'd already heard about when the court was in Vienna, fifty years earlier, at the time Transilvano was in Valladolid listening to Pigafetta talking about the Straits discovered by Magellan. When people talked about Melvicius, they embroidered their tales. He was, they said, a mysterious, elderly man who'd never left Prague and, except for his pupils who came from the ends of the earth, no normal person had seen him except on the rarest occasions; he was, they said, a friend to half the city's rabbis, and enemy to the other; perhaps a rabbi himself, but a member of a heretical Talmudic sect, for others. They said . . . they said . . . they said . . . Pure gossip. Did that Melvicius ever exist? Griffin asked himself out loud. I doubt it, he retorted, but history's there to bear witness to the Great Faker.

Rudolph employed Arcimboldo as a mediator to commission Melvicius to build him an Iron Venus, a Fornicating Machine, an automaton with a woman's body and crane's head, and its most successful feature had to be a simulated feeling of female skin when you touched the cold metal. They say, always according to Griffin, that Melvicius created this device, and that whoever caressed the female android's polished body experienced the pleasure of a real woman's skin, that the metal was mysteriously warm: it was no doubt just talk. Nonetheless, Rudolph came to hold Melvicius in very high esteem for another reason: his incurable, chronically aching molars. He'd been suffering that ache from his youth, almost from the time he was at the court of his uncle Philip II, and suddenly experienced periodic attacks that exacerbated his irritability and arbitrary behaviour. When Rudolph II had the aches, the lives of his courtiers were in danger and worth nought. Arcimboldo searched out Melvicius, knowing that the precious stones the emperor was so fond of possessed curative qualities, it was said they proceeded from the lightning that separates life from death, and that was why they were attributed such great virtues. I saw part of Rudolph's collection of precious stones in the Kunsthistorisches Museum. Perhaps none of those mineral items had passed through his fingers, or perhaps they all had, who could tell? There were sapphires, amethysts, diamonds, topazes, emeralds and turquoise. All polished and loved by him, surely.

Arcimboldo asked Melvicius for help and promised a handsome reward if the emperor got rid of his toothache. Melvicius, Griffin explained, spurned the reward, but told the painter he was familiar with nine noble stones that used different languages depending on the time of day, and that Sea Spume was the most difficult to obtain and the one that brought immediate cure. 'But not all Sea Spumes are the same. Some are malign,' added Melvicius, 'like the one called Anatolian Drop of Blood, mere possession of which brings disaster upon its owners, who die within a few days and nobody can find a rational explanation. They seem to fall into a deep sleep or hypnotic trance from which they never wake.' The benign, curing variety was to be found in the Ligurian Sea and was white with deep pink striations. It was known as Milición. Its black side cured aching molars if mixed with salty sulphurous water. 'It is advisable to drink this concoction out of sight of others, because the very taste provokes violent sickness and swooning,' Melvicius warned. 'When the patient awakes, all pain will have gone for ever.' Melvicius was so confident of his potion he again spurned any reward, though conversely offered to cut off a hand if he didn't succeed in curing the emperor's pain.

Rudolph did everything Arcimboldo recommended, following the instructions of Melvicius. Miraculously, said Griffin, his molars never ached again. From that day onwards, the old alchemist could cross the threshold of Hradschin Castle whenever he wished, but went very little because he never forgot his hand would be severed from his body if Rudolph had the slightest twinge. However, I never saw any Sea Spume in the glass cabinets at the Kunsthistorisches. I stayed there till nightfall contemplating the items in that *Wunderkammern* and left with the last security guard.

Part of what I've just told you can be found in Rudolph's correspondence with his uncle Philip, said Griffin, together with the Habsburg emperor's enthusiasm for his magician and engineer, always narrated with an erratic, schizoid energy. He told his uncle everything: it is the only reliable source about the creation of the mechanical woman, except for the fallacious gossip of individuals who swore they'd copulated with her. He also wrote about issues that had always aroused the interest of uncle and nephew alike: their insatiable desire to communicate with the dead and no less insatiable eagerness to transform lead and copper into gold. It is well known that Philip II created a laboratory for that purpose hidden in El Escorial, about which he briefed his nephew through a rich private correspondence that circulated between the two imperial capitals via secret mail, separate from the channels used for general questions of State.

Melvicius was involved in experiments that came very close to creating gold, as he did with other distillations and convoluted formulas to create hallucinogenic drugs that uncle and nephew were so fond of. Melvicius was someone who was familiar to Philip II, a figure he'd heard about though he'd never met him in the flesh, and above all, someone whose creations counted with the favour of Rudolph and the engineers of his court, like Turriano and Acquaroni who occasionally went to learn from him. That is why, Griffin continued, when he received the alarming news of the threat posed by the English corsairs, led by Drake, to Spanish interests in the Southern Sea, the principal channel to and from which were the Straits of Magellan, Philip II decided to commission the construction, a secret sworn under pain of death, of the Cabbalistic number of one hundred and eleven automata, in the shape of awesome warriors. The Spaniard remembered that, once – but where and when and who? – perhaps in passing or whispered in his ear by a third party, in a carriage or in a corridor between offices or in church or eating the frugal fruit he allowed himself, someone had related the ingenious idea that fleetingly occurred to Maximiliano Transilvano, his father's secretary, on a day at Christmas time in 1522, of fortifying the Straits with robot *homunculi*. And who better to do that than the man who'd created the fake Venus that gave pleasure to everyone, the perfect doll his nephew Rudolph had described so enthusiastically, the invented woman the Prague mob in 1580, said Griffin, his eyes wide open staring into mine to catch my reaction, had curiously called Graciella, after a tavern keeper in Malá Strana. The order for the androids was given in 1580, the 14 November to be precise, yet again via Arcimboldo who must have noted it in the secret diary he wrote in invisible ink that is lost to posterity, since I once saw in the old Milanese palace where he spent his old age, the board covers, emptied of their innards, of the fat notebook that once contained the painter's most private jottings. That same day Melvicius had secretly completed an exact replica of the Fornicating Venus, the rabble's Graciella, that he would take to the Duke of Brunswick's castle in Dolna Krupa, as was his obligation according to the diabolical pact they'd both agreed.

24

NONE OF US SLEPT MUCH THE NIGHT WE SAILED FROM Rio de Janeiro, said Griffin, returning to the subject of his voyage. The stifling heat on the *Minerva Janela* and our pleasant memories of three days on dry land brought us all out on deck to catch a night breeze and soothe our nostalgia. The glittering skyscrapers in Guanabara Bay were still visible and Paipinho the taxi driver and his obsession with 'mad cows' came to mind. I also wondered which *favela* in Lapa harboured death for Adan Krupa, if he stayed on in Rio, death from the righteous thrust of a knife I could have dealt, if I were someone else and not myself, and I thought of Cazilda Canabrava, whom I finally bedded one night because she reminded me so vividly of Li Pao, said Griffin, and I was pleased to pay the price for that memory. The day of our departure, as we progressed along the coast, twilight streaked in purple the other long beaches separated by dagger-like promontories. The Brazilian Pereira sang out their names: Leme . . . Copacabana . . . Ipanema . . . Leblon . . . San Conrado . . . He knew them well, concluded Griffin with a sly grin, because Pereira had thrown all rules to the wind and had also bedded Cazilda. Perhaps on one of those beaches now engulfed by shadows, perhaps at twilight on the first day we docked. She volunteered as much to me while getting dressed in the Belvedere, turning her back on me, because I never interrogated her. I didn't question her afterwards either, because although she was like Li Pao, I really didn't give a damn about her gossip: it was her work.

When the light had almost faded, we could still see in the distance the black silhouette on Corcovado, high above everything else, on its isolated mountain, that huge Christ the Redeemer opening his arms out like an unlikely, blissful suicide. I imagined, continued Griffin, he was an enormous bird about to swoop down on the city and ships in flight. A bird like iron Graciella, Melvicius's automaton with a crane's head, came to mind, said Griffin; then I reproached myself for associating Jesus Christ with the Fornicating Venus, a connection quite uncalled for from a half-Irish Catholic like myself, son of Sean Griffin who'd recite in bars '*Corpus Domini nostri Jesu Christi*'.

We continued south-south-west for the next few days about thirty miles from the coast, until we were on a level with Porto Alegre, Pereira's city. When Fernando Grande announced we'd entered that latitude, Pereira turned morose, spent the day in our cabin and never surfaced. He reread Verne, solved crosswords and cleaned his fishing rod to avoid seeing the line on the horizon where his family lived and where he'd left his childhood. I recalled the *Odyssey*: 'God forbade his return'. In need of distraction, he and Amaro began an engrossing game of chess that ended in a draw two days later.

After leaving Porto Alegre on our right, Captain Branco issued instructions to head south, slightly south-west, to lead us away from the maritime traffic coming out of the River Plate. 'It's longer,' Sagna the purser told me, said Griffin, 'but it's safer and less hassle, and we'll sail across a millpond.' We did have very calm days, good weather and the crew had very little to do.

I spent the time getting to know the theosophist, Caporale, whom I was befriending.

The moment I set my eyes on him I anticipated he'd be an interesting character, and he didn't disappoint. He was an able seaman trained in the submarines of the Brazilian Navy and looked the part of an experienced sailor: woollen jerseys, cap pulled down tight over a completely bald pate, and an impenetrable, mysterious smile, replete with expressions and features that could signal happiness or evil, sorrow or horror, and he had no need to change the look of his mouth or the wrinkles around his eyes that shrunk or expanded as he wanted. He liked chatting to me whenever he had an opportunity, almost always about horses, which brought a smile to his face. One particularly tranquil afternoon en route to the Falklands, after he'd finished the task Pereira had assigned him, he'd come over and blurt out a string of trivial comments about his work. I was vegetating, sprawled over a tyre full of ropes next to some winches and, arms folded, he gazed out over my head to the waves; the only noise, was the regular, by now familiar, sound from the engine room that reached the deck via the various conduits. That afternoon he didn't speak about horses. After a few brief, anodyne comments on the voyage, to my surprise he suddenly launched into a disquisition about tunnels, a topic that had also fascinated me from my very early childhood, perhaps, might we say, because it's an amateur way to gain invisibility.

Like me, continued Griffin, Caporale remembered the uncontrollable excitement and panic he'd felt as a child upon entering a mountain tunnel in a car or train, whether it was long or short, though it was better if it was long because you felt you were floating or holding your breath. Caporale felt like a temporary guest lodged in a kind of huge whale, like Jonah or Pinocchio. 'Where are we?' he wondered. 'Is there a way out?' He and I even thought, went on Griffin, that the noise of the tunnels faded and the sound of car tyres on the road made an inaudible music, like the sound on *Minerva Janela* over the sea. Half theosophist, half shaman, Caporale told me something about tunnels I'd also intuited as a young child, and from that moment I respected him as a kindred spirit. He astonished me when he said that we cease to be visible in tunnels and become invisible.

When I heard that, I jumped to my feet and was all ears. 'In fact,' said Caporale, 'we can't see and aren't seen, and whatever speeds through at top speed is no car or vehicle with headlights on, but a ghostly, elusive illumination.' I wondered if we could really be invisible to the people driving past us in a tunnel. On one occasion, when I was a kid, we almost crashed into some cows, not those 'mad cows' that obsessed Paipinho, but lethargic cows like the holy cows of India that would have crushed us like rocks if we'd hit them. They surged out of nothingness, out of the darkness of the tunnel, lit up at the last moment by our headlights. It was one of the first physical manifestations of invisibility I'd ever experienced, said Griffin, the sudden eruption into the real world of something that was latent, that was real and existed, but was also rather unreal, unexpected and fictitious. I was afraid I might be devoured by the tunnel, like a fairground 'tunnel of fear', an enormous mouth with gigantic, bloodcurdling teeth, at once tempting and intriguing, compounded by a powerful sense of disintegration, of dissolution in apparently boundless space, where everything was as pitch black as a night on the high seas, like that night when we left the Brazilian coast behind us and Caporale talked to me about tunnels, about *his* tunnels. Caporale boasted he was an expert on tunnels. He knew the lengths, layouts and heights of all the tunnels in America that were over a kilometre long. He wasn't at all interested in small tunnels, mere holes in the Gruyère of life, fleeting parentheses 'with no metaphysical connotations', as he remarked. The big tunnels in the Rockies, the Andes, Patagonia, Alaska, even the one in La Mancha, were the tunnels that really attracted him. Although he had incomprehensible gaps in his knowledge, Griffin added, Caporale could relate tunnel disasters in Siberia in minute detail but, conversely, was totally ignorant of recent developments in modern Japanese tunnels. And he was unfairly arbitrary, and studied, when he could, the names of Alpine tunnels linking Switzerland and Italy simply because they led him to a non-existent past, the deadpan Caporale would add, alluding to his illusory forebears in the House of Savoy he'd imagined so often they'd become a stack of shifting delusions his father, Alcides Caporale, had swallowed, until he finally disappeared down another tunnel, the tunnel of delirium, because he believed he descended from the House of Savoy and completely forgot that his grandfather, a general in the revolts in the Sertao, had beaten a tubercular Italian, who was unknowingingly dying, in a game of cards and won the stake, a fake royal genealogy.

Tunnels are tied to madness, Caporale reflected, said Griffin, as in the H. P. Lovecraft novels he read avidly, again much to my astonishment, but they don't take people that far, and simply lead them to the brink of lunacy, as was the case with his father and Graciela Pavic, and when reason seems to have vanished, it is restored by the inevitable exit into the light of day. Caporale talked to me about this on the second bridge as a pleasant breeze blew under a starless sky, and spoke passionately about H. P. Lovecraft. He swayed from side to side like a child as he explained the paradoxical petrified viscosity of the monstrous characters in Cthulhu, as if they were related in some fantastic way, I thought, said Griffin, to those inhabiting the shadows in Melvicius's mind in Prague, with magicians under the rule of Hecate, his secret goddess, unreal beings he had perhaps hoped to fashion in the automata commissioned by Emperor Philip II.

I shall never forget something that will always remind me of Lovecraft's fantasies, of automata and madness, said Griffin, and it involved Caporale as the protagonist, days after our conversation about tunnels. I am referring to the tattoos he sported, that he later drew on me. It was sparked a few days later, when he chatted to me again at night, this time in the moonlight, by the tattoos I noticed on his arms: on his right was the horse he wanted to buy for the Sao Paolo races, and on his left Lovecraft's face garlanded by a ribbon that said: '*Necronomicon* by Abdul Alhazred', the mad character who was the dark soul of Howard Phillips (or H.P., however you want to put it), who, by this stage in our coincidences and happenstances, was also mad, said Griffin.

Caporale had etched those most elegant of tattoos on himself. 'Each took three hundred hours,' he exclaimed, adding that every sailor should have at least one. 'They are a reflection of our desires,' said Caporale. Griffin then recalled that some are mentioned as asides in *Treasure Island*: 'Good luck', 'Fair wind', 'Billy Bones his fancy'. Who might that Billy Bones be? I wondered while Caporale went on talking about tattoos he thought he could remember, said Griffin. Perhaps he was the equivalent to a Caporale that Stevenson once met, if we can agree that anyone who embarks on a ship will at some stage encounter his own Caporale? His enthusiasm was persuasive and I asked him to tattoo me with something connected to my desires, as he'd suggested, and he did just that the day after with the help of Charly Greene, who'd been unanimously elected the ship's official tattooist.

Griffin's next move in the Funchal bar where we sat as close to each other as Caporale and he had been on board, was to roll up his sleeve and show me a long, faded red tattoo from his elbow to his shoulder. It was the serrated silhouette of Desolation Island. Some barely perceptible birds were flying around its shores that Griffin had insisted on including, like a rash of black freckles. Caporale had tattooed them because I told him the dream Rudolph II had had, according to malevolent gossip, the night before he died, said Griffin, and that in turn the monarch told his confessor, no doubt in a delirium: 'I dreamt that one hundred and eleven huge birds were flying over an island and that I was that island.' Everybody assumed they were vultures, and that he was referring to the people who wanted to raid his collection of rare treasures, the remains of which I'd seen in Prague and Vienna, but very few people, I mean nobody, imagined it was an allusion to his uncle the emperor's plan to have one hundred and eleven androids built, a failure that obsessed him to the final moment of death. That took place on 19 January 1612, and by that time Melvicius's automaton was already presiding over the solitary wastes of the Straits of Magellan. If you look carefully, Griffin said, raising his arm towards my eyes, the automaton is there as well, in the middle of the island that Caporale and Charly Greene tattooed on me that day for eternity.

25

AS FOR THE AUTOMATON'S ODYSSEY AND LONG, SOLITARY life, in a way it all began on the night of 13 February 1579, the terrible night of the attack on Callao, said Griffin almost in a trance, as if more than four centuries hadn't in fact gone by, referring to an extensive article he'd read in a journal years earlier. It pointed out that the route through the Straits to the South Sea had been abandoned long ago, he said; the climate was awful and the place was ravaged by storms, and it was accursed: boats capsized in its waters and sailors were pulled apart and swallowed by unimaginable monsters. Because the ships so avoided the corridor, within twenty years its existence was a thing of the past, to such an extent that people believed the route had been blocked by floating islands that surfaced at its entrance, and the confident Spaniards ceased to protect that flank in their struggle against the English. In fact, as Griffin discovered through other sources, the Spanish court was *never* afraid the enemy would approach from that direction. Consequently the ship owners and the Crown began to use the route across the isthmus of Panama again, a long, secure, if arduous journey that involved disembarking men and supplies in the fortified citadel of Name of God on the Atlantic coast, and taking them on horseback overland to the other side of

Panama on the Pacific coast, where they again embarked to Peru or the settlements in Chile.

Then, unexpectedly, disastrously, according to that journal article, Griffin said, from midnight on 13 February, flames burnt well into the day in the port of Callao, and cannonballs began to destroy houses and hurtle through inner and outer walls. It was raining fire, people had nowhere to take refuge, were dying on the street or in demolished houses, and the final attack at sword and musket-point finished off the garrison and hundreds of inhabitants of the city. The Dragon had come. That was what they called the most feared corsair, the bold and brave Francis Drake.

The English had crossed the Straits of Magellan in barely sixteen days, from 20 August to 6 September in 1578, something that had never been seen or heard of before, with fair winds and the best pilot in the world. Drake hated the Spanish because he hated Catholics. Francis was born in Tavistock forty years before his attack on Callao. He was the son of the feared Protestant Edmund Drake, the visionary chaplain of Chatham Dockyard, and as a child was victim of the grim persecutions Mary Tudor launched against Protestants. Queen Elizabeth took advantage of his hatred to secretly appoint him a royal employee whose single mission was to attack all the Spanish galleons he could find and sack the colonies of her cousin's empire on its weakest flank. Francis Drake left Plymouth on 13 December 1577, with a fleet of one hundred and sixty-four men in three vessels, the *Pelican*, a name he'd later change to the now legendary *Golden Hind* in homage to the emblem of nobility – a golden hind – of his former patron and protector, Christopher Hatton; the *Elizabeth*, no doubt in honour of the lady behind the adventure, and the *Marigold*.

It was a secret voyage, and all the spies from the Court of

Philip II were duly duped and announced that they were sailing to Sicily in the Mediterranean, but Drake soon changed direction to the south. He had a stroke of luck in Cape Verde that led to the success of the expedition, said Griffin, because he took Nuño da Silva prisoner. According to my research, said Griffin, he was the best pilot of his time and his story is worth telling, as Nuño da Silva himself told the Viceroy of New Spain, Martín Henríquez, when Drake, as a mark of gratitude for services given, liberated him a few months after the attack on Callao.

Nuño da Silva was born in Oporto and his whole life shifted between Spanish and Portuguese vessels in all the seas known to man. He'd landed near Cape Verde in 1577. He saw the English reach the Island of Santiago and his first impulse was to hide, but he could find no safe haven. When Drake heard about him, thinking the young man was from Brazil and would be familiar with those coasts, though he resolutely denied it, he ordered him be taken prisoner and brought on board his ship. Besides, he needed someone with a knowledge of Portuguese, because – apart from a dubious copy of Ortelio's map of the world he was carrying, and another copy of the chronicle of Magellan's journey, probably a poor Spanish translation by Pigafetta – a secret map of sea routes, probably full of errors, had come into his possession in Lisbon thanks to a corrupt functionary and he needed someone skilled to interpret its clues and pinpoint its pitfalls. He thought the intelligent Portuguese youngster, who boasted he was a pilot, would serve the purpose well. What Drake never did find out was that Nuño da Silva was in fact spying for Philip II, or at least that's what I deduced from the books I consulted, said Griffin. Nuño told Drake he was Amador de Silva and used the false name of Silvestre Silva with other people. Be that as it may, he never succeeded in alerting the inhabitants of the colonies to the Dragon's surprise attacks, whether on Valparaíso, Callao or later in Huatulco, where Drake finally let him go, not without paying him very well for his expert piloting, that was tantamount, said Griffin, to sealing his lips, because he'd have been hard put to justify his bag of gold to the Constables of the Viceroy of New Spain.

Da Silva most probably switched sides midway through the voyage with Drake, and as a sign of goodwill offered his new captain all his knowledge of the Straits, because it was obvious he did have an expert knowledge of those waters, their shallows, currents and dangerous shores. It is a mystery how he knew so much, when boats hadn't sailed there for some time, but I expect he went on one of the many secret voyages Philip II sent to those seas, most of which sank in the Straits or its turbulent entrance. What is beyond doubt, Griffin declared, is that without Da Silva Drake couldn't have negotiated those waters in two weeks.

Da Silva concluded his account to the Viceroy by telling him that Drake had fled in the direction of China, taking the longest, most dangerous route that would force him to circumnavigate rather than the shortest route back across the Straits of Magellan. The Viceroy of New Spain didn't believe him and thought it was simply a stratagem of a spy working for Drake who'd been left behind to sow confusion about the escape route he'd taken with the fabulous booty he'd amassed in his attacks. Da Silva served two crowns, but in fact neither, and because some witnesses said his command of the English language had made him the captain's close friend and that he joked with him and was his confidant, they tortured him in Mexico to force him to confess the real route taken by Drake, but despite the Inquisition's torture and his delirious pleas to his master Philip II for help,

Da Silva finished his days as a demented cripple, since he lost one eye, had one leg amputated, and enlisted as a jester on merchant ships where they made him sing dirty ditties for a jug of wine and a flurry of kicks. Perhaps he fell overboard from one of these vessels and nobody missed him. We don't know the year, boat or place, said Griffin. What is strange is that before being tortured Da Silva did manage to write a letter that never reached Philip II, though it probably did come into the hands of Sarmiento de Gamboa, the accursed figure who pursued Drake and brought Melvicius's automaton to the Straits. The Portuguese spy noted in that letter how favourably impressed he'd been by the land on parts of the shores of the Straits of Magellan for the establishment of colonies; what really alarmed Sarmiento who communicated as much with equal alarm to his sovereign, said a Griffin now in his element, was that the chaplain of the *Golden Hind*, the Reverend Francis Fletcher was similarly impressed, and had jotted in his notebooks: 'These lands abound in fertile plains and enjoy a climate similar to our beloved fatherland.' Consequently, Drake began to cherish the possibility that the Straits might one day belong to Elizabeth's Crown, and be populated by Her Gracious Majesty's subjects.

It wouldn't surprise me, added Griffin, that Drake had in his sights the place on Desolation Island where Graciela Pavic found the automaton, and consequently the spot where Sarmiento de Gamboa installed it. But the English corsair could never have suspected its existence and wouldn't have been in any mood for flights of the imagination, since when he came out into the South Sea by Desolation Island, he didn't find the calm sea mentioned by Pigafetta in his report but a tempest that kept them in that area for almost a month, unable to move forwards or backwards, losing the *Marigold* and the *Elizabeth* amid much screaming and cracking of wood, and unable to do anything to help the shipwrecked souls who perished opposite the island's southern coast. From there to his attack on Callao, Drake was caught in a succession of adventures and chance incidents. The tempest turned into a storm that didn't relent for several weeks. The *Golden Hind* was unmanageable in such circumstances and was dragged southwards along the western coast of Desolation Island to latitude 57°. He was the first to see my island from that position, said Griffin, who there in Funchal bragged barefacedly that he knew everything there was to know about the island he was obsessed or even tattooed with, as I'd seen previously. He was also the first, in the middle of that tremendous storm, to notice that the Tierra del Fuego was a large island and the Atlantic and the Pacific joined at that point erupting in those fearful roars of which Melville speaks so much and with so much trepidation. Lastly, he was the first, Griffin continued, to observe to his displeasure the steep, desolate coasts and multitude of coves and fjords cutting between the islands, since he approached from the south-east until he could see Cape Horn, which was called something else at the time, looping round it before returning to the shores of Desolation Island, close to which he suffered a bloody attack from the Alacaloofs, who inflicted several losses. Some versions say he was hit in the temples by an arrow that almost sliced off one of his ears.

Two weeks after that protracted storm it calmed enough for him to leave the island where they were sheltering. He headed north again, and after ravaging Valparaíso in a surprise attack on the night of 13 February 1579 he sailed into the bay of Callao, Griffin had read in his journal article, entering via the Morro Solar as far as Whiting Point, all lights out and totally silent. Those who saw the boat's shadow from afar thought it must be a ship full of lost souls and lepers, and crossed themselves as it sailed by: they never thought it might augur more danger than that ghastly disease.

One by one, following the plan devised by Drake, the *Golden Hind* sacked the eleven boats anchored that week in the port of Callao, some carrying cargoes of gold and silver from Arequipa, like the king's galleon. Afterwards Drake left them all unmoored and adrift, with corpses hanging over their sides. The authorities and majority of Lima's inhabitants weren't expecting Drake's cruel attack on Peru, but some had anticipated a disaster, because barely two years before, on 7 October 1577, a rare comet had crossed the sky and its tail had remained visible on cloudless nights and, as Dominican friars wrote at the time, the phenomenon remained visible for two months. That long tail attracted attention and pointed to the Straits of Magellan, and was interpreted as an ill omen. It was held to be the sign of a divine punishment that would soon be exacted because Viceroy Toledo had killed Tupac Amaru, the young Inca.

This prophesy sprang from the magical interpretation of the three sevens in the date of the comet's appearance (day 7 in the year 77), and that coincidence deeply disturbed the astrologer and half wizard Sarmiento de Gamboa, who was living in Lima at the time under the viceroy's orders as his military leader. A man on the brink of one of the greatest, most epic failures in history, a titan with a will of iron, Sarmiento realised immediately that his destiny, whatever it might be, was linked for life to that comet and the place in the world its tail indicated. But this wouldn't come until later, said Griffin, when Philip II, frightened by the fabulous booty that Drake had stolen from him for the embellishment and profit of his cousin Elizabeth, was worried in case he might repeat his bold action not once but several times and decided to fortify the Straits of Magellan, however remote and forbidding the place was. He recalled old Transilvano's idea and decided to put it into practice.

26

WHEN OLIVER GRIFFIN WAS IN THE KUNSTHISTORisches Museum in Vienna, gazing at the treasures in Rudolph II's Chamber of Wonders, he experienced a strange vision: he suddenly relived the day when his grandfather Arnaldo, the Great Samini, retired from the stage. He was little more than a youth observing another's lifetime. He recounted this to Caporale on the *Minerva Janela* when they were ploughing through the sea near the Falklands and playing draughts, and now he was telling me the same story, in that proverbial patchwork of stories and pieces from a peculiar puzzle.

I didn't think of my grandfather, he said, when I was looking at Rudolph II's rare trophies, but when I stared at one of the museum security guards meandering aimlessly, his hands behind him, I remembered the night-time vigils I'd mounted in another museum in Madrid, a while ago, before I lived in Barcelona and met Li Pao, in silent rooms which were silent to the point of provoking panic, and I now recall them very vividly, said Griffin. I imagined the guard in Vienna like that and wondered what he'd be like later, when there were no members of the public. Would he walk the empty, eerie rooms trembling with fear? I put myself in his shoes but in that other museum in Madrid by night, also walking though shadowy rooms, quelling an acute feeling of fear in my stomach whenever the sculptures loomed out of the dark like human forms that lurked there. I then remembered my grandfather the Great Samini while I was walking through the museum, perhaps because I was lighting my way with a torch and the beam of light created a magical effect on the exhibits, as in one of his hypnosis tricks.

Where did the name of Samini come from, I wondered quite absurdly, because I knew I knew, of course I knew! said Griffin, remembering how I found out the day he celebrated his retirement. The origin of the name was a cheap novel my grandfather read when he was eleven, as he told me later, which was the age I was when I began to appreciate his importance as a magician and intuit the extent of his fame. It was the novel I found in his changing room the night of his farewell, where we all toasted and feted my grandfather with champagne. It was on a metal box behind the pots of ointments and make-up powder. I flicked through the worn copy. Its title was *Samini Against Everyone*, and was written by one Sebastian Cordelier, who is now totally forgotten.

While I read random paragraphs, I spotted the look of pleasure on Grandfather's face as if he'd seen my find. The rest of the titles in the Samini series appeared on the last page in the book. Samini was an Indian detective who solved cases by using his mental powers of anticipation. He was blind and always wore a large dark red turban, something that characterised my grandfather's appearance as a magician, Griffin continued, and his purple turban was perhaps an individual homage to those childhood novels. I'd never heard of him or read his novels, noted Oliver. The book was published in 1905 and was in a poor state, binding gone and barely legible pages where only the odd word was decipherable.

That was how I came to remember my grandfather on his retirement day in that museum in Vienna. I thought lovingly of him and the magic he created. When my grandfather transformed himself into the Great Samini, he could make things exist and stage impossible feats. But once he'd retired, would he be able to do it again, could he restore a body he'd sliced in two to a single unit, or make fake fire flame from a flowerpot or a woman come out of them, or a handkerchief turn into a snake, or a hand of cards into a stream of evanescent bubbles, or make someone invisible in front of our noses, his grand finale that people always applauded so? I thought these thoughts on that April day in 1968, the day he retired from artistic life, on his seventy birthday, 'the age when life is really fulfilled, according to Petrarch', as my grandfather, an avid reader of Petrarch, said in his goodbye speech.

I was twenty years old, perhaps the only age at which astonishingly all one imagines seems possible and when one is ready to be or see oneself as a real magician. After the performance in the theatre, the longest ever given by Grandfather that anyone could remember, his friends and relatives went to his dressing room. We were exhausted by the anxiety we'd felt that final time he donned his purple turban and large glass sapphire, willing him not to make a slip or error prompted by nerves, as had happened a few days earlier, when he cut himself on his own box of swords in mid-performance, an accident he interpreted as a definitive warning issued by his age (that age, according to Petrarch), but we were still excited by my grandfather's wonderful magic acts. He performed every single one, and most were familiar, not one was new, but they continued to enthral, even the classic turns every magician must include in his repertoire.

I went with Matilde Aguiar, my mother, whom the Great

Samini summoned up onstage, and the audience all put a face, maybe for the first time, to that famous voice they'd heard thousands of time on the radio. My father had lived in Los Angeles for several years with Analía Soler, Perla Chávez, in the bigtime, and sent a telegram to the theatre. I remember my grandfather reading it at the top of his voice in his dressing room. 'Now you'll do a trick and will make a new start. Stop. Set up another seventy years. Stop. Others will accompany you then. Stop', my father had written to his father-in-law in an amusing, acid tone. My mother merely said it was a very expensive telegram. 'Too many words,' she said.

Select people were queuing outside the changing room wanting to come in: lots of people wanted to say their goodbyes at the end of the performance. There was Veronica, my grandfather's last assistant, and Carmelita, his first. There were technicians, scene-changers, make-up people, box-office attendants, ushers and theatre staff, all wishing to shake his hand on that last occasion. Their manner was cheerful, though I only remember the faces of people I'd never seen or of some I met later over the years. I felt invisible, hugely invisible. Nothing new or odd in my life, almost my natural way of being, said Griffin. Invisible to everyone except my grandfather, who glanced at me every once in a while with a strange, warm yet severe smile.

I looked around at the photos, clothes and objects strewn over the make-up table and the mirror framed by lit bulbs. I was stifled, about to faint from the heat and jostling with all the people who wanted another glass of champagne to toast the Great Samini. I sat in a corner, almost behind the illuminated mirror. It was then I noticed the metal box and the book on top. I told Caporale all this, that pale night, as we drank Coca-Cola on the second deck and, fascinated by the celestial vault, said Griffin, looked up from our stalemated game of draughts. He cheered up when he heard the word 'box' and said boxes always hold mysteries or surprises. Naturally I found a surprise wrapped in mystery.

Graciela Pavic's letters were locked away in the metal box that was like a strong box, enamelled in silvery steel with rounded corners. They were all postmarked and arranged like files in a cabinet, one after another, vertically. I counted some one hundred and eighty-six letters. The first dated from 1924, shortly after my grandparents returned from their honeymoon. Initially they were addressed to both Arnaldo and Irene, but later there were only letters to Arnaldo, even a long time before my grandmother's death, the last letter being dated November 1947, the year Irene passed away. The letter spoke precisely of that, of the grief of loss, 'something I'm acutely familiar with', wrote Graciela in what was surely the last lucid statement she ever addressed to my grandfather.

There were no more letters with return to sender in Punta Arenas after that. Why? Who knows? Perhaps Graciela went completely mad, as the infatuated Esteban Ravel feared. Perhaps she tired of a relationship that had lasted so many years. Or perhaps, and this is the most likely explanation, said Griffin, Graciela forgot her beloved Arnaldo Aguiar overnight, forgot to write, forgot words and letters, grammar and sounds and how to articulate them, and even forgot herself.

I read all that correspondence and it was a strange hybrid model of epistle that love and madness had inspired over the years. Arnaldo and Graciela wrote assiduously to each other, with warmth, fervour and passion, and although they never met again, from what I could see, they'd loved each other intensely, their way, their respective desires like separate planets. No doubt their love was genuine, and remained so for years and years: an unusual love marked by absence, a peculiar feature of my life and the life of my relatives that is connected to invisibility: not being there, not being seen, and not existing. I experienced something similar with Li Pao, with Fabienne as well, and no less so with Elsa and Roberta. And it happened to Matilde, my mother, to Sean, my father. And to my father with Analía Soler. And in a way always happened to Irene my grandmother with her husband Arnaldo.

Maybe absence is in the very nature of love? How can you understand a love *in absentia*, a love in which the beloved, the object of that love, once held near, possessed, enjoyed in the best of cases, is only present in frantic desire that's under control though still atavistic, as it flickers into life inside your head? Griffin asked, as usual not waiting for me to reply. That was the nature of the love of Graciela and Arnaldo who never saw each other again, however much they pledged and planned to. But it was Irene and Arnaldo's love as well, because he went on tours of Spain, Europe and America, and was away from home for months on end, that is, if there ever was a home, and my grandmother never accompanied him on any of those voyages and sojourns: she stayed in Madrid with my mother.

I have sometimes reflected on my hapless grandmother's dramatic love that was cut short unknowingly on their honeymoon in Patagonia, that distant southern summer in 1923. How my grandparents met, how long they were in love, what tender or erotic words they whispered to each other or how they said them, whether they argued or not, became disenchanted or not, what the years before their honeymoon were like, in the end questions without answers, but I asked them all the same, Griffin added. I know they met a couple of years before at a dance that's part of our modest family history. He trod on her dress and it ripped and she had to repair it on the spot at the dance and he was so embarrassed by his clumsiness that he knelt down in front of Irene and in a gesture pleading for her forgiveness he extracted from his mouth a thimble and a needle that was already threaded. That astonishing performance entranced the young and unwary Irene. She fell in love with the apprentice magician for ever.

But, oh, said Griffin, a similar flash, and quite as astonishing, hit Arnaldo unexpectedly when, one morning in that wedding year, two days after arriving in Punta Arenas, he met Graciela Pavic. She'd walked down to the port very early in the morning, as she did every day from 1919, and peered at the distant Catherine's Bay, cherishing no hopes. She'd sat down among the cargoes of goods that had crossed the Atlantic on German boats; she allowed her silent gaze to disappear into the waves in a ritual she enacted alone from within her solitude and despair. Arnaldo had been unable to sleep during the whole crossing, and now paced up and down all alone from daybreak. He was looking for the cause of such turmoil, but didn't know what it was. Or who.

He did the moment he saw Graciela. He couldn't take his eyes off that woman whose gaze was so sad, almost motionless against the horizon, like a statue. Her beauty attracted him and he thought it was more powerful than he was and liked that. He saw in her features or gaze a profound, forlorn sadness that fired a curious mixture of love and desire. He ardently wanted to protect her, but didn't know from what, and couldn't yet imagine they were there to protect her from herself, after misfortune beset her and she had severed her links to life. 'I live but always on the brink of death,' Graciela later wrote in a letter. Arnaldo initially thought she was an actress starkly rehearsing her role in Greek tragedy, a Hecuba perhaps.

He approached her on the excuse that they held the world

of the theatre in common. She shook her head, but the idea left her bewildered and she liked the young Spaniard's demeanour. She looked at him in a special way. When Arnaldo went to say goodbye, he managed a conjuring trick: he extracted a small blue flower from behind Graciela's ear he'd cut when leaving the hotel, where his wife Irene was still asleep. Graciela laughed. That afternoon my grandparents visited the Salesian Regional Museum and Arnaldo was amazed to find the woman from the port there. They conversed affably and my grandfather was entranced yet again. Graciela showed them her automaton. It was the day they took the photo I've always cherished, said Griffin.

Arnaldo realised Graciela wasn't right in the head when the letters she wrote to him over a whole year described in detail what her children did from day to day, as if they and her husband were still alive. In the mid-1930s she began another cycle of letters in which the automaton was infused with life and talked. Suddenly, she nonplussed her correspondent, by relating sex scenes with the automaton, described his iron body as if it were human or else, weeks later, in reverse, she told Arnaldo what the automaton had said about him, and about the tender love he inspired in her and how much she desired to meet him and spend a long night loving him in a hotel in any city in the world.

In some letters she started mentioning Dubrovnik, where she was always about to go and was sought after by a family of Croatian relatives whose faces would now be unknown to her. For his part, he promised to come on tour to Santiago de Chile or Valparaíso, and begged her to try to journey there, possibly by plane. But they never succeeded in realising their plans. Graciela listed for Arnaldo, as I saw in her letters, prolix boat timetables and the most extraordinary combinations of transfers in ports that probably no long appear on maps. He could take a merchant ship to Peru and go from there to the Philippines and Goa, skirt round India and sail to Zanzibar. There he should board an English or Portuguese mail-boat and be in Gibraltar within the fortnight. Or take a Spanish liner and, after stop-offs in Rio de Janeiro and the Canary Islands, be back in Gibraltar. They must meet in Gibraltar, that was her fixation, 'her lover's caprice', she called it, as if she were Molly Bloom herself. In other letters Graciela then wrote page after page of information about hotels in Gibraltar, noting addresses, describing rooms and comparing prices, as if it were a tourist leaflet or childhood memory that was totally non-existent, as if she really was a sublimated Molly Bloom, said Griffin.

From 1944, Graciela's letters, written in a different, nervy, illegible hand, began to talk about the automaton as if it were a beloved human being she loves or argues with. When lucid, she recalled moments when refurbishing that being as if she were narrating the ups and downs in the lives of a son, brother or lover. Sometimes it was all confused with memories of moments she'd experienced with Esteban Ravel, who visited her every day and had even asked her to marry him, but she always mocked his pretensions, alleging she was afraid of what the automaton might think, if ever he learned of Esteban's absurd idea. In moments of madness, fantasies about the past appeared in the letters, impossible episodes from her children's lives, because they'd died when they were very young, and she talked about them as if they were growing up and learning to ride horses, read poetry, climb mountains, sing Italian ballads, cook Croatian dishes, play cards, study mathematics and have their first loves. The same happened with Arturo, who, though dead, now directed a clinic, was recognised as a doctor throughout Punta Arenas and earned lots of money from his many patients; at other times she confessed to Arnaldo that

Arturo was very jealous of the automaton's constant presence in her life, especially the time she spent with him, and, worst of all, the many occasions he'd caught them loving and kissing each other in the dark in the museum. People even said the android with the cold stare and colder body was her lover.

Clearly, Graciela was raving. But her ravings only increased my grandfather's love for her, said Griffin, or so he deduced from the sentences Graciela copied into her letters from his. Although, as her madness intensified, there was no way one could believe her, and perhaps my grandfather's letters were merely polite, friendly, affectionate ones, and not the passionate missives Graciela thought she was reading, a woman who finally mistook Arnaldo's letters for letters the automaton sent her on the sly so Arturo never found them. On another day, Arnaldo had to acknowledge Graciela's total lunacy when she asked my grandfather, as a favour and matter of decency, to refrain from speaking to her again or asking her about her children or husband, because she was alone in the world, had never married or had children, had never had any and had never wanted to have any: she liked children but had decided to devote her life to her research, investigating the history of the 'Praguen' automaton (that is what she wrote, 'Praguen', Griffin emphasised), her life's goal, her *raison d'être*, although she'd recently met a young man and was thinking about marrying him and having lots of children. When she wrote that letter, Graciela had passed her fifty-second birthday, and she never again mentioned that young man, a pure fantasy of hers.

There were lucid, even amorous moments, tender phrases like, 'If you were here', 'If only I could have you here next to me' or 'I want to feel your mouth and hand now'. The letters also mentioned fantasies, sublimated trivia, such as a game they started that particularly interested me, said Griffin. As a result of the game I discovered the strangest thing of all, Graciela, as I discovered later, in the rare lucid letters she sent, was aware of the automaton's entire history, its origin and its creator, Griffin went on. That was why she had written 'Praguen' when mentioning it. The evidence surfaced precisely in that amorous game that, in many letters over several years, they played as two young people in love.

It was a game Graciela had taught Arnaldo. It was mental exercise of a magic nature she dubbed 'The dream of Melvicius', and consisted in flying around Prague in your dreams and believing that if you flew through self-suggestion, in the end you felt you were flying for real. It was a romantic story invented at the Court of Rudolph II and given that name 'The dream of Melvicius'. Young people at the magician king's court played it, helped by embarine elixirs, a hallucinogenic drug much sought after today. Apparently, Melvicius had told his followers about the only love he'd ever had: when Jewish Melvicius was young he fell in love with a Christian girl, and his love was requited, but his love, they soon discovered, became an impossible chimera. They ended up imagining they were flying over the city and going to new places whenever they could be together and love in many, diverse ways.

What Melvicius told his disciples was that, thanks to their great desire to love one other, they succeeded in turning their fantasy into reality and, in truth, from within their dreams, they flew over the rooftops of Prague. Melvicius spent his whole life attempting to find the physical key to those flights he remembered making. He never did. At best a mixture of embarine resin with opium, a potion that plunged him into hallucinatory dreams.

Graciela and my grandfather played that game of real and fictitious flights for years. They sometimes changed location, when Graciela requested they did so. They'd go to Desolation Island and love each other there. She chose that inhospitable, windswept place because it was where she'd found the automaton she did really mount and love in the museum whenever she was loving Arnaldo in her fantasies. And Arnaldo agreed to go to that island in his imagination because it was what he felt deep in his heart: desolate. By then, Griffin continued, Graciela also wrote in her letters about the wonders and obsessions of Rudolph II, the same things I'd glimpsed in museums in Prague and Vienna. Graciela had studied the dark side of Melvicius and the shadowy world of Philip II, or perhaps had heard them referred to, because her consuming interest for the automaton made her launch into the search for the past of a love that was real and overwhelming. It was in this strange way, in the 1930s, midpoint in her morbid lunacy, that Graciela sought out her beloved's impossible genealogy and encountered the dramatic adventure of Sarmiento de Gamboa and the settlements lost in the Straits of Magellan, an adventure she came to study and know as well as I did. But why anticipate events? asked Griffin.

27

ONE NIGHT AFTER DINNER AT OS COMBATENTES, OUR favourite restaurant, Griffin leaned on the back of his chair, looking out towards the Botanic Gardens on Avenida Arriaga, in the small area built like an eave over the rest of the tables one reached via a winding staircase, a relic from a gutted submarine, and told me about Monte Sarmiento. He was highly emotional and excited and it was his way of launching into the tale of the man in whose honour that crag on Tierra del Fuego was named: Pedro Sarmiento de Gamboa. It's the highest mountain on the whole Strait, two thousand and four hundred metres high, said Griffin, an absolutely curious mountain, in the form of a dazzling white pyramid. The English sailor, Philip Parker King, who later moored in several inlets on my Desolation Island, gave it that name in April 1830 in homage 'to the great Sarmiento', who more than anyone else represents the spirit of struggle and failure, a phantom, if you look carefully, still roaming those lands. Even rats know that. Rats always do, like the ones Kowanana killed with grapeshot on the *Minerva Janela*'s cargo deck while listening to his Walkman. That peak was known as the Snowy Volcano, the name Sarmiento de Gamboa gave it, until Parker King intervened.

Its peak has only been climbed once. That was in 1956 when

Italian mountain climbers Carlo Mauri and Clemente Maffei made their dramatic ascent, the latter being a distant relative of Arturo Bagnoli, as surely Graciela must have known. Nobody else has climbed it successfully. When Darwin sailed that way on FitzRoy's *Beagle*, Griffin said, he was fascinated by that pointed peak looming high above, and was struck by the gleaming, perpetual snow, garlanded by clouds, and its foot, surrounded by expanses of mysterious black forests of Atlantic beech, as evergreen as they were inhospitable.

I've seen those forests, Griffin added, I've seen them being gnawed by beavers at the entrance to the Cockburn Canal; you can't breathe in them. Darwin defined the snowy massif as a 'sublime spectacle of frozen Niagaras'. A beautiful phrase, commented Griffin almost ironically, adding in obvious admiration that Sarmiento, the man, was pure passion and ambition, and honest and noble to boot. He was insatiably curious about every branch of knowledge and every act or feat that could be tackled in this or other worlds, however titanic or supernatural they might seem, since he believed as much in science as its opposite. He didn't know what fear was and wasn't restrained by any sense of caution. He was Renaissance Man at full tilt in his life and learning; erudite, a lover of Latin and the classics, a bold sailor, a merciless soldier, a writer and brilliant cosmographer. But he was also fond of astrology and magic and used to learn the spells of fortune-tellers by heart. That's probably why he was always being persecuted by the Inquisition that judged and imprisoned him more than once in New Spain and Peru, where fate sent him after a stint of infantry fighting on Flanders fields.

He never curbed his adventurous spirit or scorned anything human, but lacked a gift that, if he had ever possessed it, would have erased him from history: compassion. It is a virtue that perishes, a mortal gift. History disregards it, declared Griffin. Always striving to reach higher goals and peaks that were difficult to scale, like the mountain that bears his name, he had an exceptional, tireless personality, was tough, prickly, ungovernable and unbending towards everyone and especially towards himself, with whom he never relented, and was merciless when it came to demanding more effort from those accompanying him on the extraordinary expeditions he mounted because of his eternal need to surpass himself. Naturally, he had no friends. He never married. Never went to the theatre. Was not known to have lovers of either sex. His greatness, that is considerable, was never properly recognised, or perhaps lies in oblivion because his life was a rich, exhausting race into the void, said Griffin.

Soon after he'd said this, we left Os Combatentes and walked towards the port of Pontinha. It was a clear, starry night and Oliver's was the only voice . . . He continued. Philip II wanted to turn the South Sea into a *closed sea*. He wanted no more incursions by pirates and corsairs of rival powers who treacherously slipped in. The Straits of Magellan were the only route to the colonies and it was a vulnerable, unguarded spot. It must be populated and filled with fortifications, with soldiers and weapons that could destroy any boat from either shore before it could progress. In time, when the word got around, such forces would dissuade the English and Dutch from entering those fearful waters. But first they had to be made to seem fearful. Or at least that's what the emperor hoped.

Sarmiento turned the royal dream into a reality: he even founded cities in the Straits. Ephemeral cities, simulacra of cities, invisible cities, as I do to a point, Griffin explained, cities where the destinies of the settlers ended in horrible deaths, in cities soon to be abandoned by the metropolis. The idea of populating the Straits proved to be a ridiculous chimera and terrible failure. Hundreds of men and women who responded to the call to populate those remote lands, fleeing from poverty, died the slow death brought by hunger and cold. Those settlers at the world's end tormented Sarmiento to his dying day, because he was forced to abandon them against his wishes. They tormented Sarmiento alone. Nobody else remembered them.

It's not known exactly when or where Pedro Sarmiento de Gamboa was born. He must have been born between 1530 and 1535, in Alcalá de Henares or Pontevedra. Sarmiento himself stated he was from both places. He invented his own life. I'm sure his parents came from the north, said Griffin. He apparently studied at the University of Alcalá and acquired his great command of Latin at a youthful age, which allowed his reading matter to encompass all that was unhealthy and on the Index of the Council of Trent and persecuted by the Holy Office, highly unrecommended books of science, prophesies, magic, astrology, banned bibles, heterodox versions of history, lascivious novels and books of spells, as well as books by Machiavelli, Erasmus, Fray Francisco de Osuna, whose *Third Spiritual Alphabet* influenced him profoundly.

In 1550 he enlisted as an imperial harquebusier in the Flanders, German and Italian campaigns, where he showed his mettle in dozens of battles and countless vicissitudes that tempered his tough character. At the same time, while he was displaying his prowess as a leader in the field, an incredible theory began to seduce him as a result of his eccentric reading and the fantastic stories told by his troops: a legend according to which Ulysses (Homer's *Odyssey*, the one whose episodes I simplified for my classmates in that 'commentary' they all copied, desk after desk) founded the land of Mexico that later became New Spain, said Griffin. The evidence forwarded in tavern chatter and the books he found whenever he could, between battles and surrenders, first in the bourgeois libraries of Bruges and then Maguncia, where he arrived as a wounded warrior in March 1554, convinced Sarmiento, but it was of course drivel based on two facts, namely: that Greeks and Aztecs wore similar ankle-length garments ('extremely identical' to quote a *Life of Sarmiento* I read, said Griffin) and the fact both peoples used the same word or sound to refer to God: *teos* in Greek, *teotl* in Nahuatl or Aztec. It was a thesis worthy of Caporale, he remarked sarcastically. However, it became one of Sarmiento's driving obsessions that inspired him in the Straits of Magellan to the point of founding the first settlement, called City of Jesus, and thinking of himself as Ulysses. He really expected to find traces of a Greek colony in millenary Mexico, the one established by the real Ulysses, the Greek who gave rise to the myth. It was he who decided to go to New Spain without delay, as when I decided to go to Desolation Island. Perhaps it was the reason – a most carefully guarded secret – why only a year after convalescing in Maguncia that he set sail, we don't know from which port, for the Western Indies and reached New Spain in September. He must have been all of twenty-five at the time. He'd become a seasoned sailor almost overnight. I imagine him receiving orders and learning everything on board the galleon. 'Astrolabe!' Astrolabe! 'Bowsprit!' Bowsprit! 'Spar!' Spar! 'Lower sail!' Lower sail! 'Foretop!' Foretop! 'Salvo!' Salvo! He piloted expertly, deciphered navigational charts, read astronomical maps and mounted armillary spheres, calculated intricate geometrical patterns, and did so incredibly quickly. But one fine day in 1557 he fell foul of the Holy Office, when the Bishop of Tlascalal accused him of practising witchcraft and trafficking with talismans 'in order to engage and win over women'. The same happened in Peru seven years later, when the Inquisition persecuted him once again as a fortune-teller and seller of magic rings to ensure success in love, and he was imprisoned in Lima for miracle-making.

His fondness for the occult and black magic linked him in no small way to the two emperors who dominated his era, Philip and Rudolph. The years go by and his life becomes a blur. Sometimes he's in jail, sometimes he's alone on the streets of Lima where people see and fear him, and sometimes he simply engaged in skirmishes against the Chiriguan Indians. In 1567 he goes with Mendaña on his expedition to the southern seas and catches a glimpse of Australia. In 1569 Francisco de Toledo takes up the position of Viceroy of Peru, a man of talents similar to Sarmiento's, who immediately recognised him as a great governor with whom he could do business. And he did. He named him Royal Second Lieutenant and put him in charge of the army that lost so many men crushing the young rebel Inca leader Tupac Amaru in the Andes, who was sentenced by Sarmiento and executed at dawn by four horses that tore him limb from limb. In the years after he'd enthusiastically repressed the natives throughout the viceroyalty with Governor Toledo, Sarmiento withdrew to Lima to concentrate on the study of the stars and eclipses, his real passion, where he read the present and especially the future.

It isn't clear if he considered it a faith or a diversion. He probably never dared confess as much to anyone, not even to himself. And that was how he lived, in virtual isolation from social life in Lima, when wily Francis Drake struck in Callao. After the impact of the disarray caused by the corsair had passed, the viceroy ordered Sarmiento to pursue and trail him, spying on everything he did and attacking him, if the opportunity arose. The only problem, said Griffin, was that Sarmiento went in the opposite direction to Drake. The Englishman went north, and the Spaniard south. They never met. At least not in this life.

The two ships that went in pursuit of Drake left the port of Callao on 11 October 1579. Sarmiento, in the *Esperanza*, went south-south-east, towards the Straits of Magellan, and would be the first to cross it en route to the Atlantic; nobody had travelled that way before. He took his time, exploring every corner and giving names to the tangle of fjords, inlets, channels and islands he found, and slotted that entry to the Straits in its proper latitude of 52° 30′. When he entered the western approach and left from St Monica's Point on the other side, he inevitably saw part of Desolation Island, said Griffin, that was battered by every known wind; and then something strange happened that would be highly important later. Namely this, continued Griffin: the day after anchoring the *Esperanza* in Port Mercy on the northern face of the island, in search of water and calm, when Sarmiento was in the aftercastle, he was suddenly startled by a shadow passing before his eyes that the sun projected on to the wooden deck, or perhaps it was only a shadow moving nimbly across the top of a crag, above the shingle strand protected from the wind where they were anchored. It was only for a second, but it took him by surprise, said Griffin, Sarmiento was afraid and so startled that he swung round and screamed instinctively. He began to shake uncontrollably. It was a panic attack that caught the attention of his crew and left them perplexed, especially his friend Antón Pablos, the pilot, who witnessed his strange reaction and related it to others.

They all looked at their captain, who was clinging to the rigging to stop himself from falling, and then at the high peak. They saw nothing. Sarmiento tried to overcome his shock by asking if anyone else had seen figures on the crags along the shore, and if they were or weren't animals. An astonished silence. Nobody had seen anything. Pablos presumed it must have been a Patagonian Indian, most likely an Alaculoof, looking down from a peak and waving his arms as he watched the strange manoeuvres of the monster that had arisen from the sea. Everyone forgot the episode, and only Sarmiento wondered whether it had been physical weakness on his part provoked by exhaustion, or a supernatural warning. He remembered that spot when returning to the Straits two years after, and it looked to be the ideal location for Melvicius's automaton, in order to provoke a first sensation of fear or alarm from afar. What he'd experienced, if only briefly, was the sensation of being shaken in an iron grip, since nothing could be more terrifying than being totally alone, and finding oneself suddenly watched by an unknown being, whether human or not, lurking there. Sarmiento de Gamboa must have felt something similar on that occasion. But he refused to interpret it as an evil omen, it was a revelation, such was his state of mind, said Griffin. That was the place, although he still didn't know why. Ten months and eight days later they reached Spain after they had found no signs whatsoever of Drake, as was only to be expected.

28

PHILIP II, WHO NOW ALSO OCCUPIED THE PORTUGUESE throne, received Sarmiento in Badajoz at the end of September 1580. The emperor was annoyed and tense because of what he considered to be his cousin Elizabeth's humiliating jape. His anger was fuelled by the reports from Bernadino de Mendoza, his ambassador at the English court, which related how eager the queen was to see Drake reach her shores with the fabulous booty he'd snatched from the Spanish. Philip confessed that Elizabeth's mocking laughter woke him in the middle of the night like the worst of nightmares and his sheets were so soaked in sweat they had to remake his whole bed, said Griffin. In the brief audience Sarmiento was granted with his monarch, he easily convinced him of the need to protect and fortify the Straits by establishing cities and transforming the place into another colony, because it was so essential for the Empire and as Catholic as Spain. Philip II had already reached the same conclusion, and Transilvano's old idea would finally be acted on two months after his conversation with Sarmiento.

That army of automata had to be ready as soon as possible. A huge sum of money was sent to the court of Rudolph II with a view to paying Melvicius, said Griffin, and another considerable amount was set aside to equip the expedition Sarmiento would lead within the year. Philip II gave orders to the Duke of Alba, the Duke of Medina Siconia and the Council of the Indies to make the voyage a priority. He took a real interest in fortifying the First Narrows, as Sarmiento suggested. He ordered leading engineers to present designs for fortifications where the automata and garrisons of 'living soldiers' could be located in their respective moats and battlements. Juan and Bautista, the Antonelli brothers from Gaeteo in Romagna, proposed two ideas that appealed to the emperor. On the one hand, they designed a gigantic chain of lock gates, like movable doors, with large caulked tree trunks at intervals of ten metres joined by fifteen-metre-high iron halters and hinges, the like of which had never been constructed before. Bautista Antonelli accompanied Sarmiento on his second voyage there to put the chain in place close to the narrowest channel in the Straits to service the towns they intended establishing there and ensure the work was carried out satisfactorily. Additionally, the brothers conceived a series of mobile watch towers, also made of iron sheeting, that would be easy to transport and place on strategic vantage points along the coast. The automata could be placed inside and when they moved inside the small towers, they would more likely be thought of as human.

Tiburcio Spanoqui, from Sienna, Superintendent of Fortifications of the Empire, was granted the honour of designing the forts on the Straits of Magellan. He prepared plans to build fortifications on the rocks of Punta Anegada and Punta Delgada, well into the Straits where the First Narrows start. It was an impregnable location because of precipitous cliffs either side for almost two kilometres of strait: there was sufficient visibility to control all naval traffic, even if there was thick fog or heavy storms, the best possible defence, in a word, added Griffin, for the settlements they were about to set up.

Spanoqui drew plans for two symmetrical forts north and south of the Narrows, with two large breakwaters opposite each other that jutted several metres out to sea. If danger loomed, the Antonelli brothers' chain could be slung between the two forts to shut down the channel through. Experts claimed the forts were marvellously efficient bastions that wasted not a metre of space: a single expanse of ground shaped like a right-angled triangle the legs of which would house the two-storey barracks and hospital and the hypotenuse a large esplanade where the gunpowder stores and stables would be located. The esplanade continued in the form of two open arms, around the whole perimeter of the castle wall, where they would erect a few sally ports large enough to take pieces of artillery. Deep ditches leading to a dock would be dug out around the part of the wall with machicolations on each corner looking down on land. The entrance was equipped with a drawbridge wide enough for a cart to pass.

Philip II was obsessed with the idea of invading and conquering England and unconditionally approved his engineers' plans and ordered Sarmiento de Gamboa to ensure they were implemented as discreetly as possible, together with the secret project of the creation of that army of tin soldiers that would have to be transported overseas in sealed chests, when the time was ripe.

However, to everyone's huge surprise, the whole scheme foundered overnight. Within three months Philip II had issued the order at the end of February 1581 to stop the manufacture of automata. Perhaps he thought a large number had already been built, but not one had yet seen the light of day, said Griffin. Old Melvicius was making no progress: he was simply drawing designs in his head and making sketches of the mechanisms necessary for the manufacture of the most perfect automata of his time that would be the wonder of future historians. Philip II desisted because of a bad dream he had over several nights that contained an evil omen that came via a coded letter from

Rudolph his nephew and matched a similar bad dream he'd had that was also repeated several times.

The root cause was a number: the awesome 111, said Griffin. When he told Caporale this story on the *Minerva Janela*, the old sailor immediately told him, 'It is a key number in astrological charts, and what is known as a *magical constant*. The worst imaginable,' Caporale told me, said Griffin. It was undoubtedly a Cabbalistic number (the fruit of two prime numbers: 37 x 3) that formed part of a diabolical equivalence in the transposition of letters from the Hebrew alphabet and responded to a magic square, that was straightforward enough because it was a simple zigzag, but a highly dangerous one because of its ultimate meaning in the books of the Cabbala, as it represented the number 666, the satanic number of the Beast. Moreover, according to Cornelius Agrippa the astrologer, who copied Hindu astrology in a secret work of 1533 that was very familiar to Sarmiento, Rudolph and the emperor himself, entitled *De oculta Philosophia libri tres*, it gives the magic square of 6 (the addition of all its figures in vertical lines always produce 111) to the heavenly box of the Sun, 'source of all virtues and fulcrum of all disasters', said Caporale.

1	2	3	4	5	6
12	11	10	9	8	7
13	14	15	16	17	18
24	23	22	21	20	19
25	26	27	28	29	30
36	35	34	33	32	31
111	111	111	111	111	111 = 666

The dangerous unit of three identical numbers, the essence of which is different if they are separated or joined together minus one (n + n – 1), according to the Cabbala, amounted to a prediction of future disaster, since all the numbers added together, with the combined latent energy of all three, make 666. In Philip II's dreams his nephew Rudolph in a state of alarm told him of another dream he'd had over several consecutive nights in which an astonishing red sea flooded the whole of Prague and Melvicius the magician sailed across that anti-natural sea guided by Sirens asking for more money to save his automaton and issuing threats in strange tongues.

What was really astonishing was that a few days later Philip received a secret letter in which Rudolph related his repeated dream down to the last detail. The emperor immediately interpreted it as a dreadful prophecy that the Great Armada he was having built in double-quick time in Corunna would be wrecked in a sea of blood. He was absolutely certain he should halt his automata project, and demonised its creator, the Melvicius he neither knew nor appreciated, and ordered his nephew to have him killed, though to no avail, because Rudolph II perhaps remembered the aching molars the magician had cured long ago.

'That 111 was like opening Pandora's Box and releasing all its horrors,' said Caporale. Philip II believed exactly that, and believed wholeheartedly that some dreams could take control of others, said Griffin, and that his nephew's dreams had set up house within his own. He summoned Sarmiento and asked him to ensure that all the automata built so far were destroyed, and demanded it be done in his presence. Only one had been made by that time. Although there were two, in fact, if one counted the copy Melvicius always made for the Duke of Brunswick, either for gold or to safeguard himself.

Griffin went on to tell the story of the second automaton. The duke was Rudolph II's great rival when it came to hoarding rarities, clocks, treasure and wonderful figures. A somewhat literary legend has built up around what I'm about to tell you, said Griffin, elaborated by initiates, historians, if not wizards, according to which it is the second automaton, not the first, that is in Punta Arenas. How did it get there? Legend has it that it occurred in a roundabout, obscure manner. Apparently, Sarmiento was one of the few people who knew of the existence of a second automaton. And he knew because an ageing Arcimboldo was summoned to Milan, where he then lived far from the excesses of Rudolph's court, to carry out an unusual mission, since he was the person who'd negotiated the building of those one hundred and eleven artefacts with Melvicius and had been privy to the secret of the automata from the start.

The mission involved carrying out Rudolph II's pledge to take his uncle Philip the only automata that had been manufactured, so he could do what he wanted with it, once those mysterious dreams had unravelled in other ill-omened dreams. But Arcimboldo brought not one, but two automata. It happened in August 1581, Griffin related. They were both fond of card games to the point of laying absurd stakes. Rudolph had won the second automaton from the duke in a private game of cards that only Arcimboldo witnessed, by royal design, and he wanted to give it to Philip II as evidence that no other automata could exist without his knowledge. But the duke was very unhappy about his losses, particularly that one, and tried to recover it: in the ensuing struggle he was killed by a dagger thrust into in his heart by Arcimboldo, who was protected by the impunity Rudolph had granted him. Perhaps that was why he withdrew to Milan, to keep up appearances, said Griffin, or simply because of his age.

When the monarch insisted on destroying the automata sent from Prague, Sarmiento and Arcimboldo agreed to conceal the second automaton's existence and give the first to the king. It was destroyed mercilessly, unceremoniously in the Escorial before his cold gaze by men armed with mallets and tongs, just as Gamboa had dismembered Tupac Amaru. Sarmiento furtively kept the other to himself, perhaps in his own house, if he had one.

The proposals for fortifying the Straits were presented to the Council of the Indies. They were passed, on one condition: that the expedition should be captained not by Sarmiento de Gamboa, but by someone much more prestigious. They chose Admiral Diego Flores de Valdés, the worst of mariners, a loathsome, corrupt man, above all, a poor administrator who was hostile to Sarmiento from the beginning and opposed the chimera of fortifying the Straits against corsairs. As a consolation, Philip II appointed Sarmiento governor of the Straits, paradoxically governor of a place where there was nothing and nobody to govern, that was even nameless: it was an invisible posting, noted Griffin, staring at me. The long, costly preparations for the voyage were made in Sevilla, where Sarmiento saw for himself Admiral Flores' poor administrative skills and the corruption of government employees in the Contracts House when supplying goods, biscuits, ropes and rigging and all that was needed to stock the galleons and other boats. The poor quality of materials was obvious. Hold-ups in the work repeatedly delayed their plans.

In the meantime, Sarmiento opened an office to recruit settlers. His aim was to recruit 258 (115 single and 43 married men, according to his plans), but finally 204 enlisted. They all came from the poor in the city and countryside and, no less so, from prisons and jails. Some were beggars, others tramps, the lame and the blind with their guide boys, bandits and thugs, or counterfeiters and heretics. But also hungry peasants and good burghers without a trade or business. And friars. And soldiers on no pay. And whores from the slums. And constables to keep order. And clerks and actors. All were going to a certain, dreadful death: some died en route, others in the savage tempests of the Straits. All, in a word, said Griffin, were heading for the slaughterhouse.

The great convoy of vessels finally set sail from Cadiz on Sunday 9 December 1581 with sixteen boats and 2,500 people at the second attempt. A month earlier on 27 September they'd left Sanlúcar with twenty-three ships, but on 5 October rain and hurricane-force winds from a huge Atlantic storm decimated the fleet. It was a real disaster and seven boats were lost and more than 800 men perished. From that unfortunate day on, the Flores and Sarmiento expedition began to be referred to as 'the accursed expedition', both on board and on dry land. And that indeed was what it proved to be.

29

WHENEVER HE THOUGHT OF SARMIENTO DE GAMBOA, Oliver Griffin had Afonso Branco on the brain. I can't stop the image of *Minerva Janela*'s stern captain from haunting me, said Griffin. He was my captain, the man who fought despair, the man with the rock-hard spirit. I occasionally remembered, briefly, Whitman's line: 'O captain, my captain.' Anyone who has sailed in a big ship knows you know very little about your captain. He is always elusive. Firstly because you hardly ever see him, he's always hidden behind the parapet of orders he gives out to his first and second officers. And secondly, because of the principle of authority generated by the superior realm from which all captains look down on their crews, mere mortals he can fulminate at will, inasmuch as he is the master of that small island-world adrift of a boat.

The fiercest captains make you feel you are the putrid depths of a stagnant pond. The simply fierce captains ignore you. What did I know about Branco? What could I know, what was I allowed to know? These are questions I've asked myself after leaving the *Minerva Janela*, said Griffin. However, I never found out much about him, just enough for our exchange of handshakes to be warm and respectful when we said goodbye in Punta Arenas. I never imagined it would be the last time I'd see him alive. But in the time I spent under his command, I immediately understood that everything possible is done on board ship to protect the figure of the captain inside his steel carapace.

How strange it felt, when I look back, to be subject to the unchallengeable orders of that evasive man who finally hung himself from a rope! marvelled Griffin for a few seconds. One has to struggle against oneself in order not to be eliminated by something I'd call erasure with consent, he continued. Nonetheless, Branco was a good man, though not at all easy or accessible. From the moment I met him in Madeira, he seemed a subtly tortured man who avoided extended human contact. It was aversion rather than shyness. If he could, he'd run from meetings, birthday parties and meals. When he felt he'd spent too much time with any of us, on the bridge, in the dining room or in the map room, all of a sudden he'd turn tail and walk off without saying a word. His manner also had a subtle hint of invisibility that I found attractive. His inner clock warned him it was time to go; everything else was unplanned and happenstance. And he'd walk off.

I spoke to him at length on our brief stay in Rio de Janeiro, and for the first time not on the *Minerva Janela*. It wasn't that unusual, because I often chatted with the captain, he'd even summon me and say ironically, 'Oliver, you're a volunteer, not a sailor, don't get too embroiled. Stay here and let's talk awhile, they're working hard downstairs for much more money,' referring to the men in the engine room and those securing the containers on a day when the sea was calm and it was all quiet on board. But when necessary, he became prickly at close quarters and said nothing, we'd only exchange glances; he stayed at my side, or rather allowed me to stay by his on the bridge, in a silence that wasn't even broken by the quiet humming of

Jordao Navares, our helmsman and the captain's perpetual shadow. Afonso Branco's silences impressed me, and were so typical of a reserved introvert. On the other hand, he was quite different in Rio de Janeiro.

He told me about things that, curiously enough, were very similar to what Sarmiento de Gamboa might have experienced four centuries earlier. How little the sea and the men who sail her change, Griffin marvelled again, and how one keeps finding identical people on the sea of time, reincarnations of reincarnations, as karmic Caporale would say. Captain Branco, my captain, was a serious character who sometimes laughed like a person surprised to be freed of something that was torturing him, and when he recalled that secret, mysterious something, he readopted the stern rictus that preserved his perfect isolation. 'He carries our lives on his shoulders, and that's a burden he can't avoid, and much greater than any ghost from the past,' said Luiz Pereira one day, ironically or melodramatically, because Pereira always ended every sentence with a smile, making his escape through the imaginary door of ambiguity.

The first officer went on to say that in this respect life on board ship hadn't changed over the centuries: captains, from Ulysses to this day, bear the burden of the lives of their whole crew, lives they entrust to him as if they were children, innocent or under sentence, who come aboard, take their lives off like a jacket and hand it to him. It was the same trust and responsibility that tormented captains in Conrad's novels, as in the dog-eared, much reread copy of *Lord Jim* I saw in Branco's cabin, that tormented Branco, my captain, o my captain.

His face, said Griffin, seemed numbed by a secret mystery, and I now know, from what he said in Rio de Janeiro, that it was a horror he couldn't shake off, as if he too were a captain who had emerged from the pages of Melville: the dead he'd seen so far. Every captain seems haunted by a mystery that clouds his eyes, and generally it is death that suffuses that mystery, so I didn't think his words could be anything but metaphorical. What might Sarmiento's mystery have been, I often wondered when I watched Branco and recreated his adventures in the Straits of Magellan? Because I know what tormented him later in life, in his final years, when he had to abandon that place to its own fortunes with all the good and bad people he'd taken with him to found those phantasmagorical cities, three hundred souls abandoned by the hand of God south of everything that existed. But what was the secret mystery he kept to himself on the voyage he co-captained with Flores de Valdés?

Perhaps he was afraid they'd discover his secret automaton half dummy, half warrior, that was well hidden among his belongings, and accuse him of witchcraft again, and that that would frustrate his plans. Perhaps he was afraid of weakening and not advancing the task the emperor had charged him with, an emperor whose only sacred obsession was directed against the English. Or perhaps it was the blood of all the dead he'd known in life, the people he'd killed, because Sarmiento killed large numbers of people, in battles, in other skirmishes, in debts of honour. 'I've never met a happy captain,' Luiz Pereira told me, said Griffin. Was Sarmiento happy? Was Branco? Who is?

I was in fact with Pereira or rather saying goodbye to him, when suddenly I saw Branco on one of our rest days in Rio de Janeiro. It was evening. I bumped into him drinking in a small, luminous, bright green bar in the Belvedere. We greeted each other and he invited me to join him. Branco was middle-aged like me, perhaps slightly older, that was why there was an obvious intimacy between us, but we were never on really friendly terms, less so given he was my captain, if only for a short time, but one's captain, I now know, is always one's captain, even if one is never again under his command. I remember his bulbous nose and square shoulders; he was strong, with powerful hands, a born man of action, with short, whitish hair and intrepid eyes.

When I gazed at Branco in the Belvedere, I thought he was the spitting image of the Sarmiento I told you about the other day, said Griffin; Branco was taciturn, a man of few words who moved stiffly, as Sarmiento was described in the books I read about him. And my captain was similarly energetic and determined, rather suspicious and devious because of possible hostile moves his subordinates might make, men he never gave the option of befriending him except for the few who earned the privilege, like Luiz Pereira or Jordao Navares. Sometimes he had a wild, frightening look in his eyes, as when he quarrelled with Fernando Grande, his second-in-command, who mistakenly took the boat too far southwards.

The Krupa incident had also affected him. He was vulnerable to me, and wary, because he knew I'd guessed that he and Grande had given the Serb a real beating. That was why he'd blurted in my face: 'He deserved it, didn't he?' I tried to pretend I didn't really understand what he meant, but then he arched his eyebrows and clicked his tongue in annoyance. He spoke loftily: 'The Serbian sniper . . . Adan Krupa . . . deserved it.' I said nothing, even though I agreed he deserved it. What really goes on in the mind of the brave and the bold? The question suddenly came to me and I asked my captain in the Belvedere. 'Do you think I'm brave and bold?' asked Branco. I don't know, I said, I think you've no choice in your position. 'And what's brave about smashing up a bastard's face? I've more in me than that,' said Branco. I think he liked the idea I'd broached the subject. Then he said: 'Pereira knows all there is to know.' Naturally, the first officer had spent many years with him, on a number of boats and on every sea, working for Dutch, Canadian, American and Portuguese companies, and he must sometimes have seen him prevaricate before reaching a crucial decision. Naturally, I thought, Pereira knows his hardness is only a mask. 'I'm not brave, Oliver, because I'm human and am afraid of death. But I'm not a coward either. Otherwise nobody would trust me with a merchant ship, would they? Then he talked about the dead people in his life. They filled him with horror.

'Do you think a brave man is frightened by the dead?' he asked. Of course he is, I replied, said Griffin, particularly if he sees them all the time. 'I see them all the time,' Branco added rather dejectedly. Many a night the image of the dead, an image from childhood, that brought an absurd, childhood panic in its wake, woke him up when they appeared. I must admit his strange confession surprised me, Griffin said, but I continued to listen, hanging on every word, noticing how Branco's contorted mind was relaxing. What deaths had he seen? First came one he hadn't seen, he told me. Mario, his twin brother, who starved to death when he was a few months old because his mother couldn't feed him and had decided only one of the twins would survive; she didn't choose Afonso, but Mario, whose lungs bellowed from the cradle. But their mother mixed them up, for some reason, and fed Afonso as if he were Mario and left Mario with no food thinking he was Afonso. Branco discovered all this at the age of twelve, when his mother, on her deathbed – 'Another death I did see' he said – confessed to him in order to relieve her conscience. He was living someone else's life, because he'd always known his mother had mistakenly chosen him, and guilt pursued him. As if it were something I myself had experienced, I then perfectly understood Branco, said Griffin, when he occasionally told the small group on the bridge that he 'lived far from the truth in order to be a living lie'. What did he mean? I remembered Li Pao, who'd say something similar on our ardent nights of ambiguous love in Barcelona. Or did I stand in front of a mirror, after making love to him/her one night, repeating that phrase ad nauseam: 'O to be someone else.' 'To be someone else' – is that a phrase we all carry within ourselves and utter very occasionally, to a select few . . . ?

While Branco was telling me the random story of his first survival, I recalled, said Griffin, a parallel incident in Sarmiento's life: he invented himself an imaginary brother, for some unknown reason, to the point that he believed he *had* really lived at some stage; Sarmiento always stated, according to his biographers, that a brother existed who'd lived before he was born, and who died early in childhood. He was known by the same name, Pedro, and when he was born, he was given the name of the deceased firstborn. In other words Sarmiento never had a name. He also lived the life of another, a life that wasn't his, possibly even lived his life twice, because Sarmiento, like a good wizard, believed his brother's spirit was reincarnate in himself and dictated his deeds and feats: he was convinced they were deeds and feats someone had already experienced, and hence subject to destiny's rigid law. That was why he believed so strongly in the settlements on the Straits, and that was why, when they failed disastrously, he became sad rather than despairing, because he'd fully assumed that his life had already been lived once.

But more deaths awaited Branco, the ones that brought the horror peopling his nights that he was confiding to me in the bar at the Belvedere. He told me he watched his father, another sailor, die in his arms, when they were shipwrecked after their boat capsized. And worst of all: the death of his son, aged seven, the day before he reached Portugal, after a long trip from Indonesia on an oil tanker. He arrived in time to see the child in a shroud, on a white sheet in a Lisbon hospital, after meningitis had snatched him from among the living. Graciela Pavic and her children Pablo and Gaetano came into my mind. I could see their little faces as I had seen them in a photo she sent my grandfather, said Griffin, one of the photos in the letters I took from his dressing room, where Graciela's children appeared dressed very elegantly. How the photos of the dead look like photos of wax statues, Griffin repeated a phrase Captain Branco had said on that occasion in the Belvedere after he'd taken the photo of his dead child from his wallet: the photo of a child in a winding sheet, in a shroud that only left his face visible; all else was bandages. He really looked like a wax doll, I told him, Griffin said, like all the dead, and I wondered if they'd painted eyes on those closed eyelids whether he'd be a worthy automata, but with a human face.

Then I wondered if it was true that the dead obsessed Branco if he was capable of carrying a photo of his dead son in his wallet, and not of his son when alive and smiling. Perhaps that was why he told me about those other deaths: friends lost at sea, who filed through his head one by one, a captain he'd had and admired, Getulio Costa, the father of Paulinho Costa, 'my last dead man', as Branco said. I think nobody on the *Minerva Janela*, let alone Luiz Pereira, ever understood how the death of that young man constituted such a personal tragedy for Branco, at least not until the captain, o our captain, took his own life in Punta Arenas.

'In a way I felt that the old, deceased Getulio Costa,' said Branco, 'had entrusted him to me from the world beyond,' and he, Branco, had failed to fulfil that cruel commitment. Paulinho

Costa's death, the stupid accident that ended his life, was important to Branco, intolerably so. It was a crucial incident – as Pereira recognised later in Punta Arenas the day Branco hung himself – that sunk him into a depression he never recovered from, because Branco knew the young electrician well and loved him like a son. He was a family friend, he'd been to their children's christening, a couple whose photo he also showed me in the Belvedere saying, 'I took it from his wallet', even his wife was a niece, his sister's daughter.

He never got over that death and lived in fear of another impending misfortune. He told me that impassively in Rio. He coexisted with that strange obsession. 'We all have obsessions. You have your island,' he told me, 'I have the people who died on me at sea.' A few days later, en route to the Falklands, the newly recruited Caporale seemed to save him from such fears. Caporale 'the Magnificent', as he dubbed him, rescued him from that silent despair where Costa's death had plunged him, at least for a few weeks, by telling him about the transmigration of souls. Carporale promised that Paulinho Costa's karma, when he breathed his last, must have been reincarnated in another being, perhaps someone who'd be in Punta Arenas when we arrived there, someone whose presence only he, Branco, would recognise. That possibility was the only thing that suddenly made him human, like the rest of us. He took a great interest in all that, Caporale said, who, of course, seemed happy he'd accepted him as a member of the crew. 'That was a good decision,' he told Pereira. Caporale also talked to him about the existence of extrasensory mediums. He'd been a medium more than once.

It gave Branco a bittersweet hope that was short-lived. He soon became depressed and tormented. Then, of course, said Griffin, there was his pride, the pride every captain displays because it invigorates and sustains his crew's high morale. 'Nobody else will die on Branco' was written on a partition in the boat. He'd said that himself or had been heard to say it, so Greene related, just before we reached Punta Arenas, when he gazed into the pitch-black night and talked to himself, addressing his words to the sea breeze. Branco had read Sophocles whose works, all underlined, were to be found in his cabin. 'When one can't find a reason to be damned, one must look homewards and talk of failure,' Branco said, according to Griffin. But Sophocles had never said such a thing.

30

SARMIENTO AND FLORES' EXPEDITION SAILED INTO a very different Rio de Janeiro to the bustling, sensual city the *Minerva Janela* left behind with Branco's confessions floating on the breeze. The small city hidden between the peaks depended on a rudimentary port and stone jetty by the beaches, with the settlements of Campos to the north and Santos to the south, a string of scattered hovels, a kind of elongated neighbourhood, where they grew brazil wood. They moored there on 24 March 1582, as torrential rain streamed down the steep, leafy hillsides creating waterfalls in the middle of the jungle. The city authorities were there to greet them on the shore, as they were now subjects of the same Crown.

The haughty, despotic Flores scorned them and refused to come ashore until the storm subsided, and left the welcoming committee waiting in the downpour. Once they did land, he ordered Sarmiento to prepare to winter there for eight months, flourishing a letter from the Court instructing him to do so in order to avoid building cities in the Straits in the harsh southern winter. The decision to stay went against the advice of Sarmiento and his pilots, who were afraid voracious shipworm might consume the insides of their vessels, which is finally what happened.

Sarmiento countered by suggesting they sail down to St Julian's Bay and winter there. But Flores refused even to contemplate that possibility. 'We shall stay here. That is my last word. The king's orders must be carried out and I will kill anyone who disobeys,' the admiral declared angrily.

Those were indeed dreadful months. All the infirm died, and many others, in their hundreds, passed away after contracting new diseases that made them writhe in pain, foam at the mouth and bleed profusely. Their boats turned to dust, and their supplies, which were in a bad state or non-existent, soon vanished. Sarmiento discovered the boxes had been rifled as had sacks of flour, rice, maize or seeds, that were so vital for establishing settlements, and had been replaced by ridiculous objects, dozens of shoes, doublets, felt hats, coloured glass baubles to trick the Indians, oil candles for light or coal to make fires, against the cold they were expecting to find.

The thefts increased with impunity, to such an extent that the settlers were soon stripped of all their goods and chattels. They now had nothing to sustain life in the Straits of Magellan, and would have to manufacture everything in the wild, from scratch. Apart from these setbacks, they had to deal with moral corruption and lax behaviour, squabbles and duels between soldiers who spent the time on their hands betting or playing cards and fighting to the point of creating rival gangs that engaged in open warfare, like the bloody battle on the Rio beach that left many maimed, one-eyed, and dead. The upheavals were exacerbated by settlers from nearby cities, who were intent on revenging damage done to the families they'd reared, daughters who'd been raped or sons slaughtered for the sheer fun of it.

Flores wasn't able to halt the battles his officers and soldiery joined, and Sarmiento was the only one who succeeded in halting the butchery of Spaniards against Portuguese by intervening sword in hand. On one occasion, a group of soldiers wrought revenge by decapitating flocks of goats that were being kept for the future settlements. Sarmiento was driven into a fury by Flores' passive attitude. That same day he ran angrily to the house where the admiral was staying, knocked on his door and demanded Flores come down. As soon as he appeared, Sarmiento took out his dagger and wounded him in the arm, a mere scratch to incite him into a duel. Flores resisted, although his blood was boiling, because he knew Sarmiento was a better swordsman, but the latter went on insulting and cursing him. The two men finally fought it out in the street with everybody watching. Flores' hatred and Sarmiento's rage grew as they clashed swords, and Sarmiento sliced an ear and a piece of cheek off his opponent. The gushing blood meant they stopped fighting, and while several men carried Flores away, Sarmiento skewered the ear and threw it to the dogs. Flores couldn't try to arrest his rival, since he'd agreed to fight quite freely, and in any case nobody would have arrested Sarmiento. He was a man they respected. So they decided to kill him, said Griffin.

A captain by the name of Suero planted the poisonous, criminal idea in Flores' head. 'With Sarmiento dead, there'll be no need to go to the Straits,' he told Flores, who smoothed his beard and thought how he could easily resolve all his problems by eliminating the hated captain. They hatched a plan. They'd mount a lightning attack at night. Suero would lead the way and stab him in the heart while the others pinned him down. 'Do it quickly, very quickly,' stammered Flores, delighted by such a simple solution. They'd have to catch him unawares or asleep, perhaps when he was entering his house by himself, and not accompanied by his only friend, Antón Pablos, Suero suggested, said Griffin. They'd then cast the body into the sea from a nearby reef and blame it on an Indian attack or on a soldier Sarmiento had insulted taking his revenge.

Flores backed the plan saying he saw the hand of God in the stratagem, since in their months in Rio the rumour about Sarmiento working in alliance with the Devil had prospered. The myth about his Peruvian past and trafficking in talismans was on people's lips once more. At dusk on the appointed day, Suero and three men waited to ambush him in a courtyard near the Church of the Conception, at one end of which was the house where Sarmiento was lodged. A fourth man trailed him all day and when he saw the captain was on his way home, he overtook him in the dark and forewarned Suero and his men. But their attack didn't go to plan. Real life always messes up, commented Griffin. True enough, the three men who hurled themselves at Sarmiento did catch him by surprise, but he fought one off, swivelled round, pushed a second man away who fell backwards, and that gave him time to take out his dagger, turn round and thrust it into the third man's stomach. The wounded man's screams paralysed the other two. Blaspheming and shouting, Sarmiento unsheathed his sword and before they could react they were both dead in the courtyard. Suero's whimpers made Sarmiento turn round to find him up against the wall with his hands over his face, scared, shaking and begging for mercy. He grabbed him by the neck. When Sarmiento saw it was Suero, a man close to Flores, he looked him in the eye and tried to discern his expression, but the dark prevented him seeing the slightest glimmer. He showed no compassion and his anger grew. The seconds passed slowly and the only sound was the two men's hostile breathing, as Sarmiento confronted Suero. The air was still. The two men sweated. Suddenly Sarmiento made a move and placed the point of his sword on the throat of his cowering adversary whose sword was still sheathed. For an instant, Sarmiento thought he might give him a chance to take it out so they could fight, but rather than do that, while his head contemplated that noble alternative, his hand slowly pushed his sword in until a third had penetrated the trachea of Suero, who gasped hoarsely. At dawn a servant took Flores a sack containing the heads of the four would-be assassins.

November came and they finally left Rio. The hostility between Flores and Sarmiento meant their voyage to the Straits was peppered with small violent incidents between rival supporters, but open warfare only erupted once they disembarked on Catherine's Island. During their stay on the island to replenish fresh water stocks and repair damage done to the ships, there were constant squabbles and skirmishes that led to deaths on both sides.

On one ill-fated day tension rose when a handful of Sarmiento's men sank a boat belonging to Flores' fleet in the largest cove on the island. The admiral retaliated by ordering the beheading of a number of settlers on spurious charges of robbery. For his part, Sarmiento cut off the hands of several of Flores' sailors. The admiral reacted by impaling another seven settlers. Cannon-fire from Sarmiento's ship destroyed two of Flores' frigates. Each side wanted to eliminate the other, said Griffin; Sarmiento didn't need Flores to establish his cities and Flores saw Sarmiento as the obstacle to his triumphal return to Spain as a glorious conquistador.

Flores' men had a stroke of luck and managed to get their hands on weapons, gunpowder and the majority of the supplies belonging to Sarmiento's people, and on the admiral's orders a good number of his supporters were left behind on land, where later, as Sarmiento de Gamboa told Raleigh when he was the Englishman's prisoner, they were devoured by Caribbean Indians, 'eaters of human flesh'.

Flores ordered the arrest of Sarmiento and his loyal followers, and the winds began to blow so hard against them that their vessels lost masts and started drifting, and, after a week of struggling with the merciless westerly wind, a wall of gusts that threatened to sink the whole fleet, the admiral ordered them to turn back and sail northwards. A few months later they were back in the gulf of Santos, near Rio, where he locked Sarmiento securely in a dungeon. Between settlers and soldiers, his contingent had been reduced to around two hundred and fifty men, thirty-five women and fifteen children.

Sarmiento eventually threw himself into rebuilding his expedition once Flores decided to return to Spain convinced that voyage was a lunatic adventure that could only bring failure and destruction. Flores wanted everything in his favour and promised to pay good money to whoever followed him and deserted the voyage to the Straits, but he failed to persuade the settlers to turn back. What country could they return to? A man's country is his heart, said Griffin. Sarmiento had written as much at the start of this adventure, had even ordered the words to be cut into the main mast of his vessel, and that same message went out from his dungeon, via Antón Pablos, and bore fruit. The hearts of those on his side belonged to those new lands, however arid they might be, because their hearts had been veritable deserts in the mother country.

They all stayed. Better luck didn't await them on the other shore, and they couldn't have imagined worse calamities. Flores, on the other hand, went without burying an ear he never found or repairing his face, Griffin joked. They set Sarmiento free, to much enthusiastic cheering, but it made little difference: his minuscule belongings and the small number of people accompanying him were themselves a prison without bars. They began to experience endless tribulations. Diseases ravaged them, hunger set in as the impoverished settlers consumed their scant supplies, and the Brazilian settlement began to grow even more hostile, sick at having that wretched crowd on their doorstep. Sarmiento had lost everything. He had lost tools, weapons, artillery, the officers who should command his soldiers and the engineers who should build the forts.

Only the automaton remained, said Griffin, which Sarmiento discovered to his surprise that he'd forgotten about completely, to such an extent he didn't know where he'd put it, since his belongings had moved around so much. When he saw Flores set sail for Spain, he was afraid those same belongings might be travelling with him. Fortunately, however, the big chest appeared, locks intact, the android asleep, oblivious to the vicissitudes its owner had suffered. Nonetheless, Sarmiento couldn't prevent the fear of the inconceivable horrors awaiting them in the Straits from haunting everyone.

They tried not to think about it, or believe it would be like that, but their fantasies ran riot. They felt terrified, began to despair of any new promised land, and many preferred to flee into the Brazilian jungle, to inevitable death, or so the locals said. Then a cunning deceit struck Sarmiento: he invented the idea that he possessed a secret weapon, on the king's orders and with the king's endorsement.

It was a fabulous mechanical warrior who'd protect them from all evil, because their enemies, be they human or devils, would see it and be panic-stricken, given that the mechanical warrior was half human, half devil. Sarmiento ordered it to be taken from the chest and placed on a stone pedestal on the esplanade in full view. He activated the strange device invented by Melvicius and, thanks to a wind that unexpectedly blew up, the automaton began to move its arms, head and fingers. The face etched on its head inspired terror because its features were so horrible.

For the only time in its long existence, in front of those settlers, the automaton displayed its whole range of movements, face, arms, head and fingers that were the reason for its invention in the first place, movements it repeated time and again, in an endless cycle that fascinated those who saw a dummy that size rehearsing its tricks. Sarmiento set it going several times. It wouldn't stir again for centuries until Graciela Pavic restored it and made it her lover in Punta Arenas.

Sarmiento convinced everyone, except the handful of Franciscan friars who'd stayed on with the expedition, he showed the automaton as a talisman or fetish rather than a machine of war. He stood next to the automaton and exhorted his people to prepare the boats they'd bought from the settlers with Sarmiento's own capital and stock them as best they could. Hope was born anew and they cheered Sarmiento. They adored the new Golden Calf, which is what Melvicius's strange machine now was.

Captains Andrés de Viedma and Diego de la Rivera stayed with Sarmiento and presented their weapons to the automaton in a weird ceremony in which they swore oaths of loyalty to their new commander, that peculiar being who perpetually repeated the same movements. Charged with new energy, the settlers caulked the remaining ships, loaded all the provisions they managed to get from the settlers, all the cows, goats, chickens, sheep and turkeys they could buy, and sorrowfully left a handful of dying colleagues behind in Rio because they'd never survive the risky voyage now awaiting them. They sailed off once again to the entrance to the Straits in their heavily loaded vessels on 2 December 1583, a destination they reached two months later.

Unexpected, ferocious currents greeted them when they arrived that shook the boats as if they were made of cork, and they tossed, heaved, and filled up with water from waves that lashed down and swept many men overboard. A number of settlers were drowned on the three days they tried unsuccessfully to enter the Straits. Two boats sank within sight of the coast amid terrible cracking and shattering of wood, to the despair of the others who could do nothing. Those perilous seas and the fact they found it impossible to anchor made everyone on board shudder anxiously and the idea that the voyage was cursed resurfaced. The Franciscans spread the word that Sarmiento's automaton, far from protecting them, was leading them straight to Hades, because it was the fruit of a pact with the Devil, engendered by the union of a machine and a witch, such was the tale they invented for their ingenuous listeners, said Griffin. 'We must get rid of that monster right away! It displeases God and that's what he is telling us! God wants no false idols!' some shouted from the *Trinity*, the vessel where Sarmiento stood on deck. 'Into the sea with it, into the sea with it!' Others exclaimed their support and applauded the initiatives of the friars to throw that creation of Satan into the sea. 'It can only bring us misfortune! We will never survive with that idol on board!' bawled the Franciscans.

The mutiny exploded on *La Trinidad* when a strange phenomenon occurred, something unparalleled in those parts. At the very moment the rain stopped, the winds abated and the sun reappeared, a light of hope amid the thick, dark clouds, a great noise resounded, like a huge thunderclap, and lightning struck the *María*, killing a child on the spot. Everyone interpreted that terrible event as a pointer to future tragedies and voices were raised demanding the captain's head or the automaton's destruction.

Seeing there was the risk of another riot, now they were so close to reaching their destination, Sarmiento thought the best course of action to pacify the rebellious spirits would be to pretend to throw the chest with the automaton overboard. Helped by his friend Antón Pablos, who hid the automaton in a barrel he sealed with black pitch, Sarmiento put his own armour and helmet in a sack, and, before sealing the chest with the sack inside, ordered everyone on deck and asked one of his sailors to feel and half open the sack to verify that the hated automaton was really inside.

His ploy worked, and the man chosen to verify the contents was so terrified that direct contact with the diabolical figure might strike him dead as had happened the day before with the poor child, he didn't notice a substitution had been made, and simply pummelled the sack with his fists and heard a metallic sound. He immediately nodded to everyone and a band of sailors quickly shut the chest, and threw it overboard: they didn't want it with them one minute more.

The following day, spirits had been calmed by the figure's disappearance, even though the storm continued, and they succeeded in disembarking on the Cape of Eleven Thousand Virgins at the northern tip of the Straits. Sarmiento decided they should walk overland as far as they could, as long the storm took their ships out to sea. Survival was possible ashore; the sea, in its present state, implied certain death. Everyone agreed to risk going along the coast and even felt enthusiastic about setting out, now they thought the automaton no longer existed.

As soon as soldiers and settlers had disembarked with all the supplies, munitions and animals they could carry, including the barrel where Antón Pablos had hidden the android, Sarmiento placed a cross on a small hill after he carried it up on his shoulder, and when he'd erected it, they all sang the hymn 'Vexilla Regina' around the mound, raising a white handkerchief on the cross as their standard, congratulating themselves that they had finally reached the promised lands. But the territory awaiting them was barren, frozen as a rock, without a single path. They started walking north-westwards, into the interior, always keeping the coast in view, whipped by a blinding wind that cut deep as if it were jagged edged.

31

AFTER WALKING NORTHWARDS FOR SEVERAL DAYS, Griffin continued, twelve hours a day without a break, they made a halt close to the entrance to the Straits, near the First Narrows, to be relatively near the ships they'd left in the ocean still fighting the winds in their attempts to enter the Straits. Men, women and children were hungry and exhausted, but they prayed and gave thanks to God that they were still alive. While they walked in single file dragging the few belongings they'd disembarked behind them, they spared a thought for those who had died since they left Spain two years before.

The place where they stopped was as keenly whipped by the winds as the many others they'd abandoned or were to see, but Sarmiento had glimpsed minimal signs of life and his visionary mind intuited the future, growing city relishing the streams slipping between the rocks, the newly green shrubs with their red and yellow fruit, name unknown, and the reed beds on the side of a high hill that blocked their path. That stump should have forced them to take a diversion, but didn't, because Sarmiento spotted to his right a curiously shaped expanse of pastureland where their few remaining animals had instinctively rushed. The place was extensive and shadowy but habitable and sheltered by small mounds near the high hill that acted as a natural barrier against the incessant gusts. Sarmiento decided to invest himself there and then with all the honours and trappings of a governor, a title the king gave him for when he found a place where he could act as one. He took possession of those lands on behalf of his sovereign and founded the city he called Name of Jesus.

After countless setbacks and disasters, the settlers had finally reached their destination and would now raise with great hopes what was to be their home and, shortly, ay, their grave, said Griffin. They were ecstatic, if only briefly so, when two days later the one hundred and ninety-three settlers shouted and cheered to see their ships sail along the coast. They had returned and been able to sail into the Straits. A radiantly calm, sunny day welcomed them and they all saw that idyllic peace in nature as an omen of the happy future awaiting them. Interpreting events as omens telling us what we want to hear is a cruel habit, said Griffin, because we always brush out reality and jump to the wrong conclusions.

That wonderful day when the ships anchored in Name of Jesus after sighting the bonfires and jubilation on land, was merely a practical joke played by fate, a snare set by the Devil who resides on the doorstep to happiness, because *La Trinidad*, the ship carrying most of their goods and victuals, split in two when it foundered on the rocks on the coast and in no time many men and much food were lost. The day's bright sun was dimmed by the harsh conditions these poor people would have to endure for the rest of their lives, who were already given up as dead by that time at Court where Flores de Valdés had finally arrived, describing the fraudulent Sarmiento as a rebel and apostate to anyone who cared to listen. But the king had only thoughts of England and what he believed to be its absolute vulnerability. The old idea of the automata, brave Sarmiento and the fortified straits were shadows and echoes from the past in his melancholy mind.

But life, as always, opened a way forward. In his capacity as governor, Sarmiento charged Captain Andrés de Viedma with the administration of the city. He was a man who'd been loyal from the start, laconic, tough and well intentioned in what he did, as eyewitness accounts testify that I and even Graciela Pavic had access to, Griffin continued, but as a leader he lacked guile and courage. Sarmiento ordered him to start building the city at once. Viedma's first act was to make a high, resistant cross from tree trunks and lianas and paint it black, then erect it on the site of the church they began to build forthwith and which sheltered all the city's inhabitants while the rest was under construction. Sarmiento ordered another different cross to be erected in the middle of the open space that was now transformed into a public square, with a large column and centre surrounded by an outer fence where a grid of streets and buildings was sketched in. It would be a robust cross too, but one that was neither painted nor polished, where the executed would hang by their feet for all to see for three days. It was the gallows. Builders began to make long adobe bricks, blacksmiths improvised rough forges where they manufactured nails and pinions, quarrymen made slabs and foundation stones, carpenters extracted planks from tree trunks, and everyone helped dig out the furrow where the sharp pointed trunks of the palisade would be inserted.

But spirits were downcast after a few days when the adobe walls collapsed, because of the bricks' weak consistency, and because they'd salvaged little material from civilisation for their house building. They improvised shacks and cabins out of branches and poles tied together with ropes made from local vegetation and pieces of cloth sewn together. The only building that seemed to endure was the church; all the others were fragile and unstable, roofed over with reeds that let in water and the cold. They soon lived like frozen, shivering animals. In the meantime, the building programme was the responsibility of Frenchman Gaspar de Saint-Pierre, a Paris architect and adventurer, wanted by the law in his own country, which he had been forced to flee on charges of obscenity and rape. Saint-Pierre was over-optimistic and it was obvious he'd miscalculated the dryness or quality of the wood or even the resistance of the stones the quarrymen chipped off rather than cut. They faced the additional grave problem of the tools that had been lost in the storms and shipwrecks they had suffered, or simply been forgotten in ports, or more recently and much worse, as they soon discovered, replaced in their boxes by useless objects, such as tin plates or leather saddlebags. Saint-Pierre finally fashioned these plates into tools that all the settlers could use.

Everyone helped to build the city, but the city still didn't exist after a month and a half. They made a big fence from sharp-pointed logs to keep out animals or Indians who shot lethal arrows; a church with a bell; a weapons store; a shelter for the animals; a field where they sowed beans and vegetables, another set aside for vines and a third for quince; all the rest were ramshackle wooden cabins, with roofs made from branches and sails. Once the settlement had assumed a very basic shape with houses and alleyways, Sarmiento walked out one morning along the streets, some of which were paved with quarried stone-slabs and felt he was the new Ulysses, undertaking the new Homeric Odyssey, that one who had founded Mexico, according to the peculiar theories he'd believed ever since he'd served in Flanders, and perhaps because an old wound was beginning to smart in his skinny body, his obsession revived and made him believe he had now entered the annals of history, a hero with fame and glory at his fingertips. How far from the truth! exclaimed Griffin.

The Indians, who were far from being the peaceful beings Sarmiento thought they were, didn't help the building work because they started to harass the sentinels at night and the settlers during the day, when they risked going hunting. The governor created posses of explorers who searched the region to find food and locate where the natives were living so they could eliminate them. He remembered how many he'd slaughtered in Peru and how easy it was to do that with a few men and plenty of cunning. The first to return from those patrols were the ones who went to the coast. When they came back, they warned of the ferocious Indians they had met: they killed them all, but lost a few Spaniards. They also brought back a bounty of fresh food, after killing a hundred seals and fishing away from the shore. Given how things had developed, Sarmiento postponed building the fortress planned by Spanoqui. He found everything disappointing, puny and ridiculous, but he knew in his heart, and that was his strength, said Griffin, that he was putting all his energy into creating the foundations of what would one day be a great city like Athens.

The bad weather started, the temperatures were icy and his people wore rags, tattered doublets, and had no adequate clothing or blankets for night-time, no tallow for candles, no protection against the elements. Sarmiento decided to salvage what he could from *La Trinidad*, the boat that had run aground near the city, its keel open and split down the middle, so that half of the vessel now lay on the sea-floor, along with most of its cargo. This was something he'd anticipated from the start. He knew about such things, he had visited libraries in Rome and Verona and, when the Antonellis had thought up the idea of the chain to close down the Straits, he'd started to study on his own account the possibility of building fortresses in the middle of the sea, with foundations that floated if they couldn't reach the bottom.

He worked out a diving system, something he intended trying himself and had brought the necessary materials from Spain. Deep-sea diving fascinated Sarmiento as much as the impossible adventure of Ulysses reaching the New World. He was fascinated by the idea of being able to walk along the bottom of the sea as one walks on land, and of seeing the whole underwater world pass by at eye-level. Audaciously, he made his own suit, like the ones he'd seen in engravings in the Grassos' library in Verona, and decided to dive down and find the remains of half of *La Trinidad*. The other half was on the reefs in the First Narrows, its whole cargo lost, a mass of splintered wood lashed by the waves that was useless even as firewood. Sarmiento found among his belongings that had miraculously survived all those years the drawings he'd copied from originals by John Taisner de Hainault and Leonardo da Vinci in the Grasso family's library. He needed them in order to recreate the hollow diving suit. The preparations took him several days, because he had to tool very delicate hides that could withstand very close, double stitching, and in those latitudes they'd only succeeded in doing that with seal skin. In the meantime he'd been tempted, Griffin said, to use more ancient diving methods he'd also copied from a drawing by Junelo: a bell the top of which contained an air-chamber. But they didn't have big enough bells or materials to make them to hold a man, let alone to allow a man to move across the sea bottom inside it. He rejected that option and spent hours, if not days, scrutinising his drawings.

He wanted to understand them, embed them in his brain, understand each step, intuit what was difficult to develop, explain rationally what was mechanically possible in the sketches and what was simply fantasy. In turn, the drawings reproduced the artefacts the Roman Vegetius had imagined in his *De Re Militari*, said Griffin, that I saw in Mario Praz's rancid house-cum-museum that reeked of death in every corner. One drawing showed the profile of a head in a glass globe sealed with bandages and straps around the area of the neck to stop water seeping in and preserve air in the globe for as long as possible. Another was of a cage where a man, in a suit without any visible seams, enters the water wearing the same globe on his head. In yet another a leather helmet rather than a glass globe surrounds the whole head except for a little glass window over the eyes with a long, thick leather tube sticking out from the mouth to bring air from the surface. A belt carrying lumps of lead or stone is tied around the suit, as a form of ballast, and another of cork or wineskins, for when it is time to come to the surface.

When the diving suit was finally completed, Sarmiento decided he'd be the first to go down. It was the most hopeful, curious episode so far in all that had happened in the history of the Name of Jesus colony. All the settlers walked the kilometre from the city to the reefs on the coast, to Punta Delgada, where the remains of *La Trinidad* had washed up. It was a Sunday in mid-April, a foul, gusty day with intermittent, violent downpours when the northern shore was lined by men and women, some embracing, others shivering, all waiting expectantly.

On the shore, Sarmiento tottered around with the help of three men while he ensured the pane of glass set in the large leather hood was well stuck down with resins and turpentine glue. As he looked up, which meant leaning his whole body back, the figures of his compatriots seemed lifeless: it was an unreal spectacle, and he had a fleeting vision of what that formidable army of automata, the dreamchild of Transilvano, might have looked like if they'd ever been installed on those or similar cliffs. One of Sarmiento's helpers, his friend Pablos, rolled a large tube around his body like a gigantic trunk to carry air to the diver's face.

Come to think of it, deep-sea divers also put in an appearance when Graciela Pavic's family vanished, said Griffin in the bar of the Carlton where he was recounting his infinite tale on that occasion. I read about them in the letters she sent to my grandfather. They appeared a few days after the boat went down, that summer's day in 1918, when the Mayor of Punta Arenas decided to salvage the bodies of Arturo Bagnoli, little Pablo and Gaetano. As on that Sunday morning when Sarmiento was about to go for a walk into the sea, lots of bystanders were idling on the shore of Catherine's Bay. Graciela stared distraughtly at the two divers contracted by the mayor with their frogmen's suits and rubber tubes and about to board the small trawler that would take them a few metres out into the centre of the bay. They spent five hours on the sea-floor and went as far as they could, because the weather quickly changed and it would have been very risky to continue. One of the diver's air-tubes was severed and he had to be lifted out by the boat's crane. In those conditions, the other diver refused to continue looking for people who had been dead for days.

Transformed into a monster or jester, according to one's point of view, Sarmiento walked gingerly over the narrow shingle beach of Punta Delgada squeezed into his sealskin suit. Those next to him could only hear him panting. Scant air was coming through the tube and they thought he would faint as a result of the asphyxiating, drowning sensation weighing down his temples. At the very moment his iron-shod feet touched the water, an arrow hit him in the calf. Lots of other arrows wounded the men accompanying him and the settlers on the hillsides. Some were lethal hits and three or four men fell from the crags on to the beach. Tremendous chaos and panic followed that unexpected attack by Indians. Many ran towards the city and were wounded by what was a short-lived downpour of arrows and darts. Sarmiento couldn't decide whether he should struggle to reach the shelter of a cornice at the end of the beach, or jump into the water, but he was paralysed by the pain in his leg. Antón Pablos started to take off his hollow hood and undo the stitching on the diving suit. There were minutes of immense disorder and disarray, when shock silenced the captains and nobody took the lead or issued practical orders.

Women and children jostled in a huddle and the men looked anxiously for the places the attacks were being launched from, but found none. They finally spotted a dozen canoes coming from the south, manned by arrow-shooting Indians. Indians also appeared from the north on land with lances and smaller darts that soon became hundreds of lethal needles. The stampede back to the settlement left corpses in its wake, both children and adults, and Sarmiento's abandoned diving suit was laid out over the rocks on the beach, like the sloughed skin of a mythical animal, and was immediately engulfed by the tide.

When that happened, the Indians shouted out, cries Sarmiento and his men interpreted as gleeful. If the diver in the sealskin suit was a god disturbed by those invaders, he was now returning to waters he should never have left. To signal their victory or pacify the gods, an old Indian, the leader of those natives, as Sarmiento observed from the palisades of Name of Jesus, walked out in front of them all, opposite the Spaniards, in an act that seemed grotesque rather than solemn, and took an arrow, showed it slowly to everyone, then pushed it down his mouth and gullet, as far as the end feathers, before extracting the blood-covered object and beating his chest to the screams and howls of the Indians behind him. The old man writhed on the ground bleeding from his mouth and nostrils and anointing his body with the blood from the arrow. Then he got up, grimaced haughtily and turned round. The Indians followed suit. Sarmiento hobbled disconsolately: he had lost ten men and all hope of recovering *La Trinidad*'s cargo. That Sunday had ended tragically and despairingly for the settlers, who started to wonder whether getting rid of that automaton on the high seas hadn't been more of a curse than a blessing.

32

A FEW DAYS AFTER THE ATTACK, GRIFFIN CONTINUED, Sarmiento ordered the *María*, the only ship in a fit state, to sail further down the Straits. He filled her with enough soldiers, settlers and munitions to found a second city, as originally planned. The westerly winds once again proved to be an impassable wall and they struggled for days to stop their ship being blown out of the Straits. When the winds changed, the favourable current took the vessel to the place they had chosen on St Anne's Cape. Sarmiento was waiting for them with a gang of men who'd made the long hike overland from Santiago Bay to the end of the cape, at the foot of which they were able to moor in a small, sheltered inlet.

Sarmiento's journey had lasted almost as long as the *María*'s, two weeks, and the weather, harsh and merciless at that time of year, made progress difficult. As they couldn't make fires, they were forced to eat the raw flesh of reptiles and small animals they found, after sacrificing the seven goats they'd brought with them. They also began to eat the roots of plants they discovered, some of which were unknown, and even lethally poisonous, like the bitter root of the yellow cornflower. Lack of food was compounded by constant attacks from the so-called tall Indians, as opposed to the small ones they'd seen who were peaceful. The tall ones weren't afraid of the Spaniards and attacked them anywhere at any time of day. Sometimes a single native would rush at Sarmiento's column brandishing a spear and throw himself upon one or two soldiers screaming like a lunatic. In that kind of attack the soldiers usually killed the Indian immediately with firearms or daggers, but occasionally the Indian's spear wounded a Spaniard and even killed him.

On his expedition to St Anne's Cape Sarmiento lost five men and a woman, but they killed some thirty Indians. Both sick and healthy walked at a slow pace. One of the dying hid and waited to die he was so despondent. The rest of the column listened to his distant, agonising screams when the Indians intercepted him before death had. They heard him being tortured and could do nothing except put their hands over their ears.

Almost everybody had wet and sore bare feet, though they improvised sandals as they progressed; they were in great pain and it slowed them down. They also found some of the scouts Sarmiento had sent out weeks earlier to search for food and reconnoitre the terrain around the new cities. Some had gone mad, others had survived but were totally disoriented, and others had been tortured and cut to pieces by Indians. Sarmiento found part of their remains, human leftovers, said Griffin, and that led him to think they must be cannibal tribes.

He founded the second city on St Anne's Cape, and called it King Philip, although in the chronicles I read it's described as Royal Philip. The area was very different to Name of Jesus: it didn't have an open esplanade, but was on a small uneven plain, and the perimeter they drew to the north bordered on a windswept heath and to the south on a steep, overgrown mountain. Here too they began with the church, using mud and branches to build the walls and rough, uncut tree trunks for a roof that was a mass of tangled branches. Then they put up the gallows, hospital, forge and weapon store. The scant hundred inhabitants were split between two, untrimmed timber cabins. They unloaded several pieces of artillery from the ship and pointed them at the Straits. They were mounted on rudimentary platforms that would surely collapse as soon as the cannons moved, but they were never used in the short history of Royal Philip.

A few weeks later, the day came that Sarmiento had been most keenly anticipating, the day when he would finally implement his most secret plan. He left the city in the command of young Juan Suárez and made an apparently urgent excuse to return to Name of Jesus by sea with a handful of men. Shortly after they set sail he changed the *María*'s direction and sailed into the Straits. He was again driven by an obsession. He sailed towards the end, to Port Mercy, on the last of the islands in the channel, the so-called Desolation Island where fierce winds perpetually blew and where he thought he'd seen a glint or a being on the move and had been so startled five years before. The boat was carrying the barrel where Antón Pablos had hidden the automaton. On this occasion he was helped by favourable winds and in less than four days he again embarked in that port on Desolation Island that I see so often whether my eyes are open or shut, said Griffin.

The inlet was blasted by the polar winds that Sarmiento remembered and was slippery with ice and light snow that covered the rocks and ship's rigging, and his men's beards and blood. The harshness of that frozen, inanimate land prevented him and his band of four dragging the mysterious barrel with ropes and rollers from gathering speed. They sought out paths and tracks going up, perched on hills that opened the way to higher, even steeper ground and went inland and towards what Sarmiento thought must be the end of the island, the precipices looking down on the bay where the *Esperanza* had anchored five years ago and where the *María* should be now. In the polar storm that was raging the men couldn't see an inch in front of their noses and lost their way in banks of dense, freezing fog. They'd no idea how long they had been walking. They went to and fro, retraced their steps and advanced, the barrel careered to a halt, the hoops broke, they had to roll the barrel along, but Sarmiento realised that might damage the automaton and decided to open the barrel there and then in the presence of his men.

They extracted the automaton as if taking an iron dwarf out of the barrel. Then two men carried it. Sarmiento walked on a few metres in front trying to imagine where they were, and then looked back and was surprised to see the blurred outlines of three figures, the automaton and its bearers, like an engraving of a wounded man being carried away by his comrades at the end of a battle. They finally reached a place from where the Straits were visible. They'd wandered so far from where they thought they should be and sensed that it must be the north coast, concretely, the foothills of Cape Cut. Sarmiento watched the waters of the Straits crash ferociously against the raging South Sea at the foot of a steep incline leading to an abyss and listened to the waves roar.

He decided that was the right place to set down the automaton. Besides, said Griffin, the wind was so strong and unrelenting Sarmiento thought it would keep the automaton moving for years hence, if not centuries. He ordered them to dig a hole, broad and deep enough to take the android's cylinder base. It was an extremely arduous task in ground that was so hard it broke the daggers of the five men who finally had to use pieces of rock they'd scrabbled to find. They dug the hole and lowered in the bottom half of the automaton. They re-filled it with the earth they'd dug out and trampled it down. But something in the automaton wasn't working; the figure didn't move, did nothing, however much wind whistled through its body; its metal armour simply made a hollow echo when touched as if it were a large vase. The key part invented by Melvicius that Sarmiento had activated in Rio de Janeiro a few months ago in front of his men had disappeared or perhaps been lost or stolen. But stolen by whom and to what end?

For a few seconds Sarmiento thought the automaton had died but realised that was absurd in terms of a being that was definitely diabolical even in his terms. He decided to leave it where it was, confident the mere sight would inspire fear and doubt in anyone espying it from afar. Better if it didn't work, better if it lacked life, he muttered. Before turning round, retracing his steps and abandoning it, Sarmiento embraced the automaton instinctively and unexpectedly. Like Graciela Pavic, he felt overcome by a strange current of sudden emotion for that inert figure that looked remotely human. He hugged it as if saying farewell to a son he was abandoning in a desperate situation and would never see again. The men accompanying him glanced at each other, perplexed by their captain's behaviour. Branco would have done exactly the same, said Griffin, I'm sure of that.

Sarmiento ran his hand over the automaton's torso and felt an inscription under his fingertips. He wondered for a moment if he'd seen it on another occasion but couldn't remember having done so. He crouched down to take a closer look even though the polar wind was blinding him. Finally, with the help of his fingers, he read what was etched there:

MELVICIUS. PRAGENSIS.
HOROLOGIORVM ARQVITECTOR.
OMNIVM PRINCEPS.
HUMUNCULUS SECUNDO.

No, said Griffin, Sarmiento hadn't seen that inscription before, that revealed its author, the vain Melvicius (what if not vanity was that '*omnium princeps*', the idea that he was best), Sarmiento mused, and also betrayed the number of automata he'd made, evidently more than one.

As if it were the pentimento on an engraving, amazed he'd not noticed the letters before, Sarmiento started scratching them with the jagged edge of his dagger until they were illegible. He didn't know why, but he recognised his action reflected the scrupulous care of a thief or murderer, and understood that everything he'd done to that moment from when he'd appropriated the automaton entrusted to him by Arcimboldo behind the emperor's back was a crime, and like a crook he now nervously erased every trace of his crime. Perhaps that was why he did everything furtively, and not because he simply wanted to test the efficiency of that contraption against the English, as he deceived himself. When Graciela Pavic repaired the automaton centuries afterwards, she didn't notice the scratches that had been smoothed away, even though she caressed it like a lover.

When they descended the back of Cape Cut, clinging to each other's hands, trying to find a natural path and not slip or roll down to the end of the heath, the freezing fog lifted and left the polar wind to blow round them and batter their faces. The five men watched the day darken and a blood-red hoop eclipse the moon. The shadows that rapidly descended over the island struck fear and panic into their hearts. 'Like when Christ died,' said Sarmiento, paralysed by the phenomenon.

After reaching Port Mercy, they immediately set sail in the *María*, convinced yet again that that automaton boded nothing good for their lives. That eclipse, Griffin went on, doesn't appear in any records, it simply doesn't exist and there are no data about it: in 1584 there were no eclipses in that area of the world, that's evident enough. Perhaps fear led them to imagine it. Sarmiento and his four men swore to keep silent about what they'd done and never mentioned the automaton or the place where it was half buried. But the fact was all except Sarmiento would soon die, so it hardly mattered if their secret was divulged among the settlers in the two cities. Indeed, one of them spoke before he died but to no avail: however desperately they later searched for the automaton, led by Viedma, as if it were a talisman that could save them from hunger and illness, they would never find it in the huge expanse of the Straits, because the dying man never managed to come out with the name of the island where it now stood.

A week later, in the midst of a howling spring storm, the *María* sailed into Name of Jesus, the first city they'd founded. As soon as they arrived they dropped anchor between the shifting rocks on the sea-floor. That very moment, a fierce wind whipped the waves up several metres higher, catching everyone on shore and ship by surprise. The rotten anchor rope snapped and the vessel was swept into the Straits. Sarmiento was on board.

That savage wind was a foretaste of a savage, prolonged storm that lasted twenty-five days. In that time, the *María* fought against the elements in order to return to land, but was hit so hard by the raging sea it almost capsized on several occasions; some despairing sailors, against Sarmiento's orders, dived into the water with a small boat that soon sank with them. Their scant provisions on board were rapidly exhausted or swept away by the tempest and it was impossible to ration or keep them secure. Anguished at being swept further and further away from his men and friends, from the settlers who'd believed in him, Sarmiento discovered he was miles from the Straits, without masts and water, with few sailors and no energy. He decided to return to Brazil on what was a painful journey, since he'd been unable to bid farewell to anyone. The sea's onslaught had caught them by surprise, and he couldn't inform the settlers he'd abandoned there like so many orphans without hope or future.

33

AS THE *MINERVA JANELA* DREW CLOSE TO THE STRAITS of Magellan, Griffin thought obsessively about how Sarmiento ended his days. Perhaps it was also because I was drawing closer to the automaton, said Oliver, and that proximity caused all I knew about its history to rush to my brain. Whether in the engine room or idling on Charly Greene's plaited rope hammock, I imagined Sarmiento suffering at the hands of a cruel fate that had swept him far from his friends and the cities they'd sweated to erect. I admired him, I always had, and I tried to put myself in his shoes and inside his anguish.

A reciprocal sorrow hit me, he said, that I could only associate with memories of falling out of love – disturbing, disquieting memories. My grief at the loss of the Li Pao I never saw again or the grief experienced by Esteban Ravel when he finally realised that Graciela would never love him. That's the kind of intense sorrow I understand: moments of appalling emptiness, of malaise in one's whole body, when heart, head and stomach unite to produce a state of indescribable distress. That's how I imagined Sarmiento on the *María* en route to Brazil, how I imagined Ravel, and how I remembered myself, plunging into the void on a street in Barcelona, hovering between life and death on a big wheel in the Tibidabo fairground that I'd jumped on to help me decide whether or not to commit suicide. It was the only time in my life when there was the slightest possibility I might take my own life. I obviously didn't, Griffin smiled before continuing his *Minerva Janela* story.

That afternoon I'd left the second level of the engine room, where I'd helped Pavel Pavka to solve crossword puzzles from his soothing, giddy hammock. It was calm sailing in those latitudes and the tasks on board were routine. 'Too calm by half for this part of the summer,' said the Macedonian, said Griffin. It was the end of November when there were usually short, torrential storms in the region of the Straits. But on this occasion we experienced nothing of the sort; it was as if we'd never left the tropics. I bid farewell to Pavka until dinner time.

When I emerged via the port hatchway, I bumped into a taciturn, self-absorbed Caporale, reading a book the title of which I couldn't see. Rata, Tonet's dog, was at his side and barked at me as usual. I accompanied him to the poop, walking over the ventilation shafts two steps behind him. Amuntado was on duty at the far end of the poop deck, checking the control panels for the cold store containers. Caporale was about to relieve him. The two sailors wore T-shirts and I was in an old jacket; it was very hot and the roar of the sea blended with radio music, folk songs sung by Carlos Vives and we caught Amuntado swaying his hips as if he were dancing. 'You think that's funny, you bastards? Piss off! I love the Caribbean, Santa Marta, Cartagena and all that,' he said as the music rose and faded in the direction whence we'd come.

I decided to accompany Cheerful Caporale my friend for part of his watch. He soon embarked on what amounted to frantic activity for him. As it was dusk, the first thing he did was to switch on the red and white spotlights that signalled our position, then he communicated with the hold where Kowanana informed him of the levels in the ballast tanks, and a moment later with the bridge, where Branco told him about the small light on the propeller shaft. If it flickered, he should wait on orders; if it was out, he should run to the engine room and solve the problem. A listless Branco told him it was switched on. It formed part of his duties that evening, according to orders from Grande. Then he returned to his book. He told me it was about the transmigration of souls, a subject obsessing Captain Branco of late. 'Me-tem-psy-cho-sis,' he drawled, looking into my eyes to see how I'd react.

Caporale was in high spirits and one could say he naturally transmitted his vital energies to those around him. He saw me looking rather downcast while he performed all his tasks so dynamically. To tell the truth, said Griffin, I was staring across the grey ocean where the waves looked like a field of white, oscillating peaks. I felt hypnotised by their rhythm. Caporale's voice reached me as if from afar, although he was beside me. I shook my head and tried to wake up. He asked me if anything was amiss, and I told him the conclusion to the story of my much admired Sarmiento.

He never returned to the Straits of Magellan, despite making every effort. Heartbroken, he abandoned those settlers he'd recruited to their fate, people he knew individually by name, whose faces he'd never forget in the years leading to his own death. But Sarmiento wasn't aware that other greater suffering was in store. Initially, I told Caporale, said Griffin, from the day he reached Brazil he never stopped trying to return to the Straits, but met only adversity: the length of time the preparations took, storms, lack of money, everything blocked his way.

He spent two years on these futile attempts. He went from Rio to Bahia, where he lived for months, returned from Bahia to Rio and soon went back to Bahia and tried to embark once again. He received no news from the Straits, nobody knew anything, and no ships could have left the Straits and not been able to re-enter them like his. Worst of all, he received no news from Spain in those two years. He wrote two hundred and fourteen letters that he sent in boats heading eastwards, to everyone he knew in the courts of Madrid and Prague, the first missives being for the emperors Philip and Rudolph. But I expect they'd forgotten him by now. Who knows?

He even wrote to Arcimboldo and Arcimboldo in Milan must surely have torn up the letter, now he was retired and had only the haziest memories of a curious automaton he'd handed over to a lunatic Spaniard. Sarmiento never received a single reply, and if a reply was ever sent, it never arrived, either because the mail-boat sank or because the carrier of the missive died before reaching Brazil. He finally despaired of his attempts to raise a frigate to sail to the Straits of Magellan and left Bahia as a passenger on a ship bound for the Peninsula.

On 22 June he was returning to Spain in a Portuguese caravel that was attacked by English corsairs working for Walter Raleigh near Cape Verde. All those travelling in the Portuguese ship were taken prisoner. The pilot betrayed Sarmiento, saying he was an important Spaniard, and sold him to the corsairs. A few weeks later they landed in Plymouth and took Sarmiento to his new captor, Sir Walter Raleigh. By a quirk of fate, the two men spoke Latin, the language of their most fascinating books, and became friends, to such an extent that Raleigh freed him from the prison where he was bound and welcomed him into his home, offering him whatever luxury he desired: clothes, servants, food or saddles.

Sarmiento recounted all his voyages and related how he'd taken possession of the Straits of Magellan for Philip II, and finally spoke of his suffering, of the inhabitants of the two cities he'd abandoned there. Sarmiento and Raleigh were pure Renaissance men, said Griffin, cultured poets, soldiers and sailors. The difference was that Raleigh was successful in his enterprises and adventures and Sarmiento wasn't. Raleigh was a rich trader because he had had a monopoly on the sale of tobacco and had reached the peak of his career as a politician, when he became the captain of Queen Elizabeth I's Guard and, ultimately, her lover. In time his life would take a turn for the worse and become similar to that of Sarmiento, his new friend.

Under James I, successor to Elizabeth, Raleigh fell into disgrace and from 1603 to 1616 would test out the cold stone beds of the Tower of London; in his time in prison he wrote the six volumes of *A Historie of the World* that was highly regarded. He was beheaded in 1618 in the courtyard of the ancient palace of Westminster, said Griffin, after the failure of his second voyage in search of El Dorado. But when Sarmiento was his guest, the queen decided she wanted to meet the intrepid Spaniard who'd founded two cities at the end of the world. They spoke for an hour and a half in Latin about the automaton and his settlers. He became very emotional remembering them and relating the diving-suit episode when they were attacked by Indians. He told the queen of the old Patagonian who swallowed arrows and took them from his stomach covered in blood. She marvelled at Sarmiento's tales and showed a rather hypocritical sympathy, because she had her own reasons for being interested in her cousin Philip's failed enterprises.

Thanks to that conversation, Sarmiento was released, and on 30 October 1586 he left London and crossed the Channel. But his misfortunes continued in France, where the wars against the Huguenots were reaching their climax. He was arrested near Bayonne by the Count of Bearn's harquebusiers, the Count, later Henri IV of France, whose palace was in Pau.

Griffin paused and gulped down his remaining whisky. It just had to be Pau, he said smiling ironically, changing the expression on his face to tell me he remembered a postcard Li Pao sent from there a month after he'd abandoned him. It was the only sign of life he received from her before she disappeared totally to Taiwan. He knew what she wrote by heart: 'Would you kiss me all over my body now? All night? Every year of my life? Come then.' That's how it ended, said Griffin, with that sweet but commanding 'Come'. But he added no details, no address to go to, no return to sender on the back except for the 'Pau (France)' he'd scrawled. I'd already had one experience of going to a French city when I was in love with Fabienne, all to no avail, at best finding myself among graves in a cemetery as happened in Nantes. I never chased after Li Pao, and I regret that to this day, believe me, Oliver concluded.

He sighed and immediately returned to the story he was telling Caporale on the *Minerva Janela* during his watch: Sarmiento was taken prisoner in Pau, as I said. For three years – three years! exclaimed Griffin – his hair turned white in a dark and dismal cell in Mont-de-Marsan as he waited to be rescued by his king, a rescue that never happened. In the meantime, he wrote endless, dramatic letters, dozens of letters, begging for help for the settlers in the Straits.

Only one man survived, Tomé Hernández, a soldier from Extremadura. He recounted in Chile, after his rescue, that the year following Sarmiento's departure the deprivations became intolerable for the few inhabitants left in both cities. They were starving and freezing to death, driven berserk by the Indians' frequent attacks. Captain Viedma, mayor of Name of Jesus, agreed to abandon the city and go back up the Straits to Royal Philip with a handful of undernourished survivors tired of their endless trivial squabbles. They still found the energy to improvise two fragile skiffs that barely floated. It was a terrible voyage in midwinter for the women and children who had survived. Their misfortune increased when they capsized after two weeks of rowing against the harrowingly adverse sea and they advanced no more than one or two kilometres a day, after exhausting their puny reserves of strength.

One of the skiffs, the one carrying most of the women and children, began to take in water and sank in a few minutes and nobody managed to surface. The other skiff, with less than a dozen people on board, finally reached Royal Philip. Suárez, its mayor, didn't greet them with any great joy, because there was little to share out. After a great many arguments, a group some fifty strong, decided to string themselves along the coast, light bonfires and each man would try to survive with his own means and skills. Many opposed the plan, particularly the more frail and elderly, but in the end they divided up and spread along the coast in small groups.

They hoped a passing ship would spot the bonfires but none came in a whole year. I keep imagining Viedma, said Griffin, desperately making for the coast in that new, chaotic reality where the cities were no longer a reflection of Philip II's imperial dream in remote, accursed lands or the seed of the new Athens Sarmiento had so vehemently longed for, a man Viedma now considered a traitor because he'd forsaken them, a fatuous fraud whose name, along with those of his descendants, the captain cursed, blinded by his rancour and ignorance.

And there, on the *Minerva Janela*, while relating all this to Caporale, said Griffin, I imagined Andrés de Viedma suddenly remembering the automaton, the diabolical being they thought they'd thrown out to sea, but one of the men who'd accompanied Sarmiento on his secret voyage had told him on his death bed of its continued existence on a precipitous island on the southern coast of the Straits. When Viedma discovered the automaton had not only not disappeared but was presiding over the whole region from the top of some peak, he became obsessed by the capricious idea of seeking it out and using it as a totem. When he laid his hands on it, he'd decide whether to destroy it or not.

But Viedma never did find it, though he searched tirelessly for months, according to Tomé Hernández, said Griffin, who didn't really know what his captain was looking for, though he watched him sail from one side of the Straits to the other in a feverish, anxious state, on perilous voyages on precarious canoes. Like Graciela looking for her sons four centuries later, though she *did* find the automaton.

They spent two more winters in the most adverse circumstances. It was grim: they had no clothing, animals skins were in short supply, the cold froze them to the marrow, the wind drove them mad. Death was a slow, constant cadence. In January 1587, in the middle of summer, Viedma counted his men: eighteen left. Then, said Griffin, after a long pause I spoke to Caporale. I wanted to know if his book on metempsychosis said where suffering souls went and where souls still with hope went. Do they go to the same place? Are they reincarnated in the same way? Caporale thought such questions too elementary, but his replies were equally so and gave me the impression he was being evasive. 'Are there souls that don't suffer, that are only waiting for happiness? No, they don't exist. In every reincarnation, the new life has to assume part of the ancient suffering of the soul it is embodying as well as part of its hopes,' Caporale declared diplomatically, running his hand along Rata's back, and adding that it wasn't in his book, but he'd always known that was how it was.

Sarmiento's pain is now in the souls who later welcomed

his, in the same way that Viedma's rancour resides in his reincarnations, Caporale continued. 'Who knows? Perhaps Branco is Sarmiento?' he concluded. The Brazilian's statement caught my attention because it chimed in with thoughts I'd had days before, and that could explain the grief-stricken melancholy seeping from our captain's face, harassed as much by his dead as much as Sarmiento ever was. I am sure you're right, I told Caporale, said Griffin, drawing the outline of Desolation Island in the little pools of water on our table as he always did quite mechanically.

Tomé Hernández saw a vessel pass by St Jerome's Point. He jumped into a boat and went after it. He was exhausted when they dragged him aboard. He didn't know it then but he'd just saved his life, the only life that would never be on Sarmiento's conscience. The ship was under the command of Thomas Cavendish, the famous English pirate, who was following in Drake's footsteps and on his way to attack Peru.

Tomé Hernández, said Griffin, gave more or less this account of the events as they happened and the final end met by the settlers of the Straits: 'The English saw bonfires on the high peaks of the cliffs along the coast, near Royal Philip. They thought at first they must be Indian, but I told them they'd been lit by Spanish Christians who had founded settlements there. They should be saved because they faced imminent death. No one could resist a third winter in those latitudes. Cavendish lowered a skiff and sailed to the shore. He found the half-built forts, the dead rotting naked in wooden cabins, and an Acevedo, who'd killed someone in a fight over a scrap of food, hanging from a rope in the gallows. Captains Viedma and Suárez were sitting despondently in church and he spoke to them. They were with two other men. To the Spaniards' delight, they agreed the Englishman would take on to his ship every survivor, a total of twelve men and two women, and rescue them from that hell and leave them in Valparaíso. Captain Viedma went to gather them up. Cavendish promised he'd wait, but as soon as they were out of sight, he ordered his men to dismantle the cabins, salvage the timber that could still be used, as well as all the freshwater they found, and then returned to his ship in the skiff. Seeing there was a favourable wind and a good tide, he sailed off at top speed, leaving the Spaniards behind to watch their last hope disappearing into the distance. From the English ship I saw them pulling out their hair and screaming inaudibly because they knew they were going to die. They died shortly after, frozen, starving or killed by the Indians.' Thomas Cavendish, a sensitive pirate, was horrified by the sight of the corpses of children who'd choked on straw they couldn't swallow and called that spot Port Famine, a name it retains to this day.

'And what happened to Sarmiento?' Caporale asked, said Griffin. Several years later, Philip II deigned to pay a paltry bounty of six thousand escudos and four horses and Sarmiento walked out from the dungeons of Mont-de-Marsan. And what a state he was in! The man who emerged from the fortress entrance, though mature in years, was now elderly and toothless with white locks over his shoulders. He wandered like a ghost through the Court of Madrid hoping for a sinecure that never materialised. Two years later, on a luminous day in May in 1592, a stooping Sarmiento accompanied the emperor when he sailed his fleet into the great bay of Lisbon. He travelled in one of the ships as a result of an act of charity by the king, who took him into his service, and his only duty was to avoid getting in the way. Aroused by the hurrahs and cheers from the shore, he rushed from his cabin to see the city in all its glory. Sarmiento looked at the houses bedecked with flowers and garlands, their luminous walls gleaming in the sun on that calm, cloudless evening, a lively breeze wafting in his face and suddenly smiled, his face radiant, his eyes dazzled by that white sheet of intense light and he thought he had entered Name of Jesus, his city and future Athens, and before collapsing dead on the deck he thought that he heard them shouting his name: Ulysses, Ulysses.

34

LIKE PESSOA, I HAVE A PLURAL LIFE, AFFIRMED Griffin, looking up at the sky and sipping his whisky. A life full of forking paths as well, he added. I learned about that from someone I met in my youth, an old friend who died young – a paradox, right? – Roberto Fornos. He was very thin and shy, pathologically so. He lived in a state of intense alcoholic poisoning but was strangely gifted, though unobtrusively so, at least in the years I had dealings with him. He'd say one of the many lives he could adopt in order to be himself was that of a sober man he could call on at will and superimpose on the unpleasant, pathetic drunkard he might have been, if he'd had only one life to live and no ability to invent others.

He died young because he lived several lives he performed in front of his friends, like an actor, and the sum total represented a protracted life at thirty, his age when he was felled in a hospital toilet by a cirrhosis of the liver that was beyond redemption. When Roberto was admitted into the Ruber Hospital, a huddle of doctors gave him barely a month to live, such was the state of his liver, said Griffin, and he lived half that.

In the years we were friends, I always thought I was his best friend and confidant. I even came to think I was his only friend.

Roberto was a publisher by vocation, although he lived on a fortune he'd inherited, almost like myself, said Griffin. He then decided to tell me something very confidential, a kind of secret, and initially I thought it must be a dark, personal and taboo one, but to my surprise, he simply told me, very mysteriously, that he'd been witness to an extraordinary paranormal, or at least quite incredible, phenomenon and it had marked his life.

Apparently he'd gone out on to the balcony of his house one summer afternoon, a balcony looking over a large square in Madrid, and had seen a huge flying saucer preparing to land on the edge of the square it would easily fill. The curious vessel, or whatever, hovered in a kind of hesitant trance for a few seconds in the oppressive Madrid afternoon, and then shot up like a flash of lightning and disappeared into the heavens.

He stood and stared into the sky for a few minutes, saw only the gleaming brightness of the afternoon, and began to think it might be the revelation of a message about the future that couldn't be explained or understood in the present. Roberto described it as a natural, even everyday, occurrence, like going to the launderette or telling someone the plot of a film. I attributed the story to a familiar alcoholic hallucination, and although I didn't believe it, reasonably enough I made it plain I felt grateful he'd confided in me.

He never brought his friends together; indeed we all felt we were his one and only friend. When he died some of us began to meet other acquaintances of his, a few from the many, perhaps, because we discovered that Roberto Fornos was really promiscuous in terms of his friendships, but singly, separately, he had developed a whole art form. He'd never talked to any of us about the existence of the others, didn't even mention them. Each friend was a whole life apart, with his rites, psychologies, secrets, like the story of the extra-terrestrial revelation he'd confided to me. On the other hand, the few of us who finally met at his funeral, some thirty at most, had never coincided on the stairs in his house or in the pages of his diary, so carefully planned and secretive were Roberto's relationships: we came to our appointment with his funeral only after seeing the notice in the press. And I checked that he'd never mentioned the flying saucer story to the many I spoke to in the cemetery, the story he had related to me so carefully and ceremonially as if it were a crucial episode in his life.

Then I experienced what I call a forking path, said Griffin. Suddenly I felt something dividing off in my life: I put my friend Roberto to one side, whose story had concluded with his death, and opted for a new path that was opening up, the path of the friends of Roberto Fornos. We discovered that in fact he made each of us feel we were special, his most special friend. That day we exchanged our respective details: addresses, telephone numbers, professions, immediate and more long-term engagements, family photos, photos with Roberto (very few of us had photos with him, and they were always blurred, out of focus or frame), anecdotes, tastes and hobbies.

New friendships were created that in turn would be exclusive, intransferible, with special, even more special friends. Once again, one to one, as if it were Robertism writ large. Someone suggested an annual dinner to pay homage to Roberto and at the same time nurture the shoots of friendships that had grown there in the cemetery, on the random occasion of the death of our common friend (and we all thought the word 'common' was strange, if not insulting). Nonetheless, though an equivocal general consensus reigned, we never met as a group again.

After a time, one of those friends of Roberto, and by extension now a friend of mine, went to live in New York. His name is irrelevant, said Griffin, because I never found out any more about him, except that he was a friend of Roberto's who wished me a Happy Christmas every year, and with each card he reiterated, perhaps out of mere politeness, that I shouldn't hesitate to go and visit if I ever happened to be passing through. So on one occasion when I'd nothing better to do, I decided to accept his offer and pay him a visit. I arrived in New York on the off chance, taken by that wanderlust that has always inspired me and that brings me, for example, to Madeira today. Yet another forking path.

Much to my surprise and disappointment, that friend wasn't in town, or so they said on the telephone, and wouldn't be back for several weeks. Even so I decided to walk to his address, 40th on Madison, in Murray Hill, knowing full well he wouldn't be there, for the mere pleasure of strolling through New York with some kind of purpose. I went many times, taking a variety of routes, to the point that I transformed that phantom address into the focus of my stay in New York. I went up Park Avenue and zigzagged along Broadway. Or else went along 42nd from Times Square. Or else by subway to the United Nations building and then down Second Avenue as far as the entrance to the Queens Tunnel.

On the other hand, I spent many other afternoons in my room in the Gramercy Park Hotel, where the wallpaper exercised a hypnotic effect on me and made me feel empty-headed; lying on the huge bed, with its pink counterpane and deer motif, I'd stare vacantly at the large wardrobes in the bedroom, as if they were rooms within a room, and immersed myself in the green on the walls, drawing mental islands or trying to find fictitious islands in the blotches I could recall later.

Or else I sat by the sash window, raised it as far as it would go, and observed the dozens of anonymous windows on the backs of surrounding skyscrapers, and on adjacent buildings I could see water tanks sticking up that were the same greenish colour as the metal roofs of New York and shaped like the carcasses of short, stubby rockets, fireworks. The constant hum of the city rose up, a monotonous background music, and, enveloped in that liquid sound, my mind wandered inscrutably down channels I don't remember.

The Gramercy Park Hotel, where Lexington Avenue runs into Gramercy Park, was and wasn't a dreadful hotel. Another forking path, this time connected with taste. I've never liked what is perfect or unashamedly new. I need wear and tear, time and erosion, Griffin confessed. The hotel was antiquated, if not in a state of decay, that made it memorable, even enabled people like me to dream of other lives. In the dark bedroom, the carpeted hallway with its dark wood-panelled walls, or the dingy, lack-lustre passageways with red anti-fire alarms, I felt more invisible than ever, the invisibility of absolute anonymity, a chameleon even for the black staff who scowled as they made up our rooms.

I had a hallucination in that hotel, Griffin continued, very much in the style of Roberto Fornos and his flying saucer. I thought, or rather hallucinated, that Roberto himself lived there and had a different friend in each bedroom, who were strangers to each other, as was his wont, and that he went up and down, in or out of those bedrooms like his friendships, always as someone else. I also dreamt a lot on those nights in Gramercy. I dreamt vividly; I came out of my dreams with a heavy head, like someone scrambling out of a well or at least feeling it was an effort to wake up from that hypnotic hangover.

Another forking path: on a night like those I dreamt of Mexico. It was a strange dream that took me days to interpret. I dreamt of a house I didn't know, a staircase I climbed slowly and a landing where I turned round to look down on a sunny street that forced me to screw up my eyes. There was a snacks stall in the doorway, and the vendor offered me one that was piping hot and he smiled as he poured on Tabasco, lots of Tabasco, rivers of Tabasco.

The lift in the Gramercy corresponding to the part of the hotel where I was staying on the fifteenth floor, was in a quite sinister, out-of-the-way area of the hallway, indeed one had to walk a good distance along corridors, around bends, up and down steps, to reach it. The whole of that tortuous path was painted a peculiarly dark crimson, even the lift-doors, that were almost camouflaged.

On the right of the lift, next to the bellboys' desk, a small lamp lit up a framed photo. It was the only light in the darkness and it was almost impossible not to notice that photo: a family photo, taken in the Thirties, which one identified immediately as the Kennedys. A caption underneath said John Fitzgerald Kennedy had lived in Gramercy at the age of eleven. It was the age for forking paths, remarked Griffin. Hadn't Rudolph II stayed with his uncle Philip II in Madrid at the age of eleven, learning spiritualism and looking for the secret door to speak to the dead? Or seeing flying saucers in the imperial sky, like Roberto Fornos and attributing their existence to abstruse stellar phenomena that had fateful or happy consequences for their realms, depending on how they were seen? Yet another forking path: wasn't my grandfather Arnaldo eleven when he read *Samini Against Everyone* by Sebastian Cordelier, the book that changed his life and his name?

I remember, said Griffin, how I lingered awhile looking at the photo next to the lift. In the meantime, I let several people behind me go up to their rooms. Others came down. Even more went up. I stood and looked at the Kennedys, at the whole family, at the whole clan, smiling and defiant, numerous and by that time tragic for me. When I went up to my room I walked over to the window and entered one of those self-scrutinising moods when I lapsed into a kind of non-identity and saw myself as if I were someone else and my environment as if it were alïen to me. I thought of myself aged eleven.

Where was I living when I was eleven? Then, and only then, did I remember another forking path in my life: just like J. F. Kennedy I had also lived in a hotel at the age of eleven. It was a hotel in the Puerta del Sol in Madrid, the Hotel Navarra, where my mother and I moved a year after my father Sean abandoned us to go off with Analía Soler, or Perla Chávez as she was known in the cinema world. It was not for long, two months at most, but I remembered in New York that what caught my attention in the Madrid hustle and bustle was also the constant hum, the hum from the streets that never stopped in that city which never slept, like New York. Of course, it is impossible to compare the two. There is such an abyss, and it was particularly pronounced at the end of the Fifties, but I've always noted a distant similarity between the two cities that I associated with the noise that came from the street at any hour of the day or night.

I celebrated my eleventh birthday in the Hotel Navarra, and I think it was the first time I had a clear idea about what happened to my father (and to my mother) and where he was (and with whom). Another forking path, of course: men and woman change their men and women, their countries and cities, weather and states, likes and dislikes.

In New York my thoughts returned to my father, and it was then I understood my Mexican dream. I remembered the time I was getting on in years and went to see my retired, bored father in his caravan in Pasadena, in San Francisco. When I returned, rather than go straight back to Madrid, another forking path presented itself: I decided to extend my trip to Mexico City and go to see Analía Soler, if she was still alive, the woman my father had run away with forty years before. I discovered she'd given up her film career some time ago and had gone back to live in her country, though nobody knew what state she was in or what her means were.

I easily gained access to her coordinates thanks to an artists' agency based in Hollywood; it was as simple as making a telephone call from a call box. By the window of my room in the Gramercy, I remembered that the house and stairs that appeared in my dream were the former actress's. Why had I dreamt about that now? I delved into my memory: I'd taken a taxi in the Glorieta de Insurgentes, near the Hotel Estocolmo where I lodged for two nights, and asked my overweight taxi driver at the wheel of his Volkswagen Beetle smelling of a sweetish air-freshener to drive to 15 Loreto Square, way past the Zócalo.

I remember very little of that drive except for the dazzling light, but I do remember he drove down many streets and alleyways before stopping in a square with a barely visible number 15 on one corner: a hawker at street level sold bleaches, detergents and brooms all in the doorway, said Griffin, and in the main entrance a seller of tacos, his dark black hotplate smoking from all sides, with a pile of plastic containers for his ingredients, chicken, fish in brine, tamales, pineapple, figs, chopped tomato, onion, avocado, beans, pots of Tabasco and ketchup, a fellow with a moustache and a constant smile, held out a taco while I checked it was the entrance to number 15 from the pavement.

I turned down his taco, but I was dying of thirst, and the man had a small fridge full of soft drinks in the bottom of his cart. I asked him for a Pepsi-Cola that turned out to be warm, and drank it feeling quite nauseous as I climbed the stairs in the house. I'd not forewarned her by telephone of my imminent arrival on that day at that time. I didn't know if it would be a pleasant or unpleasant surprise for Analía Soler, or if she was still living there or even in the land of the living. As I stood outside the fourth flat on the right, I vividly remember ringing the bell and realising I was carrying a half-full can of Pepsi. I left it on one of the steps so no one would stumble over it. I'd pick it up later on my way out. I didn't, because when I left the flat it had gone.

At that very moment a mature woman opened the door, but not the old woman I was expecting. She must be seventy, I reckoned, but looked more like fifty. She was lightly made-up, her eyes highlighted and her black hair dyed and she still retained traces of a beauty that hadn't deserted her, now transmuted from a strikingly raw beauty into a savvy mix of elegance and passion. She went barefoot with toenails painted black and wore a Chinese dressing gown with a dragon motif and it flashed through my mind, quite absurdly, that I was living in a different era, in another imaginary future, making an appearance in Li Pao's house years later when she or he opened the door to me, like that, eyes painted, beauty embracing refined subtlety in a sensual silk dressing gown, with a dragon motif, revealing glimpses of a still supple body. But it was Analía Soler's voice that declared, 'Yes, I am Analía Soler.'

She let me in when I identified myself as Sean Griffin's son, but as I crossed the threshold I saw her smile in a way that could easily have expressed incredulity or revenge: a young boy always imagines the face of his stepmother transforming into a witch's when she opens the door to her fairy tale cottage bedecked with toffees and chocolates. The fact is I experienced a strange regression, a dizzy journey back through my life in that house, sitting on a shiny, threadbare horsehair settee, in a baroque sitting room that Analía described as 'Oriental'. It was plastered with photos from past eras of all manner of famous and unknown actors; Chinese vases; plastic flowers; Manila shawls; jade cages; bamboo sunshades; pagodas from Hong Kong; postcards tacked to the wall; three televisions sets standing inexplicably in a row; records scattered over tables; armchairs; chairs; hundreds of letters inside torn envelopes; Siamese cats, two real, three terracotta; and candles that had gone out leaving trails of cold wax. In that loaded atmosphere hardly softened by the scant light penetrating the lowered blinds, I felt like a child, the child I once was, the child who soon returned from the future. It was the child looking for his father, the eleven-year-old boy going to meet the woman his father fell in love and ran away with leaving everything, him included.

To tell the truth she didn't talk very much about my father. 'They're private memories, you know? Nobody then or now would want to listen to them,' she said, but sometimes she referred to him as lousy Sean, kid Sean, cocksucker Sean, fucking sonovabitch Sean, handsome Sean, strong Sean, tender Sean. She nostalgically recalled the passionate love that had bowled them over. 'That's all so long ago,' Analía commented severely, as if she'd thought that for a long time, for years, and had finally decided to accept the coldness of final defeat.

They went crazy, desperately squeezing every minute dry, never taking responsibility for the next because it might never exist. 'The future doesn't exist for lovers,' said Analía, Griffin recounted. 'We weren't running away, it was a new beginning, and when you cut adrift, you cut adrift, for God's fucking sake. If a boat leaves port, what's the point of looking back? There's nothing you can do, you're already somewhere new, where you're fated to be, because you can't go back, even though you're only a metre from dry land.'

And Analía Soler began to reel off trite images and clichés in her desire to describe running away with my father while she rummaged for something in her boxes of unsorted photos and papers: when two people want the same thing, a third person is in the way; the cock knows what the hen's after; if you climb very high you know you can kill yourself if you fall; only people who chance their arm are lucky; I asked nothing from life but he was ready to give me everything . . . And did he? I immediately thought to ask her, as I sank deeper into the shiny, threadbare settee. I didn't because she rattled on: 'For years he gave me everything. We were very happy and very famous. He talked about you lovingly and was always thinking about what you might like or what you might be doing at that moment.'

I didn't believe her, said Griffin, but that didn't matter and I didn't want to pursue it any further out of a sense of self-preservation, because I didn't want to talk about myself. The only point of my visit was to touch her like an unbeliever, to see if she were real, to find out whether the story of her life was true, to make sure she wasn't invisible, like everything else that happened to me. She finally found what she'd been looking for. She clicked her tongue gleefully. It was a letter.

'It's what I wrote to your father when I left him. It's my goodbye letter. I don't want you to read it, I only want to show it to you so you know there is a letter in which I bade him farewell because I was evil and had fallen in love with another man, a man I can't even remember now, the motherfucker. Except I didn't post it, I wrote it, and then didn't send it. I didn't put it on any table, didn't show or read it to him, I did absolutely nothing with it. I wrote it and put it away, packed my case and cleared off, without more ado,' said Analía, who immediately added: 'Love comes and goes, beautiful dawns and horrible twilights. Such is life, don't you think?'

She talked to me as if I was really a child who had to be given one final lesson or the scolding he was expecting. As the afternoon progressed our mood saddened. It was a desolate sadness. The sitting room began to seem oppressive. We stopped talking about my father and simply uttered hackneyed phrases about memories, pity and desire. Finally, she stared me in the eye with a sudden shocked expression as if she didn't know who I was, as if something had abruptly intervened to alienate her from me, and she asked me to leave. And I obeyed like a child. I left that house and that woman in her Oriental sitting room. When I shut the door I began to hear music from inside; she'd put a record on. I imagined her dancing barefoot by herself. It was then I looked for the half-full can of Pepsi on the stairs, that was no longer there.

My father was always saying: 'I'm going to leave.' He'd say that repeatedly, without rhyme or reason, at least as far as I could see; it was a litany he hissed between his teeth rather than saying out loud. But the fact was he was set on leaving, always longing to be elsewhere. He was a man, as they say, who was always ready to up and off. I recalled that day I visited him in Pasadena. Curiously enough, he talked to me of paths that open up unexpectedly in one's life, like Analía Soler, who was a path to a different life, destroying (or not, who can ever know) my mother's, at least for a time, time for her to discover that an impasse is a tortuous variant on the open road, a simple deviation.

Forking paths, I told him. 'Yes, forking paths,' said my father, 'that's the word. Forking paths change everything. And no one understands you, you are on your own when you make up your mind when you confront one of those forking paths, where everything is the same but different, it's the moment when you are most alone in your whole life.' That day in Pasadena my father told me he once walked through a wood and came to a crossroads, one track went left and the other right, and he didn't know which to take, because at that moment either would have taken him to somewhere new, and the truth was he didn't care where the end of the trail led.

'I took the left fork,' said Sean, 'but the whole time I was thinking what the right fork might be like. And while I continued on that path, I thought about what I was missing on the other. I imagined the place I might have reached and started regretting I'd taken the track I took, but then I had a rethink and told myself I'd taken the right one, because the one you take is always the right one, and there's no way of knowing where the other leads, and moreover it was the one that belonged to me, it was real, the other was simply part of what never existed.' Of what is invisible as well, I replied, but my father stared at me and clearly hadn't understood.

I realised that was something that fascinated Griffin: duality, the double life, understood as a life that is replicated with two realities, one lived and one imagined. He was attracted by what he called dead potential he developed in one corner of his mind and his internal monologue. Then, when he discovered that double aspect within himself, he added a new, at once double and invisible level to his life – one that evidently forked. I've always wondered about the turning one doesn't take, said Griffin, and have recreated it so frequently that sometimes I've even mistaken it for the one I chose. It's like playing the game 'what might have happened if . . .' What might have happened if I'd bought the red pencil rather than the black one. What might have happened if I'd got up an hour later rather than an hour earlier. What might have happened if I'd turned right rather than left when I went out. What might have happened if I'd sailed not on the *Minerva Janela* but on the *Soliman*, the sand-transporter I'd seen anchored in Funchal captained by a one-eyed Philippine. I don't know where it was heading, but of an evening on the deck of the *Minerva Janela* I'd often wonder where it was at that precise moment. It probably sailed as far as Panama. I expect it would have damaged its propeller in the locks, and we'd have been stuck in the canal for days waiting for the company's German divers and technicians to rescue us. I'd no doubt have tired of waiting and would have abandoned ship there and then: a ship with a hostile Singhalese and Indonesian crew. I'd have returned to Madeira much earlier and given up the idea of going to the Straits of Magellan, of looking for the automaton in my grandfather's photo, and we'd possibly never have met, and I wouldn't be spinning anyone this long yarn, and once again this forking path could be extended and become an entirely different life, never lived but imaginable with thousands of variants opening up and taking us to infinity, or replicating the lives of the whole of humanity.

What might have happened if Fabienne Michelet hadn't died in Nantes (that is, if she did die there, if she ever died) and we'd met (in Nantes) years later? And lived together, had children, a house in the country, a current account in the Crédit, two Peugeots, and another nationality? What might have happened if Li Pao hadn't disappeared so suddenly from my life? Or if he/she had continued giving classes on the wars in Europe in the sixteenth and seventeenth centuries instead of going to work in the Club Pekín? Or if I'd decided to write that biography of Grünewald and not the short monograph I penned on the Holy Grail in secret societies during the French Revolution? Or if I'd gone to a doctor who'd decided to sour his patients' lives that morning and mix up all his diagnoses for the day, and, twenty-four hours after, the nurse would have rung them one by one to calm them down and say there'd been a mistake . . . But how many lives might not have been modified by that stage? *Ad infinitum*, said Griffin, *ad infinitum* . . .

And I remember how Oliver Griffin would occasionally end his protracted parentheses and narrative that were true soliloquys, if not labyrinths, and ask. What do you think? Or even: what do you think, my friend? Of course, he didn't expect me to reply and say what I really thought, but I was happy, because I was flattered my opinion could be (or might have been, ay) important to him, or at least meaningful, relevant, at best of interest.

35

GRACIELA PURSUED A FORKING PATH THAT ENDED her life or years later ended in death, to be precise. When did she take it? Probably on 21 February 1946, when she wrote a letter to my grandfather Arnaldo, one of the last he received from her, and where she mentioned Melvicius again. The fork, which she believed in blindly, was called *golem*. The *Golem*, the Formless One, the Clay Figure.

Apparently it had all started because Arnaldo wanted to create the most prodigious act of magic ever, the most sophisticated, shocking performance imaginable, one to leave his audience shaking with fear in their seats. The only thing no magician within the profession had attempted to that point was to give life to what is inanimate, to create something out of nothing, to be God onstage. The fact that they didn't try doesn't mean they didn't want to.

My grandfather got very excited about the remote possibility he could manufacture a being that would respond like a robot at his beck and call. He even told Graciela his ideas on the subject, like the creation of a figure who made frightening, mysterious gestures activated by the tiniest of dwarfs tucked inside, comfortably so, and extremely well paid, so he didn't blab too much. He may even have thought of giving him a share in the takings, but suddenly went cold on the project, and decided that kind of creation was impossible, since he couldn't find a dwarf who was dwarf enough, said Griffin, and every attempt to build a credible figure ended in an absurd, derisory contraption, so he just forgot all about it.

That was perhaps a year before Graciela's letter, because she began the letter on 21 February by reminding him of his long nurtured desire to captivate the world with his invented device. Despite her various bouts of madness, from which the ever-present Esteban Ravel tried to protect her, Graciela told my grandfather it was the same obsession that had pursued old Melvicius, as she'd discovered in some of the rarest books she had consulted. Where do the roofs with stairways lead to in the Street of Alchemists in Prague where Melvicius lived? Graciela wondered.

To a place that no longer exists, she told herself, to a place that perhaps never existed, but which legend locates in the centre of Prague, where Melvicius set up his laboratory in the eccentric guise of a camouflaged attic (which could only be reached via the roof): a false wall behind a high painting which framed all the letters in the Hebrew alphabet embroidered in gold thread, the removal of which gave access to a spiral staircase that went down and down (four hundred steps, they said), dozens of metres below street level, leading to a maze of real false passages, that ended in the centre of the city, in a vaulted room with the thickest of walls.

It was there, so Arcimboldo told his sovereign Rudolph II, that Melvicius built his automata, and that was the truth. It was there, Arcimboldo continued, that Melvicius slept standing up. It was there that Melvicius distilled his love and magic potions. It was there that Melvicius was a magician or a wizard, according to the day and what suited. But what Melvicius really wanted to do – and Graciela had found this out or gleaned it from contemporary texts – was to create a kind of *golem*, but rather than use clay, as if making a genuine *golem*, since it must be a human imitation of the Adam God also created from clay, as its name indicates, Melvicius decided he could make a metal *golem*, born from fire and the forge, with parts whose vitality would have their origins in magic formulations of an obscure, almost secret nature. He thought the material was irrelevant since the life breathed into the android, the so-called living soul (Melvicius wrote *nefesch chaja* somewhere, which is what Graciela wrote in the letter to my grandfather that I read, said Griffin), would be what would transform it into a genuine *golem*.

When Graciela discovered that as she read, she took her ill-fated forking path and descended deeper into madness, as if it were an escape valve. Once more the possibility of life beyond everything else had sent a human being spiralling to a random, unpredictable, lunatic destination, said Griffin enthusiastically. The aberration that excited Melvicius was also what interested Graciela to the point that it trapped her in an unreflecting need for absolute certainty, because she saw it as a revelation that the dead can return, can resurrect, that what is inert can move and that what is matter can become animated spirit.

She thought a distant possibility might exist to restore the lives lost to her beloved family, to her husband Arturo, her boys Pablo and Gaetano, all drowned, and even to the automaton who, in her demented or fantasising moments, had become her beloved, the beautiful being for whom she now lived, for whom she'd turned a deaf ear to the voices inviting her to commit suicide.

Melvicius wanted to create something with more life than whatever Rabbi Jehuda Löw ben Becalel, the Maharal of Prague, who created the *golem* to terrify the frivolous court of Rudolph II, was capable of, or perhaps *he* simply erred on the side of caution. The Supreme Rabbi adhered to orthodox directives as laid down by Rabbi Eleazar of Worms in his *Sefer Jezira* or *Book of the Creation*, where he describes the key to constructing the fearful *golem*, the manufacture of which always implied an unsuspected risk for whoever built it and apparently played at imitating God on that delicate, invisible frontier that separates life from death, said Griffin.

The two sages argued fiercely as they walked the streets of the Prague ghetto, past the stalls of tanners and fullers and small shops selling perfumes from Lisbon and amber from Krakow.

Löw said: 'It must be a servant, no matter whether it's made of clay or steel, but it must be a servant, and serve the specific purposes its creators made it for and run no risk of chaos, of a force that is uncontrolled.'

Melvicius said: 'The automaton will obey the voice that created it until by its own means it finds the path of free will, like all men.'

And Löw said: 'How absurd to think the automaton can be free when man is not, because no man is free outside the Law.'

And Melvicius said: 'My metal *homunculus* will surpass your clay *golem* because it isn't the fruit of an erratic impulse to create but of a bolder search to transcend morality.'

And Löw said: 'You mean to be God.'

And Melvicius said: 'If you say so, to be God, you are right.'

And Löw said: 'And will your *golem* be intelligent?'

And Melvicius said: 'He will be because he will learn from me.'

And Löw said: 'So will your *golem* have powers of memory?'

And Melvicius said: 'He will have the gift of memory.'

And Löw said: 'Your arrogance will be your downfall!'

And Melvicius said: 'Your cowardice already imposes limits on you. Your short-sighted thinking can progress no further, cannot fly, travel or create. You will never go beyond your prejudices.'

And the sages turned their backs on each other and instead of bidding farewell, insulted one other between gritted teeth as each went to his respective home in the Jewish city.

Melvicius's obsession gradually transformed into an obsession about how to become God, in fact, just as Rabbi Löw had reproached him. Melvicius was obsessed with the thought his metal construction might think, act, feel, have ambitions and be transcendent. And perhaps love. But whom? And by the same token, perhaps kill But whom?

His child would have no defects (a presumption prompted by his pretensions rather than by any expertise as a magician) and bring good fortune to its owner (quite the opposite to what it brought Philip II and Sarmiento and his motley crew). He wrote this, under the name of his follower Haim Aboab, in the same manuscripts where he sketched and drew the automaton's parts and inner workings, texts that, years later, after surfacing and disappearing, resurfacing in libraries and synagogues and in monasteries and Masonic lodges, left their traces for ever engraved on the fantasies of men, and hence the legend that Melvicius had succeeded in creating a superior being: strong, immortal, enduring and his slave.

Melvicius argued that everything that could give life to an automaton or *golem* had been long embedded in alchemy and geometry, but as far as Löw was concerned the key was hiding tranquilly in the Cabbala and Eleazar's *Sefer*. On one occasion, when the two sages were walking alone between shops and shopkeepers, Löw wanted to know where Melvicius would put EMET (Truth), the necessary tetragraphy, to give life to the *golem* after walking the four hundred and seventy-two prescribed times around the automaton, and reciting non-stop the eighty combinations of the tetragraphy: emet, meet, etem . . . etcetera. Melvicius retorted that in his case it would be one thousand, three hundred and twenty-six times and he would have to recite the four letters every thirteen times round, which meant a total of one hundred and two repetitions. 'And would you thus destroy it?' Löw asked Melvicius. 'Unlike Eleazar, may God protect his memory,' replied Melvicius. 'I shall not have to remove the initial E to make the obligatory MET (Dead) and thus end the *golem*'s existence, but will invert the word and make it say TEME (Perfection). 'The perfection of evil,' Löw must have retorted. 'The perfection of finality,' Melvicius must have responded.

Graciela told my grandfather all this in that letter dated February 1946. She also said she'd found no trace of EMET or TEME on the automaton's forehead, although its metal body was very scratched and perhaps one was the sought after, legendary word. She also told him she had tried to follow the cryptographic formula to restore the breath of life to the automaton's inert body, right there in the museum, but she had never succeeded in walking round him one thousand, three hundred and sixty-two times non stop, as Melvicius indicated, or reciting the tetragraphy one hundred and two times, and at most had managed to get it to make the movements it had been destined to make centuries ago, thanks to her restoration of the key part of its internal mechanisms. But all that – and who today could ever say why? – after Graciela had innocently spread the word to whoever in the city was prepared to listen, Ravel, the museum's director, journalists, visitors or simple bystanders, so it became a legend spread by word of mouth in Punta Arenas, then in Patagonia, eventually extending to capital cities, to Santiago and Buenos Aires, and then to ships and from those ships to the whole world.

The word spread. Or the fantasy, because some maintained that everything connected to the Desolation Island automaton was fable and mystery invented to give notoriety to the Salesian Museum itself. For others, on the contrary, it finally became an object to be coveted, an object that was so peculiar, with such a blend of powers, that were easily exaggerated to the extent that people believed (as reported by part of the press of the time, in the Fifties) that the automaton hoarded all Melvicius's Cabbalistic secrets about the processes for converting other metals into gold.

From the 1950s onwards various people tried to steal it, and, on one occasion, in 1958, the night-time security guard, Evaristo Revuelta Esterlich, a fifty-five-year-old Chilean, was mortally wounded, and some time after Graciela herself was hurt, albeit slightly, sustaining a broken joint to a finger of her left hand, when she was pushed violently on to the floor by thieves. After that Esteban Ravel, always living in hope of his impossible love, provided bodyguards, men from the Mercedes Estate, more like thugs from Calafate, said Griffin, to protect her: she referred to them as 'my personal guards', none of whom, blast them, Griffin exclaimed, could prevent a now elderly Graciela from being murdered by a blow to the head from a hard object on All Saints Day in 1965, after she'd spent several years locked up as mad in the Lunatic Asylum of the Holiest Trinity in Punta Arenas and that was five years after she'd returned to the museum as chief curator, a post that had been held for her out of a sense of pity because she was about to retire. The instrument was undoubtedly the same builder's hammer that had been used to smash several glass cabinets and to try to break the chain chaining the automaton's feet to the iron ring that attached it to the wall, and she was struck, according to the forensics, between the hours of twelve midnight and 2 a.m., a time when Ravel's men confessed they generally didn't watch the old Pavic woman because she was usually fast asleep by 10 p.m. Who would ever have imagined that Graciela Pavic would get up yet again to kiss her automaton at such a late hour of the night? The men were sacked.

I discovered the facts relating to Graciela Pavic's death a few days after I arrived in Punta Arenas. They turned out to be yet another irony in a life full of ironies. The two men who killed her were arrested the day after committing their crime. They were staying in a dreadful hotel in the port, the Miramar, and planned to check out the day after. They didn't know the city, and came a week before 'to get their bearings', so the local press reported. After entering the museum, they tied up the night guard, who'd been dozing in the porter's office. They'd been unable to break the chain attaching the automaton to the wall, but so damaged other items and cabinets and left so many fingerprints that they were soon identified. There was a police file on them in Santiago. They were common criminals. I read about it in newspapers of the time in the newspaper library in Punta Arenas that was located very close to my hotel, the Aramis, and the news was quite the talk of the town at the time.

Apparently, over the years, Graciela was liked by almost everyone, the kind of popular affection that is prompted by compassion and pity for what people see as strange. They called her Mad Graciela, mocking or laughing at her, because she was so eccentric, what with her absurd, desperate quest and incredible stubbornness, thinking that her family would emerge from the sea at any moment after all those years, or that their bodies would be found, or at least, her final, equally absurd hope, that a few remains, some clothes perhaps, a shoe perhaps might turn up.

They'd dubbed her Mad Graciela in the last phase of lunacy, when her sickly affection for the automaton in the Salesian Museum became public knowledge. At the end of the period when she wrote to my grandfather, at the end of the Forties, her mental health deteriorated drastically. Nonetheless, Esteban Ravel protected her with an iron hand, and didn't allow anyone to touch her or interfere with her. He built a wall of medicine, caring and even deceit around her, and Graciela didn't realise she was increasingly living in a non-existent bubble.

Nonetheless, a few years later, in 1957, Ravel had her admitted into the Trinitarian Nuns' Hospital and, in fact, he died for legal purposes in 1981, a completely solitary, hollow octogenarian on the Mercedes Estate that now belonged to him, even though he'd died years before that when the Prosecutor's Court rang to tell him that Graciela Pavic had been found dead in a museum room at the feet of the automaton. But he loved her so much and couldn't stand not being near her, though she hardly recognised him, because in the years when she was interned she lost consciousness of everything around her, faces, persons close to her, it was all erased in no time. Esteban Ravel went to live in the same hospital, in an annexe loaned to him by the chaplain, Don Lucas Rodríguez, whom I got to know in Punta Arenas, said Griffin and he was the person who told me all this.

Graciela soon recovered, or at least had less attacks of lunacy, Rodríguez told me. In May 1965, she was allowed back on the street, cured and able to recognise everyone, starting with Esteban Ravel. In August, the southern winter in the same year the theft was perpetrated, she returned to the museum almost as a result of Don Esteban's charity and insistence, to facilitate her transition to imminent retirement. Then the tragedy took place.

The two murderers were common criminals who had been released from jail in the Pinochet era to become mercenary parapolice: Manuel Oltracina Barrios, aged thirty-two, and Elmer Sánchez Ramírez, twenty-eight. The latter actually killed her. They were working for a gang of Santiago smugglers who specialised in works of art, jewels and collectors' items. They supplied this material via fairly obscure networks to Luis Vayado, a Chilean entrepreneur, and in turn he sent the stolen goods to an Arab lawyer resident in Paris who was well connected with the very rich and powerful, and those objects disappeared in his accounts, as into a fog, exchanged for considerable fortunes. The Arab was Ali Amor Saud Al Jabri and was himself a collector of rare items, a kind of contemporary Arcimboldo or Rudolph II, Griffin explained.

But here lies the irony: the stolen automaton from Desolation Island was on its way (though he never knew) to a Dalmatian from Dubrovnik, perhaps a distant cousin of Graciela, one of the relatives she always wanted to visit though never did, as she was continually postponing the trip, a Dalmatian by the name of Goran Valikulik, who'd made his fortune in ship-building and now lived in Capri. Valikulik was fascinated by alchemy and was well acquainted with the work and legends surrounding Melvicius, about whom he'd written a small pamphlet in his youth that must surely have been included in one of the bibliographies consulted by Graciela.

Goran Valikulik knew nothing, however, about the discovery of the automaton until he perhaps read the news going the rounds, as a simple curiosity, about the iron *golem* in a small godforsaken museum at the end of the world in a city by the name of Punta Arenas near Port Famine, that had been created by Sarmiento de Gamboa, whom Goran Valikulik had probably never heard of either. The irony lies, underlined Griffin, in the fact that Graciela Pavic was perhaps murdered to satisfy a similar desire to possess Rudolph II's automaton, now inhabiting a distant relative of hers in obscure Austro-Hungarian Dubrovnik whence her father Miro Pavic the thief had fled. It was as if a large circle opened in Rudolph's mad head had finally been closed.

Valikulik never knew, because after the murder and subsequent arrest of Luis Cayado, the clients in Paris denied they'd ever known him or commissioned any such thing, let alone a commission involving traffic in stolen or ill-gotten goods, or a murder.

How long might Graciela have lived if they hadn't tried to steal her automaton, that strange figure that held so many secrets and magic potential it was coveted from the other side of the world, although for the two killers, it was never more than an 'iron gadget' as Manuel Oltracina and Elmer Sánchez called it? This was a fork that was never taken and that is part of Esteban Ravel's life, and I remembered what my father Sean told me: 'When you take a path, you always want to know what your life might have been like on the other path, on the one you abandoned, on the one far removed from your life.' And Ravel, said Griffin, must have often imagined the autumn of his life with Graciela, something he'd put on his map of desire in his youth when it was quite a blur, from the moment he fell madly in love (the apposite word being this, underlined Griffin: madly), but he'd never put it on the map in the real world: he'd never enjoy old age at her side, in a corner of the blissful shadows kept for old lovers who are finally free.

Reality was quite different, now that she had died, now the rites of the wake were over in hospital, and the rites of the orthodox mass in the Dalmatian church, from the funeral in calle Ángamos to the cemetery, to the solitary gravestone finally placed on the tomb where Graciela had finally agreed to the engraving of the following epitaph:

†

ARTURO BAGNOLI

Gaetano Bagnoli – Pablo Bagnoli

Their souls rest in my heart

Here there has been only absence

From 1918

Reality was quite different, repeated Griffin, reality for Esteban Ravel, in the long life left to him was limited to the contemplation of the vast plains and heaths of the Mercedes Estate that were quite empty except for the extraction towers for oil and liquid gas. He would remember the afternoon of the burial, on his way home, walking to the port, perhaps now taking up his beloved's baton and going daily to wait for the deceased spirits to arise, or going on that afternoon simply to see her spirit definitively united with those of her sons and husband who'd been hiding and calling to her for over fifty years from any of the beaches on the other shore; he'd remember how he'd once seen his father's yellow Latécoère 62 land on those fields, said Griffin, with Graciela inside descending from the heavens like an angel, trailing behind it a plume apparently made of white cotton.

36

'THE FALKLAND ISLANDS ARE THAT GREY BLOTCH lurking in the mist ' Pereira told me as he looked through his binoculars from the bridge of the *Minerva Janela*, said Griffin. We were at a very low latitude, Branco had avoided the coastal traffic from Port Desire, and we were rather close to the entrance to the Straits, on a straight line westwards, though more than eight hundred miles away. 'We'll turn west when we reach the Falklands,' said Pereira.

In fact, we sailed close to the archipelago, and with the help of Pereira's powerful binoculars could see the unpleasant beaches and windy wastes of Mount Harriet, where the battle of that name was fought, said Griffin. We could also see the leftovers from the 1982 war, remains trapped on breakwaters or nearby reefs, a grand cemetery of rusting, derelict hulks.

Metal leftovers of unidentifiable ships, all thrown together higgledy-piggedly, whether Argentine or British, rusty brown, algae, coral or islands, like the *Sheffield*, the modern destroyer and the pride and joy of Her Majesty's Royal Navy, which was barely six months old when it was sunk, or the *Ardent*, the boat on which sailors painted Elizabeth II on their foreheads and the Union Jack on their faces, or the *General Belgrano*, the antediluvian cruiser that went down with its contingent of four hundred men on board, or the *Antelope*, blown to smithereens when they were about to remove the detonators from a bomb that hadn't exploded, or the *Sir Tristan*, a ship carrying shock troops, treacherously attacked when retreating and sunk in twenty minutes, or the *Glamorgan*, the gunboat that split in two while still firing on the coast, or the *Santa Fe*, a submarine that couldn't make it back down and keeled over so badly it looked like a dead whale on its back, boats that weren't history but were now simply sea. Later, at dinner, Griffin, Pereira and other crew came together in the dining room when Bergeron was serving bouillabaisse and heard Charly Greene recount a terrible incident from that war.

Greene retold the story of his brother, a story that had been rehearsed time and again at home, as a respectful homage or gloomy ritual against oblivion. His brother, Second Officer Patrick Gwynn Greene, was on the *Sir Galahad*, a transporter ship for landing troops sunk on 8 June 1982 by Argentine air attack as it was re-entering open sea after being anchored in Port Fitzroy.

It was sunk by air-to-land Exocet missiles shot from fighter-planes and many British soldiers lost their lives. Second Officer Greene was in the gun turret on the poop deck, but the Exocets came from the prow blowing open the stores and partitions at the waterline, which meant the ship would sink swiftly and surely. Fires followed explosions: inflammable fuel-oil spurted through the air and fell like a rain of fire, burning, sizzling sheets of flaming oil on the water, lifeboats full of men, others still marooned on board because lowering tackle had been blown up, men scattered over the water looking for lifebuoys or pieces of wood to cling to, including Patrick Greene, who'd been cast into the sea by a partition wall that exploded like a champagne cork, who was swimming as strongly as he could away from the coast, totally disoriented and almost unconscious. When he started to faint and swallow water and suddenly think he wasn't there but in the kitchen in their Cardiff home, with his mother asking him to eat his roast turkey on Christmas Day, someone grabbed him by the neck, then two other men by the armpits, hauling him into a lifeboat that was strangely half empty, only eight men aboard though it had capacity for forty, and they rowed to the coast, under fire from the Argentinians, and a mortar destroyed the boat and four occupants, splattering blood all over Patrick Greene's face, who was thrown several metres up on the beach, on to sand that stuck to the blood from other men, and he went deaf, momentarily, as a result of the explosion, and his mind could only hear a hum from the outside world, that is, if he knew what his mind was, when he looked at the end of his arm and saw something was missing, a void where his hand should have been, a hand that to his surprise no longer existed where it had happily existed seconds before.

He looked at that void but didn't bawl or howl, that would come a few minutes later when he regained consciousness, although his eyes were open, though staring deep within himself at his pet phantoms and horrors, the ones that always assailed him when he imagined what it would be like to be a man who'd lost a hand. And now he was that man at that very moment. He used his belt and one of the gloves in his pockets to staunch the flow of blood as best he could. The pain was intolerable.

He noticed a sailor from the same lifeboat lying wounded on the beach a few metres away: he was sobbing and asking for help. Patrick Greene crawled painfully over to him and tried to drag him to rocks at the top of the beach, but a unit of Argentine Infantry from Córdoba started shooting from behind those same rocks. Greene took his shirt off and held it up to signal surrender. Three Argentine soldiers with blackened faces walked down to the wounded men and took them prisoner.

They were questioned in a small redoubt of rocks and sandbags by a captain who identified himself as Ruiz, a tough, fair-haired man with small eyes who looked exhausted. Neither Patrick Greene nor the sailor was privy to information that mattered. Ruiz shot the injured, quite oblivious sailor point-blank in the heart. Then Ruiz extracted a knife from somewhere behind him, a long, sharp knife he'd no doubt stolen from a dead Ghurka and brought it down on Patrick Greene's remaining hand, lopping it off with a single swipe.

Greene passed out. They left him tied to a post bleeding to death, while Ruiz's unit retreated inland, after the British landed a kilometre away. By the time his compatriots reached him, Patrick Greene had expired in a pool of his own blood. They'd also cut off his ears. Ruiz was apparently carrying them in one of his pockets. A sergeant called Raffles found them when Ruiz was killed in a subsequent battle and they were emptying out the pockets and belongings of the dead. 'Those ears belonged to my brother Patrick,' said Greene, 'and were sent in a separate package to my mother, with the coffin that was deposited in Cardiff cathedral a couple of weeks later. His medal was tied to the red strap round the box containing his ears.' After a brief silence, said Griffin, Greene told us that nobody had ever discovered why Ruiz wanted his brother's ears.

The following day we left the Falklands behind us, but our voyage through those waters was far from easy. The weather suddenly changed. We faced the awesome heavy seas of the southern hemisphere. 'Life's hard, life's happy. Off I go, off I go,' Caporale hummed between his teeth as he saw the storm blowing up in the distance. I'd heard him singing as night fell and he walked down the corridor past my cabin, and I started to think how true his words were. Perhaps it came from a song Caporale knew: he knew lots of songs, tangos, cumbias, boleros, or invented them, music included, said Griffin. 'Tralala, tralala. Life's hard, life's happy,' he repeated as he went up on deck.

I was lying on my bunk in the upper berth, trying not to worry too much about the way the ship was tossing up and down increasingly violently. In the berth beneath, Pereira was reading a novel by Philip K. Dick, *Do Androids Dream Of Electric Sheep?* for the nth time with the video of a *Star Trek* film running silently as usual before he fell asleep. He glanced instinctively around to see which things might fall and break and which wouldn't.

He said everything was stuck down by strips of sticky tape, including the cassette and video tapes, all the books and toiletries, souvenirs ('Memories of Hong Kong' was written on a pay-pay), and when I looked at it I remembered the fan Li Pao used to cover his sex in his flat, when we were alone, and he revealed the rest of his naked body as he danced for me.

'Feeling sick?' asked Pereira. No, I replied, said Griffin, I'm learning to cope with these storms. 'You can never cope with storms, Oliver, and this is going to be a particularly bad one,' said Pereira. How do you know? I asked. 'The heat. Can't you feel how oppressive it is, much worse than this morning. Well, that's always the prelude to a big storm in this part of the Atlantic, in the middle of summer. I hope God will look after us. But don't be frightened, Oliver, if we're expert at anything on this ship, it's storms.'

I found Pereira's sangfroid soothing, but it didn't prevent my queasiness and waxen complexion from resurfacing. It was true we were experiencing stifling heat. I was soaked in sweat, my clothes stuck to my skin and my forehead was burning as if I'd a temperature, but it wasn't that I was feverish: the temperature on the thermometer on the wall opposite seemed to be the same this morning as yesterday morning. Something had to puncture the atmosphere. And something did: a refreshing downpour that brought relief and also terror.

Thunder and lightning exploded, and big flashes lasting several seconds lit up our cabin porthole. The rain started all of a sudden, as the clouds violently offloaded their burden of water; depending on the way the wind blew, the raindrops lashed furiously against the glass as if someone was throwing coins or screws at our window. The sea roared even more savagely and drowned out all other noise, including our voices.

Pereira had stopped reading. He lay there still and serious, awaiting a summons that came immediately: a knock on our cabin door. It was a breathless Rodo Amaro. Captain Branco wanted him on the bridge right away. Pereira jumped down from his bunk, dressed quickly, or was already dressed, I'm not really sure, because I think Pereira slept in his clothes. He shut the cabin door with a: 'You'd better stay in bed.' I took no notice, naturally: that was when I gambled with my life and came the closest to death I've ever been, or ever will be. But we should take this slowly, said Griffin, putting a brake on his excited chatter.

I was soon on the second deck in my yellow rain cape, attached to a rail by a safety harness next to Caporale, who was pulling on a steel cable from a crane that had got entangled with a support and was pressing down on the pitched canvas protecting the tools store. I wanted to help, because I'd never wanted to feel useless on board, a passenger they laughed at behind his back. Amuntado, the engineer, was trying to extract hydraulic jacks they needed to secure the cargo more tightly, but the weight of that steel cable made it impossible to open the door to get to the tools.

The torrential rain almost cut into your face and the boat tossed more violently than ever. Caporale and I slipped several times and our feet caught in the conduits for the mooring ropes, and we could easily have broken our ankles. Nearby containers moaned and groaned anxiously whenever the boat heaved. The lightning lit up the night sky, though the sudden glare suddenly seemed to fade when Captain Branco ordered all deck lights and auxiliary spotlights to be switched on, red, white, blue, yellow lights, at a stroke, in the middle of that terrifying tempest, flickering like some panic-inspiring fairground attraction, except this was for real and the outcome wasn't at all certain. Every man jack felt on the brink (except for Tonet Segarra the electrician who suffered from astrophobia and had strapped himself to his cabin bunk where he played the tenor sax until he was out of breath in order to fight his horror of claps of thunder). It didn't mean we were paralysed, on the contrary, we felt driven by a desperate wish to do whatever we could at a frantic pace to avoid having to confront the thousand and one images of shipwrecks in our minds, starting with Géricault's vast, visionary canvas of the raft of the shipwrecked from *Le Radeau de la Méduse* that I'd seen in the Louvre.

In the midst of that dazzling glare, the *Minerva Janela* was suddenly a surreal fair of coloured lights creating a fake theatrical melodrama on the open sea. I looked at the seven containers behind me that kept screeching ominously. I had good reason to be afraid. Nonetheless, the safety ropes and holding apparatus seemed to be resisting the battering from their cargo, the noise from which was audible above the raging storm.

When I was helping Caporale and Amuntado, I remember

reading a metal tag indicating they were tractor parts packed for assembly, as was later verified in the description of the cargo (the number registered in the ship's files read: CONT. 2000002/Liberia-Chile/Fab.22122/ModAH-//22-8-1955). A second after I'd looked at that label, and I'll never forget that awful moment, the whole pile of containers seemed to shake.

I couldn't believe it. I thought I was hallucinating when I saw those objects and people dance, but I looked up and felt stinging rain lash my face, forcing me to screw up my eyes, and behind the rain I saw something I didn't recognise, a strange object looming closer and closer, a sudden streak of orange across the sky in the blinding light on deck: the striated side of a container crashing down on me with another in hot pursuit.

That was the last I saw. I felt a violent tug on my belt; I thought Caporale had pushed me on the pitched canvas we'd just piled up under the winches. I think he must have saved my life because as they fell the two containers destroyed the whole tool store and part of the rail on the second deck before they slid into the sea and they and their cargo were lost for ever.

In those desperate moments, as the containers sunk into the sea with a terrific din, I saw or perhaps thought I saw, I couldn't attest the degree of reality in what I saw because it was a panic-driven hallucination, my adrenalin shooting off high in a descent into unreality, I saw Arturo Bagnoli's boat and his two sons among the white waves, next to the hulk of our ship. I saw them capsize, said Griffin, I really did, though I know that's impossible! I saw Arturo Bagnoli trying to right the battered launch, I saw little Gaetano crash though the air swept along by a savage wave, I saw his brother Pablo scream and cling to the jacket of his father who, in turn, was desperately searching for Gaetano in the froth and foam, his son who'd sunk without trace: while his voice calling to his son and the noise of the storm blowing in Catherine's Bay combined most sinisterly. Another wave capsized the boat. I saw Arturo and his son Pablo trying to keep afloat, but they soon stopped struggling, the sea closed over their heads and down they went, never to resurface.

Then I fell into the water and I thought the water and I were made of ice, said Griffin. But later or right then, I don't remember, I thought all these images, thoughts and dreams in a single hallucination. I was convinced the safety harness was still securing me to the winch and wasn't aware of what was really happening: I was falling into the sea because the harness had broken. I saw my body sinking next to the ghostly image of Bagnoli, floating silently, in my hallucination, beyond time and history, next to Sarmiento and his men, who were also waving their arms in vain amid the waves, next to a slightly more distant Patrick Greene, desperately searching for a floating object to cling to, even if it was another sailor's body.

The feeling that I was lost in mid-ocean, if only for a few seconds, made me feel anguished as if I was breaking out of a nightmare, like the one that pursued me in my childhood, when I felt I was lost in a city of sand, comprising my house, my parents' house, the streets I knew, the same windows and neighbours, but everything, absolutely everything, was made of sand, and as I walked I sank deeper and deeper into the sand, down to my knees, and then my waist and could see my neighbours totally covered by sand, walking along the streets, for sure, but their bodies were under the surface of the sand, and that's what I saw, said Griffin, and only their hats were walking, a man's, a woman's, or open umbrellas, or a hairdo or bald pate, and when I knocked on doors or windows to get them to open up to me, they collapsed in a heap of sand. This was a despairing, physically repugnant dream, like when I dreamt for a whole month that my mouth was being stuffed with raw chicken skin and I couldn't utter a sound, because of the atrocious nausea I was feeling.

All that, phantoms, sand and chicken skin, rushed into my mind, in the seconds the container fell over the *Minerva Janela*'s stern breaking the rail on the second deck and destroying everything in its path, supports, conduits, eaves and stores and the winch I'd been attached to. I heard it clearly later on, when I was in the icy water, my mind free of hallucinations, when the silence had turned into shouting everywhere and I swam against the waves towards a lifebuoy I'd spotted a few metres away.

I'd fallen into the sea in the wake of the second container. I realised that only now. Amuntado and Caporale had thrown the lifebuoy out blindly, unable to see where I was down below. They shouted my name in the dark, but couldn't see me. I got more desperate because I couldn't keep myself afloat. And strangely enough that was when I thought of ice, or rather felt I *was* ice, as invisible as ice, frozen like ice, because I realised the invisibility that had always pursued me didn't lie in the happenstance of my name, in the lack of sensitivity of people who didn't know me or in my inability to engage with the world of reality, but was now encircling me like a great sleeve of ice cutting me off from the gaze of others.

I made one last effort and finally grabbed the lifebuoy that my companions pulled on until they'd hauled me out of the sea in a state of hypothermia. When it was all over, when the cargo was lost, the whole crew was scared and hugely annoyed. It wasn't usual for a couple of containers to come loose, for a harness to break or for a man to fall into the sea, although it was the second time on this trip after Olivier Sagna, the purser from Bordeaux, had fallen overboard, said Griffin, midway on our voyage a few days out of Cape Verde. The container incident was in fact an accident and a detailed investigation was begun, carried out by Pereira, and his findings plunged Branco deeper into gloom, who had already entered a state of depression the outcome of which we are only too well aware.

Security and surveillance were the responsibility of Second Officer Fernando Grande, helped by one sailor, usually the sailor on duty that day, and they hadn't been careful enough, indeed, had been negligent. The safety bars hadn't been tightened sufficiently, the hydraulic jacks hadn't been properly located to maintain the pressure necessary to keep the containers in place, even though storm warnings had been posted, and a strong northerly wind had started blowing and several of the grips battening the containers down were found to be open rather than closed.

It was demonstrated that all this carelessness was Grande's responsibility, and Captain Branco's anger raged yet again against his second officer, and he swore he'd abandon him on land once we reached Punta Arenas. Branco, in his depression, lost heart and spoke to no one, except Navares the pilot, who was a silent soul anyway. Our sad captain returned to his limbo of absence where he disappeared without trace, like Ahab using the sad claws of melancholy to find nourishment. To the crew's surprise, and to his friend's Pereira as well, Branco put everything that had happened out of his mind and blamed the disaster on the fateful meaning of existence that led him to end his life a few days later.

'The insurance will look after it,' Pereira told me, said Griffin, when the sea suddenly calmed at dawn. 'Rodo Amaro always takes photos for the insurers.' So what could he take photos of this time if the cargo had been lost? I asked from under the two blankets on my bunk. 'This time it's you. You're the proof of the accident for the shipping agents. You'll have to talk to them in Punta Arenas. Pure red tape. And we'll soon be there,' said Grande. Indeed, the morning of the day after the storm Pereira sent a Morse code message (-.-) to the Harbour Office in Punta Arenas, meaning 'I must speak to you', and peace and quiet returned to our lives.

37

THE *MINERVA JANELA* PREPARED TO ENTER THE Straits of Magellan on 2 December, the Turquoise stone month for magicians from the era of Melvicius to the year the Great Samini retired. It did so slowly, progressing at a speed of very few knots, as if manoeuvring. The crew was exhausted after the accident of the lost containers, and tedium and exhaustion permeated every task they performed. I'd made an instant recovery from hypothermia and was on deck, enjoying the summer sun and the gently lapping waters with which the Straits welcomed us. I wanted to be fully aware of the moment I was experiencing, to see and live in real time as it was happening, like Melville's Ishmael, whom I felt I represented on this voyage.

At last I really was entering the source of my myths, the place I'd dreamt of so often after reading my books. Somewhere on the poop deck, I recalled all those I'd devoured on the subject of the Straits of Magellan, fast forwarded them like a film, hundreds of them, remembered all the stories I'd come across, all the maps I'd seen, starting with the first recorded description, then Juan Vespucci's from 1523, who drew it after he'd seen Elcano's rough scribblings, and Pigafetta's rough sketches, Maiollo's map, Thorne's, Diego de la Ribera's, Munster's *Novus*

Orbis, Desline's, Cabotto's, Agnesse's planisphere, Gastaldi's, Velho's *Orbis Pars*, Finé's *Mundo*, Juan Martínez's, Ortelio's *Theatrum Orbis Terrarum*, and the most famous of all, Sgrotenio's, came to mind, and naturally, Sarmiento de Gamboa's, drawn from life.

I felt all its history was concentrated in that moment, and my heart raced when I reflected how it had been the scenario of the lives of so many others who, long before me, centuries even, when the Straits were called All Saints, had confronted their destinies in those waters.

What a cruel scenario of clouds and coasts that threaten and promise so much, Griffin suddenly exclaimed, raising his glass and standing up in front of me, offering a macabre toast. I drink to you, scenario of so much desire and disappointment, he said, of so much drama and bliss, of suffering, torments, scares, rescues, voyages, I drink to you, shipwrecks, struggles, loves, massacres, revolts, I drink to you, whims, hopes, spoils, glimpses, plans, strategies, misfortunes, loneliness, yes, a toast to you, accursed, fascinating place. And Griffin sat down.

I was there at last, I'd arrived at last, my body had at last reached the place of my dreams! he continued. Everything that had happened in almost five hundred years had had to take place so I could be there, in that sea, facing those shores that sailors who'd sailed those waters had imagined in their scariest nightmares were the jaws of a huge monster. The myth of my life was unravelling before me, for real, crystal clear.

It was the same landscape my grandparents Arnaldo and Irene had seen on that distant 9 December 1923, when the cruiser *Santander* entered the Straits, and they were hugging on deck, kissing non-stop and he magicked a flower from her sleeve and made her laugh. It was one of the many tricks he played on their honeymoon, tender jokes, little surprises, unexpected feints in the daily languor of the liner's routines. They were in love, and I wondered, said Griffin, if perhaps that was why they hadn't see the same landscape I saw now, years later, because they were so infatuated with each other. I was no longer in love, and had no choice but to survey those coasts and find an impulse to live beyond myself.

However, the majestic panorama of Cape Virgin was there then as it was for me now, green, dark and bare on its sea face, slippery rock cut sheer, as described by Bougainville, the end of a continent that can be observed from the nearby entrance to the Straits, and beyond that the famous Dungeness Point, where the lighthouse reveals the Straits in the shape of a hook, and is home to the strangest of frontiers. Argentina and Chile share a separating line within a few metres, a dividing line that passes through the centre of a lighthouse. Of course, all frontiers, said Griffin, are resolved in a few metres, that's obviously true, but this frontier was visible from the boat, an invisible line dying on the coast between the two countries after crossing the white tower in the south, and we were greeted, so I believed, by two frontier guards in different uniforms who struck the same stance in the same place, in parallel, a mirror-like symmetry at the top of the lighthouse.

The route taken by the ship brought us close to the northern coast, and the southern coast was visible in the distance, the landmass of Tierra del Fuego. A Chilean frigate hooted a greeting on our stern. It was level with Daniel Point, where black trees line the shore as far as the squat lighthouse on Cape Possession. From that position the *Minerva Janela* now described an equally slow parabola and headed up the First Narrows, but we didn't sail in. The busy traffic of boats and merchant ships kept us waiting for half a day near the luminous buoys of Punta Delgada. The ferry linking Punta Delgada and Puerto Espora periodically sailed past, and was greeted by a symphony of hoots from all the boats waiting their turn. Wasn't it precisely there, in Punta Delgada, that Sarmiento and the Antonelli brothers had wanted to close off the Straits with long chains and lock gates, attached to the forts planned by Spanoqui the engineer. Pure entelechy, pure fantasy, commented Griffin.

As dusk fell, we finally entered the narrow channel, a kind of funnel less than a kilometre wide, and sailed into the great summer beauty of the Straits with St Phili's Bay to the south, all purple mist, and St Gregory Bay to our stern, with the tubular structures and perennial flames of the hydrocarbon terminal. There was a heavy traffic of oil and liquid gas carriers that were always being dragged to the centre of the Straits, where the water was deepest. We quickly left the terminal behind and entered the Second Narrows, reduced speed again and went much slower, as if the waves were pulling us along. There, near Punta Ana, with Elizabeth Island behind us, Captain Branco issued the order to shut down engines and anchor for the night, as he wanted to reach Punta Arenas at daybreak.

That night I was so excited I couldn't sleep so I spent it on deck, with Caporale, talking about theosophy and magic, watching the lights and listening to the noise of tankers, tugboats and containerships going in and out of the adjacent terminals, Port Percy, Clarence or Black Cape. The next morning, two hours after daybreak, we sailed towards Lee Bay on Tierra del Fuego, but we'd hardly gone a few miles when our pilot Jordao Navares swung the boat ninety degrees south and headed down to Laredo Bay, carefully steering clear of Elizabeth Island and its dangerous currents.

When we reached Catherine's Bay, where Bagnoli and his children drowned, I was stunned by a kind of emotional concussion and imagined myself in that real location, with authentic waves, lights, breezes and smells, meeting Graciela desperately looking for her dead family, with the few Alaculoof Indians she'd paid to row their canoes up and down every coast, for weeks, months and finally years, as far as Desolation Island, dozens of kilometres further west, where she found the automaton and went mad.

They were moments of high emotion and the climax to my sense of awe was interrupted by the sudden roar of a low-flying Lan Chile aeroplane about to land in the nearby airport. Thoughts of Graciela, said Griffin, led me to think once again about Desolation Island, and how close I now was to an island I felt was mine, in the hundreds, perhaps thousands of routine drawings I'd made in my lifetime recreating its coastlines, coves, capes and bays. Then, with a burin one of the crew gave me, I etched the shape of the island on one of the reddish metal walls on the *Minerva Janela*'s second deck. A homage, I told myself, and a memento. A personal rite as capricious as it was inexplicable.

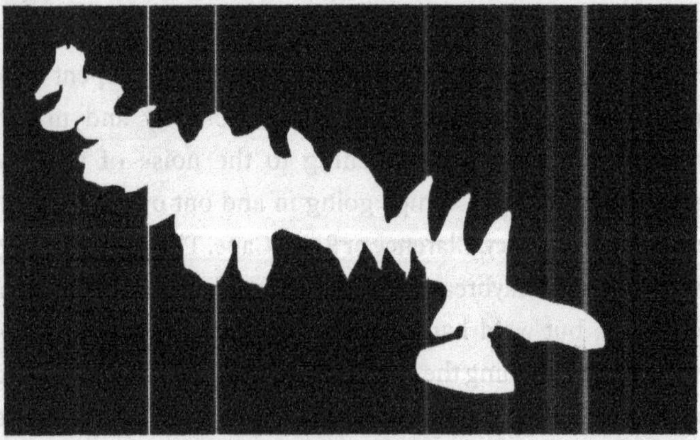

At dawn, on that third day in December, as Branco had intended, we entered the port of Punta Arenas, my journey's end. My goal was there, on land. The voyage really had been

Homeric, and I felt part of that strange, adventuresome concept of life, as powerful as it is blind, we call Ulysses. It was now time to bring my presence on the *Minerva Janela* to an end, sign off and leave, get my pay, act hard and forget, not look back as I walked down the gangway and everything else real sailors do, said Griffin, but I had to start saying my farewells, wishing all my travelling companions a long life and many a happy voyage.

I also felt very close to them, because, among other things, I owed them my life. I decided to do all that as soon as the ship had moored. Rodo Amaro began to manoeuvre very early when the electric lights in the port still blended with the blue of daybreak, aided as ever by the skills of Navares, though Pereira had to oversee the operation, since Branco had dismissed Grande that same night.

Pereira was the first I said goodbye to when I went back to our cabin to pack my luggage. Pereira was drying his face after a shave. He gave me a hug. 'Find your island, and then you won't have to draw it ever again,' he told me. What can he be doing now? I don't believe in fate and would give anything for Mick Jagger to sign that T-shirt imprinted with his face. As he left the cabin, he smiled and said: 'You almost died, for heaven's sake. Take a passenger boat next time. Don't fuck around. But if you insist on being part of a cargo boat with these bastards, then give me a call. I'm always on a boat.' He disappeared with a *ciao*, but neither of us realised we'd see each other so soon, in a few days, when he came to my hotel to inform me that Branco had hung himself.

Once again I thought of forking paths: all those I'd shared sad and happy times with over the past months were now a fork in my life I wouldn't be taking. They were already on the other path; they were already going to another place that wasn't for me. So I hugged Grande farewell, and shook the taciturn Rodo Amaro's hand, and Sagna's, with whom I'd shared the honour of being one of two men who'd fallen overboard on the voyage, the stuff of shipwrecks, and Segarra's too, whose dog still barked at me whenever I went near him, and Amuntado's, who started dancing a cumbia with me as he said goodbye, cigarette on lips, sniggering and blushing, and Pavka the Macedonian's, his headphones eternally stuck in his ears, and Greene the Welshman's, who never forgot Cazilda Canabrava, and black Kowanana's, wearing his boxing gloves, who threw a hook at me, cheek to cheek as he said 'goodbye, goodbye' à la Cassius Clay, and Bergeron's, whose cooking wasn't as bad as they said, and shy Navares', and my friend Caporale's, who insisted on accompanying me to my hotel so we could drink one last glass together, just in case, who could ever know, we shared our next reincarnation, but he was on duty and we had to postpone our drink.

And I said goodbye to Branco. It was my final farewell, as was only right. He was in his cabin, totally uninterested in the docking manoeuvre, because such tasks had never interested him, because he didn't want to leave the sea: a port for him was a place to depart, not a place to dock. Branco planned to go ashore when the whole crew was on dry land, except for the men on duty, then he'd go to the Texaco offices and sign off his second officer, Fernando Grande, after reporting the loss of cargo and the accident. That's what he intended to do, and he told me as much before shaking my hand after he'd given me an envelope with my wages and a receipt I signed on the spot. 'I don't think we'll see each other again,' said Branco. He seemed definite about that, so I tried to make our goodbyes low key. You never know, I said, the world and life are round. 'No,' he said, 'they're flat, there's a sheer drop at the end, and that's the truth.' He shut the door. That was the last time I saw him alive.

When I went on shore and trod the end of Patagonia, I stood still for a few minutes, looking around, not knowing which way to go. I saw the way out of the port, I saw the tanker refuelling platform on three steel pillars in the middle of a small inlet between stone breakwaters, I saw the ticket office for the ferry to Chilota Bay in Porvenir, on the other shore, I saw mountains of creels for catching shell fish in port, I saw a bus that said SARMIENTO CENTRO–AV.INDEPENDENCIA–LÍNEA 7, and got on.

All this was and wasn't what I was feeling as the bus drove towards the centre of Punta Arenas. Suddenly, that city of low houses, many coloured roofs and bluish light seemed a familiar world welcoming me back after a long absence, and I recognised myself, recognised who I was, surrounded by that maternal warmth. For some reason or other, from my first day in Punta Arenas, I stopped feeling invisible.

38

I TRAVELLED THE WHOLE ROUTE OF THE NUMBER 7 bus several times and that took up several hours; quite unintentionally I travelled around the southern area of the city, and was very glad to do so because it took me to the centre of my dream, to the distant days when my honeymooning grandparents reached the city. I was the last passenger to get off the bus where the route died a death. I resisted alighting, perhaps because it implied a step in the direction of reality and that's a step one doesn't always want to make. I was disoriented, and chose a random hotel near the Avenida Independencia, which acted as a bus terminus, as if it were the new fork in my life.

The hotel was 45, calle Boliviana. It was the Aramis Hotel and I chose it because I was amused by the inscription in much smaller letters under the hotel name: 'Formerly Dumas'. It was a pleasant three-storey building with few bedrooms, painted yellow with an indigo blue roof. There was a black wrought-iron entrance and a small garden with English-style chairs and tables. The interior was littered with bronze and wooden adornments and the floorboards creaked between deep-red flock walls.

The hotel's logo imitated Aramis the musketeer's name in Alexandre Dumas' own hand from one of his manuscripts. The bedrooms were decorated with framed prints, copies of all the images of Aramis the owner had collected from different editions of Dumas' work, including film adaptations. Mine, for example, room 34 (like Jacques Vaché's) had two prints: a rural landscape in which a dreamy Aramis was lying on a grassy hillock, reading a religious book by Rancé and smoking a long pipe, while Athos, Porthos and D'Artagnan rode up in the distance. The other print was a black-and-white cameo photo with a profile of the musketeer's face, straight hair and a pointed goatee from an engraving by Vitoux in the series *Noms Universels.*

I telephoned the *Minerva Janela* from my hotel room and gave them my address in case of an emergency (who'd have thought they'd ring me so soon) and I let Caporale know in case he wanted to drop by for a drink. 'Tomorrow,' he said. Then I went back out: the room had no more to offer. How does one wander through a new city? One must learn to let oneself be guided by happenstance.

I wandered down Avenida de España to calle Correa with no particular destination in mind, past streets and shops you'd find in any European city, until I finally came to a wall around a cemetery, the one where Bagnoli and his sons lay, the one, I realised, where Graciela Pavic had been finally put to rest by their side, though she was eternally alone. I followed the wall round to a maze of streets that led to the seashore, to the beaches where calle Mario Toledo met Carrera Pinto, on the Costanera.

I went for a swim in the Straits and drank a few beers I bought from a black youth carrying a bucketful of ice. At that time of day hardly anyone sunbathed or stared at bathers. Diving into that cold water was a curious kind of search and find, a lay baptism. While plunging in, I had a moment of unexpected lucidity, verging on the revelation I had anticipated: I wondered what I was doing there, what had driven me to embark on that long voyage, and something inside, said Griffin, told me it was a need to renew or fulfil a destiny that had started with my grandfather, with the way he fell in love with Graciela, though that was only the beginning, a pretext.

Can someone fall in love suddenly, once and for all, knowing it's an impossible, unstable, even inhuman love, like my grandfather's love for Graciela in that port? Yes, of course one can, Griffin answered his own question, raising his voice, one definitely can, absolutely, Yes with a capital Y, a Yes I'd only have said to Li Pao, perhaps because he was neither man nor woman, but everything simultaneously, and its opposite.

Nevertheless it was *my* destiny, though I didn't know what that might be, and simply felt it looming nearer and nearer, because I'd seen the signs. Even the waters sheltered me as if they knew who I was. I felt the waves smile, the breeze caress me, the city look at me warmly, like someone who'd seen a long awaited saviour. I was searching for something, that much I'd known ever since I'd set out on my voyage and I knew what I was searching for was connected to my arrival, as if I'd already found it, as if everything around me, except myself, knew I'd already found it. I'd reached my own private Promised Land, my personal Ithaca, feeling that I was Ulysses, just as Sarmiento had thought he was Ulysses. And Du Bellay's poem came to mind that I had translated when I was a youngster: '*Heureux qui, comme Ulysse, a fait un beau voyage* . . .'

I felt I had arrived. Had I really? Was that my final destination? The idea of arriving, Griffin said, emerging from his reverie, weighed on my mind. My father had reached his Ithaca, and so had my maternal grandfather (his final act perhaps, the compendium of all his tricks, or perhaps the overriding memory he never forgot, a face as beloved as the mother country one longs to return to).

I remembered seeing Sean Griffin, my father, in his mobile home in Pasadena. I'd hired a car and arrived very early; before knocking I hesitated on the doorstep of his *roulotte* for a few moments. I breathed in and shut my eyes. I remember how I thought that finally the cycle had closed or was closing that second: I was in San Francisco, with my father, in the city where he was born, where he'd never thought to take me, the city where my stubborn will had brought me, and I would now say goodbye to him, since my visit, generated by my curiosity, was a goodbye, however long my father went on living, because I told myself deep down that I'd never see him again. And that's true to this day. Then I pressed the standard, wheezy bell. A man opened up I didn't recognise at first because of the thick double mosquito net over the doorway to his *roulotte*; I saw a man who could have been myself, but a lot older. I thought how over time we come to resemble our parents – no doubt there's plenty of empirical evidence for that. I saw myself thirty or forty years on. We will be the old men they are now, I told myself. I still don't know if it is decreed by destiny or pure biology but it's hardly worth waxing metaphysical over. It demystified an image I still had of myself when I looked into a mirror, a reminiscence of youth and potential that had yet to vanish down the river of time. I've looked at myself in the mirror in a very different way ever since, seeking out Sean ever more intensely in my face, and daily never knowing whether or not I like what I see.

That old man I'll be one day had reached his Ithaca, and perhaps it wasn't where he'd wanted to go, I don't know, I didn't ask him on that occasion. It didn't seem, on the other hand, that he was experiencing a new stage or parenthesis in his life. Seeing him and his shabby happiness in that cheap, battered, anodyne plastic chair, I realised his mobile home had set down its roots for ever. That's what I was more or less thinking on the Punta Arenas beach.

But those waters weren't my Ithaca, Desolation Island, my island, was my real Ithaca. Then I wondered what I would do when I got there in a few days, after recovering from my accident, and my searches had thrown light on my destiny. I decided to work out how I could reach the island I draw and love in as solitary a way as possible.

That I love? I asked myself, said Griffin, perhaps it will be the perennial experience in my life, I arrive, see what I want and leave: my only love is the eyewitness I carry with me. My head seemed to enter the most disconcerting haze. I spent the rest of the day sitting on the breakwaters in Manantiales, sketching the islands in a notebook I'd bought in a stationery shop on calle Garay that I then threw into the sea, thinking the currents would wash them up on a cove on my island, miles south-east, down the Straits.

The following day when I'd put the previous afternoon's nostalgia behind me, I tried to locate where my grandparents had gone in 1923. Their hotel, the Cape Horn, along one side of the cedar-lined parade square, hadn't changed, the same impressive yellow façade and slightly Prussian air. Perhaps my grandfather performed there, if he ever did perform in Punta Arenas, and perhaps that was where Graciela came to see him, and as a result, he was contracted to give a single show on the Ravels' Mercedes Estate. I wanted to clear up all that beyond doubt and went into the Cape Horn and asked to speak to the manager, who was most helpful and took me to their archive, and surprisingly quickly extracted a box with the reservation books from October to December 1923, and on the list for 8

December I found the names and signatures of Arnaldo Aguiar and Irene Ortega. They slept in room 345 that enjoyed views of the bronze statue of Magellan. I then asked if he'd performed in the hotel.

They told me that would be recorded in another kind of book, *Shows and Reviews*, which the manager's secretary quickly produced. On Saturday 13 December, in the Chinese Room, at 9 p.m., there'd been an evening of magic created by the Spanish artist, the Great Samini, for which he was paid a hundred dollars. It was surely the first time anyone had glanced at those hotel records, and I could not but feel very moved at being there myself seventy years afterwards. I gently ran my fingertips over the Great Samini's name.

I relived that magic show in my imagination, his youthful enthusiasm, the ironic way he observed the audience's astonished or incredulous expressions, the blushes of the lady from whose ear a ring emerged, the laughter of the man who recovered his wallet that had inexplicably disappeared, the applause for the severed hand trick, the collective holding of breath when the Great Samini swallowed a sword, the amazement when five doves flew out of a small box and across the room, a small box from which brightly coloured paper had previously gone up in a cloud of thick blue smoke out of which an Indian princess had stepped, performed on that single occasion by my grandmother Irene wearing glass beads and a tight-fitting turquoise dress that clung to her beautiful body.

I fantasised about all that in the hotel manager's office while my memory heard the hurrahs at the end of the performance; a tear rolled down my cheek. The manager said photos of that performance might exist. When he came back, I was disappointed he'd found none. What my imagination had created must derive from Graciela's memories of the soirée, because she described it in letters and it was etched on my mind as if I'd really been present at that wonderful performance that earned more than fifteen minutes' applause.

In the afternoon I strolled in the port area, through the Briceño district, and allowed myself to be swept up by an impromptu decision: I joined an excursion to Fort Bulnes and Port Famine, where the last dying souls in Sarmiento's settlements had been abandoned. It was a party of Italians, Germans and Argentinians. I found an empty corner in the back of the catamaran, away from the crowd. Initially it felt strange to be on a tourist boat, after sailing in a large cargo boat. I felt brought down a peg like a vulgar intruder. It was like riding in a *bateau-mouche* along the Seine. But I suddenly decided to act like someone else, because that was what I was searching for on this voyage and had sought throughout my life.

I stood by my decision and elected to create the mental void of someone who consciously forgets his immediate past. I drank in the sun and warm weather; then observed our guide, a young Frenchwoman. It was really extraordinary how the second we left the great lighthouse of Guayrabo behind us, she started to recount the story of Jacques Beauchesne, the navigator. I paid no attention to his life, one of many filling that scenario, until I heard her describe him as the French Sarmiento. His story suddenly became incredibly absorbing. As we approached Port Famine, the guide began to describe how her compatriot Beauchesne had reached that spot on 24 June 1699, and how the sea we now contemplated was, in that far-off winter, a very cruel sea, with conflicting winds that lasted for months and paralysed all shipping.

Beauchesne served the Compagnie Royale de la Mer du Sud and his mission was the French colonisation of the Straits, and the enslaving of all the natives he could find. I found nothing out of the ordinary in his voyage, except for the fact that his plans relied partly on the stubborn vehemence of a passionate priest whose ambition it was to be the bishop of those colonies. Emmanuel Jovin the priest was accompanying him as an inflexible bulwark of morality against promiscuity, since there were men and women in the contingent, future settlers who never reached Port Famine but landed in Brazil. Jovin was an irritable ascetic and prophet of the Pope who carried a cross in one hand and a sword in the other. But he was renowned throughout France for his hobby or God-given talent, depending on how you look at it: botany and its magic offshoots, potions and concoctions for witches and Satanists. Perhaps that was why he was a member of the Holy Inquisition for years and, because of his resolute resistance, was famed as a most successful exorcist. I admit that when I heard Jovin's name on the young guide's lips, I was more attentive, even shocked, for he was familiar to me from my reading, perhaps similar to something Graciela Pavic had read, when I was looking for information about Melvicius and the automaton.

Naturally I knew rather more about that Jovin than my fellow tourists, something the French guide on the Punta Arenas–Fort Bulnes tourist route didn't realise. From my researches I knew that the reason why Jovin went to the Straits with Beauchesne was probably linked to the search for the automaton that he'd been secretly conducting for years. However, in the face of what legends said about the android's powers, Jovin didn't want to possess it or any of the hypothetical advantages it might bring: Jovin wanted to destroy the automaton, because he considered it to be a *golem*, the incarnation of evil, an instrument or latent device waiting for a diabolical voice to arouse it and for Jovin 'diabolical' was synonymous with Jew.

Jovin wandered around the Straits for months on the pretext

that he was a botanist looking for plants and vegetables, but he found no traces of the automaton on that or the other two unfruitful trips he made to the region in subsequent years. However, he came very close to finding it on one occasion when he landed in a small canoe on Port Mercy, on the coast of Desolation Island, but he took the wrong path and went south instead of north to look for Melvicius's automaton in Barrister Bay, where, of course, it had never been located. In the end, Jovin sought help from the Court of Philip V, in Spain, but no one listened to him and he was judged to be mad, like so many others linked to the automaton.

When our excursion was over, we returned to Punta Arenas at night. I didn't bid farewell to the party or our young guide. I decided to walk to the Cape Horn, where I downed a couple of whiskies to the good health of the Great Samini and his beautiful Indian assistant, my grandmother Irene, whose ghosts must still haunt the Chinese Room as they perform their magic tricks. Then, almost in the early hours, I walked along the streets to the Aramis Hotel. I saw no one I knew, none of my shipmates, that is, and a tiny bubble popped inside me, the desperate feeling that I was running out of time, the feeling I was simply in transit, and that very soon someone or other would visit Punta Arenas and watch my ghost roaming its steep streets.

Once in the Aramis I became aware of the fact I'd let a few days go by before visiting the Salesian Museum because I preferred to get a feel for the city, to know the territory beneath my feet. However, I knew that tomorrow without fail I had no good reason to procrastinate and avoid what I so much desired and feared: to have sight of the automaton. The telephone woke me in the early morning. It was Pereira down in the lobby. Branco had hung himself that night.

39

STILL SLEEPY-EYED, I WENT DOWN TO THE HOTEL reception where Pereira was inspecting the print of Aramis holding a foil or sword vertical to his face, almost brushing his nose, in salute. The photo was in fact from a silent film and the actor a complete unknown. Pereira turned round sensing I was there, his face extremely despondent, an expression I'd never seen him adopt previously now darkened his perpetually cheerful looks; he repeated what he'd said on the phone a few minutes earlier. 'Branco killed himself tonight,' he said.

At 4 a.m. he'd made a slipknot in a thin rope and left his cabin, as Amuntado testified who'd seen him walk by. He walked along the stern deck, said goodbye to Greene who was on duty, reached the poop and then jumped overboard, falling plumb until the rope tightened. 'The cracking of his neck and rush of the waves against the hull was all that must have been audible at the time,' said Pereira.

It took hours to find him, because the boat was leaning on its stern and Branco's body was only visible from the sea as it swung to and fro over the ship's name: *Minerva Janela*. Who is Minerva Janela? I then wondered, said Griffin. The ship-owner's daughter, wife or mother? Perhaps the lost love of the owner or the ship's first captain? Perhaps Branco was the only one who'd known the real Minerva Janela, being so Portuguese and suffering from *saudade* as he did, then dying against the hull where her name was painted became a posthumous homage to an impossible dream.

'Futile conjectures,' said Pereira. 'Branco committed suicide because he couldn't get over his depression, the deaths in his life, and the death of Paulinho on this trip, whom he loved so dearly, was the last straw. He killed himself because he couldn't stand any more. I understand him, because at sea you eventually understand everything: no one blames a sailor for taking his own life, on the contrary, he's admired, because at sea life becomes very relative, life slims down, becomes two-dimensional, a blank sheet blown away by the wind, screwed into a ball and thrown out to a sea that immediately breaks it down into the strange cellulose plankton that enters the whale's maw in its millions and turns into white blubber, as white as Moby Dick, as white as the blank pages on which all books are written.'

Then he hugged me, said Griffin, and told me Texaco would put him in command, as established in Merchant Navy regulations. 'I'll take Grande back on board. I think he'll work better with me. And I've changed the boat's destination, and now we won't just go to Valparaíso, but to Nagasaki, in Japan. In Valparaíso we'll repair the side you fell over and the company will contract new freight. There's a job on board for you, my friend, you're a veteran now. Come along with us, if you feel like it. I'll give you a day to think it over.'

I thanked the future Captain Pereira, but declined. I was near my goal. 'Your island?' Probably, I still don't know, but I must go if only to draw it, I answered, said Griffin. At any rate, Luiz, I'll think it over and tell you tomorrow, I added. We hugged each other again.

Before he left he told me Branco's body was in the Harbour Undertakers, what they called 'The Freezer', because they'd have to conduct an autopsy. They'd then be responsible for throwing him into the sea unless anyone gave contrary instructions; in which case they'd have to fly him to Portugal, and that would be a very long, expensive process taking months. 'I told them it would be better to throw him into the sea, that was what he wanted,' said Pereira. Then I asked him to let me do it. I'd accompany the body in that ritual and cast him into the sea near Desolation Island.

'No objections to that, my friend. Besides, when the time comes none of the crew will be here, except for you, if you decide to stay. And Caporale. I think Caporale will stay on too. We leave the day after tomorrow, and the autopsy will take a couple of days. I'll give them your name,' said Pereira.

When he'd gone, I realised what a responsibility I'd taken on: Branco's corpse and I would remain alone in Punta Arenas. What a strange twist of fate that I should give him his final burial rites on my island. Once Pereira had left, I went back to my bedroom, fell into a deep sleep and woke up in mid-afternoon with a headache. I ordered a snack at the hotel and went for a stroll around the city, and thought of Branco and his body hanging for hours from the poop of the ship.

Why did he choose that place and that kind of death? Why didn't he shoot himself (I'd once seen a pistol in his bunk) or swallow pills? How could I know why he chose to meet death that way? Perhaps he was seeking to die in close physical contact with his boat, a last, desperate embrace of the boat one loves, the boat that had become one's skin, one's body, the touch of cold, damp steel, the metallic hardness that resounds solemnly when hit, all that, perhaps, a final union with his boat, the wish of every despairing captain who's come to the end of his days.

They say a hanged man ejaculates in the last seconds of his life in a reflex, anguished movement, as a farewell to life. I imagined Branco ejaculating against the hull of his boat, even if it was through his trousers, a savage, terrible symbol, turning that way of dying into an act of love and once more I felt affection for Captain Afonso Branco and his solitary gesture.

Quite unintentionally I found myself on new streets walking towards the Harbour Undertakers, 'The Freezer', to the address Pereira had given me. I left my details with a port administrator to facilitate my taking charge of the burial on the high seas. When I'd finished the paperwork, I signed on the dotted line of a strange section headed: Guardian. From that moment on I was the guardian of Branco's body. The port bureaucrat warned me they couldn't let me see it until the autopsy had concluded, but I told him I didn't want to anyway. Besides, I could have told him what its conclusions would be, said Griffin; death from unredeemable sadness.

The following day I finally visited the museum. I left my hotel early. It was a mild morning and the sun was shining in a bright blue sky, as if blessing that special day. I walked slowly up the long calle Chiloé, where a handful of men were standing on the top of ladders pruning trees with electric saws. The pavements had grass walkways and I decided to walk the twelve blocks to calle Maipú, which I then strolled along to the corner of Avenida Bulnes and the Regional Salesian Museum at number 374. My heart was racing, my temples beating and I felt on edge.

It was just like the photos I'd seen of the museum's façade: a small two-storey building with porthole attics, fin-de-siècle balconies, old-style, would-be European architecture, painted bone-white and slate roofed. I walked through the wrought-iron entrance after lingering a while and thinking how often Graciela

Pavic must have done just that, and of the time the attendant, Kuller, carried the automaton in his arms and Graciela's murderers went in on 28 December 1965.

Once inside I was struck by the silence broken only by the hum from the air-conditioning and by the dearth of visitors. A rather old Chilean lady named Doña Magdalena Morales was now the museum director. I asked to see her straight away. She was of average build, with greying hair, a pink complexion and deep voice. She moved gracefully and spoke soothingly and that won me over. On the other hand, I was nervous and didn't want that to be obvious, though I finally realised it was absurd to hide my anxiety.

Initially, I didn't mention the automaton, but introduced myself as someone who was interested in Graciela Pavic because she'd been an old friend of my grandfather. Then I felt obliged to tell the director the story of my grandparents' journey, and did so passionately, avoiding any reference to Melvicius's automaton. Doña Magdalena invited me to visit some of the museum's rooms before going to the attic, where Graciela's belongings were kept, donated to the museum by Esteban Ravel's nephews after he died. 'At the end of the day, Graciela's only home and family was this museum, or so it seems,' said the director. I nodded because I was thoroughly in agreement. She showed me the Patagonian Zoology Rooms with dozens of stuffed animals I found at once disgusting and terrifying, and the Anthropology rooms with photos of the last Onas. 'The ones who were buried in the nearby cemetery,' she added. Then we walked past the glass cabinets with minerals, fossils and pottery and archaeological remains. And the Botany Room where I came across the specimens and drawings of plants and flowers made by one E. Jovin, doubtless Beauchesne's Jovin, as it said on the little cards next to each exhibit. And finally the

History and Fortifications of the Straits Room, which is where I knew the automaton was to be found.

My heart missed a beat, but there was nothing in the room remotely resembling a metal android. There were lots of figures in period dress, even one representing Sarmiento de Gamboa, and they made me feel desperately sad. The room was a cruel caricature of history, like a room in a waxworks museum or at a fairground. As we left I asked Doña Magdalena if she'd ever known Graciela. She said she hadn't, she'd been at the museum for ten years and had come straight from Valparaíso, her city of birth, where she'd been a librarian, in order to retire to her husband's city of birth. When she mentioned that city, I thought absentmindedly of Pereira and the *Minerva Janela*, now setting sail from the port of Valparaíso to cross the Pacific to Japan. What would be in those containers now? What storms would they endure? Who would be the man to go overboard on this trip, now I wasn't there?

I fought hard to resist the temptation to ask Doña Magdalena about the automaton, and obliged her to let us retrace our steps to the room with the historical figures. I wanted to look for myself. This time I examined everything carefully while she spoke garrulously of incidents I was familiar with. Perhaps the director thought I was interested because I wanted to know about the events leading to the creation of the Straits settlements: I let her ramble on. While pretending to pay close attention, my eyes scrutinised every corner of the glass cabinets, every enactment of fighting or daily life among Indians and settlers. It was obvious the automaton wasn't in the room where it had been exhibited for so many years, and Doña Magdalena, in her narration of the history of Tierra del Fuego, didn't mention it at all. To my astonishment, for the first time in my life I began to doubt it really existed, although it had made an appearance with my grandparents in that memorable photo from 1923. That's impossible, it must be somewhere, I thought, said Griffin, unless they'd taken it to bits, which would be tantamount to killing it, or worse: it would have been equivalent to murdering Graciela for a second time.

I was disappointed but couldn't keep the director there any longer, and followed her to the attic. The room where they kept Graciela's objects was a small stockroom with a tiny ventilation shaft in the ceiling, more like a junk room with floor-to-ceiling shelves crammed with objects wrapped in brown paper or white sheeting and bags piled as high as they could go: the big parcels and different sizes of sealed cardboard boxes sometimes jutted out perilously over the shelves. Once Doña Magdalena had finished her duties as a guide, she said goodbye and left me alone. 'Take your time, we don't shut,' she said.

Finding myself in Punta Arenas a second time with a box that contains memories about someone I'd been deeply influenced by gave me a strange feeling that I was reliving a moment of *déjà vu*. Two days ago I'd been given a similar box in the Cape Horn Hotel with references to my grandparents on their honeymoon. It was again sadly ironic that everything that was part of my story, Graciela's connection with my life through the lives of my grandparents, was now in boxes that were kept, if not forgotten, in places nobody had visited or sought out for years. The fact they were in separate boxes gave them a funeral urn aspect. But these were ashes, ashes I'd come to spread with my presence.

I realised that everything, absolutely everything held there had been waiting for me in order to recount the meaning and fate within each story, each life, each object, each being, and perhaps the only real one in all this was the one I'd yet to see: the automaton I had so longed for. I understood I'd been summoned to that forsaken place so everything might rest in peace for good.

After opening the box, I took out several bundles of letters, antiquated items from the boys' childhood, Graciela's photos and souvenirs. Among the photos, said Griffin, I saw for the first time one of Arturo Bagnoli as a very young man, perhaps before he set off on the *Emma Salvatores*, and another of the newly wed Arturo and Graciela, and of Miro Pavic surrounded by his children, with little Graciela on his knees, and of Arturo and Graciela's children, Gaetano and Pablo. I also saw photos of Esteban Ravel with Graciela on his arm strolling across the city's parade ground. In a separate envelope I found photos of the automaton, dozens from every possible angle, perhaps taken at different stages of its restoration. I was also deeply moved to find the letters from my grandfather Arnaldo and Graciela's drafts with notes to the letters she then typed in fair before sending, letters I wasn't aware of, that proved they'd had an amorous relationship that was much more intense than I'd thought, and which showed they had indeed loved each other platonically for years, during which they swore a firm pledge they'd meet in the future, though they never did.

I started to read the letters and time slipped imperceptibly by, I was so absorbed by my reading and rereading, reremembering everything: their quiet, invisible love, more powerful than any distance and their madness, but a bitter and unhappy love too. After a while, an hour or two perhaps, my neck started to hurt because I'd not changed my posture in that small room. I lifted my head by chance at that moment and leaned back with my eyes shut. On reopening them I immediately noticed an irregularly shaped package near the ceiling, and once I'd spotted it, it took a real effort to come to terms with what I had seen.

It lay on its side on the top shelf in that small stockroom where I became suddenly aware I was touching the few remaining items that belonged to Graciela, like an intruder in the sanctuary or sepulchre of her memory. But that idea soon evaporated because what was over my head suddenly became real. I saw it was a foreshortened figure, but still couldn't imagine what it was. It looked like an old toy, a papier-mâché rocking horse or large rusted tin-foil doll, though its shape indicated it couldn't be any of those things, or, perhaps, at most, the broken half of one of those figures in the History Room. However, it also looked like the model of a large demasted ship wrapped in sheets.

It reminded me of the time I saw Flaubert's Amazonian parrots in the attic in the Natural History Museum in Rouen, rescued from oblivion by my intrusive eyes. Its forlornness impressed me greatly, something resembling a degree of sorrow, a kind of pity for another species. The object I could now see was partly covered by a white sheet secured with ropes and grey with dust. Through a hole in the material one could see eye-shaped oval striations, painted on like real eyes, cold, impassive and threatening, but I perceived right away that they were inoffensive beneath the peculiar mummification they'd been subjected to. It was face down, and looking me in the eye. Then I suppressed my startled surprise as I realised with a real sense of awe that what I could see above me was indeed the automaton.

40

WHAT DO WE HUMAN BEINGS KNOW ABOUT ONE another? Griffin wondered, very little at the end of the day. We have a very superficial awareness, a trait here, a mark there, simple data that provide a map but don't lead us to the treasure. What did I know about Nemo Caporale? That he had a horse tattooed on one arm and Lovecraft's face on the other, that he was bald along superbly classical lines, like a Roman bust of Scipio, that he fantasised about his remote roots in Savoy, that he hoarded tunnels in his mind, that the aura around electricity had fascinated him from childhood and that he knew everything about the subject like a clever Frankenstein, that he was at once happy and gloomy, that he was good-hearted and always smiling and a theosophist. That's all. That's all I knew about him.

Nevertheless there was a spark of empathy between us and we'd started to be friends, as a result of affinities we shared: horses perhaps, tunnels perhaps, the stars and chimera perhaps. I liked and trusted him, and we'd struggled and worked together in the storm; our lives, for a few moments, had depended on each other on that night when the containers fell into the sea. But that obviously doesn't go far enough.

I know, said Griffin, that a black spot exists in every life, in any life, an untoward incident that is dark, unexpected and shocking, that appears and is accepted irrevocably when it occurs, as if there wasn't a will to oppose such complicity, or at least a will that looks at itself from the outside, its ego split into two, one that lives and one that looks at the life being lived, accepting the black spot, the shocking incident, which, over the years, is then dragged along like a ball and chain, a sense of remorse, of guilt, a blemish, whatever, everyone should use the word that suits their specific case, and the need for a cloak of secrecy to hide the black spot, the dark deed, is evident deep within the self, to the point that one's guard or degree of alertness must never be lowered, and one must always strive to keep the secret hidden within one's life. And every life, and I mean every life, has a secret. I am sure of that, Griffin declared.

Caporale had such a secret that he confessed to me quite naturally, perhaps to exorcise it or perhaps to turn me into an accomplice of the atrocity he'd committed, that, to tell the truth, Caporale wasn't really completely aware of. It happened when we were by ourselves in Punta Arenas. All of a sudden, one afternoon when it had rained and the air smelt fresh, he rang me. Caporale would come and collect me at the Aramis in a couple of hours and we'd go to dine in a restaurant he knew.

'A farewell or rendezvous for two shipmates, you choose the excuse for our celebration, it makes no odds, it's what we drink, like good pirates on the dead man's chest, that matters,' he told me, Griffin said. I thought he'd tried to introduce an allusion to Branco, without meaning to. He'd left the *Minerva Janela*, as Pereira had informed me, and wanted to meet up with me. 'You owe me this one,' said Caporale on the phone. 'We didn't say goodbye the other day and I'd like to know once and for all what you're going to get up to on your blasted island, because that's why you've come here, isn't it?' I mumbled that was true, that that was why I'd come. 'Perfect. If I were you, I'd never forget it. I'll take you somewhere you don't know, although you can get to know this city in a flash.'

Caporale arrived punctually at eight in the lobby of the Aramis, where I was waiting dozily reading the evening newspaper, the *Magellan Daily*. It was strange to see an advertisement for the Salesian Regional Museum. 'The Entire History of Patagonia. Newly Refurbished Rooms', read the heading. This was followed by the opening times, office hours, old and new rooms and the drawing of an Ona Indian in hunting mode flourishing a spear in one corner. After a welcoming hug and congratulating him on his elegant appearance – white linen jacket and panama hat – we took a taxi and drove down a street full of newly green monkey puzzle trees. We exchanged a few commonplaces until Caporale told me he'd arranged to meet someone he wanted to introduce to me, a friend of his he'd not seen for some time. Whenever he passed through Punta Arenas he rang him and fixed a time to go for a drink and raise a toast to their happy memories. I thought it was a good idea and really had no objections. I felt at a loss and the social contact might jolt me out of a mental obsession that meant I only thought of the automaton and the circumstances in which I'd found it the previous day.

Muller was the name of the man we were going to see and he'd recently been working as a detective at the Plaza. 'A low-key job, lots of free time and the feeling you're a guy who's struck it rich,' according to Caporale. They had agreed a rendezvous in a restaurant a good few streets to the north, in the Acapulco, where we were headed now. He filled the time in the taxi, a new, comfortable Rover, telling me how he'd met Muller, and his secret suddenly popped out; one he recounted with the natural amorality of a child casually relating how he'd just killed his mother. He decided to let me in on what was quite a dreadful secret: years ago, in July 1974, he'd reached that point in his youth when one is swept along by burning ideals one is ready to kill or die for. 'They could beat you to pulp, torture and kill you, and so could we. It was all quite natural,' he added. 'Communism and guerrillas were the scourge of South America at the time, Caporale continued, he belonged to an anti-communist movement, Patria e Liberdade, also known as the 'black warriors', linked to General Coutinha in the Bahia region. Some called them fascists, others patriots, and others even God's soldiers and that was what he felt he was, one of God's soldiers. He signed up with three other comrades to go and support the anti-communist struggle in Chile in every way possible now that General Augusto Pinochet had 'shaken the rotten crumbs from the tablecloth', going there to work politically, or not so politically, 'as life at the time was not about being over scrupulous', he said. 'That was what I was like then and how I came to be in Santiago de Chile that summer, an impulsive youth, stubbornly confident my actions could change the course of history.'

He was taken to a freezing, unlit hangar in the military airport on the outskirts of Santiago, with only cones of light in the odd corner from sad, tiny bulbs, under which other comrades smoked endlessly and waited. These included five extremely aggressive, ebullient *carabineros* in plain clothes, one or two looking daggers drawn, and next to them a group of variously aged Germans, waiting for orders, or so it seemed. His friend, Muller, whom we were about to meet, was one of these.

He got to know him personally that same day. He was young and fair-haired like Caporale, and as hairy as a brush. They talked for a while and it was soon obvious they had certain things in common, like an interest in engines. They chatted about the engine of a small plane being dismantled on a table very close to where they were standing. 'We could touch the parts, lined up ready for reassembly, and even smell the grease on them.' Muller was also a theosophist.

The hangar belonged to the Chilean Air Force, but was being used by the political police, the DINA, whose deputy-director came to give them instructions and thank them for serving the cause of freedom so devotedly in their capacity as volunteers from that fraternal country Brazil, and other such rhetoric. The deputy-director was accompanied by an older, sinister-looking man, who spoke with a foreign, no doubt, German accent, and was tall, strongly built, and wore a grey uniform Caporale had never seen before that was definitely not a Chilean Air Force uniform. Muller said it was a friend of his father, a very important man respected by the entire German colony in Chile. They considered him to be an intrepid hero. He was Walter Rauff, an old German Nazi who'd escaped the ashes of the Third Reich, like most of the German colony, to remake their wretched lives. After the coup in the previous year, Rauff had put himself at the disposition of the Military Junta to help rid Chile of communist vermin. After the brief harangue from the deputy-director that Caporale had completely forgotten, Rauff quite coldly and impersonally reeled off technical information about the contents of lorries that had just arrived, that he indicated with a nod of his head; information like fifty bodies, twenty in plane one, fifteen in plane two, ten in plane three, height four thousand feet, flight distance five miles, and other similar data.

Around fifty men had been heaped into those lorries Caporale hadn't seen arrive, but which had driven single file behind the car from which the deputy-director and Rauff had just alighted. They were fifty bruised and beaten men, bandaged all over their bodies, some on stretchers in a state of semi-consciousness;

they were all prisoners, with handcuffs and leather straps round their wrists; those able to stand up were tied up in pairs.

When they got off the lorries to get into the planes, many were pushed violently by the soldiers guarding them or beaten with clubs.

It was then Caporale realised what their task was to be. They bundled the wounded and remaining prisoners into the three Fokker Jupiter Star transport planes revving up on the runway. Rauff's orders were carried out to the letter, as was to be expected, and they assigned Muller and himself to plane two, with a total of fifteen men. 'That was the only moment I could have refused to participate,' said Caporale, 'said goodbye and cleared off, volunteer that I was.'

But he didn't and he had never thought of doing so; after all, although they all imagined what was going to happen, nobody had said anything, or made any statement at all, so consequently they knew nothing as yet. He deferred moral judgements till later, but a voice within him was already telling him it was only one of the many actions that were necessary to avoid the worse evil of a communist state in South America, a cancer, a powder-keg, a plague, that those men were in fact bitter enemies, and all that scene, the hanger, Rauff, Muller, the stretchers, the prisoners, the shouting soldiers were simply part of what happens in a war: it was that simple.

He suddenly adopted a soldierly consciousness, and repeated the slogan '*Patria e Liberdade*', its ideals, and boarded the noisy Fokker Jupiter Star via the rear ramp, after the miserable fucking communists. The planes took off. It was the first flight Muller and he took on an execution mission, because that's what those flights were: gallows planes.

'Three hours later we had to feed them more sleeping pills so they didn't get rebellious. You never know how strong a man can get when he finds out he's about to die, even if he is handcuffed,' he said. The two of them were given the task of administering the sleeping pills. Caporale finally felt useful, even though he guessed it wasn't a very honourable occupation. At a point in the flight, a plain-clothes *carabinero*, the one with the venomous gaze, went over to him and Muller and ordered them into the cabin. He remembered the *carabinero* saying: 'You've done your duty. Now go and talk to the pilot, because this isn't a job for children.'

When they were walking to the pilot's cabin, one of the prisoners, whose whole body was strapped to a stretcher, tugged at Caporale's trousers. He just had time to whisper his name, before the *carabinero* hit him in the face with the butt of his gun, no doubt killing him. He said very quietly, as if the words were struggling out from behind his teeth: 'I'm Raúl Lori, from Atacama', then the blow came and Caporale never gave him another glance. He bled from the mouth and was one of the first to be slid, stretcher and all, down the open ramp.

The altitude they were flying made it likely that the bodies would drop in the area of a kilometre around the islands at the entrance to the Straits at the Pacific end, in the area of the Evangelist Isles, the Condor Islands, and Parker and Beaufort Bay. When I heard mention of the bay located opposite Desolation Island, said Griffin, I immediately thought, as I listened to Caporale's story, that some of the bodies might have dropped into its waters. I imagined Raúl Lori from Atacama coming such a long way to die, from the north, perhaps because he was a miner or a communist or poor or a singer, and his bones landing on the island I used to draw without ever thinking it might be a grave and final resting place for hundreds of men thrown out of airplanes in the summer of 1974, in the midst of the Chilean repression, trussed up and put to sleep so they couldn't shout, swim or save themselves, if by chance they happened to survive the bone-breaking crash against waves, at the mercy of a swell that would wash them up, since they were already more dead than alive, in their death agony at best, on to one of the many coves of that steep-sided island.

'I was always sorry I got to know one of their names,' said Caporale, 'because individual reality upset me, the dead turned individual are no longer part of the anonymous dead, a long list where it didn't matter if there were ten or ten millions, one of the lists Rauff carried in his leather briefcase, and I realised right away that, if only for strategic reasons, I must keep quiet about all that. Nobody would ever understand how dirty wars can be.'

When we were near the Acapulco restaurant, Caporale merely said, by way of conclusion: 'The only other person who knows is Muller but we never talk about it. What's the point if we only see each other once in a blue moon? It was our fate, period. We went on some twenty or thirty such flights, from the Punta Arenas aerodrome, which was where they now took undesirable prisoners. That was why Muller stayed on here. None of those other wretches, on the other occasions, ever told me his name, only that Raúl Lori from Atacama, who is now a ghost from the past. It's here.' And the taxi suddenly swerved and braked in front of the restaurant door.

Muller was waiting at a table inside. He was fair-haired and still wore his hair very thick and short. He had an athletic complexion, a scar from the corner of his lip to halfway up his cheek and youthful features. He wore a white and grey check shirt. He was smoking one of those very slim cigarettes he kept squeezing mechanically into a long amber plastic cigarette holder. He blinked three times in a nervous tic. He seemed friendly enough and I thought he was smiling enthusiastically in a way that seemed happy but unjustified. When I saw him, with Caporale's story still echoing in my head, I thought of Krupa, the Serbian sniper skulking in our crew, and about what Captain Branco would have done if he'd been aware of the histories of Caporale and this Muller now innocently shaking my hand. He'd have thrown them overboard, no doubt, and perhaps he and Fernando Grande would have given them a drubbing.

As we were dining, I couldn't chase from my head the idea of men's bodies dropping head first into the waters of the Straits, an image I found difficult to conceive however much I tried, and I thought about why Caporale had said he wanted to see his friend again: to raise a glass with him to their 'happy memories'. Were the images I created in disgust the 'happy memories' uniting those two men? Then I saw that Caporale and Krupa were closer than I'd first thought, because they both blamed the war for their 'black spot', for their 'dark deed', war, that place where anything goes because nothing will be taken to court, at most will only be avenged by the winning side. That was why they were 'happy memories', because they simply weren't bad memories.

What could I do? Remake history, resuscitate thousands of Raúl Loris? I knew perfectly well I couldn't, that that was quixotic nonsense. I joined their toast to memories they'd talked about non-stop during the whole dinner. Like two old comrades-in-arms who meet up in times of peace and can only fill their present with nostalgia for the past. They laughed and kept glancing at me in a genuinely friendly way. I joined in their shamelessness and started laughing as well. Goodbye, Raúl Lori, goodbye Sarajevo, goodbye you dead millions, goodbye moral scruples. Hello bastards, I'm one of yours.

All of a sudden I remembered Pereira was expecting me to

ring him. I left the table to do just that. Luiz? I said, I'm going to stay on shore, I wanted to make sure I told you. I've had enough of boats. Have a good trip and lots of luck. Pereira said goodbye from the other end of the line with a curt, 'I knew as much.' They were setting sail that night. So it's Nagasaki then? I asked. 'Yes, it's Nagasaki. *Ciao*, my friend, don't drown in some other sea,' said Pereira.

I went back to Caporale and Muller's table. They were still swapping anecdotes about themselves and people I didn't know. Then Muller decided to tell us about his job as a detective at the Plaza. 'Nothing ever happens,' he said. 'Now and then someone wants to try it on and leave without paying or uses a credit card that has no funds, or someone registers under a false name and is arrested by the police. I intervene so it's a painless, discreet arrest, and doesn't frighten off honest customers. Sometimes old men check in with their bits on the side, on the sly so nobody knows, but you know it's an old man with his bit on the side, because they never, never, look each other in the eye.' Muller also said he could make a list of all the old men and bits of fluff who'd passed through the Plaza, their clothes, luggage, gestures, favourite phrases, petty life stories, in the past, future and in their imaginations, because everyone in a hotel, however much they disguise and hide themselves, is transparent, reveals their life, what's past and what's still to come.

While he spoke, I thought about the lists Rauff made, which led me to the lists Muller would make. Curiously enough, a few days ago, when walking around Punta Arenas, I'd thought about lists and the listed, passions for numbers, accumulation, variations on a theme, the quantity of units that make up a body, a legend, or a mosaic. Then I told Caporale and Muller about my idea of lists. In a café on the Parade Square, I thought of making two lists, one of people who've helped me in life and another of those who've harmed me.

The order didn't matter, where I started did, I said. What was the name of that guy who gave me a break as a young man, and the other fellow who tripped me up, and the one who let me go first in that clinic, garage or savings bank, and the other who tried to rob, deceive or pervert me, and the one who gave me what he most prized in life, and the other who mugged me down an alleyway, and the one who gave me a good idea and the other who let me down, and the one who saved me from being knocked over, falling off a balcony or drowning in the sea, and the other who didn't move a finger when I was in danger, and the one who got me tickets for a show, and the other who hated me for ever for no reason at all, and the one who had good reason to hate me, and the other who accompanied me on my way and the one whose path I spurned, and the man who opened my eyes, and the one who wanted to close them, and who were all those men and women I loved and who loved me, and all those I turned away or refused to love, or who refused to love me? We behave like angels and demons towards them, and they repay us in kind.

If I were a writer, said Griffin, the only novel I'd really like to have written, the only one I can imagine, is simply an account of all the people I've known in my life, to a greater or lesser extent, who've connected with me over time, and to relate, as sparingly as possible, my encounters with each of them, however brief or insignificant, starting with the baby next to me in the maternity ward where I was born, the midwife who took me from my mother, my father's friend who came to congratulate him and lifted me up in his arms, and so on to this day, for example, when I've spent time with the taxi driver who brought us here, and with Muller, Caporale's friend, the latest in that list known as Griffin's Novel.

How much might we be able to remember? Is it an impossible challenge? I admit I once took it on and realised that the effort was like repeating a third of one's life, if one discounts the time we spend sleeping or alone with our own thoughts or not seeing or bumping into anyone. I abandoned that crazy idea because it would have deprived me of the time left to me in this world.

When I stopped talking, I was again filled with that bittersweet feeling that had invaded me in the course of the evening, a mixture of harsh reality and self-reproach for being in the company of those two men, demons rather than angels, as a friend, complicit in a compromising exchange, in a charged conspiracy. And perhaps because of that fraternal spirit of intriguers that was suddenly born as the night advanced, when we were outside the restaurant and Caporale and Muller asked me innocently enough in the middle of the empty street 'what can we do to help you in this city that's the arsehole of the world?', I had that sudden flash of inspiration about stealing the automaton from the museum, so at least I could feel righteous, an angel rather than a demon.

41

WHEN I WAS A CHILD, I ONCE THOUGHT THAT I WAS a stone, said Griffin, and I never quite understood why I liked that state. I thought that stones and I shared the same motionless, static nature. It was a curious sensation, because at a stroke it erased every human action that had seemed reasonable in my life: I didn't walk, I stayed still, I didn't move, I didn't wet myself, I didn't reply when spoken to, I thought I was weighty, I hesitated about whether to breathe or not, I was even sure I could continue to live without breathing, my heart seemed to stop, my arm went cold, I intuited that time would be infinitely extended, I ceased to be myself and yet was. Most peculiar, there's no doubt about that.

Stones, I then thought, are and are not, they both know and don't know that they are stones; they simply exist, are there and remain there. In the course of one of my nights in Li Pao's house in Barcelona, he told me about some Chinese monks who think themselves into this stony state and can stay still for weeks on end without drinking or eating, aware they have entered a dimension of eternity. In that trance, they can't feel someone pricking them and don't shift from their static state even if pushed. 'My father,' said Li Pao, according to Griffin, 'saw one of those monks roll downstairs and fall as if he were a statue, not moving a muscle.' They are the rock men of Huankongh whose senses are dormant.

I felt this was a variation on the theme of the visibly invisible. I couldn't stop thinking about the automaton's strange invisibility camouflaged in the museum's small stockroom at the top of a shelf. Half wrapped in a sheet, looking like a stone totem waiting to be moved, to be planted in a garden or thrown to the bottom of a river or the sea, to become yet another stone alongside the many already there and thus belong eternally to the immobility of time, and even go beyond the realm of time. It also looked like a shroud, and I thought of the stony nature of the dead. When I saw it, I guessed that the automaton and I shared that stony state, and consequently were invisible despite being visible, at last united in a special way. This will strike you as strange, but that set of inert parts excited me, as an individual excites the person he loves and desires, as it excited Graciela Pavic to the point of loving devotion. I felt attracted, a deep, loving tenderness, to that robot half swathed in a white sheet, its pretend face on a level with mine, though further away than it often was from Graciela, when it was simply a few centimetres and she thrust her lips towards the figure's mouth that she kissed, eyes shut, searching for Arturo Bagnoli or herself.

When Graciela died, the automaton was condemned to definitive invisibility, as if struck by an additional curse; people wanted to erase the fact it had ever existed. They could have destroyed it, an option the museum director had carefully considered, then rejected, despite the pressure he was under, given that Graciela's murder was an event that upset the whole of Punta Arenas. The automaton was simply put into storage and out of sight: isolation acquiring the status of a symbolic prison sentence.

Doña Magdalena later told me, Griffin said, that first they kept it in that backroom to guard against theft, because of the morbid influence myths about its magic powers wielded over weak and ambitious minds; then they decided it would be best to remove it from there to avoid gossip-mongering about malign repercussions from possessing or indeed exhibiting it. That was surely a drastic decision taken by the most timorous of directors shortly after Graciela's demise. But over time, as we all know, prevention yields to apathy and apathy to neglect, the gateway to complete oblivion. In a word, the automaton became petrified even in the memories of those managing the museum. Or rather was petrified again, as happened for centuries on Desolation Island when it fused with that basalt wasteland.

That night when we'd said our goodbyes and they left me in the hotel entrance, I saw Caporale and Muller walk down an empty, poorly lit street. They strolled like two people with clear consciences, two mates who'd put their crimes behind them; from where I stood, one would have said they were two good friends on holiday.

I went up to my room feeling the alcohol that had gone to my head and knew that I was in for a sleepless night. I stretched out and again scrutinised the picture in which Aramis the musketeer smoked a pipe while his companions rode up in the distance. I thought Aramis had adopted a different stance to the one I'd seen previously. He was now about to look up from the Rancé book he was reading and turn round to wave a welcoming hand, because (and this was another sudden impression) I also thought Athos, Porthos and D'Artagnan were closer, had grown in size or galloped up, said Griffin, whatever. What's more, I noticed the name of the picture for the first time: *The Bucolic Musketeer*.

That abrupt change of perception took me into a brown study

where sleep and hallucination joined forces and summoned Alexandre Dumas himself, guffawing perversely and supporting Aramis's shoulder and both mirrored the 1923 photo of my grandparents with Graciela next to the automaton. I suddenly woke up, Dumas' wild laughter still echoing in my head.

It was clear that the dream I'd just had wasn't without its own logic, since I'd read somewhere, I'm not sure when or where, that Dumas was a great fan of mechanical devices, had intended writing a very different novel from the one he finally produced, and even got to the point of imagining that the Gascon D'Artagnan was a robot manufactured by the three musketeers. According to notes in early drafts of the novel, Athos had a background in physics and a degree in maths from the Sorbonne, Porthos was an intrepid engineer and nautical expert and Aramis a brilliant, subtle artist as well as a skilled draughtsman. Together they would create a mechanical model able to wield a sword and imitate their most famous and secret moves, like Athos's double thrust or Aramis's lethal zigzag, an articulated model whose powers of resistance would drive Richelieu's troops mad and seduce Milady. I even wondered, Griffin said, whether Dumas might have heard of Melvicius's automaton or known about Jovin the fanatical priest's search for it in the same period when the musketeers rode abroad.

I realised I was sitting on the bed and that the sun had risen some time ago. I tried to act as if awake, although my whole body was floating in a mixture of sleep and paralysis. It was then the disturbing figure of Dumas faded from my head and I sensed my fate was simply to restore the automaton to its rightful place on Desolation Island, the Desolation Island that occupied so much of my life. I grasped that after Graciela's death it was meaningless to keep it in the museum, hidden out of sight and totally neglected.

Why had it been punished and rejected like that? I had a sudden insight in my bedroom and knew that the parable of the automaton's life and lives of all who crossed its path over the centuries from 1580 would now come to an end thanks to me: I would return it to the place it had been snatched from, where Sarmiento had erected it in the north of the island, to the location for which it was created by a visionary mind in Prague, a city of visionaries.

Metaphorically, I also felt like an automaton coldly executing movements someone had set in motion ever since I'd set my eyes on that photo in my adolescence. Indeed I viewed all my most recent years, nay my whole life, in a new light, as the implementation of a plan that would climax in the automaton's historic reinstatement.

Thus my two obsessions came together for ever: Desolation Island and Melvicius's automaton. What would I do for the rest of my life? I wondered. Tell the whole story, as I'm doing now, as I've been doing for days, Griffin said. I felt I was Sarmiento de Gamboa, as he in turn had felt that he was Ulysses: creators of eternity.

I reached my decision after several hours of meditation, when I sat on the bed and looked out at the changing sky over Punta Arenas, as changing as the picture of bucolic Aramis, and at midday I rang Nemo Caporale to ask for help. You're the only person I can rely on, I told him, I don't know anyone else. My voice had yet to assume the imploring tone I was prepared to adopt, given I could never do what I had to do by myself. The words 'I need' slipped in. I need your help. I need you, my friend. I need a helping hand.

Caporale didn't respond immediately, no doubt weighing up the likely or unlikely consequences. I could hear him breathing at the end of the line. I felt he was hesitating and I was impatient for a reply. Then he said, 'Yes, of course, Oliver, count on me if you need help, one sailor helping another, of course, my friend, I'm ready,' said Nemo, now as enthusiastic as ever. He'd understood straight away, he even said he understood why I had left the *Minerva Janela*. Like a good theosophist, he spoke about destiny, about his destiny in this city and joked that crime also linked him to Punta Arenas, whatever he did and whenever he came.

Caporale knew the city, but not well enough. He said, 'We can't do a thing without Muller.' Two hours later, the three of us were agreeing on the detail in a bar on calle Amalfitano, the Ribeiro, the one where I'd met the pisco drinker on a previous night, who'd told me about his father bankrupting himself by betting his all on Saint-Exupéry's truncated flight, on that famous raid in 1938. Caporale and Muller hatched a plan of action in a corner of the bar that we then carried out to the letter.

It would be a night robbery and would leave no trace. 'Four breakages but no blood,' said Caporale. Muller and I nodded, said Griffin. That same afternoon, as the sun was setting, we met in the old garage-shed Muller used for his motorcycle hobby at the back of his house, on calle Eusebio Lillo, in the west of the city, a way from the centre. Muller had agreed to buy a large wooden box a few hours before and take it to the garage he'd filled with old newspapers and pillows wheedled from one of the maids at the Plaza.

We drove from there and Muller parked close to the museum in a side street off calle Maipú, between a fruit shop and a billiard hall, next to a tradesman's entrance in a wall leading to a wrought-iron door. The door opened on to the museum courtyard with a flagpole in the middle. I remember being nervous, on edge, the moment before the robbery, I had the uncontrollable palpitations I always got, but then became cold and calculating and told myself: Learn to erase any trace of yourself. What did that mean, why should I say something that implied I was feeling guilty?

Isn't it strange how at times quite inexplicably we wonder whether or not to leave a trace of our impact on things or other people's lives? When I was about to break in through the service door that had a single padlock, I wondered about the traces I'd left on others, on the lives of those who appeared in the list in Griffin's Novel, as I described the list of all the encounters one has in life. If one erases those traces one disappears, and one wants to be innocent and keep on the safe side, Griffin pondered absentmindedly yet again, before adding, Consequently it's one more way to be invisible. I can never release myself from myself or from the trace my name carries: the indelible invisibility within my surname. And standing next to that door Muller was deftly forcing with a hook, I caught myself thinking the same thoughts as Manuel Oltracina and Elmer Sánchez, the killers from Santiago who came to steal the automaton and left after killing Graciela, since both wanted to remove all trace of their presence in order to remain innocent and I was replaying their performance, sweating their sweat, fearing their fears, taking the same steps as they had in the yard, through the gallery to the exhibition rooms and across the worn flagstones in the corridors.

As we had waited until the early hours, it was all very easy. The security guard, the only one on night duty, was nodding off in front of a television with the volume on low. I noticed he had a large bandage plastered over one eye. We saw him dozing in an armchair with his bare feet up at the back of a small office with a table littered with books of crossword puzzles. He didn't walk round the rooms, ever. Muller made fun of him, imitating his one-eyed look, then went back to the car and waited for us with the engine running.

Caporale and I walked stealthily through museum rooms in total darkness. We'd pulled woollen socks over our shoes so we didn't make any noise. We found our way with the help of the light from a torch that lit up the stairs as we went up to the attic where I'd seen the automaton. The stockroom door was locked, like last time. Caporale forced it with Muller's hook and it opened easily, making a small noise the guard didn't hear. We took the automaton down from that top shelf. I removed the sheet, took a good long look and covered it up again. My impression was that it was in perfect shape, although its surface wasn't shiny or at least not as much as I'd imagined it would be, and was dotted with rust and abrasions caused by a chemical product that had been poured on it.

When I saw the painted features of its face, everything we were doing so furtively took on an unreal, almost grotesque dimension, as if we were in a toy museum. We tied several coils of adhesive tape around it. I suddenly felt like my grandfather, the Great Samini, doing one of his disappearing acts, and my fingers instinctively looked for a gap in the folds of the sheet to check the automaton was still there. It was; I could feel its cold touch.

Caporale and I carried it slowly downstairs, making sure it didn't scrape against the walls. It weighed less than I'd thought. We went back through the gallery and out into the courtyard. Once we were in the alley, Muller shut the service door, although the padlock was broken and he had to leave it open. We lifted the automaton carefully into the boot of the car. The theft had taken some twenty minutes. We drove back to Muller's garage in silence and boiled up some coffee to steel our wills. Everything had gone according to plan and now, as dawn broke, we had to finish the job.

We put it in the box, on the pillows and paper. That was when I scrutinised it most, when it was nearest to me. And I thought it was really unimpressive, it was just an old dummy, an antiquated toy. Was it worth very much, would anyone pay real money for *that*?

I'm fascinated by the difference between myth and reality, said Griffin, and always conclude discouragingly that the difference is frustratingly huge and unbridgeable. I faced that fact and relived the period when my parents separated, Sean's guilt, the need to be forgiven and the struggle between self-pity and truth. And I imagined what my mother must have thought: what had been so beautiful was now petty and insignificant; heroic, handsome Sean was suddenly so remote; their previous life now seemed so commonplace, their bodies, loves and smells so vulgar, giving way to disgust and contempt. Overnight, in my mother's eyes, that man who'd been her husband, whom she'd loved, was lost in the astronomical distance between past myth and present and future realities. And that's what I felt about the automaton in Muller's garage.

Graciela was no longer there to love it and nobody was there to live in fear of it. And it didn't inspire fear, though its appearance and unusual cylindrical shape were rather horrible, because it looked lifeless and yet somewhere there was a cold, inscrutable heart, the secret part animating it, the part Graciela recreated, for whom the automaton was this device in all its being and solitude. It was the *golem* there in front of me. What would it bring me: luck, life, death or failure?

We nailed down the lid, as if it were a dead human being (hadn't it died in a manner of speaking?). Then another image came to mind: from a corner of the harbour where Branco's coffin was waiting, also with its lid nailed down. We put the automaton in the shed, switched off the lights and left. I said goodbye to Muller and was yawning quite shamelessly.

I walked back to the Aramis Hotel with Caporale. I wasn't conscious of what I'd done, but now I was about to take the automaton to Desolation Island at the first opportunity, tomorrow perhaps, if I got a call from the undertakers. I began to feel I was a demiurge, a creator, and the master of the automaton's fate. I then turned towards Nemo Caporale and asked him if the limpid light of dawn and that moment absorbing us were the same he'd experienced years ago, after one of those aerial incursions and if once their sordid, murderous deeds were done, they walked like fearless Cains, into that blue light facing the ocean of all culture, like two men on Judgement Day after they have heard their sentences, as Dante says: *da bocca il fredo, e dalli occhi il cor tristo*. Caporale didn't look at me or stop: he just said yes, yet again.

42

VERY EARLY THE NEXT MORNING, I WAS WOKEN BY AN untimely call from the Harbour Undertakers. Everything was ready for the funeral at sea. They wanted to know the exact place the corpse would be sunk. I told them Port Churruca, the first name to come to mind from the many on the coast of Desolation Island, said Griffin. They informed me they had made a motor launch available for the trip and burial ceremony, and that given the distances involved, they'd have to leave in a couple of hours, just after daybreak. They also told me it would be necessary to spend the night in some local port to be decided by the skipper of the boat that had been baptised *Charlotte*.

I quickly informed Caporale who was still asleep, dressed and took a taxi to pick him up and the same car drove us to Muller's shed to load up the box with the automaton. Muller wasn't there, but his wife let us have the keys. It was all unravelling too quickly, or at least that was what I felt, Griffin said, because we'd only taken the decision to steal the automaton twenty-four hours ago and that deed was done, and I don't remember if I wondered whether it was a dream or not, now we were about to transport it many kilometres. Action never stopped, life never stopped.

The taxi drove to the Asmar dock where the *Charlotte* was

waiting for us tied to bollards on the quayside by heavy ropes. It was a fast, modern, grey and blue boat with two decks and outboard engines. It was very early but one could hear the stevedores shouting everywhere and echoes of distant clatter, bangs and hooters, the hullabaloo of a port that always impresses me because it is the sound of new departures and epiphanies.

We greeted the skipper, Griffin said, a tall, aloof, sharp-featured Chilean who introduced himself as Captain Martín Murature. He had a judicious expression that I warmed to. The three other men on the boat didn't say hello. Murature pointed his chin in the direction of Branco's coffin in a space on the portside, towards the poop. When he saw our other nailed-down box, he asked what it contained. I told him it was a personal, private item with sentimental value, an old family heirloom we had to leave on the island, I'd tell him exactly where, but not very far from our destination. Murature shrugged his shoulders to show his indifference. I asked him where we were going to sleep the night. 'Maybe in the boat, in St Felix Bay, there'll be no need to go ashore,' Murature retorted drily.

Caporale and I placed our box next to Branco's coffin. A few minutes later we were sailing southwards, hugging the shore. There was a limpid light. As we gathered speed, I scrutinised the two boxes, curiously both made from the same light-toned knotted pine. My immediate thought was that they were what they appeared to be: two coffins, two boxes containing the dead, one a man and the other a boy, and that sad and serious insight led me to contemplate the bitter irony of that situation, time and place, and I again imagined the bodies of Bagnoli and his sons, represented by Branco and the automaton in that marine scenario and in a curious regression also imagined history had happened differently, that it was a summer's day in 1918 and that I was an invisible bystander in the sloop that finally returned them to their mother, a few days after their boat capsized, and that they'd already been put in coffins because of their terrible state of putrefaction.

It took us more than half a day that threatened rain to reach Desolation Island. Caporale and I barely exchanged a word with the crew, three grim, solidly built individuals, with close-cropped hair, obviously not enjoying their labours. They weren't what you call pleasant. 'They're sailors working off some sanction or other,' said Caporale. 'This is their punishment, you might say. They do this rather than go to jail.' Caporale explained that the Undertakers belonged to the Merchant Navy Christian Association.

I forgot them and their duties and made myself comfortable on the poop deck and let myself feel how close I was to my island, remembering the times I'd drawn it, as if I could recall every single one. I'd invented it whenever I drew it, and its outline and very existence were an obsession or shouldn't I perhaps say that my real obsession was to go there, step ashore, walk in its black undergrowth and arid wastes at the mercy of its foul climate, impelled by a powerful, destructive force? It was the same mixture of fascination, fear and power that drives people to want to go to another planet, to step on Mars, for example. And I have always wanted to step on Mars, to be the only human being to step on Mars. That was adventure, true adventure and a perfect voyage: that immense void and moment when one may be struck by lightning, when life and death are in abeyance.

While my mind rambled thus, the *Charlotte* sailed swiftly past Port Famine and Fort Bulnes: nothing to look at; those places were familiar to me from my excursion a few days ago with the Italian, German and Argentine tourists. A little later, the beautiful green coast that surrounds Lomas Bay appeared on the portside, deep and high as a canyon, on the great Dawson Island, with a ribbon of small brightly coloured buildings along the shore. We sailed closed to Joaquín Point and at once reached Froward Cape, the southernmost tip of the continent mentioned in the accounts of all the great voyages, like a round, imposing amphitheatre. From there the Straits climb in a north-westerly direction and the water gets shallower. Big boats have to be alert or they will go aground.

A few hours later the famous Charles III Island came into sight, shaped like an almond and visible from afar. The mariner and geographer Churruca observed it similarly on his voyage in 1788; we both saw its escarpments, the sparse vegetation of blackish, spindly trees and expanse of emerald-green rocks, ever wet and shiny. We chugged slowly along its left side, left the fleeting image of the shore on our stern and entered the Narrows of Ulloa. To my delight we finally sighted Desolation Island.

Griffin paused for a while and looked at the motley plants in the Carlton Bar, where we were sitting, as if contemplating the infinite or wanting to retrace his thoughts. He seemed to need a break, a breath of fresh air, but immediately resumed his narrative, remarking that he'd always been interested in Lieutenant Cosme Damián Churruca because he had so many connections with his island. I once saw a portrait of him by Albano Carreño, in some museum or other, from when he was a brigadier. It was a large painting and he must surely have posed several times for the painter in Cadiz. It's a full-length portrait of him apparently looking Carreño in the eyes; he seems intrepid and dreamy, as if he'd always resisted relinquishing his youth. He's old now, though not overly so; by the date, November 1804, one deduces he is forty-three. He's not got long to live but he's not aware of that; death will come a year after in Trafalgar, with Gravina. His bright sparkling eyes seem absent, as if his thoughts are elsewhere and a sad, melancholy air makes him rather handsome; as Galdós said when describing him, 'it was impossible to look at him and not feel irresistibly drawn to love him'. He seems frail and his slight body defenceless, but his fragility is an illusion: I only know one thing for certain: that appearances are deceptive, Griffin said. He's as resistant as a reed of bamboo and combined that with the aura of a romantic hero like Lord Byron, though he is in fact taciturn and scientifically minded, very determined, and not at all fatuous. He boasted he read Horace.

Perhaps it was a youthful reminiscence from years before those sittings, that was clouding his gaze as he posed for Carreño the painter. In 1788, while the preparations were underway for the expedition to the Straits of Magellan that he would join, he travelled to Kew, by order of the king, charged with purchasing from the Royal Society a superb collection of instruments to employ in observations and experiments: the O'Toole collection was held to be the most modern set of geographic and cartographic tools in existence. He was entrusted with a huge sum of banknotes for their purchase and credentials to present to the Spanish ambassador and English Crown.

As described in the *Natural Review of London*, the O'Toole collection comprised a Brevet pendulum, two pairs of convex lens achromatic binoculars invented by Albert Bartholomy, a large theodolite, a quarter-circle with a radius of two feet, maximum precision sextants, quadrants and octants, brick and chisel geological hammers, gutta-percha pails, two Hewitt telescopes, a marine barometer, two hundred-foot-long chains, an air-tight sample box and a Dnieper tree. All that hugely valuable material, paid for in banknotes endorsed by the Spanish Exchequer, was loaded into fifteen special boxes and sent to Plymouth in a carriage that left Kew a day before Churruca.

When Churruca reached the port, there was no sign of the carriage with the boxes, even though it had left a day earlier. After enquiring in all the city's coaching inns and stables, taverns and churches, Churruca had no option but to wait patiently, although he got increasingly agitated. After two interminable days with no news, he decided to retrace his steps and find out himself what might have happened to the boxes he had already given up as a lost cause, while anticipating the trouble in store over the disappearance of such valuable instruments, the failure of his mission and the loss of the State's money, something nobody would credit in the Court in Madrid, which implied prison, demotion in rank and naturally the end of his career.

He travelled the entire route back from Plymouth to London in sombre mood, stopping and enquiring in post-house after post-house, inn after inn and farm after farm. Nobody knew where the phantom carriage had ended up, nobody had seen it pass by or knew the coachman. Churruca realised he was desperately alone. When he set out on the third day of his search, now a few kilometres from the metropolitan area of London, somebody finally knew something at the post-house of one Jack Caldwell. The carriage had apparently arrived three days before very late into the night. The young man and the middle-aged man – possibly the coachman – in the driving seat got down to eat and seek a bed for the night, then started drinking furiously on the pretext that they needed to chase the cold from their bones. They drank glass after glass, one after another, until they were blind drunk. They then quarrelled viciously, for no apparent reason, shouted, insulted each other and started a knife fight. The older man was more deft and stabbed the youth in the ribs when he was off his guard and he collapsed moaning, but as he was strong, he put a hand over the wound to staunch the flow, got up with his last ounce of energy, grabbed the older man from behind and beheaded him with his knife. The youth dropped his knife and fell on the other's man back as dead as he was. The people in the post-house were horrified and didn't know what to do with the carriage. Jack Caldwell claimed the horses in compensation for all the expense and upset and put the carriage in the stables while some person of authority decided its fate.

They hadn't opened the boxes, although Caldwell did try to force one or two locks to pry into the contents, as Churruca discovered when counting the fifteen boxes of instruments individually. He was forced to buy the four horses back from the inn-keeper at an exorbitant price, animals he'd already paid for in London, and he mounted the driving seat with another coachman to ensure the boxes reached Plymouth in time to be shipped to Spain. Then at last young Churruca could relax.

While the *Charlotte* chugged on, said Griffin, I thought of Churruca reflecting on all that while sitting for Albano Carreño and mentally revisiting that moment when happenstance might have changed his destiny. Forking paths yet again: one taken, one spurned, that eternal game. And when I looked at his portrait, I saw the only man I was linked to by a mutual love for Desolation Island. He too adored that island, but nobody ever found out why, and he never said or wrote down why. I know he adored it because he spent ages wandering across its heaths and valleys, exploring its shorelines of gulfs and beaches.

Churruca touched, stroked and loved the island and I knew he did because I intended to do exactly that; he went up and down the island three times, often drew it, mentally as well, throughout his life, described its coast in detail, lingered in the midst of storms and dreadful weather and collected samples of vegetation, fossils and minerals. As he recorded in writing, he found lamp and curculio shells, various species of elderberry and an earwig; he charted each hill and gulley; he suffered, drilled and smelt the island that, as he said to someone, 'he loved deeply'. However, he never saw the automaton and that's really surprising. The horrific climate, icy winds and constant downpours meant his clothes were permanently soaked and he was shivering all the time, and that protected the automaton (or protected Churruca), by placing a thick curtain of water between the two of them.

It was on that journey that he gave his name to the bay where we were now heading: Port Churruca on Desolation Island, a large, beautiful bay with an idyllic waterfall cascading down at its centre, a tumult we heard long before the *Charlotte* reached there. It was the spot chosen at random to sink Branco's corpse and now I could see it, I was sure it was the best place on earth for the captain to rest in peace. Midday passed, clouded over and in mid-afternoon we anchored opposite, as twilight and the first drops of rain descended on our foreheads.

At last I could gaze at the long shoreline. I tried to savour that longed-for moment: my island was staring at me and I was staring back. An extrasensory dialogue, as Caporale might say, was commencing between a human being and a wild landscape, something the Greeks and Romans have always praised. Did Churruca read as much in Horace? Did Homer really know about dialogues with rocks and untamed coasts? I then asked myself, Griffin said. I began to concentrate exclusively on what I wanted to do, on listening to my island that would soon receive the automaton, and on throwing Branco's coffin overboard. The sky had gone a dark grey streaked with red. It rained even more heavily. For some reason or other everything had suddenly become tragically solemn, like a painting by Friedrich.

The silence was barely broken by cormorants and seagulls and the waves beating against the helm of the *Charlotte*, after Murature had ordered the engine to be switched off so the boat could heave to. The shore was full of rubbish: black plastic, oxidised drums, bits of tree blown off by the wind, piles of mouldering timber, remains of tents improvised from rags, empty bottles, old paper scattered over the brush, small dead animals; the magical and the horrific, the filthy and the spiritual, the limpid, as I'd heard Muller say the other night in his peculiar Chilean accent, and the opaque, the earthly and the heavenly.

The sight of the black waters of the Straits prompted me to imagine the many marine figures quite different to those I'd thought of when on board the *Minerva Janela*, first of all, the monsters De Bry dreamt up in his engravings, giant fish with huge eyes devouring Jonases with their sharp-pointed teeth, then wild-eyed, frightened marooned sailors who must have sailed there over the centuries and also the hopes that must have been dashed hundreds of times on those barren wastes, the fear gripping so many men facing the desolation and the mirages that drove them mad, and the barbarity they must have been forced to employ in that forsaken spot, surrounded by that unique stretch of water, on remote territory outside the habitable world.

Murature had given the order to place the coffin on a wooden plank as was the custom, and after an evangelical blessing (we'd discovered that Branco was Protestant), the sailors readied to slide it and him into the sea. As the waves were about to close over Branco's coffin, with a short, sharp splash, as it gashed the watery surface, I grasped why the sea wields a fatal attraction over suicides. It is a summons as irresistible as the

Sirens' in the *Odyssey*. In a way, a suicide was now sinking to the bottom, because Branco hurtled down in his heavy pine-wood coffin weighted down by strips of lead, like a deep-sea diver.

I shut my eyes and imagined his heavy, rapid descent, banging into all sizes of barrels, bits of boat, cannons and naturalists' steel boxes, trunks full of crockery, and cannon-balls, trunks full of books and decorations, and lost treasure, fabulous jewels and coins, and upturned keels and masts and boat partitions, probably sunk in skirmishes nobody now remembered, and coffins of other men, maybe as suicidal as Branco, dead and thrown overboard there like the young sailor Avellaneda, Churruca's friend, killed by a spear hurled at his neck by an Ona Indian on the Córdova fjord, near where the body of our old captain was now sinking.

Next to me, Nemo Caporale also luxuriated in a personal litany of his ideas of death. From what he said, he imagined death in many ways and with many omens that were sometimes seen and sometimes dreamt: the Lady in Blue, the White Knight, the Silver Fox, the Dolphin Chariot, the Transparent Serpent, the Cold Flame, the Hypodermic Needle, the Circular Ray, the Open Balcony, the Placid Lake, the Illuminated Glass, the Painless Pain and Mute Voice.

When the coffin hit the water and sank, the small ripple of waves soon closed in an eddy over its point of entry. It disappeared, was swallowed up and buried in watery territory before our eyes. Caporale said, 'Death, the hand that hides.'

I remembered Calypso, the nymph who lived on the Mediterranean island of Ogigia, whose name means 'that which hides' and who welcomed the shipwrecked Ulysses, cherished him and kept him for ten years. Could I stay on Desolation Island for ten years? Was it Calypso who kept the automaton on that island for so many years, hiding it from the sight of all comers, including Churruca? At that precise moment, as the short ceremony Murature had started came to an end, rain began to fall. It was a constant, gentle rain, like the rain I remembered from Ireland.

The *Charlotte* raised anchor and continued to sail close to the shore until it reach the new place on the island I'd indicated to Murature: Cape Cut. Night fell when we moored opposite the cape. The skipper asked us to hurry up, as he wanted to spend the night sheltering in St Felix Bay. He thought that would be best, as the weather was getting worse.

I went ashore with Caporale in a rubber dinghy with an outboard motor, the automaton sticking up in the prow as the rain beat down. Once on the steep, crushed shell beach, we began our march into the interior of the island, dragging the box behind us with the help of ropes. We lit our way with a powerful torch, the same one, I thought, that Nemo took to the museum on the night of the robbery.

We made considerable headway inland, climbing muddy slopes and others dotted with rocks that tore our clothes. It rained non-stop and the night was black as pitch. We progressed painfully with visibility under one or two metres afforded by a distant amber glow. Caporale didn't panic but he wanted us to postpone our task to the next morning. I told him bluntly it had to be now or never and imagined Sarmiento de Gamboa reacting similarly in such adverse conditions.

An hour later, I chose a spot between some rocks at the top of a hill from the precipitous side of which we looked down on the lights of the *Charlotte* flickering below, and we dug a deep hole with the dinghy oars Caporale had had the foresight to bring. It wasn't easy, because the downpour softened the earth and kept filling the hole with black mud. When we thought it was deep enough, we extracted the automaton from the box like an embalmed mummy or landmine about to explode and left it half buried again on the island where Graciela Pavic had found it more than seventy years before, perhaps in the same place, whatever.

Drops of rain streamed down our faces and its metal body and magnified my acute sense that we were abandoning that disturbing android that was now returning to a limbo where it would probably be lost for some time. I glanced back at it, planted there like a defenceless doll, and thought I glimpsed the spine-chilling stance Melvicius had tried to fashion, which, I expect, had captivated Graciela and all who contrived to have sight of it. For an instant, but only for an instant, I thought it really was a malign being that must be repelled, a *golem* of evil and madness.

There it stood on the lichen, sheltered by rocks, like Ulysses on his way back to Ithaca. It was endgame and grand finale to a caprice that had been stillborn centuries ago. We climbed down, keeping a few metres between us. The rain intensified, the distant glow receded and the darkness deepened. It was then that Caporale and I turned round and looked back at the automaton and saw nothing. We screwed up our eyes to focus our gaze through the violent downpour and saw only saw hazy objects, the rocks and the automaton that was now one of them behind a watery curtain gradually forcing us to slide down the hill. 'It's disappeared,' said Caporale. No, it's there, I said, it's simply become invisible.

I then understood why it went undiscovered for so long, why it wasn't seen by Sarmiento's men or Philip II's inquisitors, why they sometimes lost sight of it in the Salesian Museum, why Churruca passed it by, perhaps, and didn't notice its presence. For a reason no one could pinpoint, probably to do with the material of manufacture, the automaton had the gift of invisibility. And recovered its material form very rarely and in the presence of a highly select minority. Maybe only those of us who, from time immemorial, had recognised that we too were invisible despite ourselves.

People say Melvicius died in the belief – like Verne's Wilhelm Storitz – that he had granted his automaton the power of invisibility, because he'd discovered, just that once, a hybrid between steel and glass, perhaps, as Verne describes it, an impregnating substance that dissolved light in chameleon-style, something Melvicius never succeeded in doing again in all his competitive experiments and heated arguments with Rabbi Löw. It was an exceptional discovery, alongside his many failures, that he interpreted as a divine revelation, the purpose of which eluded him for his entire life.

The purpose may merely have been so it could endure eternally on the frontier between the visible and invisible, on the remotest island at the world's end, visible and invisible to no one, as if condemned for potential evil that never was, evil that those who approached the automaton and set its diabolical machinery to work expanded of their own accord. Melvicius couldn't have foreseen the redeeming love of Graciela whose good fortune turned sour when she discovered the automaton on the island and it brought her unhappiness, or that I would restore it to its location, doing so and being the instrument to that end, yet still not knowing what good fortune or misfortune it would bring.

I thought fleetingly of the menacing world in Lovecraft's books, read by Caporale with such enjoyment on the *Minerva Janela*, whose face he displayed on one of his tattoos. I imagined that metamorphosis was the last attribute of perfection Melvicius decided to grant his metal monster.

'Come on, it's getting late,' said Caporale at the foot of the hill we had climbed down so perilously, slipping on the wet undergrowth as if it were a snow slide. I looked up one last time to the spot where we'd left the automaton. I saw nothing. Everything was as it should be.

Captain Murature was smoking small Navarino cigars that looked like cigarettes. His profile was silhouetted against the penumbra of the distant sea and grey smoke spiralled up from his aquiline nose. He was an amusing distraction on the *Charlotte* while Caporale and I drank wine and warmed up in the cabin, in clean clothes one of the sailors had lent us as we proceeded back up the Straits to St Felix Bay, where the sight of the lighthouse soothed our skipper. I was seized by a sense of fulfilment and closure. Here ends my adventure, I thought, Griffin said. We spent the night on board, anchored at the foot of the lighthouse. Lulled by the water and the passing hours, wide awake, much to my surprise, I felt full of the wonders of life and everything it offers, if one knows how to live it.

43

YOU'LL NOT GO BACK, YOU'LL NEVER GO BACK, I TOLD myself, adrift between melancholy and glee, said Griffin, as the *Charlotte* sailed back into the Punta Arenas harbour basking in the golden promise of twilight. And it's true that I have never returned in all the years since and it's not anything I'm contemplating right now. Why return? I sometimes wonder. The automaton is now invisible, chameleon-like or dissolved like a burlesque artifice in the island's wet, windy fastnesses. How could I ever find it, if I returned to that spot I've wrenched from my memory? And as for Desolation Island, I stopped drawing it at some stage, and the truth is my hand hasn't drawn its coastline ever again, like someone who's spontaneously triumphed over an addiction. No, going back didn't and doesn't enter my plans for the future, whatever they might be.

The sun was going down and once we'd moored in the harbour that was as busy and noisy as ever and were ashore, Caporale and I said goodbye to skipper Murature who was hidden behind the spirals of smoke from his Navarinos and walked in silence to the Aramis Hotel. Only a day had passed, but my body was exhausted after wandering for years in the backwaters of history. A heavy atmosphere of festering farewells hung over the streets of the city and I couldn't help feeling it was all rather tedious now that I'd tramped them and satisfied my traveller's curiosity, as if I'd drained the last dregs from a bottle of wine.

A letter from Pereira was waiting for me in the hotel reception that I decided to open when I was alone. I shut my eyes, took a deep breath and turned round and hugged Caporale who was standing next to a window between Aramis riding along the edge of a forest and a devious Aramis caricatured by Daumier. We'll meet again, Nemo, I told him, in this life or another, and with an instinctive gesture of friendship, one that comes rather awkwardly to sailors, which is what we felt we basically were, I tried to thank him for everything he'd done for me. Caporale gripped my arms and, unexpectedly, became very shy as his strong hands squeezed my elbows. He removed them as he searched for the right reply.

'I'll look after your island,' he said very slowly, as if he'd carefully weighed his words. 'Wherever I go, there'll always be a place in my thoughts for that island and it will also be a place for my friend. And whenever a ship sails me here, I'll return to the island, even though there's nothing there. Or will there be? Will *he* still be there?'

Yes, he will, I replied, knowing we'd both been involved in an act that was private and exclusively so, yet one that was historical, if not transcendent, who could tell? Caporale looked me in the eyes with a sparkling smile, and exclaimed, 'I'll find more tunnels, but you make sure you don't get into any more scrapes!' and disappeared out of the lobby and hotel door that was open to the city's cool night air. I'd never see Muller or Caporale again and didn't hear any more from the German during the rest of my time in Punta Arenas.

When I was in my room I opened Pereira's letter. He wrote that the *Minerva Janela* had reached Valparaíso a few days ago and he'd post his letter from there where they'd be docked for several weeks until they found out their port of call in Japan. As if in a vicious circle he gave me another chance to enlist and was even ready to wait for me and pay me a lot more money, if I accepted his offer. 'You're one of us now,' Pereira wrote in his letter, Griffin said. I glanced up at the window and the evening lights on the other distant shore, perhaps the land occupied by the Ravels' Mercedes Estate, then tore the letter into four and didn't reply that night or the other nights I stayed in the hotel.

It was my past, and the past never returns or changes: it only exists in our memory as a fragile image, a prey to fantasy and oblivion, a mere reminiscence that comes back in illusory fashion to shape our nostalgia.

The next few days I meandered around the city, as I'd done every day since I'd arrived, especially on quiet, solitary nights when I transmuted into more of a phantom and a spectator. Out of a sense of dignity, I waited rather anxiously on local news; not a word about the theft of the automaton, nothing in the press, on the radio or television. An absolute silence, perhaps they'll never realise the automata isn't there any more, since nobody will ever again ask after it.

At the back of my mind I feared naively that we might get into trouble because of what we'd done. What might that mean? Being arrested, put on trial, nasty prison, even if only for a short spell, the payment of a ridiculously large fine? If it had ever happened, I'd have thought it absurd, way over the top for a dummy that was lost and forgotten in a hidden corner of a fourth-rate provincial museum. Nonetheless, my feeble nature or lurid imagination led me to pay a return call one last time before departing, to see whether anything was amiss or it was the usual stagnant backwater.

I checked that everything and everyone was in their rightful place; the atmosphere was one I recognised, the same tedium and empty exhibition rooms. I even tempted fate and asked them to tell the director I wanted to say goodbye. But when Doña Magdalena appeared, she was as pleasant and solicitous as before and made no reference to the automaton or Graciela Pavic, let alone any recent mishaps on the premises. While she talked, I glanced out at the courtyard, where we'd made our entry. I'd never thought they might find incriminating evidence. I was blessed by impunity.

On the evening of that same day, I realised that my story and stay were coming to an end. The following night, as planned, I flew back to Madrid via Santiago de Chile. Before leaving, while I was waiting in the departure lounge, the image of myself reflected in a mirror led me to meditate on the good fortune one must have in life to get where one is, to that instant in time when one can say: I'm still alive and here's what I've achieved so far. All those mistakes, failures, disappointments, moral dilemmas, collisions, dangers, injustices, one's sorrows and the sorrows of others, heartaches and humiliations that occur in one's life, and each and every one involving a last breath, a possible farewell to this world, random chances that lurk there waiting to disrupt everything. Forking paths, yet again.

I often remember friends who have died, who have departed this world as a result of a mistake, illness, depression, a bad move, friends who aren't here and can't ever be, who didn't get past the next step. And then you see yourself on that other step, with many others, and it's only then that you know you're still a survivor, if only for a minute. Forking paths. Forking paths that respond to the obtuse logic of survival. I thought of my grandfather, my grandmother, my father, Sarmiento, Melvicius, Graciela, Caporale, Muller, Li Pao and myself, as if ripped out of myself, as always happened because of that rare sickness or quirk of behaviour I suffer from, so they say, and I thought that they and we are all survivors from something or someone in this life.

When I left Punta Arenas, my last thought in the plane went out to those dozens of settlers Sarmiento never succeeded in seeing again because a survivor's forking path took him elsewhere. And I wondered how long those who were irrevocably going to die sooner or later in that bleak place must have felt they were, in their turn, the survivors, since they were sadly of the belief that it was Sarmiento who had really perished.

And no less a survivor was the automaton those settlers sought in vain, perhaps the only genuinely real survivor in this whole story I insist on recounting like a fable, and that's like shifting sands, the elusive grains of which engulfed me for years, leaving only my head visible, which will be swallowed up by lethal quicksand at any moment.

In one letter Graciela even told my grandfather that she had survived but didn't know what. She admitted that for a long time, in rare moments of lucid despair, she would have liked the automaton to kiss her. That was her greatest hidden desire. She would have given her most valued possession to be able to transform that dummy into a human being and for its lips to offer a protracted, nourishing, vampire's kiss of love. Forking paths, forking paths . . .

In that same letter she even wrote that on one occasion, driven by a nihilistic sense that she could never be kissed by the automaton she loved so much, she had walked up the square tower by the Cross lookout point and wanted to throw herself into the void, but at the last moment had had second thoughts, had run down the steps of the tower and walked to where the automaton was kept, driven by a sudden onset of bliss prompted by the belief that it was all a nightmare and that she'd dreamt her husband Arturo had turned into a metal dummy and that now she remembered his lips and, awake at last, was in hot pursuit of flesh, blood and passion. She would be kissed and would survive, like in childhood fairy tales she could barely remember. But it was all a dreadful mistake, nothing woke her up to reality, because reality was what she preferred to think was a dream. She was the one who kissed the slightly raised, icy edges of the automaton's unchanging, fearsome face, a permanent tribute to survival as hapless Graciela knew only too well.

Five years later I now occasionally spend time in Madeira in case I might see my crewmates, Pereira captaining the *Minerva Janela* or another boat, or Nemo Caporale betting his fortunes away on an exotically named racehorse. It has never happened, we've never met up, said Griffin, though you never know, we might one of these days.

He said, Goodbye. Or I think he did. Because . . .

After the morning of Friday 21 January in the first year of the new century, Saint Inés's day, the month of the *Shebat* in the Hebrew calendar, I saw no more of Oliver Griffin. That was the exact date. After seeing each other almost daily for weeks in Os Combatentes, the bar at the Carlton, the cafés in the port or on interminable strolls along Funchal's steep streets, not to mention our prolonged post-lunch or supper conversations, Griffin's perorations via which he explored his own and other lives and related every incident, a true voyage in words, since in the end that's what our encounters were, I had simply listened to his stories and his disappearance was like the withdrawal of a drug or vital fluid I'd become dependent on.

I walked the streets of Funchal and frantically crossed the city, looking for him in the cheapest cafés and darkest taverns, though I knew I was unlikely to find him. I went all over and was occasionally startled when I thought I glimpsed him among passers-by. It was then that I realised how little I'd noticed about Griffin's physical appearance. True he must have been fifty-five, sixty, as I'd imagined from the start, of average build and handsome, with a wispy, days-old beard, but I couldn't tell you the colour of his eyes or whether or not he wore glasses, I'd swear he only wore sunglasses. Did he smoke? He dressed well, but always casually, light tones, and usually wore a hat he almost never took off, and when he did he'd sweep his hair back over what was a considerable bald pate.

He sometimes wore a natural linen jacket, and that was the garment I looked for when I thought I'd spotted him among the crowd, on the Marina or in the hustle and bustle of people walking down Avenida Arriaga. I remember the last time I saw him, that Friday 21 January, when he left, I looked at his back and his shoulders seemed firmer and younger than usual. I felt I was watching a friend walking off, a lifetime acquaintance, yet really the man was a nobody as far as I was concerned, I didn't have his address, telephone number, any reference point at all apart from his stories. Seeing him vanish into the distance I thought: There goes Oliver Griffin, storyteller *par excellence*, but who is he?

I didn't realise how distant and part of the past he was becoming. I'm not sure whether past or future, certainly in another different space, a huge void. It was the space filled by his extravagant tales full of true or false stories and I wasn't really worried if it was pure fable with transformations appropriate for a body in the course of creation, an embryo gestating inside his inscrutable mind.

Griffin was on his way, and as I watched him that last time, I don't remember where, perhaps in the shade of a café terrace, his final words were still ringing in my ears, that day when they were extremely sparse in terms of his narrative, because he only spoke about drinks and the hot weather before telling me about the Great Samini, his grandfather's death agony when he heard him utter the name of Graciela, just before he died, linked to a vision of the automata smashed to pieces, dismantled and unusable at last, as Emperor Philip II had ordered, an order Arcimboldo had ignored, a vision that had left his grandfather with a look of horror in his eyes in his final moments that it took Griffin many years and journeys to understand.

I started my search for Griffin subsequently. I went to his hotel. They said he had indeed stayed there, that he still had the room reserved, but must have gone out. I went back several times but to no avail. Whatever the hour of day Griffin was never there. Or perhaps he never replied to the calls made to his room from the hotel lobby. Perhaps he was hidden in some corner of Madeira, recounting his story, this story I'm now writing, to someone else, who was no less under his spell?

Finally, after a while, I understood his disappearance was down to the fact his long story had simply run out of steam. Last full stop, sudden interruption, book closed, end. That was all there was to it. Griffin no longer sought me out as I did him because he had nothing else to tell. One day I waited and waited, but to no avail. He seemed to have evaporated. He didn't return to his usual haunts where I sat and reflected on the stories he'd told me. I saw inexorably that the story had come to a conclusion, that Griffin the narrator had told all. He'd become invisible, and his life also seemed invisible, or at least opaque, look how little he'd said about himself and yet I know that I had finally got to know exactly what he wanted to tell, his tissue of words within other words that in turn were within other words.

As far as I was concerned Griffin no longer lived in his hotel, however much reception thought he'd be back. I was convinced he'd left Funchal and Madeira again. He'll return, but I won't be there to see him. When I became conscious that I'd turned into one more character, I shut myself in my hotel, placed the red, gold, green dragon next to me, the one Li Pao had given to Griffin as a present and, like a faithful, anonymous scribe, I tried to retain every word he'd said, I strove to hear his voice again within myself and took notes of everything he'd told me, the testimony which you the reader now have.

My only desire now is to go to Desolation Island. I have unthinkingly started to draw its contours on a piece of paper: its fjords, capes and coasts. Even with one's finger it's easy to sketch its pointy shape in furrowed, ever hazy lines. I think we all draw invisible outlines of invisible islands. Can Griffin really have become invisible? Will I become invisible too? Haven't we both always been invisible?

www.vintage-books.co.uk